A DARING SHIP HIJACKING
carried out by the world's most successful and
savage terrorist, Alain Dureau . . .

A PACIFIC ISLAND MANHUNT
led by a fanatical U.S. Marine Corps colonel,
Sabbath Spangenberg . . .

**A DISCOVERY IN A
MOSCOW LABORATORY**
where Nikolai Lubentsov, a chess-obsessed
computer genius, comes to a conclusion that
spelled global madness . . .

**A SUPER-SHOWDOWN
ON THE HIGH SEAS**
where surface and submarine fleets of
every nation speeds toward nightmare
confrontation . . .

AND A PLUNGE INTO PERIL
as Cas Bonner and Steve Chaffee, a pair of
master U.S. divers, backed by a nervy woman
scientist, try to do the impossible to stop the
unthinkable. . . .

THE PANJANG INCIDENT

THE
PANJANG
INCIDENT

Charles Ryan

A SIGNET BOOK

NEW AMERICAN LIBRARY

PUBLISHER'S NOTE

This book is a work of fiction. Names, characters, places, and incidents either are the product of the author's imagination or are used fictitiously, and any resemblance to actual persons, living or dead, events, or locales is entirely coincidental.

Copyright © 1989 by Charles Ryan

SIGNET, SIGNET CLASSIC, MENTOR, ONYX, PLUME, MERIDIAN and NAL BOOKS are published by NAL PENGUIN INC., 1633 Broadway, New York, New York 10019

First Printing, April, 1989

1 2 3 4 5 6 7 8 9

PRINTED IN THE UNITED STATES OF AMERICA

To Helen

. . . damned, most subtly and most malignantly! damned in the midst of Paradise!

—HERMAN MELVILLE, *Moby Dick*

Prologue

Coral Sea
January 17
1420 hours, Queensland Standard Time

Two hundred miles off the southeastern tip of Guadalcanal, an ugly gray freighter churned wearily at sixteen knots through a long southerly swell. The Liberty ship *Panjang* was alone on the sea, inbound for Australia. Her hull plates bore streaks of rust along the weld lines and the paint on her upper structures and king posts had oxidized to a whitish powder. Her single brass screw boiled up a dirty yellow wake.

In her master's cabin, Captain Sigurd Gotchok stared thoughtfully at the litter of papers on his desk, absently listening to the creaks and thuds of his ship, to the faint, rich rush of her triple-stage turbine. The sounds were as familiar as his own heartbeat. He had captained the *Panjang* for nearly all of her forty-five years. She had run the C Track during World War Two; after refit she began her new life, ferrying naval supplies under commercial contract. Studying the papers once more, he felt that twinge of disquiet he had experienced when first opening his shipping orders.

There were two sets of orders. The first, registered with the shipping log in San Diego, consigned him to Brisbane and Rockhampton. The second, in code, in-

9

structed him to turn the *Panjang* north at a point two hundred miles from the Australian coast. He would skirt the Great Barrier Reef to the Tamarand Estuary near the tip of the desolate York Peninsula of Northern Queensland.

Gotchok shook his head. It was going to be a tricky business, a series of tight maneuvers in shoal grounds to a secret landing deep in the estuary.

The buzzer over his bunk rang. "Captain, Bridge."

He tapped the intercom button. "Go."

"We're getting a blip on radar, sir. Bearing zero-three-five. Looks like a low-flying aircraft."

"I'm coming up."

Renfro, the redheaded third mate standing bridge watch, was peering through the wheelhouse with binoculars. Gotchok paused at the radar screen, then stepped onto the port wing. Renfro followed him out with a second pair of glasses.

The captain scanned the horizon slowly. There was a heavy salt haze and the sun made flashing diamonds on the water.

"There he is," Renfro called out. "Three points off the port beam. It's a chopper."

Gotchok swung his glasses back and forth until he picked up a small black dot skimming just over the surface. "What in hell's he doing out here? Tell radio to raise him on aircraft frequency."

"Aye, sir," Renfro ducked into the bridge.

The copter grew steadily larger in Gotchok's binoculars.

Renfro returned. "We're getting a helluva burst of static, sir. Just started. Radio says nothing's coming in."

In two minutes the aircraft was visible to the naked eye. It was coming fast; a camouflaged fuselage, the sun flashing on the rotor blades. It was so close to the water the downwash dimpled the surface.

"It's a Cobra gunship," Renfro said. "I seen them in Nam."

Gotchok lowered the glasses and squinted at the approaching craft. He felt a sliver of foreboding and swung around. "Go to emergency frequency. See if you can raise the military channel out of Manila."

Renfro darted away.

The copter was a mile out now. Gotchok lifted his glasses. He could make out the men aboard. Four—no, five, dressed in battle fatigues. One sat in the open blister, his legs dangling.

The captain's heart turned to ice. Resting on the man's thigh was an assault pistol, and just above his head poked the muzzle of a machine gun. He tore the glasses away and plunged his head through the doorway. "Alert the crew," he yelled. "And break out the gun closet."

Renfro, halfway across the bridge, turned, stunned.

"*Move.*"

"But, Captain—" Renfro stammered. "The closet key."

Gotchok reached into his shirt and tore a chain from around his neck. He tossed it and the key it held to the third mate. As he swung back, the copter was on them. It rose like a huge dragonfly coming up off the ocean, the sound of the blades whomping and crackling in the air.

It flashed overhead, so close the downwash of the blades whipped Gotchok's clothing. He gripped the railing, his body pounding with adrenaline. He shot a glance through the wing door. The helmsman was ducking behind the wheel column, staring wild-eyed at him. Renfro appeared in the after door carrying a shotgun and pistol.

The copter reappeared, bursting into view thirty feet above the bridge, the roar of its engine coming with a sudden clap of sound.

A hot rage took Gotchok and he began shaking his fist at the aircraft. "This is my ship!" he screamed. "Stand off, you sons of bitches, stand off!"

The copter's machine gun opened up. Bullets went zinging off the railing. The bridge windows shattered in a shower of blowing glass. The helmsman was stitched across the back with a string of bullets and fell violently to the deck.

For one stop-action moment Gotchok stared up at the faces of the men in the helicopter. He saw the tip of a dark, pipelike thing protrude over the shoulder of the sitting man. It flashed. Something struck him in the chest and flung him off his feet through the wing door. He slammed against a bulkhead and crumpled to the deck. The thing in him was coiling, hissing, sending jolts of excruciating pain through him.

In a half-conscious red haze he stared through the plateless wheelhouse window. The copter, buffeted and jerked by its own ground wash, was synchronizing to the movement of the ship. Lines suddenly appeared from the blister. Men were crawling out onto the struts; the buckles of rappeling harnesses flashed in the sun.

He closed his eyes. Opened them.

The timed grenade in his body exploded, throwing hunks of bloody flesh and fragmentation debris across the bridge of the *Panjang*.

Four thousand miles to the northeast, Chief Petty Officer Leroy Radabaugh, duty man for Naval Communications, Pearl Harbor, glanced up as a tiny red light began flashing on his computer console. He watched it a moment, then punched several numbers into his keyboard. Within seconds the computer screen lit up with an ident sequence: CODE TTS—C35 SAM/AKA PANJANG—USS/COMPAC: DD/MSC—LL 172200ZHT—SIGSIG 1011 S/1641 E—16 KNOTS, CALM/ DES 1A.

Radabaugh grunted and glanced at his watch. It was 5:22 P.M. Hawaiian time. He entered another series of numbers that initiated an automatic scan tracer through the network of Naval Communications stations in Westpac Command. Each MSC vessel was equipped with a black-box tracker that was linked to the internal navigation gyro and sent hourly fix reports of the ship's position. He lit a cigarette, waiting for verify.

It came within thirty seconds. All stations reported *Panjang*'s track normal.

Radabaugh cursed softly. He knew what had happened. Some jerkoff machinist aboard the ship had accidentally cut through the tracker-box power unit. He typed in an override request to headquarters to set up a retrack on the *Panjang* in ten minutes.

Helmless, the freighter began a gradual drift off her heading.

Below, in her machine room, Chief Engineer Jack Gray paused beside his control board, listening. He thought he had felt a shock come down through the ship a moment before. It had been soundless in the rushing surge of the giant turbine, yet Gray, like all enginemen, had a sixth sense tuned to vibrations and movements outside the normal range of operation. He stepped to the grate railing and called down to his second engineer. "Hey, Jerry, you feel that?"

In the engine pit, Jerry shook his head.

Gray returned to his panel and picked up the ship' phone. He buzzed the bridge. There was no answer. He tapped the telephone box. Still no answer. Frowning, he replaced the phone, stared at it for a moment, then stepped to the grate rail again. At that instant the rapping sound of automatic gunfire came clearly through the machine-room hatchway.

Gray froze.

Below, Jerry's head jerked up. "What the fuck was that?"

There was another sharp burst of gunfire, followed by a single echoing scream.

Gray leaned over the railing. "Get the others up here," he roared. "Arm yourselves."

He dived back to his control panel, dropping to his knees. He kept saying, "Oh, Jesus!" over and over. He wrenched the cabinet door open and pulled out a Winchester riot gun wrapped in oilcloth. He tore the covering off and fumbled shells out of a box on the lower shelf. His hands shaking violently, Gray began jamming rounds into the load tube.

A minute earlier, four raiders had come swinging in across the railing, their harnesses and strapped Ingram machine pistols jingling as they hit the companionway. Moving with silent precision, they raced to the bridge-deck hatchway and disappeared into the ship.

Gathering on the second deck, they fanned out, sprinting down alleys, slipping through hatches. Crewmen jolted out of details by the explosion and scurrying feet were coming out into the corridors, openmouthed. They were instantly cut down.

The raider leader darted into the master's cabin, made a quick search, and came out again. His name was Alain Dureau, a strikingly handsome dark-haired man. His black eyes were blazing; energy seemed to smoke off him. A second raider appeared down in the companionway. Dureau pumped his arm, indicating a ladder to the lower deck. The raider dropped down into it like a viper going into rocks.

Bent over, Dureau scurried through a short alleyway into the bridge. The radio operator staggered from a side room. His shirt had been blown off. Dureau shoved the machine pistol into the man's belly and fired.

The bridge was filled with smoke and smelled of cordite and blood. The third mate was sitting against the starboard bulkhead. He was half-conscious, his left arm in shreds. Blood had pooled around him and trembled from the deck's vibration. Dureau put the pistol against the man's forehead. The bullets smashed into his brain, violently jerking his neck. He groaned once, rolled over, and lay still.

The ship, responding to the torque of her shaft, was moving heavily into a port turn. Dureau leapt to the helm and steadied her. Through the shattered window he spotted a crewman cowering behind a forward anchor winch. He threw a long burst onto the foreward deck. The rounds pinged and whined all around the winch. The crewman, panicked, leapt up and started running aft. Dureau's second burst flung him disjointedly into the scuppers.

Another raider came running through the after doorway. He was a short, powerfully built man with a blunt, cretinous face. His name was Pellegrino Villachio.

Dureau was lashing the wheel with bungee cords. He glanced over his shoulder. "How many?"

"I count twelve."

"Four up here and one on the forward deck. That makes seventeen."

"The men in the engine room sealed themselves in. There should be four on the watch."

"Twenty-one, all told. There's three more crewmen somewhere on the ship. Where's Kaneshige and Stedman?"

"I sent them to check the after house."

Suddenly the *Panjang*'s engine stopped. The two men exchanged glances. The ship began to lose headway immediately. The bungee cords on the wheel were stretching as she started to yaw again.

Dureau gripped the spokes and, straining, brought her up. He swore in French and shouted at Villachio. "We must get into that engine room, Grino."

The *Panjang*'s engine room formed a large compartment below the main mess deck. A narrow alleyway led around the curve of the funnel core to a companionway lit by overhead lights. The air was filled with gunsmoke. A crewman's body was sprawled at the foot of the second ladder. His blood was dripping from the step.

Dureau and Villachio approached the sealed hatch. Alain put his hand lightly on the metal, then reached down and unsheathed his boot knife. He tapped one of the dogs.

Silence.

In Morse code he tapped the message: OPEN UP.

The answering tap was almost instantaneous: FUCK YOU.

Squatting, Villachio had been testing the dogs. He glanced up. "We'll have to blow them."

Dureau nodded.

"I'll need padding."

Dureau hurried back up the companionway and went up the ladder. In a moment he was back, carrying three bunk mattresses. Villachio had already placed tiny charges of gelignite on each dog lock. They stuffed the mattresses around the door and strung the charge wire back up the companionway.

The explosion was muffled and blew a cloud of ticking back up the corridor. Tiny burning filaments drifted in the air. They waited a moment, then stealthily returned to the hatch door. It was slightly ajar, the dog locks blown away. The Italian gently began pulling the door open. The blast of a shotgun roared and pellets splattered against the inside of the door.

Villachio put the muzzle of his Ingram through the crack. He let go a short burst. "Cover me," he hissed, and sent in another burst. Then he wrenched the door open and dived through.

Dureau fired over him into the engine room. It was answered by two quick shotgun blasts. Then Villachio was firing, the deep, rapping sound of the Ingram echoing up through the overhead boiler pipes and feed conduits.

Dureau started through the hatch. A man loomed up off the deck, swinging a long metal bar. His face was bloody, grimacing with rage. The bar smashed into the bulkhead just above Alain's head. The man started a backswing. Dureau put six bullets into the thick muscle under his armpit.

He crouched, listening. The grunting, *wuffing* sound of hand-to-hand combat came up from the grate pit. Another shotgun blast. This time the charge punctured one of the boiler pipes. A cloud of steam exploded through the rupture, hissing violently among the intertwined conduits.

He dived to the deck. It was oily and hot, and he could feel his heart thudding against the metal. A head appeared over the pit grating. It was Villachio. He came up the ladder slowly, wiping the blade of his boot knife on his pantleg. His blouse was covered with blood. He held up four fingers.

Dureau pushed to his feet and raced to the control

board. He scanned the dials and fixed on the four fuel indicators, large glass circles with brass frame locks.

"She still has too much fuel in her," he shouted to Villachio. "We've got to get her down to twenty thousand pounds."

The compartment was beginning to heat rapidly as the steam kept pouring out into the upper spaces. It was condensing on the cooler bulkhead plates, running down in fat droplets. Dureau looked up. "Get more mattresses," he snapped. "I'll try to divert out of that line."

Villachio headed for the hatch, slipping his knife back into its boot scabbard.

Radabaugh sullenly watched as his computer printed out radio track relays: TT-RECON VIA MANILA: NEGATIVE . . . TT-RECON VIA NZ A/S TERMINAL: NEGATIVE . . . TT-RECON VIA MIDWAY: NEGATIVE . . . On and on it went from stations all around the Pacific's middle and southern quadrants. No one was raising the *Panjang* on retrace.

He checked his watch. It was 6:03 P.M. The ship had been out of track and radio contact for forty minutes. He took a last drag on his cigarette, squashed it out, and picked up his phone.

It was answered immediately upstairs: "Nav-Com Stat, Seaman Wilkins."

"Frank? Leroy. Collins around?"

"Yeah, hang tight."

There was a click, then: "Lieutenant Collins."

"Lieutenant, this is Chief Radabaugh. I got something here I think you better have a look at."

"What is it?"

"We've lost total contact with one of our MSC ships."

"How long?"

"Forty minutes."

Collins sighed. "Okay, I'll be right down."

He showed up three minutes later. "So what have you got?"

"It's the *Panjang*, sir, inbound to Queensland."

"What was her last position?"

"Two hundred miles southeast Guadalcanal. Two minutes after the position fix came over, her box went dead."

"You tried retrack yet?"

"Yes, sir. Everybody's negative."

Collins frowned. He was chewing a thick wad of gum, a none-too-successful substitute for cigarettes. "Well, what do you think? Another clumsy crewman?"

"I figured that at first, sir. But it's been too long now. And she's not sending or receiving on emergency. I got a feeling something's bad wrong."

Collins straightened. "All right, put an emergency through to Air/Sea and get a code to Aussie Coast Watch."

"Aye, sir."

Collins started away.

"Sir?"

"What?"

"The *Panjang*'s tagged triple-red category."

Collins made a face. "Oh, no. Now we'll have to contact Naval Intelligence and write up a DES report to the fucking Pentagon."

It took them seventeen minutes to cap off the ruptured steam line. Dureau and Villachio worked on a mobile scaffold. They scorched their hands as they jammed mattresses around the break. The flow of steam had dropped to a single jet that whistled through the edges of the break.

McCullom, the Aussie pilot, came below. He had landed the copter on the afterhouse and chained it down. He said the others had killed two more men and were prowling the ship looking for the last crewman.

Finally they got the line sealed, and Villachio began baffling the steam head down into the turbine. Dureau watched a moment, then signaled McCullom. They went up to the bridge deck and into the wheelhouse.

The Aussie stopped short at the door, his eyes squinting with repugnance at the carnage. A breeze was washing through the windows. It had dried the blood and gore on the deck, and there was a raw, slaughterhouse stink in it.

Dureau stepped to the helm and released the bungee cords. The *Panjang* was gradually picking up speed. He swung hard rudder, putting her into a starboard turn. He could feel the ship tremble as she came up into it, rolling as the swell moved fully into her hull.

He watched the compass indicator in the binnacle head. It was swinging past heading points: 290 . . . 299 . . . 004 . . . 020 . . . The compass card rocked like a crazy pendulum for a moment, then settled, holding on the new heading of zero-four-zero degrees. Straight for Guadalcanal.

Dureau twisted around. "Get up here and take the wheel," he shouted to the Aussie. McCullom walked through the drying muck like a man walking barefoot over glass. "Hold that heading," Dureau commanded. "I'll be back in fifteen minutes."

Number-two hold stank of bilge water and rust and rat feces. Carrying a shoulder bag of tools, Dureau climbed slowly down the companion ladder. Above him the tiny oval of light coming through the hatch shrank until it was no more than a pale moon.

He flicked on his flashlight. On either side of a center row of stanchions were stacks of palleted cargo crates of machine parts, huge generators, Quonset frames, drilling shafts, tanks. Steel cargo nets covered them, their ends chained to eyebolts in the deck.

He moved slowly aft. Rats rustled furtively under the netting. His light picked up a scaffold built of wooden six-by-sixes. The scaffold formed a grid of twelve separate sections.

Each section contained an upright metal canister. Fifteen feet tall, the canisters were four feet wide at midsection, and then narrowed near the top like an artillery round. The metal casings shone like polished silver. Each was snugged into the gridwork with rings of polystyrene and cross cables.

Dureau played his light over the scaffold. The hold was stifling hot; sweat slipped along the small of his back. He chose one of the outer canisters. Bracing his boots into the beam junctures, he climbed up until he was about three feet from the tip.

He wedged his flashlight through a cable eye, focusing its illumination directly onto the metal surface. Feeling with the tips of his fingers, he searched the casing. He found a seam and traced it out. It formed a square inspection door. Eight lock screws held it closed. Their heads had been so finely milled there was no break in the surface.

Using a self-powered pressure drill from his bag, he began taking the screws out. His hands shook with tension. Finally they were all out. He affixed a rubber suction cup to the door plate and pulled it off.

The exposed compartment was jammed with electronic components that were fitted around a central shaft about the size of an automobile driveline. Covering the inside of the casing were antimagnetic coils. Between the coils and shaft were six gold-plated disks, each backed with a circuit board. Plastic-wrapped wires led from the disks up through slots in the shaft to a reservoir terminal on the top of the compartment.

Dureau drew out a small computer from his tool bag and set it on a beam near the casing. He flipped the top up. It was a tiny screen and below it was a keyboard.

He leaned close to the top of the door and studied the reservoir terminal closely. Several color-coded leads came from it and went up through the overhead plate into the canister tip. He searched until he found a bright red one. With lock pliers, he gently loosened the lead flange bolt into the terminal. Into the empty socket he inserted a wire from his computer, locking it in with alligator clips. He flicked on the computer. Instantly the tiny screen glowed green.

From around his neck he produced a chain with a metal dog tag. Stamped into the tag were the letters USN and six sets of numbers, each containing five digits. He studied the first set, holding it close to the flashlight. For a moment he blinked sweat out of his eyes. Then he punched the first set into his keyboard.

The moment the last digit went in, the machine began rapidly scanning all possible combinations of the series. The numbers flashed like quivering insects on the screen. As each variation was displayed and rejected, there was a tiny blip signature. They were coming at such high speed the signatures made a soft electronic chirp.

Ten seconds passed . . .

Twenty . . .

Abruptly the flashing numbers stopped, holding on one variation. Instantly the bottom gold disk began to revolve with a minute purr of internal gears. Tumblers fixed and the disk stopped, locked into a new position.

Dureau's heart trembled. Sweet Virgin! It was working. He had broken into the unit's system.

But would it accept all the series?

He punched in the next set. Within seconds it had located the proper variation, and the second gold disk moved and locked in. He went through the remaining sets, one by one. Each was accepted. As the sixth repositioned, the reservoir terminal began to hum.

A shrill whistle went off.

Dureau, jolted, jerked away from the opening, nearly falling off the wooden scaffold. A screeling echo rebounded through the cavernous hold. Near panic, Dureau frantically searched for the source of the whistle. He saw the core shaft coming up. The top of it slipped into a bevel space on the bottom side of the terminal box. It swiveled, locking.

The whistle stopped.

He was trembling violently. His ears still vibrated with the banshee wail of the whistle. He gritted his teeth, forcing control. Slowly, slowly he quieted.

He quickly entered a command into his computer: CANCEL MAIN AGC INPUT . . . SYNCHRONIZE TO SECOND PHASE OF FIRING SEQUENCE . . . ENTER OVERRIDE COMMAND: 345600 SECONDS . . . NOW.

The letters disappeared from the computer screen. A single dot of light formed, flashing on and off. A second later letters flared: OVERRIDE COMMAND ACCEPTED . . . UNIT NOW ON INTERNAL POWER . . . LAPSE COMMAND ACCEPTED AND ON SCAN: 345600 SECONDS . . . HOLDING.

Dureau's eyes quivered in the reflection from the screen. Blood was making tendrils of pressure across his temples. He entered the final command: BEGIN COUNTDOWN . . . NOW.

The letters vanished off the screen and were instantly replaced by the numbers 345600.

A second, like an eternity, riffled through the heated air.

345599 . . .

Another.

345598 . . .

Dureau expelled a rush of air from his lungs. It was finished. The unit was primed and locked into its time-sequence command. In ninety-six hours the terminal would reach zero state and automatically initiate final firing sequence.

Once done, nothing could stop it.

Lieutenant Collins was smoking again. He was on his third cigarette when his desk phone buzzed. It was Rear Admiral Cal Brooks, adjutant of the Fourteenth Naval District's Communications Command. Brooks waived courtesies. "Goddammit, Lieutenant, what the hell is going on down there? I just got an urgent verify on your request for satellite scan."

"Sir, we have a major problem here," Collins answered. Quickly he explained the situation.

"But a goddamned scan? Why?"

"Sir, the ship's running a triple-red category."

There was a pause. "Well, shit! What's Air/Sea picked up?"

"Nothing yet, sir. They've dispatched two search aircraft out of Station Thirty-four in the Gilberts and sent a code-priority watch to all ships in the area."

"What about the Aussies?"

"A Seagull aircraft from Brisbane and two Coast Watch corvettes from D'Entrecasteau Island in Papua."

"When do they figure convergence?"

"They're probably already there, sir."

"What was the ship's last fix?"

"Approximately two hundred miles southeast Guadalcanal."

"Did you run anything out of there?"

"No, sir."

"Well, Jesus Christ, why not? With that damned conference about to start, there should be all kinds of available craft on the Canal."

"That's just it, sir. It's so confused down there, I didn't know who to liaison with."

The admiral sighed. "All right, I'll get on the WC line and find out procedure."

"Yes, sir."

The admiral was gone.

Collins slowly lowered the phone into its cradle and stared disconsolately through the glass partition of his office at the rows of communications consoles in the outer room. As he watched, Radabaugh suddenly appeared, weaving his way through the units.

He burst through the door. "Lieutenant, you gotta see this."

"I can tell from the look on your face, Leroy, I ain't going to like it."

"No, you won't, sir." Radabaugh was holding a dispatch report. "I got to wondering about the *Panjang*'s cargo, you know? So I contacted a buddy down at Logistics Terminal. She was freighted for construction gear. But look at what else she was carrying." He slid the dispatch onto Collins' desk.

The lieutenant leaned forward to read. His eyebrows shot up with a look of shock. "Holy shit."

At 5:34 P.M. Guadalcanal time, Dureau ordered the *Panjang*'s turbine shut down and her boiler fires extinguished. The ship went dead in the water, rolling lazily. To the west, the sun was still twenty degrees off the horizon, but already the sea was taking on the deepening blue-black solidity of dusk.

Stedman and Kaneshige had assembled the corpses of the crewmen on the foredeck beside number-three hatch. They were neatly stacked on a cargo pallet and covered with a fine-mesh cargo net.

Stedman squatted beside the pallet, riffling through a pile of personal possessions he had pilfered from the bodies. He was a rangy American with shoulder-length blond hair and a badly mangled right ear received in the last, vicious days of Nam. Dureau had recruited him in Sydney, where he lived with a Chinese prostitute who fed his voracious addiction to cocaine.

Kaneshige was sitting off by himself, silent and aloof. A student from Tokyo University, he was a member of the Sekigun, the Japanese Red Army. A true fanatic, he had participated in the hijacking of a Japan Airlines flight to Bombay in 1977. Yet a change had come over him ever since the killing aboard the *Panjang* began. His eyes were haunted, confused, as if something in himself that he had always believed solid was now fragmented.

Above on the bridge, Dureau and Villachio watched the two men. "Where's McCullom?" Dureau asked.

"Warming up the chopper."

Alain squinted at the lowering sun. "All right, it's time. I'll bring up the charges." He turned and nodded toward the men below. "Finish them."

Vallachio nodded and moved out to the port wing and down the companion ladder.

Stedman glanced up as Villachio appeared on the foredeck. He grinned and held up a thick roll of American currency. "Hey, *paisano*, look at this. One of these suckers had twenty grand on him." He giggled. "Must have been smuggling dope, the motherfucker." He tucked the roll into his blouse and bent to probe further through the watches and rings spread out on the deck.

Villachio slipped a short-bladed stiletto from a scabbard in his pack harness. As he approached Stedman, he dropped his left shoulder slightly, bending his knees, and plunged the knife straight down into the conjunction of Stedman's neck and collarbone.

The American gasped and instantly fell onto his face, scattering his hoard. Across the deck, Kaneshige sprang to his feet. Villachio's Ingram burst caught him in the chest and knocked him hard to the deck. He began thrashing wildly about, trying to get up.

Villachio walked over and stood watching, his small dark eyes expressionless. Kaneshige's muscles went into violent spasms. He fought for breath for a moment, then went limp.

Villachio laid down his weapon and picked up the body as if it were weightless. He tucked it under one arm, walked over to Stedman, hooked a hand under his harness, and carried both men to the pallet. He laid them down and began loosening the net.

The bodies were secured by the time Dureau came along the starboard weather alley carrying two satchels. He tossed one to the Italian. "You start in the after holds, Grino. I'll work back from the forepeak. Remember, place the charges precisely on the spots marked on your blueprint."

Seven hundred miles over New Zealand, the American weather satellite SeaSat 3 received a radio command from Naval Track Monitor Station Jordan on Phoenix Island north of Samoa.

Holding in a synchronous orbit above the southwestern Pacific, the tiny vehicle was capable of scanning over two million square miles of ocean every thirty-six hours. Its microwave instruments, reading in radio-spectrum signals of 1,000 to 300,000 megahertz, could produce high-resolution photos that relayed data on wind, temperature conditions, and chemical assays.

Now the satellite's thematic mapper console swung slowly into position to focus on the northern limits of its range. Primary mirrors swung out to pick up the last rays of the sun. Its infrared sensor camera triggered every thirty seconds as the vehicle's field of vision moved steadily northward.

Within forty-five minutes it would cross the Solomon Archipelago.

It took twenty minutes for the *Panjang* to die.

Dureau and Villachio, using gelignite charges cemented to designated weld seams, had gradually worked their way toward each other. They moved swiftly, dogging down the hatches of compartments that would not be flooded.

It was wild, dangerous work. The charges went off with muffled impacts, followed instantly by explosions of water as it blew through the fractures.

By the time they finished the demolition, the ship was listing slightly to starboard. Tall geysers of water were shooting up through her vent horns, flooding onto the main deck. A faint, deep rumble came up through her plates, punctuated by dull impacts as the flooding waters smashed loose gear against internal bulkheads.

Dureau and Villachio came out onto the bridge deck. Far astern on the after house, McCullom was waving them in. Behind him the copter blades were idling.

They raced down the after ladder and worked their way aft. Water from the horns was a foot deep now, and it kept washing back and forth in countering waves as the ship rolled. They reached the after house and scrambled up to the deck. McCullom was already in the pilot's seat, squinting intently through the Plexiglas.

"Where's the others?" he shouted as they pulled themselves aboard.

"They had an accident," Dureau yelled back.

McCullom stared at him. "You can't bloody well leave them."

"They're both dead."

McCullom's mouth opened.

"Move, dammit," Dureau ordered. "She's going under any minute."

McCullom swung back to the controls. He put power to the engine and the copter lifted off, roaring. They hovered fifty feet above the ship.

She was settling rapidly. Small bits of debris floated on the main deck. Lower and lower she went, sinking even-keeled now as internal flooding was beginning to equalize throughout the ship. Great bubbles of air exploded around her hull, staining the ocean brown.

A huge vomiting of water blew through the wheelhouse windows. It cascaded like rain onto the forward deck, where the pallet of corpses shifted in the flood, straining against the net cables.

The main deck went fully under. Water poured over her bulwarks in powerful waves that erupted when they met in her midline. Only her mid structure and king posts protruded above the ocean now. Soon these, too, sank out of sight. Only the fading outline of her hull beneath the huge patch of roiling, stained water marked her passing.

The men aboard the copter watched for a long time after she disappeared. On the western horizon the sun threw long orange streaks across the sky. Dureau tapped McCullom's shoulder. The copter banked sharply and headed north toward the low strip of purple cloud that was Guadalcanal.

The *Panjang* went down in lingering protest, creaking and groaning as the remaining air in her flooded compartments escaped. Fragile light from the surface played on her superstructure, shimmered in dappled patterns across her empty decks. Down she went, as level as if she still sailed the sea.

Gradually her air eruptions diminished. Light faded. She sank into a twilight that thickened into blackness.

Two hundred feet . . . four hundred . . . six . . .

Her descent was slowing. The only sound coming from her now was the soft chirking of straining metal as the hull began to respond to the increasing pressure.

Seven hundred feet . . .

Deep within her, unflooded compartments began to stabilize her drop.

Eight hundred . . .

Nine . . .

She stopped completely. She had reached a point of neutral buoyancy: the trapped air in her unflooded compartments precisely balanced the downward pull of her flooded ones.

Like a dark, ungainly bird, the *Panjang* hovered in blackness and silence. The sea current began to nudge her gently, to the south.

At that moment a tiny pressure fracture appeared in the weld between plates in a deep ballast tank below her engine room. From it a stream of bubbles, delicate as beads of mercury, wobbled toward the surface.

One

91 hours, 42 minutes

Marine biologist Cas Bonner watched the jeep turn off the deserted boulevard and wind down the long, curving road to the docks of Honolulu's Kewalo Basin. Its lights flashed through the jacaranda trees. It came up onto the wooden apron of the dock and inched along, the driver playing a small flashlight onto the nameplates of the moored craft.

Bonner's fingers went still on his guitar. He'd been playing softly, sitting on the transom of his charter boat. Hawaiian slack-key, good finger-picking stuff. It always helped ease tension out of him.

Tonight he needed it. It had been a long, frustrating day. Late in the afternoon his boat had thrown a main shaft out in the middle of the Molokai Channel. Four car dealers from Portland, Oregon, had chartered him for some night diving off Ilio Point, Molokai. He finally got the boat repaired enough to limp home, but the clients were pissed. They bitched all the way in and got puking drunk on his Budweiser supply. When they reached Kewalo at midnight, Bonner had dutifully returned the charter fee. Minus the cost of the beer.

The jeep came abreast of Bonner's boat. The flashlight swept across the stern, then up into Cas's face. The vehicle stopped.

"Bonner?" a man's voice called. "Is that you?"

"Get that damned light out of my eyes."

It went off. A moment later the jeep's headlights also went out and the engine died. The driver got out and walked around to the head of Bonner's slip. There he stopped, looking the boat over. Cas could see now that he was a naval officer, dressed in summer tans.

"What you call this barge, Bonner?"

Cas stiffened, recognizing the voice. "My God! Chaffee?"

The officer laughed and came on down the slip and onto the gangplank. Bonner met him there. They shook hands warmly, slapping each other on the arms. At last Cas stepped back. "Well, I'll be damned. What're *you* doing here this time of night?"

Chaffee didn't answer. He glanced at the neighboring boats. One was a day sailer with its sails in canvas bags, the other an old sampan that creaked softly on the tide. He came back to Bonner. "I need to talk to you. It's important."

"Oh?"

"Somewhere private."

"Sure, let's go below." Cas led the way down into the cabin. It was cluttered with equipment: diving tanks, hose lines, slings, netting. It had the thick aroma of stale salt water and wet wood and neoprene.

Chaffee had to duck coming in. He was tall and slender with close-cropped red hair. Yet he seemed adroit in moving in small spaces. His body molded to corners and projections. He found an empty box and sat down.

"You want a beer?"

"Yeah, sure."

Cas dug a couple of cans out of his ice chest and tossed one to Steve. He slid onto his bunk, popping his. He was a big man in his late thirties, six-two, with broad, muscular shoulders honed by years of diving. His skin was tanned the deep brown of a *kukui* nut thrown onto the beach by the tide. His hair, naturally a light brown, was burned golden by the sun.

He studied Chaffee. In the light he could see the man had changed. He had dark circles under his eyes, and his face looked pale and gaunt. His long, delicate fingers kept tapping his beer can.

Bonner and Chaffee had served together in Nam. Unit Six, the Coastal Recon Section of Naval Intelligence. When the war was over, Steve transferred to the San Diego Center for Submersible Development. A graduate of Woods Hole, he held a Ph.D. in deep-sea environment and had always intended to get into the SD program.

He used to write long letters to Cas. The intensity of his passion for submersibles was as sharp as a bright flame. He managed a transfer for Bonner. For eighteen months they worked together on the R-and-D phase of the Navy's EN-145 Diver, an early deep-exploratory vehicle.

Steve was glancing casually at the cabin clutter. "Not exactly cruiser station."

"Keeps me in Bud and pretzels. How'd you find me?"

"I checked with Hawaiian Marine."

HM was a highly respected research-and-development outfit that specialized in marine technology and oceanic biology. For a time Bonner had been their chief biologist. He had been married to the daughter of a former senator, whose influence had gotten him the job in the first place. When they divorced, Carolyn took her daddy's patronage with her. But that was only part of the reason for his troubles with Hawaiian Marine. Bonner was a rebel. He did things in unorthodox ways, he challenged accepted theories with a zeal for the truth and a disregard for the theorists. That made enemies, and such enemies usually controlled the doors and funds for research. Now he was a pariah, all but locked out of the normal channels of oceanic research.

Chaffee shook his head. "I was sorry to hear about the way things turned out with you over there. It was a pretty good deal while it lasted, wasn't it?"

"While it lasted."

"Well," Chaffee said. "Screw 'em. They threw away a good man."

Cas grunted and took a pull on his beer.

"See, I told you to stay in the Navy."

"No, thanks." He nodded at Chaffee's collar. "I see you made full commander."

Steve nodded, thumping his fingers on the can. Tiny slitted frowns flicked on and off between his eyes.

Bonner lay back on one elbow. "Well, you gonna get to it?"

Steve's eyes came up slowly. He seemed to be inspecting Bonner's forehead. "I need a copilot."

Cas tilted his head. "For a deep dive? Man, I haven't been near a submersible since I left Dago."

"I know that. But this is an emergency. I'll be using a vehicle with very little field time. I need a backup man I can trust."

"What about regular division roster?"

"My assigned dive coordinator got sick. There just aren't any reserves for this type of dive."

"What're you telling me here? There's nobody in the whole friggin' Navy who could qualify?"

"There isn't time for them to orient to the Saran. She's not your typical submersible; her whole design purpose is different."

"And you figure *I* can?"

"Now hear me out. You were the best DC I ever saw. You've got the instincts, Cas. Down inside. A man doesn't learn those things."

Bonner shook his head. "This is crazy."

Chaffee stared at him. "This is going to be a hard run. A lot of powerful people will be watching this one. If I screw up here, my career's gone."

"What's so special about this one?"

Steve averted his eyes. "I can't say until you agree to come along."

"Bullshit."

Steve reached up and pinched the skin of his forehead between thumb and forefinger. Finally he straightened. "Okay. But this is high Q5 stuff, right?"

Cas nodded.

"We've got a freighter on the bottom of the Coral Sea. I have to go locate her. Real fast."

Bonner's eyes narrowed. "Are men trapped aboard her?"

"We don't know. We don't know much of anything, actually. She just disappeared off her track."

"What was she hauling?"

"Secret cargo."

Cas snorted derisively. "That's what I thought. The cloak-and-dagger boys with their tit in the wringer, right?"

"Something like that. It's my job to verify her cargo."

Cas had started to take a drink. He stopped. "Verify cargo? What're you talking about? A deep breach?"

"If necessary, but I don't think it'll come to that. The Saran's equipped to sonar-scan the freighter's holds from the outside. We'll relay data to Comm Div on Midway for computer enhancement. If we're lucky, we'll get adequate shape ident on the cargo to verify."

Shape indent? Bonner thought. They were looking for something specific. "What if you're not that lucky?"

"Then we breach her."

Bonner's skin tingled at the prospect. A deep breach was something he had only read about. With the Diver they had merely probed the depths, observing, cataloging what they saw. Back then, actually boarding a ship at depth was still on the horizon.

Chaffee read his thoughts. "My vehicle can do it, Cas. Believe me. She's got the best gear in the world for a deep breach. A lock chamber that can tight seal beyond twenty thousand feet. And her lasers can cut through six inches of carbon steel."

"Wait a minute, I don't figure something here. Why run the risk of a breach at all? Why not use a robot probe?"

Steve shook his head. "I wish it could be that easy. But the Navy only had one operational robot unit, and that was lost off Newfoundland six months ago by a team from Woods Hole."

"How about the one they used on the *Titanic*?"

"No, they don't want any commercial or foreign outfits in on this. Besides, nobody really knows where Ballard is. Last anybody heard from him, he was doing deep tests off South Africa. He hasn't been in contact for weeks."

Bonner shifted his legs on the bunk. There was a restless tingle in his muscles. He took a drink, stared at Chaffee. "How deep is she?"

"The last position report put her over the Prescott Plateau. Maximum depth in that area is four thousand feet."

Cas's mind brought up the image of the Coral Sea. He'd worked there several years ago on an HM contract to the Navy: dolphin tests along the outer rim of the Great Barrier Reef.

"You're forgetting one little thing, ain't you? The Murchison Trench runs through that sector. We're talking thirty thousand feet there."

"I haven't forgotten," Steve said. "If she's in the trench, well, that's it. I'm hoping she's not."

Bonner drained his beer can, thinking. Chaffee's request was coming from way out in left field; he was reaching, desperate. That kind of desperation could make even the simplest sea operation hairy as hell. And another thing: he knew Steve wasn't putting the whole story on the table. The rest of it was energizing Chaffee with jolts of tension, like a teenager firing speed.

Weird.

During all the years he had known Steve, the one thing that had always marked the man was his cool under pressure. Cas had never seen him panic. He remembered one time in particular. Aboard the Diver they'd run into trouble off the Bahamas. The vehicle became fouled in salvage cables. Only one directional rotor was operating and all internal circuits had blown. They were helpless at eight hundred feet, in total darkness, with less than an hour's supply of air.

Bonner had come very close to panic that time. But Steve had touched his shoulder in the blackness, his voice calm, assured. With curt, crisp commands he had gotten the Diver free and back to recovery depth.

But the man sitting opposite him now wasn't the same Chaffee.

"There's thirty thousand dollars in it for you," Steve blurted abruptly.

Bonner snapped out of his reverie.

"I mean it. Thirty big ones. Whether we find the freighter or not."

"How in hell did you get the Navy to kick in that kind of money?"

"I didn't. It's mine."

"Whoa! How'd *you* get so flush?"

"That doesn't make any difference. What's important is, I need you."

Bonner fell silent. Outside, a night bird went flapping softly over the boat. "I have to be honest," he said finally. "You've changed. I see wires in you."

"I'm okay."

"We both know the cardinal rule. A deep man with something on his mind stays on the surface."

"I tell you, I'm fine." Chaffee's eyes flashed for a fleeting moment with something deep and on fire. Then they softened. He gave an embarrassed smile. "You know how it is, Cas. A new vehicle, the virgin on her wedding night. As soon as we climb aboard the Saran, it'll be like old times."

Well, Bonner thought, here we are. Doubts pulled at him like lead weights tied to his legs. Still, there was something else pulling at him to do it. The old curiosity, that hunger to go have a look at unseen things, to run his fingers along the razor-sharp edge. It had always undercut his rational conclusions, sometimes made him terribly foolish, but it had never bored him.

He crushed his beer can and tossed it into the galley sink. "So, what the hell? Let's give her a shot."

He threw some shaving gear into a ditty bag, sealed off his boat, and they walked back to the jeep. Chaffee swung the vehicle around and headed back toward the boulevard.

The night was silent. Behind them, buoy markers formed a drifting necklace of red flares in the channel. Steve stopped for the light at the boulevard. Across the road a drunken sailor was weaving slowly along the sidewalk, trying desperately to hold to the center.

Cas lit a cigarette and flicked the dying match into the air. He drew a lungful of smoke down and turned to Chaffee. "This freighter of yours was carrying nuclear loads, wasn't she?"

Steve sat very still, said nothing for a long moment. Then he nodded. "Twelve Trident 3A missiles."

Bonner chortled sardonically. "Figures."

At precisely 7:15 A.M. Washington time, the President came into his private conference room adjacent to the Oval Office. A tall, handsome man with a tan acquired from a recent visit to his ranch in Colorado, he greeted no one but went straight to his chair at the head of a long mahogany table. At the door two security men took their places, one on each side.

The four men who had been seated immediately stood. They were: Tim McQuisten, chief adviser of the National Security Council; Philip Rebbeck, director of the Central Intelligence Agency; Admiral Walter Smith, chief of Naval Operations; and Paul Lirette, a personal adviser to the Chief Executive. Two others of this inner group were absent: William Aldrich, Secretary of State, was in London, and Roger Glayshod, Secretary of Defense, was attending a conference in Brussels.

The President sat down and waited for the others to do likewise. He scanned the faces around the table. "Well, gentlemen," he said quietly. "Let's have the details."

The men were stiffly uncomfortable. All except Lirette. He eased back into his chair and folded his arms. He was a small, wiry man with a shock of unruly white hair. An ex-governor of Wyoming, he was very close to the President, who seemed to enjoy his ribald speech and blunt honesty.

Admiral Smith cleared his throat. "Well, sir, we don't as yet know all the pertinent facts. The ship simply lost contact yesterday at 5:22 P.M. Hawaiian time."

"I already know that much," the President said curtly. He found the news very disturbing. The *Panjang* and her cargo were all part of a complex and highly secret agreement he had personally worked out with Scotty Cox, the prime minister of Australia. Under the pact, the U.S. would build and man, in total secrecy, three nuclear submarine bases in Australia: at the Tamarand Estuary, at Point Fowler in the Great Australian Bight, and at Dongara on the Indian Ocean. After six years, ownership of the bases would pass to the Australian navy. It was a mutually sensible agreement, one that would greatly increase allied undersea tactical and strategic positions in the western Pacific and Indian oceans. Unfortunately, the whole thing was a blatant breach of ANZAC treaty injunctions. "What I don't know" he continued, "is what the hell is being done about it."

"Well, as soon as we realized the ship had had some major emergency, a priority call was sent to Air/Sea Command at Pearl. Code relay was then sent to all stations in the southern quadrants, including notification to Australian Coast Watch."

Lirette held up a finger. "Admiral, you're saying this *Panjang*'s radio just up and went dead?"

Smith turned slightly to face him. The admiral was a tall man with a prominently elongated bald head. There were heavy pouches under his eyes. Six months before, he had experienced a heart seizure. "More precisely," he said, "she lost contact in her tracking unit. All subsequent efforts to raise her on open-frequency channels were fruitless. Her power, for some unknown reason, was incapacitated. But that would not have affected her emergency radio. We simply don't know why she wasn't transmitting anything."

Lirette started to ask another question, but the President held up his hand, silencing him. "So, Smitty, where are we now?"

"Frankly, sir, I think she's down."

"Why?"

"Primarily because our satellite photos show no trace of her. Since she was running red category, my people called up a satellite scan. The SeaSat 3 sent back data on the entire Coral—"

Rebbeck cut him off, "You used the SeaSat? Why wasn't the military Sopac-13 used? It's got a damned sight better surveillance capability."

"We had no choice. The 13's scan area is restricted to the Indonesian and South Philippine area. The Coral Sea is out of its range."

The President was watching this exchange intently from under his brows. "And the photos were empty?"

"Completely, sir. Despite the fact the SeaSat is capable of picking up a ship's boiler heat even in last stages of cooling."

The men all drew back, mulling that over.

NSC adviser McQuisten was the first to speak. "Mr. President, isn't it possible we're focusing too much attention on this freighter?"

"How do you mean?"

"We're moving in some extremely delicate areas here. We all know the absolute necessity of establishing leadership at this Pan-Pacific conference. Every major nation involved in the southern Pacific will be present. Many at plenipotentiary level. If we stumble on this *Panjang* incident and the whole secret agreement with the Australian Prime Minister comes to the surface, it could be devastating to our credibility in the region."

McQuisten paused, staring first at the President and then at the others. Satisfied that the full import of what he had said had sunk in, he went on, "I feel we should discontinue any further search for this vessel immediately. It can only hurt us."

"Jesus Christ," Lirette cried. "You mean just leave the damned thing sitting on the bottom of the Coral Sea carrying what we know she's carrying?"

"Yes, that's precisely what I'm saying. What can we do about it anyway? At this moment, Guadalcanal is crawling with media people. Sooner or later they're going to start homing in on this if we continue. As I see it, we can either cancel all search operations or pull out of the conference."

"Impossible," the President snapped. "Backing off now would create bigger questions."

"Then call off the search, sir," McQuisten pleaded. "You're scheduled to be on the Canal in two days. If some hotshot newsman opens the lid on this thing while you're there, my God, you'd be caught—" He stopped suddenly.

Across the table Lirette chortled. "With Jockey shorts waving in the breeze?"

McQuisten flushed. "Mr. President, I didn't mean—"

The Chief waved it off and sat thoughtful for a moment, lightly tapping a silver pen against his thumb. He nodded. "I think Tim's correct. It would be discreet to low-key this thing as much as possible." He turned to Admiral Smith. "But I've got some serious questions before we do that. First off, is there any possibility, any, that those missiles could detonate?"

Smith shook his head emphatically. "Not a chance, sir. All power systems within the canisters are inert until activated by the firing computer aboard the carrier submarine."

"What about radiation contamination? These are five-thousand-megaton units, and there's twelve of them."

"The nuclear masses involved, even if they did leak, would be insignificant once dispersed in the ocean."

"And what about any men aboard who might have gone down with her? Could they still be alive?"

"I'm afraid not, sir. It's been over thirteen hours since contact was broken. Any air pockets in the ship would be contaminated by now."

The President tapped his pen again. "All right, Smitty, call off the search."

The admiral's eyes went dark, but he nodded. "Yes, sir."

Lirette moved forward and put his elbows on the table. "I think there's one possibility we haven't considered here."

The President glanced at him. "What's that, Paul?"

"That the damned *Panjang* was sent to the bottom deliberately."

On the other side of the table Rebbeck stiffened. "What are you saying? The Russians?"

"Maybe."

Rebbeck scoffed. "No way." The muscles in his lean jaw tensed, forming little convolutions under the skin.

Lirette's blue eyes narrowed. "How in the hell can you be so sure?"

"Think about it. Why would the Russians do that? To get what, a few warheads?"

"Maybe Paul's got something," McQuisten put in. "If they could produce just one of those missiles, they'd have proof we were arming a base in Australia."

"What proof would they have if the ship was sunk?"

"Maybe they took one off before they sank it."

"My God," Rebbeck cried derisively. He swung to Smith. "Smitty, what does one of those missiles weigh? Ten, twelve thousand pounds?"

"Nine thousand."

"All right. Nine." He gave McQuisten a sarcastic leer. "What do you figure they did, put one of the damned things down a submarine hatch?"

McQuisten didn't answer. He stared at the table, stung by Rebbeck's sarcasm.

. Lirette said, "As much as I hate to admit it, I have to agree with Rebbeck. From the Russian point of view, a stunt like that would be lunatic. But what if it wasn't Russian?"

Rebbeck's head snapped around. "Then who would it be?"

"Maybe a third-world country, with enough bucks to finance a ship and crew."

"Oh, now we've got a terrorist navy?"

Lirette's face reddened. "It's possible, goddammit."

"No, it's not possible," the CIA director shot back. "Anything of that magnitude would have been picked up by my field agents like that!" He viciously snapped his fingers.

"Like they picked up the embassy takeover?" Lirette dug in with diabolic relish. "Like they tagged onto the Munich massacre?"

Rebbeck's face went ashen with rage. Before he could speak, however, the President sharply rapped his wedding ring against the table. "All right, enough of that." He stared at the two men until they drew back, glaring at each other like stalking lions.

He returned to Smith. "What's your opinion on this aspect?"

"Well, sir, it's unfortunately valid."

The skin around the President's eyes bunched up with cold, sharp intensity. "How valid?"

"Early last night Naval Intelligence ran a contingency/ option construct on the *Panjang*'s disappearance. Three possible scenarios emerged. One, she's still afloat out there somewhere with no power or radio capability. Two, she went down very quickly, taking all her drift debris and fuel with her. And three, she was attacked and deliberately scuttled."

Everyone at the table had moved forward as he spoke. The President was the first to respond. "Are you saying there is a possibility some of those missiles are not aboard that ship?"

"It is a possibility, sir. But one that both NI and myself consider very remote."

"Dammit!" the President hissed. He lunged from his chair and strode to the broad window that overlooked the Rose Garden. The others exchanged hard, silent glances. Even Lirette said nothing. The President returned to the table but didn't sit down. He leaned forward, placing his palms against the tabletop. "Does NI have any speculation as to who would do this?"

"The scenario suggests a fast-moving corvette or PT, not a submarine. A smaller craft would be harder to detect, yet would still be capable of deck-loading at least one missile. However, this type of attack would almost certainly be from pirates, and that would change the scenario."

"Pirates?" The President looked surprised. "I don't understand."

"The entire Indonesian–New Guinea ocean quadrant is infested with local pirates. They're scavengers who attack ships that have somehow wandered out of the normal shipping corridors. But that fact creates a dichotomy. If pirates did strike her, they couldn't have possibly known about the missiles. The attack would have simply been a standard ambush. The *Panjang* would have been looted, then scuttled. But her debris and oil would have left a wide slick on the ocean. Pirates don't have the heavy firepower to put a ship down quickly. They open her petcocks and flood her, and that takes a very long time to put her under. As I said earlier, nothing was seen of her or any oil slick."

He paused, expecting a comment from the President. When none came, he continued: "On the other side of the picture, that is, if the missiles *were* the prime target, it has to be assumed the strike force was from an organized nation with a sophisticated intelligence network. It would then have to be the Russians."

Across the table Rebbeck started to say something. Smith held up his hand. "Let me finish. It's precisely this aspect of the hijack scenario that makes NI consider the whole thing remote. I think we all agree the Russians would never mount such an attack at this time and place."

"But, Smitty," Lirette asked quietly, "what if the Russians already know about the Tamarand base?"

"They probably do. Their own scan satellites would have picked up the freighter traffic up the Estuary. It's just not conceivable they would do anything militarily at the moment."

The President bored in on Smith. "It all sounds very neat, but it's still speculative. I can't act on assumptions, not in this case."

"I agree completely, sir," Smith answered. "It's because of this that I initiated action last night aimed at proving definitely that those Tridents are still aboard the *Panjang*. I ordered the Saran submersible unit to the Coral Sea to locate the ship and verify her cargo."

McQuisten gasped. "A full-scale submersible search? My God, you'll have every journalist on Guadalcanal chartering a plane to go out and have a look. It'll be a bloody circus."

"No, it won't," Smith shot back. "The operation will be totally covert. A single antisubmarine P-3C aircraft will be used to run a sonar search. When they find her, the support ship will move in alone. Diving operations will be conducted at night."

"Can this Saran make a hundred-percent verify?" the President asked.

"I believe so, sir. We've got the best submersible officer on this, Commander Steve Chaffee. The vehicle can sonar-scan the ship from the outside to identify even the smallest items of cargo. And if that fails, she has the capability of actually breaching the ship."

"What are the depths in this area of the Coral Sea?"

"Approximately four thousand feet, sir. The Saran is operational at five times that depth."

Everyone turned to the President, waiting for his decision. At last he straightened. "All right, Smitty, I want you to push that Saran crew to as much speed as is humanly possible. I want constant updates on them."

"Yes, sir."

McQuisten tried to recover something. "Sir, could we at least place an embargo on both shipping and aircraft traffic in, out, and around the Canal?"

The President glanced at Smith. "Possible?"

"Yes, sir. In fact, I'd say it would be a wise move. Not only to expedite the secrecy of the diving operations, but as a general security precaution for the conference."

The President nodded. "Do it."

On Guadalcanal it was still pre-dawn. Alain Dureau stirred in sleep, shifted on his straw mat, and opened his eyes. He was in a hut. It was dark save for a flickering light that came through a hole cut into the wall of the hut. The room smelled of marijuana, and beneath it the stench of fish and garbage. A dot of orange light glowed brightly for a second across the hut, and Dureau's eyes darted to it. It faded, glowed again, faded. In the faint light from the window he could make out the young Melanesian girl who was McCullom's mistress. Kalima was smoking a long reed pipe. Now she put her head back against the thatch wall, holding the smoke in. The movement jutted her naked breasts forward. Her nipples shone in the flicker like whorls of ebony.

McCullom's shack was located beside a muddy estuary that fingered in from the sea. The hut had a corrugated tin roof and thatched walls, and stood on heavy coconut pilings to keep it dry during the heavy-tide season. A reef lay several hundred yards out, and now and then the hissing sound of surf could be heard.

Yesterday evening, McCullom had landed the copter in a small clearing that the girl had marked with kerosene lamps. As they came in, the copter's landing lights illuminated her standing at the edge of the clearing. She was completely naked.

The girl prepared a meal for them while they changed out of their fatigues; vinegar rice balls and strips of dried fish and cups of a thick yellow mash liquor. McCullom didn't eat. He kept downing cupfuls of the liquor, his eyes flashing with excitement. "Damn, mates, we done it!" he kept saying joyously. "We bloody pulled it off. Them fuckin' Yanks'll have a bitch tryin' to find that bleeding ship."

The Aussie was a dope runner. Weekly he took loads of hemp out to rendezvous with freighters headed for Brisbane and Rockhampton. The hemp was grown by Tikapi Indians in the lush forest of the Maragud Ride, west of Guadalcanal's capital city of Honiara. Sometimes he hauled bundles of raw cocaine processed and transshipped in from New Guinea.

He was an ex-ANZAC chopper pilot who had flown British Gazelle AR-3's in Nam. Afterward he'd run guns and ammunition to the Communist rebels in New Guinea and aborigine girls from Australia to the slum houses of Honiara and Tasimboko.

Dureau sat up. "Where is McCullom?" he asked softly.

"Gone to wait for the boat." The girl's voice was soft and drugged-lazy.

He reached out to Villachio, who was stretched beside him. Instantly the Italian sat up. Together they stepped through the door and down a long ramp to the beach. Somewhere along the rim of the estuary, a crocodile roared in the night.

McCullom was squatted beside a small fire of coconut branches. He glanced up as they approached the fire. His face was sweaty and dulled by drink. "Well," he said sullenly, "have a bloody good sleep, did we?"

Neither man answered. Villachio hunkered down and idly played with the coconut coals with a stick. Out near the reef a flashlight blinked several times. McCullom pulled a flashlight from his pocket and returned the signal. He poked it in the sand and looked at Dureau.

"All right, the boat's here, Frenchie. It's settlin' time."

"Of course," Dureau said pleasantly, and squatted on the opposite side of the fire. "How much was it, now?"

"You bleeding know how much it is. You gi' me fiddy thousand right off, I got fiddy more comin'."

Dureau nodded. Behind McCullom the Melanesian girl wandered into the firelight and stood watching. Her eyes were heavy-lidded. Dureau studied her casually. She stood with a relaxed sensuality, her weight on one hip, her skin made coppery by the fire.

"She's lovely," Dureau said.

McCullom's mouth opened in a yellow grin. "You like that, do you?" He turned and looked possessively at the girl. "Aye, Kalima's lovely, all right. Especially her dark little *pingo*." He swung back, his eyes slitting with sudden drunken comradeship. "Lemme tell you, when she's soaked with the stuff, she'll suck your bleedin' guts right through your cock."

"Ah, yes."

McCullom waved his hand. "Enough cunt talk, let's get to the money, Frenchie."

The sound of Dureau's silenced Beretta 9mm was like the quick snuffle of a lead weight flung into a still pool. McCullom took the first bullet without moving. Only his mouth burst open. "Bloody hell," he gasped.

The second bullet knocked him onto his buttocks.

Kalima stiffened. Instantly Villachio leapt to his feet and grabbed her roughly by the arm.

The Aussie was rolling around on his side, feeling with his hands like a delirious man trying to find the edge of things. He cursed softly. Dureau rose and moved around the fire. He shot the man in the back of the head, twice. McCullom went limp and blood spurted onto the sand. It glistened in the firelight.

Dureau walked to Villachio and the girl. He stood looking at her. She didn't seem particularly frightened. He touched one of her nipples. It felt as smooth as a polished gemstone. "Lovely," he said, and lifted her chin. "Do you enjoy life, Kalima?"

She stared at him.

"Do you, love?"

"Yes."

"Good. Then you will go off into the jungle and find yourself another man. Mm?"

She nodded.

"Go."

Villachio released her. She walked slowly up the beach, the firelight dancing on her buttocks. In a moment she had disappeared into the darkness.

Villachio said, "Was that wise, Alain?"

"She's seen killing before. This one will mean no more than the others."

They walked down to the water's edge to wait for the boat. In a few minutes it loomed out of the night. The boatman, a strapping Melanesian in tattered khaki shorts, stepped out and pushed it onto the sand.

The boat, a native *palimi* canoe, was more than twenty feet long and constructed from a single mahogany log.

An old six-cylinder Ford engine was mounted near the stern, and its propeller shaft extended far beyond the transom.

"Where Cullom?" the boatman asked.

Dureau nodded toward the fire, where the Aussie's body lay as if in sleep. "Drunk," he said.

The Melanesian shrugged. He bent to hold the *palimi* steady as Dureau and Villachio climbed in. The seats were narrow and a bed of dried coconut leaves lined the bottom. Alain settled himself near the bow. The boatman turned the craft around, gave it a powerful shove, and slipped into the stern. He paddled for a few moments, until they could feel the surge of the channel buffeting the canoe.

The boatman started the engine. It throbbed throatily as they eased up the channel. The surf residue off the reef soughed softly off the bow.

By the time they reached open ocean, Dureau was asleep again.

Two

81 hours, 22 minutes

The sun came out of the eastern sea like the rising mushroom of a nuclear explosion. Its light washed with sudden brilliance across the nine-hundred-mile-long chain of the Solomon Islands. In a small hill cabana nestled among eucalyptus trees just outside the capital town of Honiara, site for the upcoming Pan-Pacific Conference, Marine Colonel Sab Spangenberg lay naked on a large *punee*, a native bed, and smoked quietly, watching the new morning filtering through his blinds. Beside him lay a young Melanesian woman, also naked.

After a moment he slipped softly from the *punee*, picked up a half-empty bottle of gin from the bed stand, and walked to the window. He was a lean, muscular man in his mid-fifties. His grayish-brown hair was close-cropped. His eyes, narrowed against the light, were the gray of storm clouds over the Arctic. He took a long pull from the bottle and gazed through the blinds at the grassy slope that slanted down to town.

Sabbath Richard Spangenberg was the possessor of twenty-eight citations for valor, including the Congressional Medal of Honor. He was a genuine hero who had, in storybook style, won it all the hard way. As a twenty-year-old master gunnery sergeant in Korea, he had won his first battle promotion on the Chosin Reservoir. Subsequent grades had come quickly. In Nam as a light colonel, they had called him Slam Dunk Sab, head of a crack raider regiment that made insurgency forays against the Khmer Rouge. On a hill named Quen Tok, he and seventeen of his troopers had stood off three battalions before being relieved. That action had garnered him the Medal and his silver eagles.

But war and its glories fade. The idiosyncrasies of field heroes transported to the delicate elegance of Washington dinner parties make an abrupt and embarrassing impact. Spangenberg was a satyr. Word of his hunger soon tarnished his medals. Desk jockeys whispered that the colonel possessed a grotesque, insatiable appetite, and he was shunted into the shadows. On Guadalcanal he had been assigned as a liaison to the local constabulary during the Pan-Pacific Conference.

He took another deep draft of gin and returned to the *punee*. He slid a knee onto the coverlet and bent to lightly kiss the woman's exposed breast, the nipple thick as a thumb of chocolate. She sighed, half-awake. The taste of her skin heated him into tumescence. He lowered his body beside her and entwined a thigh between her legs.

She opened her eyes. "Sore," she whispered.

"No, angel," he cooed gently into her jet-black hair. He twisted downward, drawing a tongue line over the rise of her stomach. Her opening was swollen, redolent of the night's debauchery. He licked, devoured. She cried out when he penetrated her. Eyes closed, he plunged on. At last orgasm trembled through him. Again and still again. Sweat limned the woman's face.

He disengaged. She lay gasping into the pillow. Spangenberg sat on the edge of the *punee* and stared dully at the floor. The old savage hunger receded like a tiger fading into brush.

An hour later, in knife-creased summer tans, he strode into the Quonset hut designated Marine Liaison Group One on the edge of the newly constructed conference complex. A young sergeant stood as he came through the door. Sab went past him into his office and a moment later the sergeant followed with a cup of steaming coffee.

The colonel dropped into his chair behind a massive *koa*-wood desk he had won in a crap game two nights before with a Chinese pimp in the Slot, Honiara's red-light district. He lit a cigarette. The sergeant produced a sheaf of papers and began droning off the night's events. "The military police picked up one of the base marines last night, sir. Sergeant Rawlins. Made him on a D and D."

"Where is he now?"

"Over in the brig in Numura."

"Get him out."

"Aye, sir." He moved on to other items. "We got a priority DM from Pearl at oh-four-hundred. We are to investigate presence of local terrorists."

Spangenberg's head came up. "Local what?"

"Terrorists, sir. Pearl wants a complete rundown of dissidents in the area from local constabulary."

Sab snorted. "Local constabulary wouldn't know a terrorist if you shoved one up their ass."

"Yes, sir," the sergeant said boredly. He finished the night's report and departed.

The colonel sipped at his coffee, then pulled a bottle of cognac from his desk and spiced his cup. He lit another cigarette. Local terrorists, he thought. The idea was absurd. He had spent enough time in these southern islands to know that the fanatical personality type of the typical terrorist simply didn't exist here. The goddamned natives were too stupid or impassive to generate the intensity of fomentation cells and revolutionary rhetoric.

Of course, terrorists from the outside, that was a different matter. The magnet of this coming conference would attract them like hounds to a bitch in heat. But that wasn't *his* bailiwick. Oh, no, let the jerkoffs from CIA and British Intelligence and the French Morovine Group handle that shit.

Still, something about the early-morning dispatch nagged at him. Why the sudden concern? During his prestation briefings in Sydney, no mention had been made of local terrorists. He snapped his chair around and picked up his phone. He dialed the constabulary headquarters. There was a double ring and a man answered: "Honiara Constabulary, Fa'uza here."

Jacob Jacob Fa'uza, chief constable, was a grizzled islander who had fought the Japanese in 1943.

"Jacob, Colonel Spangenberg."

"Ah, Colonel, how good, how good."

"I want to know something. You people find any evidence of local dissidents?"

"Dis-si-dents? What is this dis-si-dents?"

"Fuckups, Jacob. People who don't like the way things are run."

"Oh, no, Colonel. We keep very good peace here."

"What about weapons? You ever find guns?"

"Guns are forbidden on Guadalcanal."

"I know that, Jacob. But what about the fishing fleet? Could they bring in guns?"

"Oh, no, sir."

"Have you checked?"

"Yes, we check for hemp. We find much hemp. It is terrible how much hemp we find."

"Fuck the hemp, Jacob. I'm talking guns and explosives."

"No, no, there are no guns and explosives. We police very expertly."

Spangenberg blew a ring of smoke. "All right, Jacob. You keep a close watch, you hear? You find any artillery coming into this island, I want to know about it."

"Oh, yes, Colonel. We will be very watchful."

Sab hung up and settled thoughtfully into his chair. The day's heat was filling the room like a dragon's breath. Annoyed, he drew a lungful of smoke and spewed it upward, where it dissipated in the slowly revolving overhead fan. He was powerless to act on his instincts, the guiding force in his life. Jacob Fa'uza and his ragtag force of *lavalava*-clad constables offered little comfort.

He sighed. This whole operation was shit-face. One big fuckup run by bureaucratic assholes. He'd seen them,

resplendent in dinner jackets, wandering through the dives
and shanty whorehouses of the Slot. Their faces were as
pallid as the underbellies of rotting fish. Liaison men,
guidon bearers, fussily preparing the way for the big
honchos who would follow. He despised such people, as
all warriors despise those who sit in the rear echelons and
count spears.

And yet perhaps the garbage had brought others.
Terrorists.

He shifted in his chair restlessly, the old blood scent
rising. He rolled his cigarette between his fingers and
stared moodily at the slow swing of the overhead fan.

Bonner slept through the whole flight from Honolulu.
Fifteen minutes out of Midway, Chaffee woke him. They
walked aft through a sophisticated sonar room to the
aircraft's galley. They were aboard one of the P-3C Orions
from SVR-4, the antisubmarine tactical force out of Pearl.
They'd taken off before dawn, and it was now late
morning.

Steve handed Cas a cup of coffee. Chaffee looked
exhausted. Bonner found a box of flares and sat down,
stretching his legs. "You look like shit," he said. "Didn't
you sleep at all?"

"No, I was going over marine contour maps of the
Prescott."

"It's gonna be a bitch finding that ship, isn't it?"

"I'm hopeful. These SVR boys are pretty sharp."
Chaffee rubbed his neck, opening and closing his bloodshot eyes.

"You better get some sleep," Cas said. "You're going
to need it."

"Yeah, I will on the leg south."

The aircraft's engine pitch was audibly changing. There
were a few buffets as it moved lower into thicker air. Cas
peered out a porthole. Far below, the ocean made a flat
blue carpet. Just off the starboard wing he caught sight of
the tip of Midway. Cas came back. "Assuming we find
her, how do you think she'll be sitting?"

"Last night I talked with a machinist mate who served on Liberties. He said all the Sam boats had flat bottoms. That means if she didn't plow in or break up, chances are she'll be flat and upright on the floor."

"Let's hope so. We'd have clear scan of both sides of her hull."

"That's true, but it could also complicate a breach. We'd have to come down right on top of her. Could be very hard getting through her upper works and deck gear. If we have to go in, I'd prefer a shot directly into her hold from the side."

"Which hold are we looking for? Do you know?"

"According to her load chart, the missiles are in number two."

Cas took another sip of coffee. It was very strong and drove the last wisps of sleep from him. "Will the scan tell us which compartments are already flooded? If we go cracking a seam into a flooded hold, we're gonna have real problems."

Chaffee frowned. "The scan gear's capable of it, but I'm more worried about another problem."

"Like what?"

"This machinist claimed the Liberties, particularly those that had gone in for refit, had double hulls with a three-foot space between plates. If that space is empty and filled with air, it'll distort the readout."

"Why wouldn't it be empty?"

"The machinist said that sometimes captains pumped fuel up into it to stabilize the ship in heavy weather."

Bonner grunted. There were no storms at those latitudes this time of year. "You figure anybody's still alive on her?"

Chaffee shook his head. "No, it's been too long."

For one long, bleak moment Bonner pictured what it was going to be like going aboard a sunken ship lying on the bottom of the ocean. Darkness. Bulkheads like slabs of ice. Cavernous, compacted silence. And the thick, putrid smell of death. . . .

He shook the image from his mind and watched through the porthole as Midway rose out of the sea.

While the Orion was being refueled, Chaffee borrowed a line jeep and they drove over to the administration center, around a long curving bay where water-skiers were out and young girls sunned on the beach. The base commander was Captain Karo, a short man in his late fifties. He greeted them pleasantly in a spacious office furnished in rattan. "Well, Commander, you certainly must have talked a hellish line to CINCPAC. They've not only given straight-through permission, but they've even classified you a Code Five priority. I'm impressed."

On the ride over, Chaffee had explained that Karo knew nothing of the *Panjang*'s cargo. He was assuming that Chaffee's interest in the ship was simply due to the fortuitous opportunity to test the Saran in an actual salvage situation. "Thank you, sir. They were more receptive than I had hoped. Have you alerted your analysis section yet?"

Karo nodded. "We've also sent entry codes to the *Voorhees*." He was referring to USS *Claude Voorhees,* the Saran's support ship, which had left Midway before midnight.

"Very good, sir." He stood up and Bonner followed. "I certainly want to thank you, Captain. You've been extremely helpful."

"Oh, by the by," Karo said, "that geologist of yours was tearing around the base early this morning looking for you. It seems nobody told her the *Voorhees* was leaving. Why is that?"

"She's a civilian, sir. I thought it best to leave her here rather than hassle over regulations."

"Ah?" Karo's gaze moved to Bonner. "He's a civilian."

"Bonner's ex-Navy. He was with me in Nam and on the Diver project."

Karo's eyes narrowed slightly. "Incidentally, what about your ex-copilot, Eckhart? Do you still intend to press that thing?"

"Yes, sir," Chaffee snapped.

Karo nodded. "Well, what do you intend I do with your geologist?"

"I'd appreciate it if you could assign her quarters for a few days. Until I can confer with her employers at Sutter Oil."

A faint smile touched the captain's lips. "I understand she's a mite waspish. Chewed hell out of my yardmaster."

The base cafeteria was crowded with civilian workers and a few military dependents. Bonner and Chaffee found an empty table on a patio overlooking a seaplane anchorage. Two old PBY's were moored to buoys offshore. The water was very clear, showing rock formations on the bottom.

Bonner wolfed down his food, but Chaffee ate listlessly, gazing off over the ocean. "Christ," Bonner said between chews. "What's the matter with me? I haven't asked how Denise is."

Steve's head snapped around. In his eyes was a sudden bleak hardness, "She's left me," he said flatly.

"Hey, I'm sorry." Cas formed a mental picture of Denise Chaffee. Tall, slender, pretty in a frenetic way. He remembered her always rambling on with a feverish rush, as if hysteria were hiding in the next moment. "What happened?"

Chaffee shrugged and looked away. "I guess the pressure finally got to her. She always hated the diving operations."

"I remember."

The hardness in Steve's eyes melted. Now there was pain. "No, that's not true. It wasn't the dives. She was having an affair."

Bonner stopped chewing.

Chaffee's gaze banked off his face and returned to the ocean. "An ensign with the Recon Command at Dago." He snorted with bitterness. "A lousy fucking ensign."

"Where is she now?"

"Who knows?"

Bonner looked away. There was nothing to say. He watched a small detail of sailors lethargically policing the lawn. At that moment a pretty young woman came into the cafeteria, her stride long-legged and determined. Her hair was sun-bleached and ruffled from the sea breeze. She wore shorts and a pink tank top emblazoned with SAVE THE WHALES, ASSHOLES.

Bonner had caught her entrance out of the corner of his eye and stiffened. "Jesus! It's Napah Gilchrist!"

Chaffee jerked around. "Where?"

"Right there. What the hell is *she* doing here?"

Chaffee cursed. "That's all I need now. Let's get out of here."

"You know her?"

"She's the geologist with Sutter Oil."

They hurried down the patio steps and crossed the lawn toward the parking lot. Steve glanced at Bonner. "Where do you know her from?"

"She was in some of my classes when I did that lecture series at Scripps a few years ago. A mite waspish? She's a goddamned fireball. Challenged everything I said in the lectures. Drove me nuts."

"Yeah, that's her."

They reached the jeep and climbed in. Chaffee fumbled with the keys and finally got the engine started. There was a screech from the patio, and they swung around. Napah Gilchrist was wildly waving her arms at them.

Chaffee slumped. Gilchrist sprinted across the lawn, breasts bouncing under the WHALES and ASSHOLES. The sailor detail paused to watch appreciatively as she galloped past. "You wait right there, Chaffee," she yelled. "I want to talk to you."

As Cas watched her come on, he remembered with sudden clarity that her eyes were green. She used to sit in the front row of the lecture hall, intensely attentive, constantly questioning. Out in the demo tanks, she could swim like a fish, those long, damnably lovely legs propelling her with the force of a fleeing dolphin.

She pulled to a stop on his side of the jeep, the emerald eyes flashing. "All right, buster, where the hell have you been?"

"Gilchrist," Steve said patiently. "I can't explain anything right now, but—"

"You damned well better."

"Now, listen—"

"No, you listen. I've been running around this damned base for the last eight hours trying to find somebody who'd tell me what the hell's going on. First you disappear, then the *Voorhees* takes off like its ass is on fire. Dammit, I came here to do a job, not get screwed around by you Navy types."

"I'm sorry, there's an emergency."

"You have an emergency? I've had Sutter headquarters burning my ears off since six this morning wanting to know why the field tests have been scrapped. That's an emergency."

Chaffee frowned. "Who the hell told them that?"

"How do I know? Thanks to you, I don't know anything."

Bonner touched her arm gently. "Look, why don't we discuss this someplace more private?"

Gilchrist focused her green fire on his hand. "Do you mind, Bonner?"

"For God's sake, Gilchrist," Chaffee said, "get in the jeep. We've got a matter of national security here."

"What?"

"Get in the goddamned jeep."

She pushed Bonner's shoulder. "Move it over."

Cas climbed into the back and Napah slid onto his seat. Chaffee jammed the gears in and they took off. Two sailors in the yard detail whistled. "The field tests have been temporarily suspended," Chaffee said over the whine of the engine. "That's all I can tell you."

"Temporarily? How long is temporarily?"

"Two weeks."

"Why?"

"I said, that's all I can tell you."

"Great! And what am I supposed to do in the meantime? Feed the goddamned goonie birds?"

"We'll be back."

"No."

Steve lost his patience. "Goddammit, I told you this is a matter of national security. That overrides everything. Your people will just have to wait."

Gilchrist shook her head stubbornly. "No way, pal. You got a problem? Fine. Either I get explanations, or I call Sutter Oil and tell them you've backed out on our contract."

"You can't do that."

"Hide and watch."

They reached the end of the anchorage. Chaffee viciously swung the vehicle onto the road to the terminal. They flew along in silence for a full minute.

"All right," Chaffee said at last. "Okay, you want to be in on this, you're in."

Bonner's head snapped up. "What're you saying? We need her like we need a load of rattlesnakes."

"She goes," Steve said sharply.

Napah turned around. "Why don't you butt out, fella?"

Bonner settled morosely into his tiny seat, glowering at the back of Gilchrist's neck. Her hair blew in the wind, sending waves of perfumed air washing over him. It smelled lemony, like fresh rain. He reached out and tapped her on the shoulder. "Still the hardass, eh, Gilchrist?"

Her glance back was long and withering. "And you're still playing Mr. Macho Man, eh, Bonner?"

Cas sighed. Sweet, he thought disgustedly. This is going to be real sweet.

Lieutenant Commander Frank Hillar of the *Voorhees* grinned devilishly across the chessboard at his exec, Matt Costello. "You never learn, baby."

Costello searched the board, finally spotted his error. "Well, shit! Not again?"

Hillar triumphantly moved a knight. "Check and mate." He leaned back, folding thick, muscular arms covered with hair the same rich red as the thatch on his head. He was an easygoing skipper. His crew called him Coach because, twenty years before, he'd played guard on a semipro football team out of Seattle.

"One of these days, buddy," Costello said. He pushed away from the wardroom table and poured himself a cup of coffee.

"How much you owe me now?" Hillar teased. "Five hundred?"

"Who knows? I lost count."

The intercom crackled. "Coach, Bridge. Engine says we're getting a little chatter in number-two shaft."

Hillar cursed. "I knew it. Goddammit, I hate pushing her like this." He lunged to his feet and slapped the intercom button. "I'm on my way."

Droplets of water made trails on the bridge window. Two hours before, they had run into a fast-moving squall out of the northwest. But the sea was calm, long swells under the gray sky.

Hillar paused to check the compass, then stepped onto the starboard weather wing and looked astern. The *Voorhees* was an icebreaker refitted into a submersible support ship. She carried a high prow triple-steeled for cutting floes. Her amidship structure was four stories high, which gave the ship an ungainly, top-heavy look. The stern had been modified with a cutaway transom made into a slide ramp. Surrounding the ramp was a bevy of launch and recovery gear, including a tall swing-out crane. The Saran vehicle itself sat on a pedestal, its fore and aft struts chained to the deck. Hillar studied the ship's wake rolling away from the stern ramp before returning to the bridge. "She's lagging to port, all right. What's our position?"

A seaman called it out from the chart room.

"We also got a code from Midway," the bridge officer

said. "An Orion with Commander Chaffee aboard will rendezvous with us at 1010 S, 1640 E at ten hundred hours tomorrow."

Hillar returned to the port wing and squinted astern. Costello joined him. "Well, looks like Chaffee found himself another copilot," he said.

"I hope whoever this copilot is," Hillar snapped over his shoulder, "he's better than that flake Eckhart."

"Yeah, the kid was a little hyper, wasn't he? Incidentally, scuttlebutt says he isn't in sick bay at all. He's in the Midway brig."

Hillar swung around. "Is that right? On what charge?"

"Striking a superior officer."

The ship was drifting off her track again, and Hillar bellowed through the door. "Goddammit, Philpotts, steady her up."

The young bridge officer echoed the call and glared at the helmsman. Slowly the *Voorhees* came back.

Dureau trudged behind Villachio along a scorching plantation road toward Honiara. The mass of green jungle rose on either side of the road, thick and airless. It was nearly noon, and they had been walking for three hours. The road showed patches of coral stone where plantation gangs had covered rain channels.

Dureau was exhausted and drenched with sweat. He wasn't used to such physical labor; he thrived in the salons and casinos of Europe, or the sumptuous homes of oil barons and gunrunners of the Near East. Despite that, his body was lean and trim. His finely chiseled features, the glossy sweep of sable hair, showed the youthful vigor of his twenty-nine years.

His reputation in the dark world of international terrorism far outweighed his age. An elusive, brilliant jackal, he was known by many names: Assassin 13, Jeaumeau, the Viper, code names tagged to files in every major police organization in the world. Yet despite this notoriety, no picture of him existed. He moved in swift anonymity, one day in Istanbul, the next in Venice, the third in Paris.

Alain's instinct for movement was genetic. All his male ancestors had been sailors. His father had died of syphilis, his mother, an Alsatian prostitute, of an overdose of heroin. As a boy he had lived with his maternal grandmother in Touraine. She was an unstable woman who cursed the neighbors and sometimes threw rotted vegetables at the police. At fourteen, Alain's good looks had enamored him to a local widow named Angel Costinou. During sweltering afternoons he made love to her. In return, she taught him good manners, a taste for poetry, art, Bordeaux wine, and an abiding sense of his own power.

In 1968 Madame Costinou took him to Paris. He stood on a sidewalk and watched the student riots of that summer, thrilling to the roaring, malevolent power of mass movements. It created a fascinating dream.

When he reached nineteen, he was sent off to the Sorbonne, where he studied mechanical engineering and political science. Within a year he joined the Gascon Revolutionary Guard. In shadowed cabarets he discussed Marcuse and Ché Guevara and he met a man named Rudolph Sheltzer, an anarchist lawyer from Prague.

Sheltzer's wife, Enide, was a Renaissance painting come to life: thighs of robust thrusting power, breasts that could envelop. She fell madly in love with Alain. In an artist's loft beside the Tuileries they mated in constant and delirious abandon, and Enide whispered that his destiny lay in anarchy.

He killed his first man, a usurper to the leadership of the Gascon movement, when he was twenty. He used a short-barreled Walther that put a hole in the man's head the size of his thumb. Afterward he wept in Enide's arms, aflight with a strange ecstasy. Soon after that he met Ulrike Meinhof of the Red Army Faction, a cretin with wild eyes and a lesbian lover named Andreas Baader who was more violent than he. From them he learned that beliefs needed the backing of explosives.

For four years he drifted through elite European terrorist organizations: the Italian Red Brigades, the Breton Front de Liberation de la Bretagne, the Spanish ETA. Yet he slowly began to understand that there was something essentially sterile and pointless in these subterranean political movements. The true believers killed for an ideology, not for personal gain. To Dureau, this was stupid. But he took from them what he needed. He became expert in weaponry and explosives. Soon he branched out on his own. He would kill anyone, anywhere, anytime for the right price.

Eventually Europe became unsafe. He moved his operation to festering Beirut, where he formed links with the PLO and Black September. He met Pellegrino Villachio, a Sicilian deserter from the French Foreign Legion who had fought in the brush wars of Central Africa. The powerfully built, gorilla-faced man brooded in silence, yet possessed a dark code of personal honor. They became inseparable. Villachio was the only human Alain Dureau trusted.

Internecine bloodletting soon lost its lift for him. Slaughter is an addiction that demands ever more powerful sources of stimulation. He dreamed of ultimate supremacy in his chosen field. An assassin of historical proportions. He watched and waited. Then, through a chance remark by the Greek mistress of a Russian envoy to The Hague, Alain learned that the Americans were doing something very interesting in northern Australia.

It took Dureau months to put all the pieces together from a network of covert sources. And more months to isolate a mole strategically located in the San Diego Logistics Depot, a swabbie with a real hard-on against the U.S. Navy. He gave Alain the three key elements of the plan: the designation and departure date of the *Panjang*, the precise position of a specific Trident in the loading hold, and a wax imprint of the latest break-in numbers for that missile. His payment was to be a hundred kilograms of raw cocaine. Instead he got a Cadillac engine block chained to his chest and sixty feet of water off the Tenth Street Pier in San Diego harbor.

They heard the vehicle coming from a long way off, the whine of its engine riffling and fading through the jungle. Dureau paused and lowered his pack to the ground. Up ahead, Villachio glanced back. A British Land Rover covered with dust came around the bend. A man in a wide plantation hat was driving. He slowed and stopped beside Alain. He was a ruddy Englishman with a short gray beard and watery eyes. "Hello," he called cheerily. "You chaps need a lift?"

Dureau smiled. "Are you going into Honiara?"

"Yes."

"Thank you, *monsieur*." He slung his pack into the back of the Land Rover. Villachio came down and silently climbed onto the rear seat. Alain got in and the Englishman drove on.

"Tourists?"

"Yes," Dureau answered pleasantly. "Working tourists, actually. I'm doing research on a book."

"Ah, a writer."

Dureau introduced himself as Paul Soison and Villachio as Anthony Garibaldi. The Englishman's name was Mathew Mott-Smith. He owned a plantation near Toombar Grove on the southern end of the Maragud.

"Are you from Paris, by any chance?" he asked.

"Yes."

"Ah, indeed. My wife would love to meet you. She's from Paris too. Longs for the homeland sometimes. Personally, I find Paris a bit too bohemian for my tastes. No offense. Prefer Italy myself. Eh, Garibaldi? Bloody drenched in history, that country."

"Yes," Villachio said.

They drove awhile in silence. Finally Mott-Smith said, "Damned nuisance this conference, don't you think?"

"Oh? Why is that, *monsieur*?"

"All these powerful nations coming here to carve up the bloody area. Makes me damned sick. For years no one cared about the South Pacific. Sleepy natives, swaying palms, and all that rubbish. Now the bastards have run out of contending ground elsewhere, so here they come."

"Will this have a bad effect on your business?"

Mott-Smith snorted. "Bloody well has already. Those bleeding Americans have placed a damned embargo zone around the island. Nothing in or out without their permission. I've got a load of copra sitting in Honiara right now that should have left this morning. Bloody cheeky Yanks." His face contorted with rage. "Well, I'll damned well make the ears of the commissioner of shipping burn when I get there."

Dureau glanced sharply over his shoulder at Villachio. "This embargo," he said to Mott-Smith. "Does it apply to the small fishing boats too?"

"Applies to everything that moves. Even bloody aircraft."

In the trees beside the road a flock of mynah birds suddenly burst into the sky, spooked by the Land Rover's engine roar. Dureau watched them scatter, cawing furiously. His eyes were thoughtful.

"Bloody Americans," Mott-Smith grumbled.

Jim Gillespie, U.S. coordinator for media coverage to the Pan-Pacific Conference, had a blistering headache. Last night he had attended a journalists' cocktail party at the newly constructed main hall in the conference complex, and had vague memories of swimming with all his clothes on in a swampy place.

At the moment he was gloomily seated in the Lead-bottom Lounge, one of the five bars built to cater to conference personnel.

The conference complex covered four hundred acres gouged out of the jungle a half-mile south of Honiara. Over the past six months massive construction had created a small city of dormitories, dining halls, a gymnasium with adjacent swimming pools and tennis courts, and numerous administration buildings and delegation offices. Everything was built in concentric circles around the main conference hall, a low, windowless structure of yellow sandstone that looked like a huge blockhouse.

A Washingtonian, Gillespie had been here for two weeks. In the heat a maddening rash had erupted under his testicles. He was a thirty-four-year-old back-slapper with a receding hairline. At one time a journalist, he had found government service more conducive for establishing contacts. One day he hoped to become a publisher.

The Leadbottom Lounge was sunk in semidarkness. The bartender, a morose Melanesian in a see-through *balagong* shirt, was taking bottles out of a wooden case at the end of the bar and putting them on a back shelf. A man and woman came into the lounge, flushing the bar with white-hot sunlight for a moment. They stood just inside the door, adjusting their eyes to the gloom. They spotted Gillespie and came over.

"Jimbo," the man said, and clapped him on the shoulder. "Blowing the cobwebs?"

"Hi, Frank. Martha."

They slid onto stools bracketing him and ordered drinks. The bartender sullenly mixed them and returned to his case. Martha Camarillo, Asiatic correspondent for United Press, sipped her drink through a long straw and watched Gillespie with sweet hazel eyes. "You almost drowned last night, Jimbo." She laughed, the tinkle of it rich in the empty room. "Why didn't you tell anybody you couldn't swim?"

"I was drunk enough to think I could."

Frank Evern, an independent stringer for several magazines, said, "You know what I found out this morning from my houseboy? Crocodiles come into the area we were in last night."

"I'm really glad you told me that, Frank," Jimbo said sourly. "Now I can spend the rest of the day wondering why I'm still alive."

They drank in silence for a minute before Evern said very casually, "I just got a cable from San Francisco. You people have a ship in trouble out here?"

"What ship?" Gillespie asked innocently.

Evern exchanged glances with Martha.

"Really, what ship?" Jimbo said. "I don't know any ship."

"Come on," Martha said.

"He's not mellow enough," Frank said. He snapped his fingers. "Hey, give this man another . . . What're you drinking?"

"Bloody Marys."

"A menstruating Marie."

The bartender brought it. They waited until Gillespie had taken a sip, then Camarillo said, "So?"

Jimbo shifted his glass so that it fit perfectly into the water ring the other had left. "Okay, yeah, I got word a freighter was having some problems south of us."

"What kind of problems?"

"They didn't say. Her cargo shifted, somebody forgot to feed the squirrel. What the hell do I know about ships?"

"Is it bad?" Evern asked seriously.

"Come on, you guys. It's no big deal. Air/Sea jumped right on it and it's probably all cleared up by now." He downed his drink and stood up. "I gotta go."

"Have you had a stand-down report yet?" Martha asked.

Gillespie ignored the question. He waved to the bartender. "Another round for the vultures here." He tossed a ten-dollar bill on the bar.

"About this ship," Frank persisted.

"Look, I'll dig into it and have something for you at this afternoon's briefing. Okay?"

"Okay. Oh, Jimbo, was it Navy?"

"Slick, Frank. The off-guard question. Slick." He waved and headed out. He pushed the leather-padded door open. An excruciating burst of sunlight and heat struck him like an explosion. Head down, he scooted across the compound toward his office.

Far to the southeast, the *Panjang* drifted in primordial darkness. She shifted to momentary surges, coming around, moving abreast, then sterning into the two-mile-an-hour current. A massive pirouette in slow motion.

She had settled nearly two hundred feet deeper since her initial plunge. The tiny seam break in her deep tank had disturbed her equilibrium. As she sank deeper, pressure began to probe for other weak points in her weld seams. Plates groaned and whinnied softly in the undersea night.

At last a small weld blew in her ballast space beneath number-five hold. It went with the crack of a rifle shot, and water hissed in.

Three thousand feet below her were the undulations of the Prescott Plateau. Over the last six hours, the bottom had gradually risen. Deep-pressure cracks and canyons appeared. Fifty-three miles to the south rose the upthrust foothills that rimmed the thirty-thousand-foot abyss of the Murchison Trench. . . .

Three

75 hours, 48 minutes

Five hundred miles to the southwest, the Russian Delta-class submarine *E.R. Sabir* had just completed a radio run. A small, towed radio capsule skimming just below the surface had received her twice-daily signals from the Russian Mish-4T communications satellite. In her officers' lounge the skipper, Captain Second Class Yuli Lapshin, was drinking a cup of tea and going over statistical reports.

There was a soft knock on the door. "Comrade Captain?"

"Come in."

Lieutenant Lev Orserov stepped in. "A dispatch from Cam Ranh Bay, sir. They report a rapid concentration of American warships developing in quadrant fifteen. Also Intelligence reports an embargo has been set up around Guadalcanal."

Lapshin shrugged. "Not unexpected."

"But something is peculiar. Radio intercepts indicate a standoff area two hundred miles south of the island. Even their military ships are being advised to detour away from it."

"Oh?" Lapshin was a thoughtful, quiet officer. His narrow, down-curving eyebrows gave him a faintly sardonic look when appraising someone. "Does headquarters have any suggestions as to why?"

"No, sir. They advise we proceed there to reconnoiter. They are deploying N-189 and N-57 to cover our station."

Lapshin sighed and rose. With Oserov following, he made his way along the main corridor, sunk in orange light, to a curving stair that took him to the main control room. His executive officer, Lieutenant First Grade Iskander Chernov, was standing watch. He gave Lapshin a silent nod and vacated the pedestal chair located in the center of the control deck. Lapshin settled into its thick leather folds. Directly ahead of him were several television screens. The rest of the control space was taken up with computer consoles, electronic banks, and panels of operational indicators.

"Bring up quadrant fifteen and focus on northwest sector."

Instantly the center screen flashed a grid map of Guadalcanal and the adjacent Coral Sea area. A flashing white dot far to the south blinked on and off, indicating the *Sabir*'s position. Lapshin studied the map a moment, then snapped, "Helm, come to bearing three-zero-five. Go to three-quarters speed."

Chernov echoed the order and the helmsman repeated it. The deck tilted slightly to port, and there was a gentle inertial pull as the ship's speed increased. "Steadying on bearing three-zero-five," the helmsman called out. "Fix—now."

"Maintain running depth, Iskander. Stand by for hundred-percent sonar ranging."

"Aye, sir," Chernov answered, and quickly moved to a secondary panel of instruments on the after bulkhead.

Lapshin studied the screen, trying to visualize the stand-off area. It seemed a tactically void space. What are the Americans up to? he wondered. Curious, he turned his head slightly. "Give me water depth in grid thirteen-point-eight."

One of the console men repeated the order. A moment later numbers began to flash onto the screen adjacent to the designated grid: TRANSLATERAL AA: 1.4 KILOMETERS, AVERAGE SOUNDING: 3,800 METERS::::SURROUNDING TOPOGRA-

PHY: EE IDENTICAL//SS ABRUPT DECLINE TO 25,000 METERS (AE MURCHISON TRENCH)//WW IDENTICAL//NN SLOW SHALLOWING OF PRE-ISLAND RISE.

"Switch off."

The numbers disappeared.

On the edge of very deep water, Lapshin thought. Interesting.

A bar called the Singapore was in a small alley near Geoffrey Street, the main drag through Honiara's Slot. A Chinese girl in a tight-fitting red dress and stiletto heels was sitting on a stool at the door. Her lips were blood-red, her face heavily powdered. She gave Dureau and Villachio a sleepy-eyed smile. "Hi, jacks. Fun and game inside."

They paused a moment to accustom their eyes to the semidarkened room. The tables were crowded mostly with sailors, and the air was filled with smoke. On a small platform in the rear, three Melanesians in white *lavalavas* were playing calypso music, using a guitar, a tall wooden drum, and a native flute.

The bartender, dripping sweat, scurried down the bar. "G'day, mates," he hollered over the music. "What'll it be?" His face was so battered it looked as if it had been thumb-pressed in soft wax.

"Two Foster's," Dureau said.

"Right ya are, mate."

A Vietnamese girl barely fifteen slid between them. She put her hand on Alain's thigh and smiled at him. Her heavy mascara gave her a weary, desperate look. Her breasts, tiny as robin's eggs, were nakedly visible under her blouse. "Hi, jack. You buy me drink?"

Dureau grinned at her. "*Ah, bon jour, ma cherie.*"

She tilted her head. "You France guy," she screeched. "I born Saigon. I can do many French loveliness. You take me in back?" Her breath was tainted with the acidic scent of amphetamine.

"*Non, ma cherie.* Perhaps later." He took her hand and pressed an American twenty-dollar bill into it. The girl scowled. She put her forefinger against her nostril and blew slightly in a gesture of contempt. Then she strolled away.

Dureau was staring at several framed photographs as the bartender slid two tall bottles of Foster's onto the bar. The photos showed him in boxer's tights, standing in front of several makeshift rings in the Australian outback.

"A fighter?" he asked.

The bartender laughed. "Aye, mate. When I was young and had blood in m'balls." He glanced over at Villachio. "Your mate there looks as if he's stood a few lines hisself."

The Italian nodded. "A few."

Alain leaned forward congenially. "Listen, we're looking for a man. Perhaps you know him?"

The bartender's eyes grew wary. "Whot's 'is name?"

"Ramasingh Jaywedeen."

"Sorry, mate, never 'eard of 'im."

Quickly Dureau laid a hundred-dollar bill on the bar. The bartender looked down at it, then up suspiciously. "You constabulary?"

"No."

"I still ain't 'eard of 'im."

Dureau put down another hundred.

The man looked at them, then shrugged. "Well, ain't no skin off m'bleedin' arse." He scooped up the bills and tucked them into his apron. "They's a alley two blocks over. Go to the end. A blue door on the bottom floor." He hurried off to serve two Aussie sailors banging on the bar.

The alley was narrow and smelled of garbage and feces. Clotheslines were strung between the buildings. At the end the alley opened onto bamboo walkways with small skiffs and native *palimis* tied in.

Jaywadeen was a petty contraband runner who made weekly trips across the northern reaches of the Coral Sea from Bougainville and New Guinea. He had been hired by Stedman to take the assault team from the Canal to Queensland. According to Stedman, the Indian's boat, a modified *sampan*, looked like a wreck, but carried twin

Hall-Scott engines and could do forty-eight knots in open ocean.

The blue door fronted a dilapidated apartment building. A lean-to of tin had been thrown up beside the door and inside it were stacked grimy corrugated washtubs and an ancient wringer washing machine with all its porcelain cracked off. Alain tried the door. It was locked. He pounded on it. A few seconds later a small window beside the frame opened and a dark face peered out.

"What you want?"

"We're friends of Stedman," Dureau answered.

The eyes that studied them had a yellow sheen in the whites. "I don't know you. Go away." The window slid shut.

Dureau lifted his leg and slammed his boot against the door. It flew open. As he darted inside, he caught sight of a half-naked man disappearing into a side room. Villachio took off after him.

The air was heavy with the cloying stench of opium smoke. A woman lay on a filthy cot near the opposite wall. Her yellow cotton dress was pulled up, exposing her hairless pudenda. She sighed softly, eyes closed, obviously drugged.

Villachio returned with the man in a headlock. He was short and stocky, and his face was pockmarked. He had on nothing but a sweatshirt. He glared at Dureau. "Why do you do this? What do you want?"

"The completion of our bargain."

The Indian's eyes slid away from Alain's face. "You are the Frenchman?"

"Yes."

He shook his head. "I cannot take you now. There is a restriction on all boats."

"I know. But you will take us anyway."

"No, it is too dangerous now."

Dureau smiled faintly. He had expected this. The embargo was complicating his plans. At first it had infuriated him. Yet over the last few hours he had become tantalized by it. The prospect of cutting the line sharper, of tempting fate more brazenly, exhilarated him.

The Indian was glowering at him. "Besides, I do not know you. Where is Stedman?"

"Dead."

The first sliver of fear stole into Jaywadeen's yellow eyes. "It is too dangerous," he repeated. "I will take you next week."

"Now."

The Indian began to plead. "I cannot, I swear. Look, I will give your money back."

"No."

"Let me go and I will go and get it."

"Where is your boat?"

"I . . . I don't know. I gave it to some friends to hide."

"You lie."

"No, I am truthful. Please, take back the money and go away."

Alain stared thoughtfully down at him. Then his eyes went flat, gelid. Quietly he asked, "You are Muslim?"

The question confused the Indian. "What you say?"

"Are you Muslim?"

"Yes."

"Then you believe that when you enter Paradise, all of you must enter. Is that not so?"

Terror erupted in Jaywadeen's face. He struggled for a moment against Villachio's hold, but it was too strong. He slumped, watching Dureau with beseeching eyes.

"Where is your boat?" Dureau asked again.

"I do not know. I swear."

Alain slipped his Beretta from his pocket and shoved the silencer tip against Jaywadeen's penis. The Indian gasped. His eyes flew open, and he tried to squirm away from the touch of the cold steel.

"Where is your boat?"

"Oh, sweet Allah," Jaywadeen moaned.

Dureau fired twice. The Indian screeched with pain. Behind him Villachio jumped back, startled. Jaywadeen crashed off a wall and onto the floor. He clawed at his groin. Blood was pumping from his buttocks. He whimpered and heaved, his eyes wild.

Alain stepped in and shot him in the base of the skull. The Indian slumped. Across the room the woman on the cot mumbled something. The sound drifted off into a sigh.

"*Mon Dieu*, Alain," Villachio cried. "He was our only way off the island."

"Then we'll find another." Dureau knelt and gathered up the spent cartridges and put them and the Beretta into his pocket. He stood. "Let's go."

Villachio fled out the door. Dureau started after him, then paused, looking at the woman. After a moment he walked over to her, lifted the hem of her dress, and covered her nakedness. He closed the door softly when he left.

Commander Ron Kitchens, chief pilot of the Orion, didn't like this flight. Going out on a night run to locate a goddamned sunken ship. Jesus, what for? Anybody aboard that ship had long since bidden good-bye to the world. He and his people were trained to hunt Russian submarines, not go wandering around the Coral Sea looking for steel on the goddamned bottom.

A handsome black man, Kitchens was a career officer. He'd come up the hard way, from enlisted man to warrant to flight officer. He was a good pilot, and kept his men sharp; they zeroed in on ASW runs. Stupid excursions like this only took the edge off.

His copilot, a sandy-haired lieutenant named Wally Klinch, tapped his shoulder and pointed forward. They were flying at twenty thousand feet. Ahead, they could just make out the green humps of the Florida Islands, located twenty-five miles north of Honiara. Still farther west was the tiny cone of Savo, like the tip of a coolie's hat. The water separating these islands from Guadalcanal was called Leadbottom Sound for all the ships that had gone down there during World War Two.

Kitchens swung his frequency dial until he picked up

Approach Control at Henderson International. He would not be landing there, however. A Flash code from Midway had advised him to use a jungle runway called Kukum, made of Marsden mats laid out by the Marines in 1942. According to the aero map, they'd have to clear hogback ridges getting in.

"Henderson NDB Approach, this is Navy Orion zero-four-niner, fifty miles northeast at flight level two-zero, inbound for Kukum, over."

Henderson Approach came back instantly. "Orion zero-four-niner, we have you on scope. Continue heading one-niner-zero until vector notice to Kukum. Lower to approach altitude. Traffic is single outbound Japan Airlines seven-two-seven, heading zero-five-one. Wind two knots, one-eight-one. Altimeter two-nine-nine-zero. Will call on vector change when you pass over Savo, over."

Kitchens acknowledged traffic and field instructions. He flicked the intercom: "Secure back there. We'll be coming in in fifteen minutes." He leaned forward and began dropping power.

The panel chronometer read 1730 hours. He swore softly. They were already two hours behind schedule because of a delay during refuel in the Marshalls. A minor problem with number-one-engine oil lines. He hated disruptions in schedule. They created further disruptions down the line. You never caught up.

And there was something else. A woman was aboard. That was a bad omen. As a kid in East Bay, Oregon, his father had worked on the salmon docks. He used to go down to watch him, sit around and listen to the fishermen swapping stories. Their superstitions made a strong impression. One of them was you never took a woman to sea. Especially if she was menstruating. The way things were going on this trip, Kitchens was sure Napah Gilchrist must be pumping blood like a stuck pig.

Sixteen minutes later, they rolled to a shuddering stop on the rusted Marsden matting of Kukum.

Evening was coming on. Already shadows had begun to

lengthen in the lower valleys to the west. The Orion waited silently at the north end of the Kukum runway. Some of the crew had gathered under her starboard wing to play penny-ante poker. Bonner and Napah were in the game.

For the fifth straight time Gilchrist burned them. She'd pulled an inside straight in seven stud. Cas was the only one who had anything close. Chief Petty Officer Mathias, sonarman, disgustedly tossed his cards in. "Good Christ, woman. Don't your luck ever dry up?"

Napah chuckled. "Only when I sleep."

"Yeah, I'll bet your luck is hellish when you climb into bed," Bonner said.

"Getting testy when we lose, are we?" she countered.

"Deal the damned things."

She gathered in the cards and coins. "My, my," she teased. "This is just too easy. I'm getting bored."

"Look at this," Seaman Third Rick Kamaski laughed. "She gets bored winning money." He and Napah had spent a lot of time at the sonar consoles during the flight, going over Navy procedure.

Gilchrist squared the cards and laid them down on the Marsden. She stretched. "I think I'll go for a run. How long is this strip?"

"Thirty-two hundred yards," chubby, balding, Lieutenant Buchanan said. He was the sonar officer, a graduate of the University of Minnesota. "Both ways."

"Ha-ha," Napah said. "Anybody care to join me?" The men chortled. She stood up and looked at Bonner. "How about you, macho man? Let's see if you can run any better than you play poker."

"Forget it," he said sullenly.

Laughing, she turned and started off.

Slowly Bonner began to deal. The others were watching Gilchrist. Buchanan sighed. "Man, I wouldn't mind getting a little taste of that."

"It'd poison you," Bonner said.

"Well, to each man his own poison."

"Come on. Five-card draw, deuces wild."

The men turned back. Cas dealt himself zilch. On the draw, he pulled more zilch. He tossed his cards in, drew up a knee, and rested his chin on it, gazing down the runway.

Napah was down near the end already. She made the turn and headed across to the opposite side, long legs pulling high, hair bouncing with each stride. Gilchrist annoyed him with her caustic, challenging female flippancy. A woman with a quick-click brain like that kept a man forever in a stew.

Yet she was damnably feminine. She had a certain delicate turn of the hand, a way of unconsciously brushing back her hair. And from what he'd heard of the conversations between her and the sonarmen, her questions had the clipped zing of knowledge. He mused idly whether Napah's fires could be banked and controlled. And decided it probably wouldn't be worth it.

Napah ran easily, skirting the field. The matting bounced slightly under her weight, puffing tiny bursts of dust through the metal holes. The jungle pressed in close here, huge banyans with vines clawing all over the trunks. There was the smell of denseness and rot. The remnants of a World War Two military truck lay in the fringes of the jungle covered with creepers. The windows were all gone and someone had sprayed an obscenity on the hood.

She felt her blood pumping, the steady rhythm of her feet hitting the mats. She loved the solid pound of her heart singing, creating a bright, swift feeling.

She'd always been a runner. Way back, before the fad hit. Her father, an engineer, had run regularly too, sometimes with her around the rain-pocked track of her high school in Livingston, Illinois. People used to stop and stare at them, puzzled by such displays of energy on those long summer evenings.

Her father always told her, "Slow running is for the birds, honey. You gotta sprint. That's the way to go, hard and fast. Test the body." It was true. Wind sprints made her legs wobbly, her stomach near nausea, but her soul soared.

At the University of Colorado School of Mines, Napah had run every night. Something had gone wrong there. A geology major, she began to flounder. It was one big party, everybody laid back on drugs. But she always felt a gnawing sense of uselessness the morning after, and ran to catch up to something that seemed to be slipping terribly away.

In 1978 she pulled out. She transferred to the University of Alaska at Fairbanks, the best damned geology school in the nation. In the summers she worked on a salmon boat running the inland waterway out of Bilson. She was partners with a hunchback named Billy Hardcastle: gentle and shy with the softest eyes she'd ever seen on a man. It was hard, aching work. They'd leave the dock in the darkness, sweating like stevedores hauling in line drags. She still wrote to Billy and he to her, in penciled sixth-grade words that filled her heart with joy each time she received a letter.

The light was dimming, and the jungle trees held a soft gold. She began to sprint back to the Orion. The evening light streaked the plane's fuselage with platinum. The card players were still at it.

She thought about Bonner, and chuckled between pulls of air. He was such a clunk. She recalled the lectures at Scripps when she was making up marine-biology credits. He had looked uncomfortable on the lectern, like a beach-comber who had wandered in out of the surf. She had pinioned him with questions. He'd fidget with pencils and paper, and she could see he was trying real hard to keep his patience. It had been glorious.

The damnedest thing, though, was that right from the beginning she had thought he was the sexiest man she'd ever seen.

Chaffee was lost in a deep, inexplicable dream. He was swimming with long, desperate strokes. The water was warm, murky, all around him. He could feel his heart pounding from the exertion. Tendrils of terror snaked through his consciousness.

Something moved through the gloom. It was shadowy and moved with a slow, sinuous grace. Sounds riffled through the water, like steam escaping. It went higher, pitched like a whistle. His ears hurt.

He touched something hard. Metal. His fingers scurried across the surface. Rivets. It was a bulkhead. He seemed to understand that something precious was on the other side of the barrier. He couldn't hear it or smell it, yet he *knew* it was there. He felt a terrible hunger for light.

He began to claw at the steel bulkhead. In frantic slow motion. He was aware he moaned. Like the other sound, it climbed higher, and then he himself was climbing on the wall, slipping back, enclosed, breathless, his lungs sucking at the thick water, trying furiously to draw oxygen from it. . . .

"Steve!"

Chaffee came out of the dream. Directly in front of his face was the Orion's bulkhead. For a horrible moment dream and reality merged. He felt someone shaking his shoulder. He swung around to see Bonner's anxious face peering down at him.

"Steve, you all right?"

Chaffee groaned and fell back onto the bunk. He was drenched in sweat. He felt the mattress trembling with the vibration from the plane's idling engines. Finally he sat up, his head pounding.

"We're ready to take off," Cas said. "Damn, where the hell were you?"

Chaffee swallowed phlegm, managed a weak smile. "Just a bad dream." He peered out the porthole. Far to the east, he could see the pale crescent of a quarter-moon. "What time is it?"

"Nearly eight o'clock."

"God, I need coffee."

"You'll have to wait till we get up. Everything's secured for takeoff."

"Yes, of course." He swung his legs off the bunk and dropped to the deck. "Okay, give me a minute. I'll be right up."

Bonner gave him a long look, then ducked through the hatch.

Chaffee rubbed his face. His hands were ice cold and his body was still trembling from the dream. He reached into his top pocket and withdrew a bottle of pills. He shook two into his palm and tossed them into his mouth. Without water, he had to swallow several times before they went down.

Everyone was strapped in the sonar room. He advanced to the command platform. Both pilots were busy running through preflight checks. Chaffee touched Kitchens' shoulder. "Mind if I sit up here, Commander?"

Kitchens didn't turn around. He flicked a thumb, indicating the small observer's seat behind Klinch. The Orion's landing lights threw twin fans of powerful brightness ahead of the craft. Beyond them, everything was black.

Chaffee felt the edge of the amphetamine rush in his skin.

Kitchens was talking to Henderson Approach Control. When he was cleared, he put his right hand on the four engine throttles, the fingers spread wide. Slowly he began to push them forward.

With a sudden, rising roar, the engines took power. Chaffee's seat began to shake violently. Higher the engine thundered as Kitchens held full brake for maximum power before rolling. Pebbles and strip debris were being flung up under the plane's fuselage by the prop wash.

At last Kitchens released the brakes and the aircraft lunged forward. Lumbering at first, it began to pick up speed. Chaffee's fists beat a rapid tattoo against his thighs, the drug's lift in his blood synchronizing with the surging power of the engines. For a moment it was as if his body were leaping, itself taking flight.

Two hundred yards out, the landing lights picked up the sheer green wall of the jungle. The Orion lifted off, hesitated, then lifted again. The pitch of the engines changed slightly, droning now as the aircraft pulled free of the ground. For a flashing moment the treetops loomed directly in front of the Orion's nose, and then they disappeared under it; the landing lights made twin, misty cones into open air.

Kitchens banked to the east, gaining altitude. Below them the lights of Honiara looked like scattered coals in the darkness. They continued around in a wide, climbing turn and then Kitchens leveled off at six thousand feet. They headed into the blackness over the open sea.

Chaffee rested his head against the back of his seat. He closed his eyes and felt his heart racing.

Four

67 hours, 12 minutes

Spangenberg, senses quivering, stalked around Jaywadeen's corpse. He sniffed the air, studied trajectories, scanned the floor. His starched fatigues rustled in the thick silence.

A half-hour before Fa'uza had called his cabana. "Colonel, there has been a killing."

"Where?"

"In the Slot. A man we have suspected of smuggling hemp."

Sab relaxed. A lousy drug runner who got caught taking too big a scoop of his cargo. "You handle it."

"No, Colonel, I think you must come. The man had guns."

"All right, stay there. I'll be right down. And don't talk to anybody about this yet."

Now he squatted at the body's feet. Jaywadeen was still lying in the fetal position in which he had fallen. Spangenberg could see that the right buttock had been nearly torn off where the bullets had exited. There was a thick pool of partially coagulated blood under the body. It smelled raw and rancid.

He shoved the corpse over onto its back. There was a soft, squishy sound as it settled. The crotch was now exposed, the legs drawn up rigidly. The position looked grotesquely lascivious, the genitals shrunken.

He bent closer, squinting. Two small punctures, nearly

bloodless, were located at the junction of penis and groin. There were tiny flecks of burned tissue around each wound where the gun's explosions had seared the skin.

Fa'uza came into the room, closing the door gently. A big Melanesian in his sixties, he stood very straight. He wore a khaki shirt, the sleeves rolled to the biceps, and a brown *lavalava*. On his head was a white pith helmet with a brass eagle on the front.

Without turning, Sab asked, "Anything from the woman?"

"No, Colonel. She is still very confused from the opium."

"Other witnesses?"

"None."

"Something stinks bad here," Sab said. He stood up, walked around the body once, letting his senses work again. In Command School at Quantico, he had led all the U-and-I exercises. Uncover and Identify.

"Where're the weapons?"

Fa'uza disappeared into the side room, returning with a revolver and a sawed-off shotgun. Sab took the revolver, an old Smith and Wesson .22. The hand grips were gone, showing the cross frame. He smelled the barrel. It hadn't been fired.

He tossed it onto the table and took the shotgun. It was an Australian Inchler 12-gauge. He cracked the breech. Empty. A strip of electrical tape was wound around the stock where it had split. He snapped it shut and thoroughly hefted it in hands. These were trash guns, owned by a man who didn't know weapons but who happened to be in a business where a gun was needed.

Quietly he laid the shotgun down on the table. "What do you have on this poor prick?"

"We are sure he was running hemp," Fa'uza said. "He has a very fast boat he hides in the mangroves up north. But we could never catch him with contraband."

"I want everything you have on him. Friends, any arrest records anywhere, whatever."

Fa'uza nodded.

"And I want this killing sandbagged."

"Sandbagged? I do not understand 'sandbagged.' "

"Keep it quiet, Jacob. No talky-talky."

"But I must prepare reports."

"Do what you have to do. But you put him away quickly and silently. If anybody comes nosing around, you send them to me."

Fa'uza looked troubled, but he agreed to do as he was told.

"You people have a medical examiner here?"

"Yes. I waited for you before I called him."

"Good. When he's finished, I want to see a copy of his report."

"Yes, Colonel."

"I'll be back."

Sab walked up the alley to Geoffrey Street. It was crowded with jitney taxis and motor scooters and military staff cars. The street vendors had tiny strings of lights on their umbrella carts. The streetwalkers strolled with predatory casualness in their Lycra pants and needle heels.

Spangenberg stood at the head of the alley, arms folded, scanning the crowd. His eyes, shadowed, moved slowly under the brim of his cap. They held a bright, hot gleam. The hunter hunting.

Twenty minutes from Kukum, Kitchens took the Orion up to fifteen thousand feet. He needed altitude so they could set up a precise fix on the *Panjang*'s last position. They used the signals from Marou Station on the Canal, KIRA on San Cristobal, and the Talimoko Lighthouse at Rennel Island.

Kitchens gave the controls to Klinch and came aft. He tapped Mathias, sitting with Napah at the sonar console, on the shoulder. He jerked his head at Bonner and Chaffee, who immediately stood and followed him, along with Buchanan and Mathias.

In the galley Kitchens poured himself a cup of coffee and squatted with his back against the hatch sill. "Well, gentlemen, here's the skinny," he began. "We'll be over the freighter's last position in thirty minutes. As you know, a P-3C's primary mission is to locate and track submarines. She's set up to home on noise and heat. Unfortunately, what we're looking for has neither. We'll have to rely solely on our magnetic anomaly and sono-buoy scans."

He paused for a sip of coffee. "Instead of going in with immediate buoy drops, I've decided to make loop passes over the area with the MAD scan first. I've set up a target area of approximately twenty-five square miles with the last fix as center point. If we turn up likely reads, we'll concentrate on them with the buoys and Torpex charges. If we're lucky, we might get enough bounce for the analyzer to resolve."

"What are your buoy capabilities?" Cas asked.

Kitchens nodded the question to Buchanan.

"We're running PD-12 models," the sonar officer said. "Straight passive systems with no side scan. But they're good gear. A short streamer with extremely sensitive double sets of hydrophones and an on-board analysis unit to read ambient temperature, salinity, and density factors." He paused and turned to Kitchens. "How deep you gonna want the pressure chambers set, Skipper?"

"Let's go sixty feet."

"Right."

Kitchens explained to Bonner and Chaffee: "Depth placement is a matter of tit for tat. We place the buoys too shallow, the phones will pick up surface turbulence. If we place them too deep, we sacrifice scan area. My TPO maps indicate four thousand-foot depths here. The loss of a single degree of scan arc at the surface could mean several hundred yards on the bottom. So we'll go to shallow drop and keep the surface as quiet as possible by using only two engines and as little flap as I can safely carry."

"Very good, Commander," Chaffee put in.

Kitchens shot him an irritated look. He wasn't asking for agreement. "If I continue running with only two engines, we'll have enough fuel to stay on site for about sixteen hours. But Pearl wants us down at Kukum by dawn, so we'll break off operations at approximately oh-four-hundred hours and be out here again at ten hundred hours when the *Voorhees* is scheduled to arrive at fix site."

He turned back to Chaffee. "By the way, Commander, what's the sonar setup on the *Voorhees*?"

"She carries both passive and active systems," Chaffee answered. "Very good multichannel seismic profile capability and a fairly decent MAD scanner. But she doesn't have the analysis gear to high-resolve the traces."

"That's what we're here for. She can patch her bounce signals through our computer."

"Midway A-and-D is on alert if we run into anything we can't handle," Chaffee added.

"We won't need them." Kitchens finished his coffee and smiled faintly at Bonner and Chaffee. "One other thing. I don't know how much air time you people have had, but we're going to be working low and slow on these runs, and that'll mean lots of ground-effect turbulence. The aircraft'll shake like hell. Just stay cool." He paused, waiting for any questions. None came. "All right, gentlemen, let's do it."

Jimbo Gillespie's fork stopped three inches from his mouth as he caught sight of a man passing the commissary door. His name was Hal Worthington, correspondent for the BBC.

A second later, Worthington returned to the door, grinned at him, and came in. Jimbo swore silently and lowered his fork. Ever since the afternoon press briefing, he'd managed to dodge press people. He'd been forced to renege on his promise to have something more on the ship off the coast. He'd turned up nothing.

There had been a few pointed, accusatory questions about it, especially from Martha. But he'd managed to field them with decent enough equivocation to cover. As soon as the briefing was over, he'd scooted out before anyone could get a tight hold.

Hal slid into a chair, still smiling. "Well, James. Hiding?"

"Working late."

"Ah, such dedication." Worthington lit a cigarette with faintly effeminate grace. He silently watched Jimbo go back to his dinner. At last he shook his head. "Good God, James. How can you possibly eat that slop? What *is* that thing? Looks like a masticated piece of cardboard."

"Chicken-fried steak. Very big in the States."

Hal sighed. "Yes, another example of your American frenzy over nostalgia. Looks absolutely ghastly."

One of the staff secretaries came into the commissary for coffee. She was blond and pretty in a disheveled way. Her name was Christine something-or-other. Jimbo had heard rumors that she was an easy lay, and made a few halfhearted remarks to her, preparatory to asking her out. She gave him a big smile as she left.

Worthington leaned forward slightly, as if they were two spectators at a chess match. "I say, James, have you been able to chase anything down on this ship thing?"

"Not a thing."

"Rather strange, isn't it? Ship has a bit of a problem and nobody seems to know the slightest detail. I've even tried wheedling a bit of news from our ministry. They don't seem to know anything either."

"Because there's probably nothing worth knowing. I figure it's all cleared up by now anyway."

"Ah?"

"Ships have minor problems all the time, Hal. A gasket blows out, somebody forgets to oil a bearing. Obviously it was something like that."

Worthington stared at him. "Yes, I suppose." He held the gaze and Jimbo forced himself to return it.

At last Hal sighed heavily and squashed out his cigarette. "Well, I suppose it *has* to be done. That ghastly lunge across the quadrangle." He stood up. "I say, James, if you have a moment later, why don't you stop in at my quarters? We can share a gin and tonic and regale each other with our astounding sexual exploits."

"Yeah, I might just do that."

"Splendid. Well, cheerio." He strolled away.

Gillespie shoved his unfinished plate away and leaned back to gaze thoughtfully at the ceiling. This ship thing was picking at him. Something about it was definitely *not* kosher. The journalists were already picking up the scent.

Take Max Wilcox, undersecretary for the delegation team and Jimbo's direct superior. *He* was playing it cool about the ship. Very casual and offhanded. That smacked of play-down.

But why?

Gillespie knew the bureaucratic penchant for manipulating the possession of information. You show me your tidbit, I'll show you mine. The same old power crap. But what in hell could be so important about a lousy old freighter in the Coral Sea? He'd at least gotten that much out of Wilcox, that it *was* a freighter.

He felt a belch rise from his stomach, hot with acid and the after-tang of catsup. Inexplicably the sound brought Christine what's-her-name to mind. Idly he considered walking down to her office and asking her to have a drink with him.

He immediately felt contrite. Since marriage Jimbo had allowed himself two affairs. Short-lived, sweaty little things with girls in the department. Each time he'd been drenched in feelings of guilt. To assuage it, he resorted to a sham. Whenever he sent his mistress of the moment a dozen roses, he sent his wife *two* dozen. This recognition of precedence was pathetic, really, but enough of a penance to cut the edge off his guilt.

He sucked at a sliver of steak that had lodged between his teeth and thought of Christine. There was a chance he might pick up some information on the ship from her. Sure, why not?

Sufficiently augmented with a justifiable purpose, he left the commissary and headed up the hall to her office.

Bonner watched the night ocean come gently up to them like a misty, moon-dappled plain. Kitchens was bringing them down to the exact spot of the *Panjang*'s

last position report. Behind him the tactical room was
coming alive. The overhead lights had dimmed, replaced
by a soft blue glow. In it the dials and screens were a
glaring white.

Kamaski and Buchanan were seated in front of the
terminals wearing helmet earphones. Napah, also hel-
meted, leaned on Buchanan's seat, intently watching the
consoles. Mathias and the other sonarman, Seaman Third
Tippit, were below in the launch bay preparing the sonobuoys and Torpex canisters. Chaffee was in the forward
command platform.

Buchanan turned and signaled Cas. He pointed to his
helmet, then at a small intercom outlet above Bonner's
seat. Cas flipped the switch, letting Kitchens' voice come
in: ". . . AD on flex status. Entering final glide. We'll
hold at one hundred feet. Heading one-niner-zero."

Cas felt power coming back into the engines. Kitchens
was opting to use all four on the MAD runs. They
settled. There was a slight jolt as the air brakes went
down along the trailing edges of the wings. This was
followed by a steady tremble that moved through the
fuselage as they began picking up some backwash off the
ocean.

"Commencing primary run. A-and-H for sixty seconds
. . . now."

Bonner looked down. The sea slid past just below the
wings. Long moving hills of gray-white, the rounded
crests polished by the moonlight. When he turned back,
three of the sonar screens were showing blotches of flashing light.

"How's the receive, Bobby?" Kitchens asked.

"Lots of scatter. There's a helluva lot of magnetic
garbage down there," Buchanan answered.

"My God!" Napah cried suddenly. "The bottom's loaded
with ferrous deposits."

"What?"

"You're picking up iron ore, Commander. It's all over
the damned place."

"Coming up on sixty seconds."

The Orion lifted sluggishly and they banked, first to the right, then left and around as Kitchens realigned them for the second pass. Once more the aircraft settled, leveling.

"Second run commencing."

Napah tapped Buchanan's shoulder. "Bobby, you're not going to be able to MAD-read here. This isn't normal ocean crust. It's a subduction zone."

"What the hell's that?" Kitchens' voice snapped.

"This bottom was formed by tectonic plate displacement," Napah said. "Ordinary ocean crust is formed by basaltic magma. You've got continental rock here."

"Sixty seconds coming up . . . now."

They realigned for the third pass.

"Skipper," Buchanan said, "we're getting anomalies all over the place."

"Isn't the computer filtering?"

"Negative. There are too many of them."

Napah pointed at one of the screens excitedly. "Look at that! We're flying over oil deposits."

Chaffee slipped through the forward hatch and stood looking at the screens. His face in the blue glow was agonized.

"Sixty seconds coming up . . . now."

For the next thirty minutes Kitchens determinedly continued the MAD passes. Then he took them to a thousand feet and began a slow circling. He came aft.

The Univac-enhanced trace tapes were replaying on the screens. Napah and the two sonarmen were studying them, exchanging technical comments. Kitchens watched a moment, then tapped Buchanan, who glanced around and slipped off the headset. "There ain't no way, Skipper. Trying to find that ship with the MAD would be like spotting a single leaf on a forest floor."

Kitchens squinted his eyes and swore softly.

Napah looked at him. "There's something else, Commander."

"What?"

"Whenever you've got this kind of plate displacement,

you've always got an area of sediment buildup followed by a sharp decline. Judging from the slope direction of the seamounts down there, I'd say there's a deep trench somewhere south of us."

"That's right. TPO maps show the Murchison Trench about fifty miles southwest."

Napah shook her head. "If your ship's down in that thing, that'll be all she wrote. Besides, even if it isn't, the Trench will cause problems with your Torpex drops. All ocean trenches have freshwater conduits seeping from the walls. The denser salt water above it forces some of it up and over the lip of the trench and out onto the adjoining plain."

"Oh-oh!" Buchanan put in. "That'll mean a density discontinuity all along the bottom. It'll raise hell with the buoy probes."

Napah nodded.

Kitchens was staring at her. "How come you know all this shit?"

"It's my job," she answered. It was true. For the last three years she had been running sonar scans for oil deposits aboard Sutter Oil's exploratory ship *Clipperton*. First off the Alaska Peninsula and then along the Peruvian coast. She could read MAD- and sonar-scan traces like open books.

Kitchens looked sour. Wordlessly he turned and went forward.

During this conversation Bonner had been quietly listening. Mostly he watched Chaffee. As each new problem was discussed, the man's face looked as if physical blows were pummeling it. His eyes bored into the screens as if he could through sheer will suck information out of their circuit boards. A moment after Kitchens left, he went back to the head.

Despite what Napah had told him, Kitchens stubbornly stuck to his original plan. They circled for ten minutes while Mathias and Tippit readied the three buoys for drop. Cas, restless, slipped down into the launch bay to watch.

The sonobuoys were narrow aluminum tubes six feet in length. They would be fed into an air-pressure chamber and then fired out below the aircraft. Once free, a set of rotor blades would flange out and allow the buoy to drop gently into the sea in an almost vertical position. The impact would release the blades and deploy a radio antenna on a long feed line. Water-fed batteries would click on the radio transmitter and uncoil the hydrophone streamer.

Finally they came down out of the circle, Kitchens still carrying four engines. They leveled out at three hundred feet and made one dry run while Mathias timed his firing sequence of forty-five-second intervals. Then they went into a sweeping one-eighty and came back along the same track.

The first buoy went out of the firing barrel with a slamming rush of compressed air. Mathias waited a moment to allow residual pressure to dissipate, then cracked open the chamber breech. A surge of salty air blew back in the bay as he and Tippit slid the second buoy up the feed trough and down into the firing tube like an artillery round. Twenty seconds later, the buoy was automatically fired.

They ran through the entire procedure again and the third buoy was gone.

Mathias called forward: "All buoys out and away, sir."

"All right, set up the Torpex. Let me know when you're ready."

Hurriedly he and Tippit began loading the canisters into the feed trough. There were nine in all. Laid end to end, they jiggled and tanged against the trough as the Orion heeled hard to port and Kitchens took them around.

Cas returned to the tactical room. Chaffee was back, hunched forward on his observer's seat with all the intense despair of a high-school football coach watching his team and his job disintegrating before his eyes. Silently Cas slipped into his window seat.

The ocean was floating past close beneath him again. The inactivity of the flight was making him reflective. He watched the sea move by, remembering. Bitter memories. This particular ocean, or at least the western part of it, the Great Barrier Reef. . . .

Six years ago, he had been running dolphin open-ocean recover tests with Hawaiian Marine. The Barrier Reef run was the last in the series. It was on that one he lost Zim, a bottle-nosed dolphin. He had loved her with that inexplicable bonding that sometimes comes to a man and an animal.

The series had bad omens, right from the start. The night before they left Hawaii, Cas was served divorce papers. Right on the dock, from an apologetic Japanese lawyer dressed in an expensive Italian silk suit. That was like Carolyn. She liked to inflict the knife dramatically. Carolyn was the beautiful, kinky, self-indulgent daughter of the publisher of the Honolulu *Sentinel* and a former senator from Hawaii, Adrian Silham.

They had met at a fund-raiser cocktail party in Manoa when Cas was still in the Navy. In his whites Carolyn thought he looked like Robert Redford. They got wildly drunk and went surfing naked at Makapuu. Afterward they smoked grass with a group of beach bums and ate roasted hot dogs and Spam sandwiches. They watched the dawn come up in a place called Cockroach Gulch, where Deborah Kerr and Burt Lancaster had made love in the surf for the movie *From Here to Eternity*. They repeated the scene, furiously coupling as the surf overwhelmed them and the mica in the sand glistened like black diamonds in the new sun. Carolyn murmured a phrase from the *Kama Sutra* in orgasm, and they rolled and laughed and she said she was unbearably in love.

Two weeks later they were married at the Seven Pools of Hana on the island of Maui. Judge Kale Gilstrap, an old family friend, presided. Carolyn wore a sarong, barebreasted with only a Queen Liliokalani *maile* lei around her neck, looking like a jungle princess.

The first year was a sleigh ride. Cas resigned his commission and Adrian Silham's influence got him appointed to the directorship for biological research of Hawaiian Marine. The second year, Carolyn got pregnant and cursed him for it. She got an abortion without his knowledge. By the end of the year she was indulging in flagrant affairs and doing coke. Hard and fast. He tried desperately to slow her down, and she despised him for the effort. One day he came home and found her with a beachboy from Kuhio, screwing on the kitchen floor. Cas promptly threw the beachboy through the glass door, packed his gear, and left.

So the divorce papers weren't a surprise. Yet it hurt, filled him with a sense of failure. That night, for one last time, he and Zim went swimming around Kaneohe Bay, with the moonlight like metal on the water and the lights of Chrisholm Island throwing stencils of color. Zim stayed close beside him, the wash of her fins tight, as if she sensed his disquiet.

He lost her on the third dive of the Barrier series: a pinging canister drop into an area of fanning reef ridges. The water was crystal clear; he could see three hundred feet down. Zim worked the ridges like a hunting dog, sniffing out the pings. Cas had pulled up at sixty feet, watching her work. Gradually he became aware that she was becoming disoriented in the ridgebacks, her sonar ranging confused. She grew more and more frantic, burrowing into tight crevices, scurrying over sharp coral heads. They wounded her. He could see a trail of blood coming off her underbelly, pale as smoke in the blue-gray depths.

He somersaulted in the water and started down to her. By the time he reached the hundred-foot depth, she had located the canister. Deftly she wriggled into the harness loop. Then, joyous as a dog, she swept up toward him, coming straight up, the canister wobbling in her slipstream.

With her gleeful clown's grin she went rocketing close by him. His hand riffled along her flank. And then the canister struck him just behind the right ear. There was a jolting explosion in his head and he went out.

The next thing he remembered was hands grappling for him. Shouts, the sharp reports of rifle fire followed by the whomping impacts of the rounds going into the water behind him. Zim had brought him to the surface and her blood had brought the sharks.

Half-unconscious, he lay on the gunwale of the Zodiac recovery boat and watched them come in. Four dark brown shapes hissed through the water like blurred ghosts, homing on Zim. Ordinarily sharks did not attack dolphins. But Zim was alone and wounded and her speed was encumbered by the trailing canister. They caught her.

Bonner, bellowing with helpless fury, grabbed a rifle and began pumping round after round at the now-bloody water. When the weapon was empty, he flung it at them, grabbed up a scuba tank, and hurled that out too. But Zim was gone.

He sat on the Zodiac floor and wept like a child. It was only the second time in his life he cried. The other was when his father was killed on an archaeological dig in Baja California when he was thirteen.

Back at Kaneohe, he was dismissed from Hawaiian Marine. They cited emotional instability. He had freaked. It wasn't the real reason. Adrian Silham had deftly withdrawn his backing. . . .

The first Torpex charge caused all five console screens to blaze with light. Slowly they faded, the audible feed warbling and quavering off. A second passed. Another. The upbank screens began picking up bursts of light as the returning impulses were gathered by the buoy hydrophones. The tactical room cracked with the static of the audible monitor.

Cas glanced out the porthole. Until that moment he hadn't realized that Kitchens had shut down two engines. They were very close to the ocean now. The Orion seemed to struggle forward, sideslipping. She slammed and jerked as heavy surges of propwash came up off the water.

Kitchens' voice snapped through the intercom. "Twenty seconds coming up . . . let her go."

"Number two gone and away," Mathias called.

Another pause, and the second Torpex explosion blew light onto the screens.

Chaffee had risen from his seat and was pacing nervously back and forth behind the sonarmen, his eyes glued to the screens. The third canister was fired. Kitchens lifted the aircraft into a slow, thundering climb, forcing Chaffee to hurriedly grab for support.

"What're you getting, Bobby?"

"That density layer's there, Skipper. But we're getting some clean return off the tops of the sea mounts. If we're lucky, that ship's on a hill."

"What do you advise on next pass?"

"I'd hold four degrees off. The salinity rate's high as hell and boxing our parameters."

"Will do. Stand by."

They came around again and dropped toward the sea. Kitchens called out the approach. Number-one canister went out, then number two. Three seconds after it was deployed, his voice burst through the intercom.

"Nellie, I'm getting pressure drop on number one." Nellie Carpenter was the Orion's flight engineer.

"I've got it, Skipper," Nellie answered. "It's that goddamned sump— Jesus! There she goes!"

Bonner froze in his seat. Only his eyes moved, just in time to see a burst of flame shoot out of the starboard inboard engine. The sight of it sent a burst of adrenaline through him.

A Klaxon went off, blowing harsh sound through the console static. Mingled within the bursts was Kitchens' voice hurling commands.

Instantly Buchanan and Kamaski began frantically securing loose gear on the console boards. Chaffee jerked upright, gazed for a fleeting second at the screens, then dived for his seat and began strapping himself in.

Cas grabbed for his seat harness. He had just about

jammed the buckle together when he glanced up and saw Napah standing behind the sonarmen, looking confused.

"What's the matter?" she cried loudly. "What's happening?"

Bonner leapt out of his seat and grabbed her around the waist. She let out a sharp squeal. Her earphone helmet banged him in the forehead. Cursing, he shoved her down into his seat.

"Strap in and bend forward!"

Napah's green eyes stared at him, fear flicking through the depths.

The Orion was rolling and plunging crazily. Cas grabbed for one of the console seats and went down hard on one knee. Just above him, Bobby Buchanan's face loomed, pudgy and strained. Bonner finally crawled up and into the seat and rammed home the buckle.

Forward on the control platform, Kitchens and Klinch were fighting to keep the aircraft in the air. She was bucking hard and the controls were very heavy. Kitchens had instantly realized what had happened when he saw the flame. The main oil line of number one had blown. Immediate shutdown of the engine was necessary. Without oil in the casing, the engine would seize up within twenty seconds and tear itself off the wing mounts. But he couldn't shut it down; that would leave him only one engine eighty feet above the water. He had to keep number one running until he could get the outboard starboard engine started. He shot a glance out the window. At the first burst of flame, Klinch had set off the extinguisher-flooding rings inside the engine cowlings. The fire was almost out.

The instrument panel was shaking violently, clinking and tanging as the Orion neared stall. Kitchens dropped his right hand to the engine controls and rammed number one full forward.

The control wheel jerked violently to the left and back as the roaring engine rolled up into power, the prop grabbing great chunks of air and hurling them back across the horizontal stabilizers. Kitchens put his full weight against the wheel and bellowed to Klinch: "Manual-prime number three. Give me full flaps and twenty degrees on the cranking prop."

Lunging with furious haste, Klinch activated the prop hub switch and watched the tiny indicator above it crank to twenty degrees.

"Number three ready and primed," he yelled.

"Hit it."

Klinch punched the starter button. There was a high whine and the huge four-bladed propeller on the outboard engine began to turn slowly. A burst of white smoke blew out of the exhaust vent. Faster and faster it went. But it wasn't catching.

Kitchens was listening to the sound of number one. The steady thundering roar was breaking off now, discordantly, out of synch. As the remnants of oil evaporated in her crankcase, pistons, con-rods, and cylinder heads were rapidly heating from fiction. The heat was driving it into auto-detonation as incoming fuel was igniting at the jet ports. Within seconds the engine would blow itself and the starboard wing off the Orion.

Kitchens yelled into his mike: "Hold tight. We're going in."

His hand shot out to cut off both numbers one and two. At that instant the outboard engine caught, blew smoke, partially died, then caught again. With the throaty roar of new life, it rolled up into power, slewing the aircraft to the left.

Kitchens held on to the wheel as best he could and shut down number one. The engine faltered a moment, trembled violently, and continued firing for a few seconds, then died. Holding full power on numbers two and three, he gradually pulled the Orion up and away from the sea.

Dominique Mott-Smith could not take her eyes from Alain Dureau's face. She sat transfixed, letting her gaze wander like touching fingers over his exquisite profile.

They were sitting on the veranda of the Mott-Smith

plantation house. A cool breeze drifted up off the river across a long expanse of lawn, where cicadas hummed in the hibiscus. A bat darted now and then from the shadows, catching bugs in the air.

Dureau was demonstrating a coin trick. His hands moved like the heads of sinuous vipers, playing with the light. An American silver dollar flipped across his knuckles, fled back. With a quick toss he sent the coin high into the air, caught it, made a pass, and it was gone. He reached out and pretended to retrieve it from Dominique's long brown tresses.

She felt a tremble ripple along her spine and fuse out to touch delicately at her nipples.

"Jolly good!" Mott-Smith shouted, clapping his hands. "I say, Soison, what marvelous dexterity you have."

Dureau smiled, letting his eyes linger for a fleeting moment on Dominique's face. She immediately flushed and wondered in tiny panic if he had noticed.

"Could you teach me that?" Mott-Smith asked loudly. He was half-drunk, his tiny eyes bright and dancing above his sunburned cheeks.

"But of course. It only takes a little practice."

"Good fellow. Do you know, I've always found magicians a fascinating lot. They do for entertainment what the bloody politicians do for greed. Make you see what isn't really there, eh?"

Dureau chuckled. "A good comparison."

He and Villachio had arrived at the plantation house earlier that evening in a jitney taxi from Honiara. In her small studio Dominique had been painting the same subject she had been laboring on for months: a small Chinese pine in the backyard. By now she had painted it dozens of times, in all sorts of light, in rain and wind. Yet she could not get it correct. It seemed to represent some unattainable thing that haunted her soul.

Her husband was in the garden. A perfect English garden, with neat cobblestone walkways and set patterns of colorful flowers. Every evening he wandered through it, absently switching his leg with a short bamboo walking stick, now and then bending to snip an insect off a leaf.

Dominique heard the jitney pull up. Visitors were rare, so she walked through the house and stood in the veranda doorway. She was a trim, attractive woman in her late twenties. Her large eyes seemed to gaze at the world with a look of sad innocence.

She watched as two men got out of the jitney. She immediately noted that one was breathtakingly handsome. Her husband smiled happily and hurried out to greet them. The jitney went on around the oval driveway and headed off as the three men came up onto the veranda.

Her husband called up to her, "Oh, love, I have a wonderful surprise. Remember I told you about the two gentlemen I picked up this morning? Well, they've come to see us."

He introduced them.

Dureau took her hand, bowing slightly. "Such a pleasure to meet a fellow Parisian, *madam*," he said in French.

She felt the warmth of his hand and it sent an almost tangible tingle of electricity up her arm. She returned his smile. "Thank you, *monsieur*. Welcome to our home."

"*Merci.*" He turned to her husband. "I'm afraid our visit is not totally social. My partner and I find ourselves in a rather frustrating situation. We were hoping you might offer a suggestion as to how we might resolve it."

"Of course, anything I can do. But come in, come in."

The front room was spacious and cool. There was no ceiling, as such. Instead the roof beams were left exposed, allowing the heat to dissipate. The furniture was made of dark *koa* wood. In one corner, beyond the dining table, there was a tall gun cabinet containing at least a dozen heavy hunting rifles.

Mott-Smith mixed gin and tonics for everyone. When they were all seated, Dureau explained: "It's this American embargo. We can't seem to find anyone to take us off the island. And it's extremely urgent that I be in Rockhampton within the next forty-eight hours."

"That damned embargo again," Mott-Smith growled. "It's shinnied up everybody's bloody business."

"By the way, were you able to get your copra out?"

"No, blast it. And won't, either, till the idiotic conference is over." He took a long, angry pull at his drink. "By then the load'll be bloody maggot food."

"I'm sorry."

"It's these damned Americans pushing in like blasted footmen!" His little eyes screwed up. "But someone will pay, you can bloody well bet on it."

"Mightn't Hedges fly them across?" Dominique suggested quietly.

"By God, that's it," Mott-Smith cried. He laughed. "It'd titillate that silly bloke's sense of poetic justice to thumb his nose at the Yanks. Never has forgiven the bastards for stealing his wife."

"Who is this Hedges?"

"A chemical flier works for the sugar companies down south island at Marau. A bit of a lunatic but a damned crack pilot. He's got a twin-engine could pop you over to Rockhampton in a jiff."

Dureau glanced at Villachio.

"I'll give him a jingle straightaway." Mott-Smith winked gleefully. "But I hope you chaps won't be squeamish about skimming the ocean all the way over. Hedges hates to fly higher than twenty feet. Claims it's bloody boring."

"That won't be a problem."

"Good, good." He finished his drink and stood up. "Fix up another round, will you, love? Be back in a moment."

It was quickly settled. Hedges agreed to fly them out late the next afternoon in exchange for a case of Napoleon brandy. Mott-Smith insisted the men remain for supper and the night. In the morning he would drive them down to Marau.

Supper was roast beef served by a young Melanesian houseboy named Tombo. Dominique wore a moonlight-blue *longyi* with gold bracelets and the faint scent of sandalwood on her skin.

Mott-Smith turned to Villachio, sitting back in the shadows. "I say, Garibaldi, you're rather a silent fellow, eh? That name, Garibaldi. Any relation to the famous one?"

"No."

"But I'll wager you've been a soldier. Correct?"

"Yes."

"I knew it. You've got the look of the warrior in the eyes. Invincible stoicism and all that. Used to be in the ranks myself, the Korean thing. Wasn't old enough for the bloody big one, but had a decent run at right square march, nonetheless." He chortled. "Damned near froze my bloody manhood off on that trip, I did. Where've you served?"

"In Tunisia," Villachio said. "And Central Africa."

"Ah, a mercenary."

"Yes."

"By God," Mott-Smith breathed. "Fascinating occupation. Tell me, what makes a man fight just to fight?"

"Money."

"Yes, of course, money. I say, would you like to see my gun collection?"

Villachio shrugged.

"I've some fine pieces. Come on, as one campaigner to another." They rose and went into the house.

Alain leaned back in the wicker chair and gazed down the sweep of lawn. Tiny lights on the river bobbed and scooted.

"What are those?" he asked in French.

"Tikapi fishermen. They use kerosene lanterns to attract and mesmerize the fish."

Dureau turned to her. "Those paintings in the house, they're yours, aren't they?"

"Yes."

He nodded. "I thought so. They possess the same sensual power you have. And, like you, they are repressed."

Dominique caught her breath. She glanced at Dureau, then away. A bat flitted across the light and then swooped back into shadow.

"How long have you been away from Paris?" she asked nervously.

"A year."

She brushed her hand through her hair, suddenly aware of its soft, full body. "Sometimes I get terribly homesick for France," she said quietly, wishing that her stomach would cease its faint trembling. Her physical reactions were confusing her. She did not ordinarily respond to men in this manner. Yet there was something utterly magnetic about Soison. His presence seemed to leap out at her, to envelop her.

"How is it you are here?" he asked evenly. "With him."

Again she glanced at his face, then veered away. When she spoke, it was as if to the night air. "We met in New Caledonia. I was working with the French consulate there."

"What made you leave Paris?"

"I'm not sure."

He was smiling. "An impossible love affair, perhaps?"

"Yes." She said it so quickly that it startled her. Yet the word, spoken, triggered remembered sexual passions, suddenly real and powerful in the darkness. She felt a furtive tendril of arousal warm between her legs.

"You're very beautiful," he said. "Much too beautiful for him."

She whirled. "That, *monsieur*, is an insulting thing to say to me."

His smile played across his lips. "But it's true. And you know it's true."

Her eyes held his only for a moment, then sought refuge in the lights of the river.

"I want to make love to you," Dureau said.

A flare of adrenaline of such intensity flew into her blood that she gasped. Its force propelled her to her feet. Brushing past him, she stood at the railing, her heart trembling.

She heard his wicker chair squeak softly. A moment later, his body pressed against her back. She stiffened, felt his breath on her neck. His hands flowed over her hips, dropped to cup at the confluence of her legs. Electricity leapt from his fingers through her dress, through the filament of panties, into her vagina.

She inhaled sharply. "*Mon Dieu*! Please don't."

He held her. She could feel the partially risen penis against her buttocks like a fire wand. With a soft, arrogant snicker he released her and returned to his chair just as Mott-Smith and Villachio came back onto the veranda.

It was several minutes before Dominique could compose herself enough to turn away from the railing and pretend interest as her husband recounted his famous tale of the ribald wife of the brigadier of the Fifteenth Lancers.

Five

---

66 hours, 12 minutes

As dawn approached, Red Square lay under a heavy blanket of white. The few pedestrians at this early hour scurried along with their greatcoats pulled up and their faces muffled. In front of the Moscow Academy of Sciences, a Russian naval staff car was parked at the curb. The driver, a young sailor, stood under the portico of the building, stamping his feet and blowing on his gloves.

On the third floor, Professor Nikolai Lubentsov headed down the chilly corridor toward his laboratory. Halfway down, he noticed his door was open, a light on inside. He was startled to find a man gazing out one of the windows.

"What's this?" he demanded angrily. "Who let you—?" The man turned. Instantly Nikolai's face broke into a surprised smile. "Friedrich!"

The man laughed and came across the room to greet him. He was Vice-Admiral Friedrich Tsander, deputy naval chief of the Kremlin's Tactical Analysis Section. They embraced warmly, then stood apart, holding each other's shoulders.

"Nikolai," Tsander said. "It's been a long time."

"Yes, my old friend. Too long." He held up a finger. "But first, our vodka." He hurried to his desk and withdrew a bottle and two glasses. A moment later, each man held up his glass in a solemn, silent toast.

For years this had been a ritual between them, this

salute to fallen comrades who had fought with them during World War Two. At the battle of Kryukova, where the Nazi panzers had finally been turned from Moscow, both men had won the Order of Lenin.

Friedrich quietly surveyed the array of computer terminals and data banks that filled the room. "Very impressive, Nikolai. They tell me that at the university you're considered a genius with these things."

"No, merely a technician."

"Good. Technicians make the world run. Genius only dreams of doing it."

Lubentsov laughed. "A valid observation." He settled back and studied his guest, slowly rolling his glass between his forefinger and thumb. He had long, slender fingers like those of a concert pianist. His long, lean face was still youthful at sixty-seven. The shock of white hair, always unkempt, exuded a bohemian air.

That initial perception was not totally incorrect. He could speak four European languages, was an expert in subjects as disparate as the French Impressionists, early American westerns, Dixieland jazz, and Italian opera. He had read most of the literary classics of both Russia and the West. In fact, he was never without a frayed copy of Walt Whitman's *Leaves of Grass.* Although disagreeing with the author's frantic patriotism, he found in the powerfully sensual passages a link to his own visions of man's oneness with nature.

"I heard of your promotion to the TA Section, Friedrich," he said. "Congratulations."

A shadow passed through Tsander's eyes. "It did not make me happy. I would rather be at sea." He had once been commander of a nuclear cruiser task force in the Adriatic. "All this talk of *perestroika*, restructuring the old ways. It's all foolish and weakening."

Nikolai eyed him closely. "Something is troubling you, comrade. Come, tell me."

Tsander shoved himself out of the chair and walked to the window. He was silent a long time. "I would ask a favor."

"Of course. Anything."

"Are you aware that the Americans and their allies are holding a summit conference at Guadalcanal?"

"Yes."

Tsander snorted bitterly. "They want to carve up one of the last untouched places on this earth. For their own imperialistic aims. My God, it's China all over again."

Nikolai shrugged. "It's in the American psyche to spread their democratic system to lesser nations. They perceive it as missionary."

Tsander walked slowly back to his chair. He stood with his hands in his pockets, eyes dark and intense. "This time there's more to it than missionary zeal."

"Ah?"

Friedrich dropped into his chair and leaned forward earnestly. "Nikolai, we've been getting steady reports that an unusual buildup of naval force is developing in the South Pacific. The Americans have issued an embargo around the Solomons. They've moved elements of their Seventh Fleet out of Subic Bay in the Philippines to enforce it.

"At the same time, a large battle fleet of the Royal Navy is moving through the Indonesian quadrant to deposit their Prime Minister at the conference. And for the last six months, the French Navy has been running nuclear tests in French Polynesia to the east." He shook his head. "I find this all extremely foreboding."

"What does TAS say?"

Tsander gave a short, disgusted growl. "My young colleagues in the section see this as normal movement. They're inflamed with *glasnost*, the imbeciles. They fail to see the bigger picture."

"What exactly do you think the bigger picture is?"

"I don't know," Friedrich answered passionately. "But I feel the Americans are up to something." He thumped a clenched fist against his chest. "In here, I feel it. It burns."

"And how can I help?"

Tsander swept his hand, indicating the computer and

data banks. "With these, Nikolai. I am told you can predict the future with them. Is that true?"

"Under certain conditions, yes." For the last year Lubentsov had been working on long-range climate forecasts, utilizing analogue models. By coding into mathematical expressions all known historical weather data along with the basic principles governing weather systems, his computers could calculate probability curves for weather phenomenon as far ahead as a hundred years.

Tsander picked up an attaché case that had been resting unnoticed against the desk. He laid it gently in front of Nikolai. "Here is all the classified information you'll need. Deployments of our Pacific fleet, including approximate positions of our nuclear submarines. There's the known positions and strengths of American naval power in the area along with analyses of observed responses and strategic moves the Americans have used during their sea exercises. I've even included personal profiles of leading commanders."

Lubentsov's face showed alarm. "Friedrich, this could be very dangerous. You've smuggled out classified material."

"No one will know," Tsander cried. "Please, my friend, take this material. Add to it whatever you know or can find out about the American psyche, as you call it, and let your machines tell me what the Americans are up to."

Nikolai stared at the attaché case. "That may not be possible. We're dealing here with human factors. Such things can't be traced precisely."

"Do it," Tsander pleaded heatedly. "Not for me but for your country."

Nikolai looked at the admiral and sighed. He knew what was behind this: not Mother Russia but Friedrich's own survival. He was being pushed out of the military hierarchy; his assignment to TAS was only the first step. With the new General Secretary of the Party, Yuri Markisov, everything was changing. Youthfulness was a goal. The old ways and the old warriors had become expendable. *Perestroika*. Friedrich needed a coup. And Friedrich was his friend.

"All right, I'll try."

Tsander relaxed. "Good. If you need any further information, contact me personally and you'll get it immediately. But understand, time is essential. How long do you think it will take?"

"I don't know. I'll try to have something for you late this evening."

Tsander stood, and held out his arms. He and Nikolai embraced again. "Thank you," Friedrich said. He turned and walked to the door, where he paused, smiling. "Give my best to your wife."

"Yes, of course."

Tsander closed the door very softly.

Nikolai stared at the attaché case for a long time. He was afraid. Yet beyond that there was the enticement of challenge. Could he predict American strategy? A fascinating concept. His mind began probing avenues, methods.

At last he scooped up the case and hurried to his computers.

Christine what's-her-name turned out to be Christine Shumbacher. For the last hour she had brought Jimbo Gillespie to physical collapse. Gasping and limp, he sought refuge in her bathroom.

He gazed blearily at his face in the mirror. It looked sucked dry, like a marathon runner's at the tape. He straightened, feeling a slight dizziness, the remnants of the potent joint he and Christine had shared before the onslaught. He urinated, noting with consternation that his penis seemed more reddened and shrunken than it had ever been. He washed his face, braced himself, and returned to the bedroom.

Christine's quarters were in the last wing of the American staff dormitory. Sterile and functional as a cheap hotel. With a sudden wrenching of his stomach, he wondered if Christine's ecstatic yelps and moans had penetrated the walls. He could imagine numerous other secretaries sitting upright in their beds, listening. He was sure that by morning news of his liaison would be rampant in the complex.

In momentary quiescence, Christine was stretched on the rumpled bed, smoking another joint. Her fleshy breasts and buttocks had been slimmed during daylight hours by corset panties and high heels. "God, they grow good grass on this island," she said lazily. "I'm going to smuggle a ton of this shit when I leave."

Jimbo settled wearily onto the edge of the bed. Christine patted the covers. "Here, honey. Right here."

"Let me catch my breath." He stared forlornly at her stomach. It was laced with stretch marks. They looked like tributaries flowing down to the delta of her crotch.

He thought of his wife, wondering what she would be doing at that precise moment. He tried to figure the time difference. It would be morning in her part of the world. Snowing probably, with the kids already off to school. His wife would be watching Phil Donahue in her faded blue housecoat. The image filled him with guilt.

Christine offered a drag on her joint. He shook his head. She kept pushing it at him. Finally he took a small pull. The smoke burned his throat. Her hands began to play over his back.

"Chris?"

"Mmmm?"

"Do you know anything about this freighter in trouble south of us?"

"Nope." After a moment, though, she added, "But there were two guys from NI to see Wilcox this afternoon."

Gillespie stiffened. "Naval Intelligence came to see him?"

"Yeah."

"Why?"

"I don't know."

Jimbo pushed off the bed. "Look, Chris, I've got to go."

"What?"

"I've got loads of stuff to do tomorrow." He wandered around the bedroom, looking for his discarded clothes.

"Party poop," she said. "I'm just getting wound up."

Jimbo located his balled-up Jockeys and pulled them on. Buttoning his shirt, he sat on the edge of the bed again. "Look, I want you to do me a favor. Okay?"

Her hand reached around his hip and probed his crotch. He grabbed her wrist. "No, listen. Come on, listen. I think something's funny about this ship thing."

She flopped petulantly back onto her pillow. "You do, huh?"

"Yes."

"So do I."

"Yeah. Why?"

"I don't know. But I was talking to one of the girls in the MIC pool. She told me she was doing transcriptions for CC Division and there were high-level clearances coming in on it. I mean high. Like the State Department."

Gillespie swung around. "Is that right?"

"That's what she said."

"Dammit, I knew it." He stood up and began angrily pulling on his pants. "Chris, you gotta do me this favor. Keep your ears open, okay? You catch anything more on this ship, you let me know."

"You make it worth my while?"

"A hundred times over."

He headed for the door, carrying his shoes. He opened it and peered out into the hall. It was brilliant with light. He glanced back. "See you."

"See you," Christine said.

He slunk furtively along the hall to the rear door. The tropical night was still hot. The entire complex was lit with bright arc lights, and crews were still working on the outer edge. He slipped into his shoes and hurried across the quadrangle. His sense of outrage increased with each step. Naval Intelligence? High-priority relays from the State Department? He was being left in the dark deliberately. And sure as hell, some hotshot journalist would snoop it out and *he'd* be standing there with his thumb up his ass.

No way! He had a few chits to call in back in Washington. He'd damn sure get to the bottom of this thing.

It was nine o'clock sharp when Admiral Smith was ushered into the Oval Office. The President was alone, sipping coffee at his desk. "Ah, good morning, Smitty."

"Good morning, Mr. President."

"Sit down." The President studied the admiral. "Are you feeling all right? You look pale."

"It's nothing, sir. I didn't sleep too well last night." He wasn't telling the whole truth. Ever since three o'clock that morning, when he'd awakened in a sweat, his left arm had felt numb.

"Neither did I." The President settled back into his chair. "Well, what've you got for me?"

"I'm afraid it's not too good, sir. The aircraft we sent out to make initial search runs for the *Panjang* drew a blank. It seems the ocean bottom in that particular area is filled with ferrous deposits. They completely fouled up the sonar readouts."

The President sucked thoughtfully at his lip and took another sip of coffee.

"Also the aircraft developed engine trouble and had to break off any further runs. The pilot, rightfully, opted to go to an alternate landing site rather than return to the Canal. It would have seemed unusual for a Navy plane to be getting repairs at a commercial airfield."

The President nodded.

"They're headed for the Hinchinbrook Light Station off the Great Barrier Reef. Aussie NGH has already been contacted and they're sending a crew of technicians out from their air base at Mungana. Oh, and there's one other thing, sir. COMMPAC tracking in Hawaii indicates the Russians are affecting deployment shifts in their undersea force in the South Pacific."

"Oh?"

"At this point it doesn't seem too abnormal. Or at

least not major yet. Personally, I think it's just a bit of nosing around the Canal. However, one of their attack boats has been tracked moving toward the *Panjang*'s fix area."

The President's eyes narrowed. "I don't like that." He mused for a moment. "Tell me, Smitty, what do you really think our chances are of finding that freighter?"

"Well, the Saran support ship will be arriving on site by ten hundred hours, their time. She carries a fairly decent sonar capability. I think working in conjunction with the P-3C should give us a pretty good shot."

The President sighed and rubbed his neck. He had a headache starting. "Okay, Smitty, keep me informed."

"Of course, sir."

"And get yourself some rest."

Six

60 hours, 53 minutes

Kitchens picked up the Hinchinbrook Light Station signal a hundred and fifty miles out: twin bursts of sound followed by a hum and another double burst. The station was situated on a small rock upthrust seven miles from the Australian coast, inland from the northern tip of the Great Barrier Reef. Fishermen from Cook and Nan Point hunted the bonita schools in these waters, and sometimes the southern storms caught them, which was the reason for the lighthouse.

The runway was a narrow strip of tarmac used by Alpine seaplanes during rescue operations. The lighthouse itself was at the high end of the strip, right on the edge of a five-hundred-foot drop to the ocean. As Kitchens made his approach from the north, the runway lights seemed to be floating on the dark sea. The lighthouse looked like a gigantic jewel flashing its occulated bursts. Nestled below it in a cluster of weaker lights were the barracks and station offices.

He brought her in low with full flaps. The wheels touched, skidded, touched again. Kitchens yanked back on the wheel. As the Orion settled, he hit the brakes and the aircraft lurched. Klinch's hands were flying over his side of the control panel, reversing props. Outside, the runway side lights flew past and then the props were pushing and gradually the plane slowed. She came to rest fifty yards from the edge of the cliff.

The technicians from Mungana had arrived a half-hour earlier aboard a Stormbird helicopter. Four Australians in gray coveralls with patches of the Australian Northern Air Force on their arms set up a scaffold beside the two small corrugated tin hangars of the Alpines and went to work on number-one engine. Kitchens and Nellie Carpenter supervised while the sonar crew, with Chaffee and Gilchrist, remained aboard, going over the run tapes to see if they could decipher anything.

Bonner watched the technicians for a while. Then, bored and restless, he walked up the runway to the cliff. A cool ocean breeze came up the sheer wall with the tart smell of guano. Finally he went over to the lighthouse and up the curving staircase to the control room.

A young Coast Watcher with deep sideburns and thick glasses was sitting with his feet up on the control panel. "Ah, Yank." He grinned. His teeth were yellow from chewing tobacco. "Bit of excitement, aye?"

"A bit."

"Those blokes from Mungana are cracks. They'll have you out of 'ere in a blink."

Cas wandered around the small room. The walls were made of riveted steel sheeting. Overhead, he heard the steady whir of gears as the light lenses revolved.

"Care for a coldie, mate?" the sailor asked.

"Yeah, thanks."

The Aussie got a tall liter bottle of dark ale from a small reefer. The ale was icy cold and thick in Bonner's throat. He nodded toward the cliff. "What's at the bottom?"

"A bit of beach and some tumble rock."

"Is there any way down?"

"Aye, a walkway cut into the rock."

"Any chance I could borrow a light and snorkel mask?"

"Right-o, mate." The sailor pulled open a drawer and withdrew a mask and a long flashlight encased in plastic. "Goin' to do a bit of explorin', are you?"

"Might as well."

"Best stay away from the deep water. You'll get shark-'et for sure. They come big and fast hereabouts."

"I know," Cas said quietly.

"Here, take a couple coldies along wi' ya."

"I appreciate it, but let me buy them."

"Away with ya, Yank. No more than you'd do for me, aye?"

The cliff walkway had a rope railing running through eyebolts driven into the limestone. Gulls scuffled and squealed as he descended, his light disturbing them inside their rock caves. He came out onto a small crescent of beach. The ocean rustled softly against the tumble rock. There was no reef or waves, indicating the water beyond the rocks was very deep.

He took off his clothes and, naked, went into one of the bigger pockets formed by the rocks. He drifted out into the center, pulled on the mask, and dived under. The pool was full of a soft clicking and creaking music from the animals that lived in it. He reached the bottom and moved along one of the walls.

Although Bonner was an expert in cetacean studies, his first specialty was reef biology. As a boy in California he'd spent endless hours probing among the reef lines of La Jolla. Studying, cataloging, but mostly just observing. Sea life fascinated him, its sheer diversity, its pure symmetry. He wasn't a particularly religious man, yet he'd discovered a certain theology from the ocean. Everything was so beautifully planned and coordinated. In a fundamental way this had formulated his expectations of existence onshore. In that he was disappointed. Humans, including himself, he found, continually veered off into irrationality. And they usually ended up by screwing themselves and everything they touched.

A moray eel darted from a crevice at his hand. He tapped its head with the flashlight, and the eel zipped back into its hole like a string of spaghetti into a fat man's mouth. The wall face was broken with crevices and several long slits that opened out into the ocean. Little

schools of sergeant majors swarmed curiously around
him, attracted by the light. They darted and fluttered
like striped leaves in a wind.

For nearly an hour he wandered around, peering into
holes, prying off sea urchins and teasing crabs. He switched
off the light and hovered in the darkness, watching little
clouds of phosphorescent algae, like glowing smoke, drift
through the slits on the tidal surge. He turned his light
on a sudden flutter in the algae. A huge barracuda had
slipped through one of the slits, its eyes rotating slowly,
watching the light.

Cas respected barracuda. They were lightning fast and
prey for nothing in the sea. Unlike the blind, bullying
rapaciousness of the shark, the barracuda remained aloof,
struck only when he wanted to. When he did, nothing
escaped the strike.

Cas hissed softly at it. With a flash of tail too quick to
see, the fish was gone. Bonner swung around and his
beam picked him up again. Now he was hovering three
feet away. Cas gently tapped a fingernail against the
flashlight housing. Again the barracuda disappeared from
the light. Bonner flicked it off just in time to see the faint
whirl of phosphorescence where the big fish had rocketed
through the slit and back into open water.

Chuckling, Cas lifted his face above water for air.

High above him someone was coming down the cliff
walkway. He could see the flashlight bobbing on the
limestone. Figuring it was one of the crewmen coming
down to retrieve him, he decided to make one more pass
around the pool before getting out. He hated to leave.

Through the water he could see the light come down
onto the beach. It paused at his pile of clothing. In a
moment, whoever it was began to build a small driftwood
fire.

Bonner surfaced. As the firelight grew, he saw that it
was Napah. She sat down beside the fire, her legs drawn
up, looking out at the ocean. For a moment he sculled
his legs, undecided. Then he swam over to the edge of
the pool and got out. He retrieved the two bottles of ale

he'd stashed in a crevice and nonchalantly strolled up the beach to the fire.

Napah turned and silently watched him. When he reached the light, he tossed one of the bottles to her. Then he quietly bent to pick up his shorts and began pulling them on. Unabashed, Napah continued watching him.

"How's the plane?" he asked.

"Kitchens said it'll take another two hours. He suggests everybody get some sleep."

"You get anything on the trace tapes?"

"No." She twisted the cap off her bottle and took a pull. She made a face. "God, that tastes like bitter molasses."

Cas squatted shirtless, cracked his own bottle. "It's good for you. Makes hair grow on your chest."

"Lovely."

They sat looking out at the ocean. It seemed to whisper back at them with a vast, breathlike sound. In the sky, the moon had passed beyond the crest of the cliff.

"I never thanked you," Napah said.

"For what?"

"What you did up there when you thought we were going to crash."

"No need to."

"You know what was really neat about it? Nobody else gave me a thought."

"I just didn't want you to fall on me when we hit."

"You're so gracious." She tasted the beer again. "We got pretty close to it, didn't we?"

"Pretty close."

"Would we have been killed if we went in?"

"That's hard to say. Kitchens is a good pilot, but if that engine had blown on him, we'd have gone in with one wing down. Definitely not the proper way to ditch."

She hugged her legs. "I came that close once. In a storm off Alaska. It scared the hell out of me. I was twenty-two and thought dying was for other people. You just don't think about it when you're young, do you?"

"That's why they draft young men to be soldiers. They're just stupid enough to be brave."

"Are you brave?"

"You mean, am I stupid enough to be?"

She rested her head on her crossed elbows, watching him. "I'll bet you are, when it gets to the nitty-gritty."

He didn't comment on that. He took a drink instead.

"I read about you getting blackballed after Hawaiian Marine."

Bonner looked surprised. "Yeah? Why the interest?"

"Oh, I just came across an item in the *Ocean Journal.* I think it was cruddy the way they treated you."

Again there was no comment from him.

"How old are you, Bonner?"

"Thirty-nine."

"Married?"

"Once."

"Oh, lemme guess. She was a beautiful showgirl who chose her career over you, right? No, wait, that's not it. She was a society snob who thought you looked resplendent in a dinner jacket, but found out she didn't like beer and pizza."

He gave her a sharp look.

"Sorry. That was tactless." She straightened, began toying idly with the label on the ale bottle. "You don't like me much, do you?"

"Not much."

"Why? Because I was rough on you at Scripps?"

"That didn't help."

"But there's more to it than that, isn't there? Tell me."

"You got a two-by-four on your shoulder."

"You figure I come on too strong."

"A mite."

"You prefer sugar and lace."

He chortled and rested back on his elbows. "It's always one or the other, isn't it?"

"You tell me." Her voice had stiffened.

"Damn, all you feminist types are hell-bent on being

like a man. Why? What the hell is so hot about being a man?"

"If you were a woman, you wouldn't have to ask."

"Psychiatrists call it penis envy."

"That's a crock."

"Well, at least we agree on one thing. But tell me, why do you have to be so hard-nosed about it?"

"Maybe then you jerks will notice."

Bonner shook his head sadly and appraised her. "Listen, Napah, out on those sonar runs, you impressed those men in that aircraft. ASW men, in the business. Hell, you impressed the crap out of me. You probably know more about sonar analysis than all of us put together. And they weren't looking at your tits when they were impressed. You understand what I'm saying?"

She was silent.

"You've arrived in a man's world. Okay? Maybe it's time to shift gears a little."

He took another drink, as if the words had parched his throat. They were both silent for a while, yet something seemed to move in the air between them. Bonner could feel it. A stillness, like before the first crack of lightning.

At last Napah turned her head and looked at the ocean. "Is the water cold?"

"No."

She spun the bottom of her ale bottle in the sand and stood up. Very deliberately she began to undress. First the dungaree shirt, then the trousers Buchanan had loaned her, then panties and bra. Naked but not looking at him, she walked down to the pool he had been in and dived into the water.

Bonner felt a surge of lust. He watched her surface, the firelight shimmering off her wet hair. The yearning thumped at his temples. He stood up, pulled off his shorts, and went down to the edge of the pool.

"It's glorious," she cried. "Come on."

At that instant he saw through the water a whirl of

phosphorescence lift off the ocean side of the pool wall. He froze. He said, "Napah, don't move."

"What?"

"Stay absolutely still."

She caught the tenseness in his voice. "What is it?"

"Stay still, dammit. And shut up." He felt along the edge of the pool until he found a loose rock. Another. Gently he lowered them into the water and began knocking them together.

The surface suddenly erupted like a steelhead taking a lure. Napah let out a squeal and began thrashing toward the edge. Behind her, the phosphorescence whirled again and drifted against the far wall, following the turbulence out the slit.

She lunged out of the water. "What was that thing, Cas? My God, what was it?"

Bonner looked up at her. She was staring down at the water, a little girl peering fearfully into a darkened bedroom from which a terrible sound had just come. He started to laugh.

"Damn you," she said furiously. "What the hell was that?"

"A barracuda."

"Oh, my God."

He fell back on the sand, still laughing.

"What the hell are you laughing at, you fool? That damned thing could've taken my leg off."

"Or a tit." He roared. "I would have gone for the tit."

"What the hell's the matter with you?" she demanded. She smacked him on the top of the head and fell to her knees beside him. "Stop laughing."

"Your face," he blurted between spasms of laughter. "You looked like somebody'd shoved a poker up your butt."

"Oh, you're hilarious," she said, still angry. She started to get up.

"No, wait." His laughter died, just like that. He could feel her knees touching his skin. He reached up and ran his fingers over the smooth wet sheen of her hair. Did she shiver?

A shrill whistle drifted down from the cliff edge. "Bonner," someone called. "Hey, Bonner. Come up."

Napah smiled down at him. She put two fingers against her lips and touched them to his. She stood up and walked back to the fire. He got up and followed her.

Wordlessly they dressed.

Dureau woke to the sound of pigeons cooing on the roof. Through the mosquito netting he saw the sky pearled with fresh light. He flexed his muscles, stretched his legs under the thin sheet. He'd slept soundly, without dreams. He glanced at the floor where Villachio had slept in his bedroll. He was gone, the roll neatly bound and resting against the wall.

The room was white and airy. A woman's room with a canopied bed and an ornate gold-and-white dresser. It had the comfortable feel of occupancy. He wondered, smiling, whether Dominique slept here. Alone, allowing her husband only furtive conjugal visits.

A movement beside the door caught his eye. He sat up. It was Dominique. She was standing just inside the frame, watching him with the frightened look of a fawn about to flee.

"What is it?" he called.

She put her finger to her lips to silence him. Quietly she closed the louvered door and came to the side of the bed. The folds of her white peignoir draped her body like descending mist. Beneath it she was naked. She lifted the netting, pulled it aside.

"Where's Garibaldi?" he asked.

"Gone with my husband to shoot crocodiles," she whispered. Her eyes were fearful and intensely bright, like a woman watching her child being born. "Don't speak. Say nothing." Her voice was hoarse with excitement. "Just take me and be done with it."

Smiling with faint scorn, Dureau lowered himself slowly

onto his pillow. He watched her, not moving. A look of shocked doubt flashed across Dominique's face. With a quick snap Dureau flung the sheet aside, exposing his nakedness. Dominique gave a small gasp as her eyes found his distended member. Without taking her gaze from it, she disrobed and climbed in beside him.

At first she was tense and stiff. He could feel her skin trembling like a frightened animal's. Then her mouth opened to him; her breath came in short, frantic gasps. Her hands flew over his flesh. She twisted, took him into her mouth, and moaned as his fingers probed into her.

He rolled away from her. She gave a startled cry and glanced up. He drew her to her knees, slipped deftly behind her. She arched, her mouth wide. "Yes," she moaned. "Oh, God, yes."

With one powerful thrust he was deep inside her. The chain on his neck tinkled softly against the dog tag as they rocked forward and back. The sides of the bed creaked, the frilly tassels shook. When Dominique reached orgasm, she tore at the pillow as if suffocating.

Dureau took her repeatedly, their bodies glistening with sweat. She wept as if in terrible sorrow. Yet the weeping bore her to new heights of passion. At last, exhausted, they pulled apart. Dureau flopped onto his back. Dominique curled away from him, gazing through the window, now flooded with sunshine. The sound of their labored breathing filled the room. Ignored by both of them was Dureau's watch, ticking on the night table. It was nearing nine o'clock.

Three minutes later, Mott-Smith came through the door.

Dominique gave a tiny scream, bolted upright, and frantically began pulling the sheet up to cover herself. Her husband stood framed in the doorway, momentarily motionless with shock. His khaki clothes and his boots were splattered with river mud. His mouth worked but nothing came out. Then his features contorted with rage. Blood flew into his cheeks, thickened his neck. With an incoherent bellow he charged across the room, his bamboo walking stick raised.

Dominique, whimpering with terror, tried to get out of the bed. The bamboo stick whipped through the air, slashed across her neck. She screamed and fell to the floor.

Dureau had already leapt to his feet. He started around the bed. Mott-Smith met him there, raining blows, cursing savagely each time the stick cracked across Alain's upraised arms.

Dureau gave way, falling back, trying to protect his face. The Englishman went after him. Villachio appeared at the door, then bounded into the room. He threw his arms around Mott-Smith's shoulders, pinning him. They struggled back against the bed and the canopy fell down.

With brute strength Villachio flung Mott-Smith back against the wall. A mirror shattered. The Englishman gave a cry of pain and fell to the floor. His head lifted, eyes blazing.

"You filthy French swine," he screamed. "I'll kill you!"

He stumbled to his feet and headed for the door. Villachio caught him before he got through. Mott-Smith struggled feebly for a moment, then crumpled, sobbing.

Beside the bed, Dureau was looking at the welts on his forearms. They were red and the skin was already puffing. His eyes were hard and flat. In one leap he was beside Villachio's bedroll, tearing at the straps.

Villachio let Mott-Smith slide to the floor and stepped around him. "Alain, for God's sake."

Dureau got the bedroll open and shoved his hand down into the folds. It came out with the Ingram.

At the sight of the weapon Mott-Smith gave a wrenching wail. He began to plead. "Oh, no, please! Dear God, no!"

"No man whips me," Dureau announced coldly. He rammed the receiver back, let it slam home. In one move he lifted the Ingram and fired. The explosions cracked hard and fast in the small space.

The bullets lifted Mott-Smith up off his knees and flung him back through the doorway. He crumpled onto the corridor rug. Dominique screamed and went on screaming.

Dureau let go another burst. The Englishman's body jerked from the impacts. The blasts were still echoing through the house as Villachio darted through the door and sprinted down the corridor. On the other side of the bed, Dominique, letting out short, hysterical shrieks, was trying to crawl toward the window.

Dureau lowered the Ingram. "Shut up," he muttered. When she continued, he flung himself across the fallen canopy, grabbed her by the hair, and wrenched her head back. He put the muzzle of the machine pistol against her cheek. "Shut up or I'll blow your head off."

Dominique stared at the weapon. Her eyes were glazed with horror. Trembling violently, she fell into gasping silence.

There was a pistol shot outside. Dureau dropped her, leapt off the bed, and scurried to the window. He peered cautiously over the edge of the sill. Villachio was in the backyard. "The houseboy," he called. "He's run into the bush."

"Never mind about him," Dureau shouted. "Let's get out of here."

Fifteen minutes later, with Dureau at the wheel of Mott-Smith's Land Rover and Villachio and Dominique in the back, they headed down the plantation road toward Marau, a hundred miles away.

The *Sabir* had reached the southeastern approaches to the Coral Sea.

In his cabin, Captain Lapshin was awakened from his nap by the intercom above his bunk. It came on with a sound as delicate as a billiard ball striking a table cushion. "Comrade Captain?"

He brushed his hand across the tiny cell beam that activated the unit. "Yes?"

"Sonar room, sir. We have a contact."

"I'll be up."

Lapshin rose and stepped into the main corridor. It was drenched in subdued red light. On the surface it was dawn. Soon the lighting would automatically fuse into yellow, maintaining the human need for the cycles of daylight.

Lieutenant Chernov was watch officer, Orserov OOD. "It looks like a surface convergence, Comrade Captain," Chernov informed him. "Bearing zero-four degrees twenty-two hundred meters."

Lapshin leaned his arm on the pedestal chair. "Ident?"

"Computer engine resonance indicates one Russian, the other American. Light tonnage. CIC signatures the Russian as a whaler. The American's speed indicates a corvair, H Class."

"Home on F Sector."

The screen directly in front of him went into tighter focus. The blips of light showing the converging surface ships became as large as dimes, then nickels.

"What's their separation?"

"Three hundred meters, sir," a man called from his left.

Chernov said, "The American is certainly closing fast."

Lapshin grunted noncommittally. Many years ago he had learned to control his emotions in front of his crew. It was a matter of simply clamping down the external movements of his hands and face. If these were held in check, the rest of his body would follow.

"SRS?"

"Surface conditions excellent, sir. Long swell, two-knot wind, twenty-eight degrees centigrade, sixty-two-percent humidity."

The blips continued on their collision course. Lapshin's eyes narrowed. He suspected what was happening up there. The American corvair was bullying the whaler, trying to force him to yield his heading.

Would he? And if not, would the American actually ram him? In such an event, what would he do? Surface for rescue operations and thus expose his ship? Or sit helplessly by while his countrymen died?

"Shall we stand by radio buoy, sir?" Chernov asked. "Perhaps we can find out what is being said."

"Negative. Separation distance?"

"One hundred fifty meters, sir."

As he watched the blips flying together, he felt a welling of pride. The whaler was not giving an inch. The blips closed.

"Control, Sonar. We have countercavitation on the whaler."

Lapshin slumped imperceptibly. His countryman had just capitulated. In his mind he pictured the scene, the American corvair slicing across the whaler's bow in an obscene gesture.

"Control, Sonar. We have another target. Bearing zero-eight-seven degrees, range nine thousand meters, depth two hundred meters."

"Focus."

The screen scrambled into wavy lines, then cleared. The two original targets were now in the north corner. Coming in from the east was a sharper blip, moving rapidly.

"Control, CIC signatures new target as American nuclear submarine, 688 Class."

"All stop. Target heading and speed."

The engine command was echoed and the *Sabir* immediately began to lose headway.

"Target heading zero-eight-seven degrees, holding. Range eight thousand, six hundred meters, speed thirty-two knots."

Suddenly the blip disappeared off the screen, lost in a flurry of light bursts. The 688 was throwing out an electron shower to hide from the *Sabir*'s sonar probes.

"Go to resonance track," Lapshin snapped.

Two seconds went by. "Control, RT indicates heading holding to zero-eight-seven degrees, speed has increased to thirty-four knots, range seven thousand, nine hundred fifty meters."

Lapshin stared at the screen. The flashing lights made

tiny, momentary images on the retinas of his eyes. He thought: Another obscenity? Not this time.

"Go to two-thirds," he called out.

It was obeyed instantly. The *Sabir* began to move again.

"Right full rudder."

"Right full rudder, aye."

The *Sabir* heeled, moving sharply into her turn.

"Steady up on zero-eight-seven degrees. Call turn."

The helmsman snapped: "Swinging through zero-one-zero degrees."

As quickly as it had come, the flashing lights on the screen disappeared. The American blip was clear and sharp again. Lapshin watched his own blip fix coming about.

"Coming up to zero-eight-zero degrees. Fix. We have zero-eight-seven degrees."

"Target?"

"Heading holding steady, speed increased to thirty-four knots. Range six thousand, four hundred meters."

"Full ahead."

"Full ahead, aye."

Now the *Sabir* was rocketing through the water. On the screen the American's blip was dead ahead. Lapshin felt a tiny thudding in his neck. Eyes still fixed on the screen, he willed it to calmness. In a moment he no longer felt it.

"Range?"

"Target range, two thousand, four hundred meters, speed thirty-eight knots."

The blips on the screens were flying together.

"Control, Sonar. We detect slight course change to zero-eight-nine degrees. Speed holding thirty-eight knots."

A faint smile touched the captain's lips. In an instant he removed it.

"Range?"

"Target range, nine hundred fifty meters."

Lapshin's eyes could now detect the slight divergence of the American's blip relative to the *Sabir*'s bow line. He would pass to starboard.

"Target range, three hundred meters. Speed holding thirty-eight knots."

The 688's cavitation was clearly audible in the control room now. It grew louder. Forty-three seconds later, it passed the *Sabir* to starboard, boring through the water. Gradually her noise faded as the sonar room kept calling the increasing separation distance. At last Lapshin allowed himself to relax. He glanced at Chernov, who was smiling broadly. "Take her to cruise speed and return to original heading, Lieutenant," the captain said.

"Yes, Comrade Captain."

Lapshin left the control room.

Seven

56 hours, 3 minutes

Lubentsov's first runs added up to a confused jumble of untenable projections. He was not surprised. He was dealing with a massive amount of information that had to be fed into his computers. In addition, there was so much human factor, not easily reducible to mathematical precision.

Throughout the day he and his five assistants had correlated and transcribed into digital code the information from Tsander's attaché case. As the hours passed, Nikolai became more and more obsessed with the challenge of the task. At five o'clock he dismissed his assistants, primarily for their own protection. They had no idea that the information he had was current. Twenty minutes later, he began his first run.

It was now after seven. He stood at the window of the lab, sipping a fresh cup of tea and looking pensively out at the night coming over Moscow. He could see the lights of the skating rink at Gorky Park, could hear the faint strains of a Viennese waltz. It had not snowed all day but there were ice pools below his window, and the leafless trees along the river looked like pen sketches against the streetlights.

The problem, as he saw it, was in isolating specific mental responses to a factual situation. His input of previous American moves, even augmented by the personal profiles of strategic American commanders, was proving insufficient to pinpoint the process by which the distinctly American mind created and then sought out goals. If he could fix on that process and then filter it into mathematical parameters, he would be able to predict what all the other factors indicated about the Americans' aim in the Pacific.

He turned back to his computers. It was very cold in the room, but he ignored it. Computers worked better in low temperatures. He wandered among the banks, mumbling softly to himself. What did he know of the American psyche? What pattern of behavior was endemic?

He sat down at his input console. His fingers were cold. He flexed them a moment, and began feeding in conceptual factors.

SPECIES: AMERICAN:

His mind swiftly scanned memories, images, tidbits of information long stored. One rose into focus. It was black-and-white: two gritty figures walking toward each other on a lonely street. Confrontation. A moment of suspense. Then hands clawed at weapons, gunfire, one man fell.

CORRELATIONAL CHARACTER OF RESOLUTION: CONFRONTATIONAL, CLIMACTIC, SUBJECTION OF OPPOSING FORCE . . .

Numbers flashed across the console screen as the machine codified the concepts, assigned mathematical groupings.

His mind again scanned. Dixieland jazz. The concerted focus of scattered soloists that always reached a crescendo of purpose. Blatant but fused, powerful and stunning.

SECONDARY CHARACTER THRUST: COLLECTION OF ELEMENTS WORKING TOWARD SINGLE CRESCENDO . . .

More numbers silently arrayed themselves across the screen.

Now he plucked fragments from his beloved Whitman, his unconscious subtly injecting phrases unremembered:

Not wan from Asia's fetishes,
Nor red from Europe's old dynastic slaughterhouse,
   plots of thrones, with scent left yet of wars
   and scaffolds . . .

These virgin islands, islands of the Western
   shore . . .
To . . . the new empire, risen from the sea,
Promised long, pledged, to be achieved in glorious conflict.

TERTIARY CHARACTER THRUST: AIMS OF CONQUEST AND
DOMINANCE IN SOUTHERN SEAS . . .
Lubentsov meticulously formed the conceptual design,
the *anima humana* known as American, delineated and
codified into the purity of numbers. When it was completed, he rose and walked back to the window. His
senses were highly tuned. Outside, the Viennese waltzes
had transformed into thunderous Wagner. A roll of drums
rumbled through the skeletal trees like distant cannon.

He returned to the console. Without pause his hands
darted, threw switches, punched buttons.

His final run was on.

At precisely 0916 hours, the *Voorhees* arrived at the
coordinates of the *Panjang*'s last position fix. Hillar had
brought his ship down through the wide channel between
New Britain and the northern Solomons in the dark. At
2:30 in the morning, they'd run into the outriders of the
American cruiser force out of Subic. The ocean seemed
filled with ships and their running lights. The air was
filled with ship cross-chatter. One of the corvairs knifed
across the *Voorhee's* wake to check him out.

Now they were alone. Hillar, a mug of coffee in his
hand, returned to the bridge. Costello was watch officer.
He had the *Voorhees* doing wide three-sixties at five
knots, holding fix position.

"You raise the Orion yet?" Hillar asked.

"Not yet, Frank."

Hillar checked his watch. "All right, let's set her up for the drag. We'll come around to zero-one-zero and start pinging on the southwest corner. Get Peddie up here."

A moment later the loudspeaker cracked: "Sonarman Peddie report to the bridge."

Hillar watched the ship's bow straightening slightly, then stepped into the sonar room inboard the port wing. It was a small room crammed with electronic gear. A panel of screens took up one side. The three in the top bank were television monitors for the Saran's onboard cameras. The bottom bank contained sonar visuals, each with its own computer board. On the starboard bulkhead were the impulse-frequency controls and transducer relays.

A short, stocky sailor came in and braced. "Sonarman Peddie reporting as ordered, sir."

"Crank her up, Jack. We'll begin streamer deployment in fifteen minutes."

"Aye, sir," Peddie sat down at the main console and started throwing switches. The bottom bank of screens came to life.

Hillar returned to the bridge. "Heading?"

"Crossing through zero-three-zero, sir."

He picked up his radio mike, keyed the loudspeaker. "Streamer detail, stand by." To the helmsman: "Start bringing her out of it. Set up heading to zero-one-zero."

"Helm easing off, aye. Maintain zero-one-zero."

"Give me three knots."

The ship's speed dropped immediately.

"Coming up to zero-one-zero degrees . . . we have it."

Hillar checked his watch. "Let go streamer."

Thirty seconds later, the divemaster's voice came through a secondary speaker: "Streamer away and trailing."

The radio operator poked his head around the door of his room. "I've got the Orion, sir."

"Put it overhead and key my mike to frequency."

There was a burst of static through the speaker. ". . . vector to you, fifty miles due west. I have you visual."

Hillar keyed, thinking: West? What the hell's he coming from there for? "Orion, this is Captain Hillar. We have started sonar run and pinging in southwest quadrant of search area. Advise."

"*Voorhees*. ETA approximately three minutes. We'll trail and track your first pass and then align for Torpex drops."

"Understand."

"Expect a lot of splurge off the bottom. The place is littered with ferrous deposits."

Hillar cursed softly before keying. "Roger that."

"Start transmitting your tapes to us in sixty seconds. Use frequency two-three-zero-point-five."

Hillar repeated the frequency. "We will contact you when aligned for second pass. Over." He turned to the sonar room. "You got that frequency, Jack?"

"Yes, sir."

He walked out to the starboard wing and looked aft. The streamer cable laid across the ramp trembled with the pull of the hydrophone array. He watched it for a while, thinking: Ferrous deposits? Here? Jesus H. Christ!

The *Voorhee's* tapes were transcribed and displayed on the Orion's screens after a six-second delay. Buchanan and Napah were working the console now. Cas and Chaffee were sitting in the observer seats, watching intently.

Cushioned from the steady engine drone, the tactical room was filled with tiny sounds. The steady clicking of the varible-displacement-indicator, the soft whir of tapes and reels, the wavering pings of the *Voorhee's* probes that impulsed solidly, then modulated into scatter as the array phones began picking up the rebound from different angles. The P-3C's computers digitalized incoming information, amplified it, and isolated the individual returns, spreading them on a multiline readout. The resulting track showed the washed bottom along a four-hundred-yard strip.

Kitchens came on: "How's the read?"

"Not bad, Skipper," Buchanan answered. "We're on enhancement cycle now. Those Torpex shots should come off the bottom like floodlights."

"Gilchrist," Kitchens said. "Will the ferrous deposits screw us again?"

"I don't think so. We've got enough hydrophones in the water now, we'll be able to pick up vein lines. The ship would show up as one big chunk of iron."

"Let's hope so."

Bonner tapped Napah on the shoulder. When she turned round, he gave her a lifted eyebrow and flicked his thumb toward the flight deck as if to say: "See?"

She smiled and winked at him.

Below them, the *Voorhees* completed her first pass and started an angulated turn. Kitchens took the Orion out into a wide sweep. He turned the radio over to Buchanan, who immediately began communicating directly with Hillar, coordinating the ship and aircraft headings and timing sequences.

"Initiating drag run now," Hillar called up.

Far ahead of the Orion, the ship moved slowly in a shimmering, sundotted sea. She seemed to drift toward them as they came up, her white sides brilliant.

"Stand by Torpex," Buchanan ordered. His eyes were fixed on the chronometer above his console. "Let go number one."

A soft jolt.

"Number one away."

Kitchens gave the engines power and they gently pulled away from the sea. Six seconds later the screens flared with a brilliant white explosion of light. It rippled and flamed, then gradually disintegrated into highlights that slowly faded into spots and blotches like a city seen from way up at night. The VDI clicked furiously.

"Looking good," Napah cried happily. She and Buchanan exchanged grins.

For the next two hours the *Voorhees* and the Orion worked together, the aircraft skimming astern like a hovering hawk. Up the tapes came, reeled through the analyzers and enhancement cycles, projecting bottom tracks as clear as a motion picture.

They found nothing.

*   *   *

Lubentsov's run sheets clicked and hummed through the computers with sharp dotlets of sound. Above the panels, reels spun, halted, reversed under their glass viewing windows. He prowled around the corners of the machines, nervously sipping tea. Outside, it was pitch dark.

Nikolai walked over to his desk and took out the bottle of vodka. He drank from it, letting the fiery liquid go straight down. It spread a soft glow through his chest.

The computers clicked into silence.

Lubentsov returned the bottle to his drawer and crossed the room. The readout sheets were neatly counter-turned in their outfeed rack. He began scanning the results. First skimming down columns of decoded number groups, then back, reading in depth. His heart started pounding. When he reached the last sheet, he started over again.

There was no mistake. The projection was clear, parameters defined, decodification synopsis firmly propelled toward a single entity: *the Americans were initiating the early stages of a major nonnuclear naval engagement with Russian forces in the South Pacific.*

Eight

52 hours, 27 minutes

Spangenberg slowly rolled three spent 9mm cartridges in his palm. Each had a slight nick in the edge of the base, an ejection mark he immediately identified. Mott-Smith had been killed with an Ingram M-10. A terrorist's weapon. Light, smaller than an Uzi, with a rate of fire of one thousand rounds a minute. He smiled coldly, satisfied that his instincts had again been correct.

Fa'uza and one of his constables were wandering around the bedroom, stunned. Jacob came over and stood helplessly beside him. "Oh, Colonel, how terrible this is. I was familiar with Mr. Mott-Smith. A nice man."

"Where's the priest?" Sab barked. Father Sebastian of the local parish had been the one to report the murder. Tombo, nearly incoherent with fear, had fled to the parish house.

"Outside with the plantation boys."

Sab put the casings into his pocket and walked through the living room to the veranda. A cluster of workers, Tikapi indians with machetes hanging from leather thongs from their belts, were gathered around the priest in the driveway. Spangenberg whistled for him to come up. Father Sebastian's face was pale and grim as he came up the veranda steps.

"Have you discovered anything?" he asked in a slightly Bostonian accent.

Sab ignored the question. "Where's the houseboy?"

"Still at the parish house. He's terribly frightened. He refuses to come back here."

"Tell me precisely what he said."

Father Sebastian glanced through the door before speaking. Mott-Smith's legs were visible in the corridor. He shook his head and leaned against the railing. "Two men came here yesterday evening. Apparently Mott-Smith knew them. He invited them to stay the night."

"What did they look like?"

"One, the younger man, spoke French with Dominique." His eyes screwed up with emotion. "Poor woman."

"What did they *look* like?"

"The one who spoke French was apparently quite handsome. Tombo said his mistress seemed quite excited when she looked at him. The other man didn't speak much. He was large and had a face like a *cuscus*—a jungle monkey."

Sab's head snapped around suddenly. Two of the workmen were creeping up to the house, trying to see through the window. "Hey, you," he shouted. "Get the hell away from there."

The priest held up his hand. "Please, Colonel, be gentle with them. They are merely curious. Mott-Smith had no relatives. All these poor souls are out of a job."

"Tell them to back off."

Father Sebastian called quietly to the men, speaking Tikapi. He turned back to Spangenberg, drew air before speaking, then continued. He recounted the sequence of events up to and following the killing as told to him by Tombo. The boy had hidden in the jungle until the Land Rover left.

Sab's eyes slitted. "What direction did they go?"

"Tombo was too frightened to look. But some of the workers said that they saw the Land Rover headed south."

"What's there?"

"Nothing but jungle, really. Five miles from here the road splits. One fork goes over the mountains to Cape Hunter. The other is a jungle road that goes along the foothills to Paron Bau and Marau in south island." The priest was thoughtful for a moment. "Something else Tombo remembered. During supper they were speaking about a man who lives in Marau."

Sab stiffened. "Did he get his name?"

"Yes, Hedges. He's an Aussie pilot who flies for the sugar companies in south island. Rather disreputable fellow, from what I hear."

Spangenberg walked up the veranda, thinking. Was this a terrorist plot? Now a pilot was involved. He could feel anticipatory bursts of energy starting in his chest. He came back to the priest.

"This Englishman's wife. What do you know about her?"

"She's young, quite charming, and pretty. As a Catholic, she occasionally came to Mass. Once she told me she was from a small town south of Paris, Châteaudun, Châteaufrun, something like that."

"How long has she been here?"

"Two or three years. She lived in New Caledonia before marrying."

"Was the houseboy positive it was Mott-Smith who knew these men, and not his wife?"

"It was Mott-Smith. Tombo heard him introducing them to her. Tell me, Colonel. Do you think they've murdered her too?"

"I don't know," Sab answered curtly. "This place have a phone?"

"Yes."

Sab went back into the house. For the first time, he could smell Mott-Smith's corpse. He found a phone in the kitchen and called his office.

"Marine Liaison, Group One, Sergeant Burke."

"Listen, I want you to get over to the SP barracks and requisition two automatic weapons and ammo."

"Sir, the quartermaster won't release weapons without your signature."

"Then forge the fucking thing, asshole."

"Yes, sir."

"Bring them to the parish house at Nolitoto. In thirty minutes. You got that?"

"Yes, sir."

An old panel truck had pulled up in front of the house while he was on the phone. A short Japanese man in a rumpled dungaree jacket was talking to the priest on the veranda. After a moment he came into the house. He stopped short when he saw Spangenberg.

"Who you?" he challenged.

"Marine liaison. Who the fuck are you?"

"Dr. Sakai, medical examiner."

Sab jerked his head toward the hall. "All right, do your thing."

Down the hall, Fa'uza and his man came out of the bedroom. Spangenberg signaled him and walked out of the house and down to Jacob's battered constabulary jeep. When Jacob came down, Sab stared into his eyes for a long moment. Then he asked, "You still remember how to kill a man?"

Fa'uza's brow furrowed. "I do not understand, Colonel."

"We're going after this prick. Just you and me. He's headed for Marau. If we're lucky, we'll catch him in the jungle before he gets there."

Jacob studied him. Something moved in his brown eyes. A remembrance, a whisper of lost glories when he fought the Japanese, now disintegrated across the years. He nodded. "Yes, Colonel, I remember."

They loaded the priest's bicycle onto the jeep and drove back to Nolitoto. The village was nestled amid a grove of coconut trees. The houses were propped on stilts, scattered down the slope toward the river. Father Sebastian left them in the jeep and walked toward the mud-brick chapel to say a mass for the Mott-Smiths. The heat was intense out in the road. Naked children with protruding bellies and sores on their arms came up from the village and stared at the men waiting in the jeep.

Fifteen minutes later a Honiara taxi roared into the village. Sergeant Burke was sitting in front with the driver, and the barrels of two M16s poked out the window.

Burke started to get out with the weapons. "Put them in the back seat," Spangenberg ordered. Burke obeyed, then got out.

"Them boys in Ordnance was plenty hot about this, Colonel," he said.

"Screw 'em. Come on, Jacob, we'll take the taxi. It'll make better time." He walked around the front of the vehicle and pointed at the driver. "You, out."

The driver was a burly Melanesian with very dark skin. He looked Sab up and down scornfully. "Who you, man?"

"We're commandeering your vehicle for police business. Now, get your fat ass out of there, boy."

"What you say?" the driver yelled. "Try say again?" He shoved the door open and lunged out. He thrust a thumb at Spangenberg and began cursing him in Pidgin English.

As quickly as a cat, Sab stepped in under the pointing arm. His left hand snapped around the man's thick wrist, jerked it forward, and then slammed his elbow up under the driver's bicep. As the man reared back with pain, he kneed him in the lower stomach and stepped back. The driver fell to his knees, gagging.

Burke, on the other side of the taxi, watched with his mouth and eyes wide open. Fa'uza made no comment.

"Sergeant," Sab snapped. "Take the jeep and this asshole back to Honiara. When he comes around, tell him he'll get his vehicle back when we're done with it. And you wait at the office until I call."

"Yes, sir," Burke said. He scurried around the front of the taxi and gingerly touched the driver's shoulder.

"Let's go, Jacob."

Still silent, Fa'uza opened the passenger door and climbed in. Sab got behind the wheel. In a whirling cloud of dust he spun the taxi around and roared back to the main road.

For the first time in two days the President was in a good mood. His speech was going excellently. The Chamber of Commerce executives repeatedly interrupted him with bursts of applause. He was working solid ground, his record on the economy.

Two-thirds of the way through, he glanced into the wings. Secretary of Defense Glayshod was standing just beyond the curtain, arms folded, watching. When the President saw his face, he instantly realized something was terribly wrong.

Ten minutes later, Glayshod ushered him into a dressing room.

"All right, Roger, what is it?" the President asked as soon as the door was closed.

"Admiral Smith is dead, sir."

"What! When? How?"

"About an hour ago, in Boston. A heart attack."

"My God!" The President sat down on one of the folding chairs in front of the dresser. "I knew it. He looked terrible this morning."

Glayshod shifted his weight, crossed his arms. It was an instinctive body position of his, closed. He was a taciturn man with undeviating habits. It was said he ate the same meal three times a day: oatmeal cereal with vanilla ice cream.

"Poor Smitty," the President said, and sighed. "Well, this puts us in a bind, doesn't it? Smith was the only military man who knew all the details of our freighter incident."

Glayshod nodded.

"Who's next in line?"

"Admiral Hawkins is automatic acting CNO."

"What do we know about him?"

"A fair commander. He was CIC of the Atlantic Air Wing for four years before assignment to Washington." Glayshod frowned.

"Problem?"

"Hawkins has a tendency to fraternize too freely with his staff people. Lacks a hard-rock control. There were rumors of informational leaks in his command when he was with AAW."

"Oh, Christ, that's all we need. Can't you override and make a temporary appointment?"

"That would take several days. And if we shortcut like that, it would cause a hellish amount of curiosity."

"The last thing we want now." The President tugged thoughtfully at his right earlobe. "What do you suggest?"

"I think we should leave Hawkins as CNO but simply bypass his office on anything concerning the *Panjang*."

"How can we do that? The whole operation is geared to come through Smitty's network."

"Hawkins will be faced with an overwhelming inflow of duty assignments right now. We divert to Naval Intelligence any transmissions about the freighter operation."

"Wouldn't that seem obvious?"

"It could take weeks before Hawkins' staff got wind of it. By then the situation will be resolved and the whole thing could be written off as an oversight created by the confusion of Smith's death."

The President was silent for a few moments, then nodded. "All right, we'll go with that." He stood up.

"Incidentally, when are you scheduled to leave for the Canal?" Glayshod asked.

"Tomorrow morning at seven."

When Alain Dureau was seven years old, he had been almost buried alive in the basement of his grandmother's house. While playing one day, he discovered a small brick tunnel. It was five feet deep and just wide enough to allow him to wedge his body in. Often he would hide there, listening to his grandmother yelling upstairs.

The old bricks were crumbling into powder. One day, lying there staring up at them, he worked one loose. Instantly a shower of dust and tiny stones fell onto his chest. He felt the weight of the house shift. It terrified him for a moment.

Then, very deliberately, he jimmied another brick loose. Once more there was a crumbling shower. His heart was pounding wildly. He wanted to squirm back out of the tunnel, but he didn't. The suspense was unbelievably

fascinating. Would the next brick crumble the whole shaft?
Would the house come down and crush him into darkness?

The third brick came out easily and there was a very
feeble shower. Disappointed, he immediately began pulling out another. As it came loose, the roof of the tunnel
groaned. Panicked, he slid his body out and squatted at
the entrance, peering in as a cloud of dust erupted from
the tunnel.

It took him nearly thirty minutes to work up enough
courage to reenter the shaft. He could feel jagged pieces
of brick under his back. His eyes stung from the dust.
With steady hands he felt along the roof of the tunnel.
Large gaps were open now and the light from the basement was obscured by dust. He felt the corner of an
exposed brick. Nearly half of it protruded from the tunnel's ceiling. He worried its corners as he worried a loose
tooth, touching it, probing and pulling, going to the edge
of pain, then drawing back. His blood hummed in his
head. His body tingled with expectation, muscles tensed
and ready to propel him away from the pain.

He yanked the brick out.

Instantly there was a thick rumble. Alain gave a cry,
knowing it was coming. Frantically he jammed his elbows into the dirt and began wriggling backward. The
weight of the roof came down onto his legs. For a terrifying moment he was pinned. The beams in the basement
creaked and popped, and the light bulb swung on its
cord, throwing dusky shadows.

His momentum carried him out, tumbling onto the
brick floor of the basement. In the tunnel there was a
rushing impact as the entire wall came down.

On his knees, he watched it come jarring down. His
heart was crazy in his chest, the fear exploding like bursts
of release as when he had diarrhea and let go his foamy
excrement and everything came out and his stomach felt
empty and quiescent.

His grandmother whipped him savagely afterward. And
then drunkenly hugged him to her breast and begged his
forgiveness.

Sitting relaxed at the wheel of the Land Rover as it bounded over the jungle road, Alain felt the same exhilaration of dangerous temptation. Only now the bricks were hours and the crushing tunnel roof lay two hundred miles away in the ocean.

The road had wound steadily upward from the Mott-Smith plantation. They passed through open savannas of *kunai* grass, tall as a man and pale as wheat, and they could see eastward all the way down to the sea. The air was cool and smelled of pine and peppermint.

Dominique sat beside him in bleak hopelessness. Once or twice he had teasingly touched her knee, and she had recoiled. In the back, Villachio cradled the Ingram in his powerful arms.

They came to a fork in the road. Alain stopped and studied it a moment. Each branch looked equally used. He turned to Dominique. "Which do we take?"

She refused to answer.

"*Ma cherie,*" Dureau said softly. "You have two options. If you do not tell us which is the road to Marau, I will kill you. Right here, now. On the other hand, if you show us where this Hedges is, you will be free." He laughed suddenly. "In more ways than one, eh?"

Dominique did not move. Somewhere in the jungle a bird sent a soft, plaintive treble through the trees.

"Which will it be, my love?" Alain asked, grinning.

She clasped her hands and put them into her lap. "That one," she said, nodding toward the road to the right.

"Wise choice," Dureau said.

Ten minutes later, they rounded a bend, and Alain jammed on the brakes. The Land Rover fishtailed to a stop. Fifty yards ahead was a tin-roofed shed beside the road. Three shirtless Melanesians beside it were looking over their shoulders at them. Up a small hill were a cluster of shacks and a white pickup truck.

The three men slowly stood up and turned to face them. Each man had a rifle. One of the men started walking toward them, holding his weapon at the ready.

"You bitch!" Dureau hissed. "You lied."

Dominique was staring at him triumphantly.

Alain grabbed her viciously by the hair. "What is this?" he shouted. "What is this?"

She cried out with pain and wrenched herself free. "Marijuana growers," she screamed. "And they're going to kill you, you bastard."

The approaching man began to run, pointing and shouting. The other two started after him.

"Cut him down!" Dureau bellowed. He rammed the Rover into reverse.

Villachio stood up and let loose a burst. Dust geysers erupted at the feet of the first man. A moment later, he crumpled forward and went down. Instantly the other two opened fire, kneeling in the road. A round exploded through the windshield, flinging glass fragments. Dominique screamed and tried to get out of the vehicle. Alain, fighting the wheel with one hand, grabbed her with the other and wrenched her back into her seat. Another round slammed into the Rover's fender.

Villachio sent out a second burst. The bullets stitched across the road and the two men dived for cover. Up the hill, the door of a shack flew open and a man leapt out. Squaring off, he began firing at them with a handgun.

Another bullet hit the Rover as Alain got it turned around and headed back down the road. Dominique was cowering in the seat well. He jammed the accelerator to the floor. They fishtailed a moment, then leapt away.

Villachio cut loose again until his clip was empty.

For the last two hours Chaffee had been fighting the panic hard. *Don't let it show,* he kept repeating to himself. *Don't let them see it.*

For four hours the *Voorhees* and Orion, working their monotonous tandem, had traversed the target area. Back and forth, radio chatter, Torpex drops, and the sinking pull-up as they rose to a thousand feet to pick up the ship's hydrophone tapes. Wide tracks of the bottom, foothills and seamounts feathering southward. The *Panjang* would have stood out like an elongated flare, the sonar pings coming off her with what Napah called a speed-read bounce.

But there was nothing. Absolutely nothing.

They were going through the motions now. The freighter wasn't down there and everybody knew it. "Maybe the ship blew up," Napah suggested. "We'd miss scatter down there."

"No, dammit, no," Chaffee said hotly. He could feel the anger in his eyes. A man's eyes betrayed him. He stared at the screens to avoid their glances. "There was no surface debris or oil slick. The ship did not explode."

"Then she must have gone on past her last fix," Buchanan said. "But where and how far?"

Chaffee growled something and left the tactical room. He went into the head and closed the door. He was sweating again and his stomach was boiling. Lights seemed to flash behind his eyelids. He leaned over the tiny toilet bowl and tried to vomit. His muscles cramped but nothing would come.

Before he went out, he took three more pills. He looked in the mirror at his face, and was startled at how strange and wild it looked to him. A peripheral thought struck him. This was the face Denise had seen the last night she had been with him. She said he was becoming a crazy man and she couldn't stand it anymore, the violent eruptions of rage, the creeping sense of paranoia.

When he went out, he found Bonner drinking a cup of coffee in the galley. Bonner's look was cold, far away. "You all right?" he asked.

"Yeah," Chaffee answered. He rubbed his stomach and felt the pills beginning to grab hold. "I guess I'm airsick."

"That right? I never knew you to get airsick."

"All these maneuvers," Chaffee said, flicking his hand. He started to move by.

"We have to talk."

"Talk? What about?"

"I don't like what I'm seeing."

"What does that mean?"

"You know goddamned well what it means." Bonner's frigid eyes were steady. "You're losing it, buddy."

Chaffee felt a sudden flare of anger, driven by the drug. He whirled around. "Listen, Bonner, I told you I was all right. Now get off my ass."

Cas stood up slowly and put his cup down. He stepped forward, bringing his cold eyes close to Chaffee's face. "You know what I think, buddy? You're not fit for a deep dive."

That went into Chaffee hard. "You can't back out on me now," he blurted.

"Like hell I can't."

Chaffee felt a violent urge to strike him. His arms and hands felt powerful, destructive. Bonner was like the others; they all wanted to destroy him. With an effort of will, he drove the feeling back. He dropped his eyes and stared at the corrugated deck. "Don't do that to me, Cas," he said softly. "Please don't do that to me."

Cas was silent for a long time. Then he reached up and touched Chaffee's shoulder. "What the hell is the matter with you?"

"Nothing, dammit," he snapped, trying to pull out from under the hand. Cas's fingers gripped his shoulder powerfully.

"Something happened to you, didn't it?" He demanded. "Didn't it?"

Helplessly Steve shook his head. "Just stick with me, Bonner. Please."

Cas released him and with a hiss of disgust stepped around him.

Steve grabbed his arm. "Please. For chrissake, I'm begging you."

Bonner reached up and pried his fingers loose. He tilted his head. "All right, I'll stick. On one condition. You lay off that shit you're taking. Get off that wire or I'm out."

Chaffee nodded blindly. "Yeah, sure, Cas. No more."

*   *   *

In an anteroom of the Moscow Opera House, Admiral Tsander had presented Lubentsov's findings to the Supreme Commander of the Russian Navy, Admiral Anton Kruchevsky. Kruchevsky was attending a ballet set to Shostakovich's Seventh Symphony, and was perturbed at being interrupted.

"What is this nonsense about a naval engagement in the South Pacific?" he demanded. Tsander's urgent note, delivered to the admiral in his seat, had mentioned this.

"It isn't nonsense, Admiral," Tsander said. "I have proof." The room they were in was stuffy, and Tsander could feel tiny beads of perspiration slipping down his spine. "It's all here, in this case."

Kruchevsky scoffed. "What proof?"

As quickly as he could, Tsander explained Lubentsov's run. The admiral listened, toying idly with one of his gleaming jacket buttons. Tsander could feel his almost tangible antagonism. Tsander had breached military etiquette by leaping over the normal chain of command. To distract from that, he hurried on to Nikolai's final projection.

Kruchevsky studied him from beneath thick eyebrows. Then he shook his head. "That is ridiculous."

"Yes, Admiral, on the surface it would seem so. But think about it. Under such a strategy, everything would be in the Americans' favor. They overpower us in that area of the world. And what better choice for a major battle than an area devoid of land concentrations? At this very moment, there are powerful elements of two other navies in that zone."

Kruchevsky plucked a cigarette from a small golden case on the table and lit it slowly with a golden lighter. He blew smoke into the air, where it hovered like a delicate fog. Down the corridor the final, triumphant strains of the Seventh Symphony rolled like distant thunder.

When Kruchevsky finally spoke his voice was softer, almost confidential. "Friedrich, you are reaching here."

"But, Admiral—"

Kruchevsky held up his hand. "I understand, Friedrich,

I do. You and I are old men, almost anachronisms, trying to hold on. Mother Russia will soon discard us to die unneeded. You see? I understand."

"Anton, please think on this."

Kruchevsky pointed his cigarette accusingly. "*You* think on it. Would the Americans send their President into a potential war zone? Even they aren't that stupid. And this—this projection of yours. What precisely does it say? That there will be a concerted action of multiple navies? What navies? The French? British? Do you seriously think they would attack us on the order of the Americans?" He swept his arm through the air. "The whole thing is preposterous."

For a chilling moment Tsander drew back into himself. The Supreme Commander had zeroed in on the two weakest points in Lubentsov's theory. Still, there must be an explanation for these things.

Kruchevsky had settled back into his chair. "How did this Lubentsov of yours obtain naval-deployment material?"

Tsander recoiled. Why had he not expected this? "I gave it to him," he mumbled.

Kruchevsky clucked and shook his head sadly. "Friedrich, Friedrich." A crescendo of clapping swept up the corridor. "Your refusal to accept the inevitable will destroy you."

"Sir, I have done wrong. But it's only because I believe our country is in terrible danger. I also believe in this man's predictions." Tsander straightened. "I will stand by my actions at whatever cost."

Inexplicably, Kruchevsky's face broke into a smile. "That is a good Russian answer. Defy all facts." He lightly tapped the cigarette ash into a golden tray and the smile faded. "Nevertheless, we will talk more about your behavior tomorrow. At ten o'clock in my office."

Tsander braced. "Yes, Admiral."

Kruchevsky nodded silently and Tsander stepped through the draperies.

The Supreme Commander remained seated, smoking thoughtfully. Finally he barked, "Lieutenant."

Instantly a young adjutant came through the draperies, snapped to attention. "Sir?"

"Contact the senior members of my staff. I want them in my office in one hour." He paused. "Also contact Marshal Petrov of the General Staff and request a meeting with him as early as possible in the morning. Tell him it is most urgent."

"Yes, sir." The adjutant disappeared through the draperies.

In his observer's seat in the console room, Bonner swore disgustedly. Hillar and Kitchens had expanded the target area on the possibility the *Panjang,* crippled, had wandered slightly from her last fix before actually going down. That ship isn't down there, he told himself. At least not *there.* All they were doing was wasting time. He didn't feel he had a lot of that to lose.

He was disgusted at himself too, because he knew that, no matter what, he'd go down with Chaffee. He had to, *they* had to. Somewhere there was a load of missiles with enough power to destroy a hundred cities, millions of people. It was up to them to find out whether that nightmare could come true or not. Besides, Steve was his friend. Or at least he had been. One of the few guiding rules Bonner lived by was loyalty.

He tapped Buchanan on the shoulder. "Get Kitchens back here. And can you run the TRM map up on the monitor?"

"Sure," Buchanan answered, looking puzzled.

"And I want to talk to the captain of the *Voorhees.*"

"What's this?"

"Just do it."

Buchanan shrugged and keyed Kitchens.

For the last hour Cas had been chewing on a theory. The more he thought about it, the more right it seemed. It was time to find out.

He was on the radio with Hillar when Kitchens came aft and stood listening. "Do you have updated information on deep-current set and drift?" Cas asked Hillar.

"Negative. But our TRM shows a fairly constant sur-face movement of the East Australian current running standard two-point-one knots, generally southeast at this latitude."

"Are you capable of running a current check at, say, two thousand feet?"

"Can do. What're we looking for?"

"A new approach."

"It'll take a few minutes to deploy."

"Roger. Keep us advised." He handed the mike to Buchanan and leaned around him to study the TRM map on the screen. This one had no surface-current informa-tion. That didn't matter. He wasn't after surface drift.

He swung around to Kitchens. Chaffee had come up while he was talking to Hillar. "I might just know where this bitch could be," he said.

"Where?"

"She's not *on* the bottom. You see, this particular ship was carrying hull tanks and they were probably empty. That means she's carrying a complete, or at least nearly complete, envelope of unflooded compartments."

He caught a quick movement in Chaffee's eyebrows, but Kitchens still looked confused. He went on, "When a ship goes down, she doesn't always go straight to the bottom. If there's enough air trapped in her, somewhere between surface and bottom she'll stabilize in a state of neutral buoyancy."

"That's it," Chaffee cried. "She's riding the current."

"You mean that thing is *floating* down there?" Kitch-ens said incredulously.

"Exactly."

"For how long?"

"Forever," Cas said. "Or at least until her metal works deteriorate enough to allow water to flood in and change her equilibrium."

"Why did you choose two thousand feet?" Napah asked.

"It's a standard depth for deep current readings, far enough below the surface to be free of wind and tidal movement. From there on down it'll usually hold steady."

He swung around to Chaffee. "What was the exact time of her last fix report? Do you have that?"

"Yes, it was 2:24 P.M. Guadalcanal time."

Bonner looked at the console chronometer. "I make it forty-eight hours and twelve minutes ago. Buchanan, enter that into the computer."

He did.

They waited silently, exchanging excited glances. Four minutes later, Hillar came back with the two-thousand reading: "CDS indicates a steady two-knot set, bearing one-eight-niner degrees. Advise."

Kitchens took up the mike. "*Voorhees,* stand by." To Buchanan: "Give us a new fix."

Buchanan punched in the drift reading. A moment later, a tiny cross appeared on the TRM map. It was approximately two miles past the northern rim of the Murchison Trench.

Nine

47 hours, 58 minutes

Spangenberg drove with icy, gleeful rage. The old Plymouth lunged over the ruts in the road, throwing dust. The interior smelled of the musky odor of crotch. A crucifix was tied to the mirror and a *kapu* necklace of black beads dangled from the cross.

Jacob sat silent and somber as a *tiki* god. After a while he reached into the back of the car and brought up one of the M16's and a clip. He studied the weapon, obviously unfamiliar with it. Yet Sab, glancing over, saw that his hands were sure on the rifle. He inserted the clip, rapped the bolt back, chambering a round, clicked it on safety, and rested the rifle between his legs, the muzzle pointing out the window. He retrieved the other weapon, did the same, and then returned to his wordless staring through the windshield. Spangenberg smiled, oddly pleased. He liked Fa'uza. He was going to be a good man in a fight.

They came to a fork in the road. A white four-by-four Toyota pickup was parked on the side. Three Melanesian men were walking around and looking down at the road. When they heard the taxi coming, they hurried back to the side of the Toyota. One man reached down into the bed.

Jocob sat forward slightly. "Be careful of these, Colonel."

Sab skidded to a stop next to the pickup. His dust engulfed them both for a moment. The three men remained near the bed of the truck, eyeing them suspiciously.

A black man sitting in the driver's seat opened the door and got out. He wore a high-cut football jersey over his massive biceps and washboard stomach. He had a red baseball cap with the insignia of the First Marine Division and a Colt .45 strapped to his hip. He squinted at Spangenberg and broke into a wide grin. "Well, looka here, if it ain't ole Slam Dunk hisself." He sauntered around the front of the taxi and stood beside Sab's window. "What *you* doin' here, Colonel?"

"Takin' a little R-and-R."

The black man' glanced at the two M16s. "Look more like you doin' some search-and-destroy."

Spangenberg glanced up at the cap. "Ex-marine?"

"That's right, Colonel."

"What rank?"

"Pickens, sir, hard-stripe E5." The words shot out, and Pickens shook his head grinning. "The fuckin' habit stays with you, don't it?"

Sab chuckled. He turned to look at the Melanesians, then back. "Got a little *gooch* going here, have you?"

"You know how it is, Colonel."

"Well, I'll tell you, Sergeant, I don't give a rat's ass what you're running here. I'm looking for two men and a woman in a Land Rover. You seen 'em?"

Pickens' eyes went hard. He looked at Fa'uza before speaking. "Yeah, I seen 'em. The motherfuckers shot one of my men."

"Where'd they go?"

He nodded toward the left branch of the fork. "Down there. But they ain't goin' far. We put a round into their tank. I'm surprised the sucker didn't blow."

"Thanks, Sergeant." He geared into first. "Good luck on your enterprise."

"You want help, Colonel? I got a little score to settle with them pricks m'ownself."

Sab shook his head. "This one's personal."

Pickens shrugged and stepped back. "I figure they'll go to bush when the Rover dies. Maybe heard for Tumai on the coast." He snapped an order to the men in Melanesian. One of them took two machetes out of the pickup and quietly put them on the rear seat of the taxi.

"Thanks," Sab said.

"Watch out for 'em, Colonel. They carryin' rapid-fire heat. Sounded like a M-10 to me."

"Right." Spangenberg gunned the engine and they roared away.

Gillespie kept to the outer fringes of the crowd gathered on the small complex dock awaiting the arrival of the British Prime Minister. The group consisted of the Australian PM, Scotty Cox, the Governor-General of Guadalcanal, Sir Albert Frizzley, the higher echelon of legation people, and the usual collection of reporters.

A red carpet had been rolled onto the small gangplank. The fifteen-piece Solomon Island National Band played a ragged rendition of "Garryowen." Out in the sound, the captain's gig from HMS *Valiant* was making its slow approach, the ships of TFS 14 arrayed beyond.

Jimbo had managed only three hours' sleep. Until four in the morning he had been on the overseas line unsuccessfully shooting info sources. Low-level bureaucratic types, mostly, who nevertheless had positions in which they became privy to a lot of high-level stuff. He also called a few inner sanctum people who owed him favors, and one big-shot New York editor who always knew everything about everything.

That last call had been a mistake. "What's this, Jimbo? You people have a ship down and *you* don't know details?"

He managed to shuffle and kick sand, pleading utter confusion on the Canal. The guy hadn't bought it, he knew. Well, screw him. The trouble was, he'd be on the line to his field people. "Something's up, check it out. Gillespie was probing *me*." Shit, Jimbo thought dismally, watch the questions *zing* now.

He had dodged that afternoon's press briefing. Sent

out standard press sheets with the usual drivel. Still, with the heads of state arriving like homing bees, there would be two scheduled briefings starting tomorrow morning.

The band finished "Garryowen" and swung into "Oh, Britannia" as the captain's gig slowed and, props back-washing, drifted in to tie up at the dock. Rose Treleven stepped onto the red-carpeted gangplank and descended, smiling brightly. She wore a pink dress, the thin fabric fluttering sensuously against her body.

The *Pink* Steel Rose, Gillespie thought sullenly. A good tag. He'd have to work that into his dispatches somehow, he decided.

Once the formal greetings were over, the cluster of people began to move up the dock. The reporters pressed in, arms poking up with tape recorders like stalks of pussy willow. The Pink Steel Rose pushed ahead smiling, with Cox lumbering beside her.

In the royal suite of the Royal Crest Hotel, Rose Treleven stepped out of her shoes and stood in front of the room air conditioner, allowing its cool air to wash over her face. Her maid was in the bedroom, unpacking.

There was a soft tap on the door.

"Jenny," Rose called. "The door."

It was Treleven's chief aide, Roger Whitcomb. "Excuse me, madam. The Prime Minister of Australia has asked if he might come up for a moment."

"Oh, yes." She slipped back into her shoes. "Send him up." She turned toward the bedroom. "Jenny, leave that unpacking until later. You pop down and get yourself tea."

"Yes, mum."

Rose walked to a large mirror near the window and fluffed her hair. She had been looking forward to seeing Scotty in private. She smiled, remembering how dignified and stiff he had been on the dock just now. But the old Aussie twinkle was still in his eyes. Once she thought he'd even winked.

Cox's knock was like the rap of a gun butt. She opened it and they stood smiling at each other.

"You look marvelous, Scotty."

"And you, luv, are positive apples."

"Come in."

When the door was closed, they hugged. Holding his hand, she led him into the sitting room. He dropped heavily into an armchair and grinned at her. "My God, woman, you defy time. I've always said your news pictures fail to do you justice."

"How gallant. Drink?"

He gave a sidelong glance.

She moved to a side table and poured two gin and tonics. She returned and handed one to Cox, then stood watching him drink it.

After a moment, she seated herself on the settee as Cox lowered his glass to grin at her.

"Advise me, Scotty," Rose said softly. "This is your home ground. Tell me the rules of the game."

"Well, luv, it's a tangled affair down here. Everybody's shifting for power bases. These tiny island nations have suddenly become important because of their strategic positions. Of course, the Yanks carry the main power. Everybody treads lightly with Uncle."

Rose nodded, pleased, and sipped her drink.

"There's the key, Rosie," Cox went on. "American hegemony in this area. It's a fact of life we accept. Let them run the world."

Rose settled back into the settee cushion. "Is that what you really want, Scotty?"

Cox sat silently for a moment, slowly twirling his glass. "Yes, isolation."

Rose looked surprised. "Isolation?"

"Exactly, Rosie." He sat forward resolutely. "Complete isolation from the rest of the bleeding world. Australia doesn't need 'em. We Aussies are a carefree lot and that's it. We sit on our damned island and drink our coldies and want no international johnny hops telling us what's about."

Treleven's eyes were serious, yet deep down there was the slightest twinkle. "Is that why the little ado in Tamarand Bay?"

He looked at her through his eyebrows. "Your Intelligence blokes *are* on the tub, aren't they?"

"You expected less?"

"Not actually." He sighed. "Understand our position, luv. Our major defense line is north of island. New Guinea, the Indonesian Corridor. It's our bloody Maginot Line. We *must* fortify it."

"How many?"

"Three."

"Eventual control?"

"Yes." Here he lied. "Twenty-five years."

Rose nodded. "Will you allow complete interlink with the Royal Navy?"

"Of course."

"Accepted."

Cox settled back, relieved.

"And, you in turn will back me on keeping the Commonwealth of Nations intact in this hemisphere."

"Of course." Then his face clouded. "With one stipulation."

"Which is?"

"I need your help to oust Malcolm Davis."

Treleven frowned. Davis was New Zealand's prime minister. "He *has* tried his best to make a shambles of the ANZAC agreements, hasn't he?"

"The man's a bloody *chook*. I'd like to crush the bastard like a rat on a drainpipe."

Rose shook her head, chuckling. "Scotty, I love your silly language."

"Will you help?"

"Davis has a powerful coalition in New Zealand and quite a few sympathizers in Parliament."

"I'm not talking London, Rosie. Out here it's a different football game. If we both go against him at this conference, we can send him back to his damned New Zealand like a bleeding whore with the shifties."

Costello was signaling to Hillar from the door of the sonar room. "Look at that new fix," he said. "If Bonner's right, that damned ship's sitting squarely over the Murchison Trench."

Hillar swore and stared at the cross-marking coordinate position on the map's plastic cover.

His exec gave him a studied look. "This could get dicey, Coach."

Hillar nodded. A free-floating ship was as dangerous as a bomb to approach. Inner bulkheads could give way at any moment; pressure shifts could build to explosive levels and blow out hull plates. If the Saran were even near the freighter when something like that happened, the *Panjang* would pull her down. And if they had already attached . . . !

Lordy, he thought, and felt a chill of foreboding.

Eight thousand feet above, readying for a radio fix, Buchanan was kneeling between the pilots' seats, talking to Kitchens. He and Napah had worked out the best pattern for the buoys and Torpex drops. The two of them had become a team; he even deferred to her opinions. It didn't bother him. Bobby Buchanan had always felt more comfortable taking orders than giving them. Besides, Napah was one sharp sonar analyzer, best he'd ever seen. She'd done computerized exploration and electromagnetic mapping, software records of explosive and thumperram core charts. She was amazing in seeing through peripheral scatter to base read. Still, he knew enough about his skipper to downplay her to Kitchens. There was something about Gilchrist that got under Kitchens' skin.

"TRM maps shows a gradual rise in bottom as we approach the Trench," Bobby explained. "They're seamounts. The whole phenomenon is called thrust overlap. On this heading, water depth should shallow out to about a thousand feet. If the freighter's approach was below that level, she'll be sitting out there on one of those seamounts."

Kitchens listened quietly, staring through the windshield. The horizon made a thin blue misty line across the glass.

"If she's cleared the mounts, she's sitting in open water. That's better. We'll get definite bounce separation on the down vectors, and side scan off the sheer. The computers will enhance her out clear as a bell.

"We figure the best line to buoy drop is just south of the mounts. Maybe two degrees. Three drops at fifteen-second intervals. Then we lay in the Torpex at five hundred. This way we pick up at least the top three hundred feet of the mounts and still get a solid picture of open water off the SS transducer."

Kitchens nodded. "You got the headings worked out yet?"

"Yes."

"Okay, I'll let down in thirty seconds. Vector me when we hit a thousand."

"Right, Skipper." Buchanan started to leave.

Kitchens stopped him. "Tell me, Bobby, what do you think? Is that ship out there?"

"I think so. I ain't no deep-water man, but I got a feeling Bonner's correct. I think she's smack dab out there in open water over the Trench.'

Kitchens shook his head, sucked air through his teeth. "That's one deep mother."

"You got that right," Buchanan agreed. "I know one thing. I'm glad as hell it ain't me going down in that titanium can."

The bullets tore through the jungle to Spangenberg's right. Sab pressed his face against the wet earth, grinning. They were probing, he knew, trying to draw return fire. He lay very still, hoping Fa'uza, down across the road, would not be suckered into firing. The bursts stopped, leaving the impression of sound floating through the trees. They were close, and they wanted by. Bad.

Around him the jungle was an explosion of sultry green: buttress trees covered with creepers, tanglebrush, dripping water, bamboo stands dotted with flaming *cannas* and spider orchids. Over it all hung the poisonous stink of perpetual decay.

Spangenberg pushed his nose into its green mold and inhaled. He loved the jungle. It was like a woman, fecund, heated, ripe.

Forty minutes earlier, topping a low rise in the road, they'd spotted the Land Rover turned partially across the road. An ambush. Fa'uza glanced at him. "We go through?"

Sab nodded. The huge Melanesian, cradling one of the M16's, rolled over the back of the seat into the rear. They crept forward. The Rover was down the slope a hundred and fifty yards away. Something sparkled at the edge of the road, a tiny glint of gold. A woman's hand, her body. She had slumped forward grotesquely on her hips as though she had fallen straight down.

So much for Dominique Mott-Smith, Sab thought coldly.

"Jacob, take the left," he said. He reached down for his own M16 and brought it up, resting the barrel on the passenger-side window. "Ready?"

"Yes."

"Here we go." He rammed the accelerator to the floor. The old taxi jerked as its ancient carburetor jets blew in a full load of gasoline. Then it lifted and bounded forward, the engine screaming. They tore toward the Rover, rapidly building speed. Sab edged the wheel over a little, aiming for the front corner of the vehicle.

The fire came from both sides of the road simultaneously. Quick, sharp bursts. The windshield disintegrated. Sab peered through the glassless windshield frame at the precise spot in the jungle from which he'd seen the muzzle flash, and threw a burst at it. Fa'uza opened up, firing out the left window.

Twenty yards . . .

Ten . . .

They plowed into the Land Rover with a violent wrench. The steering wheel was torn from Sab's grasp and he was flung against the door. The Rover was knocked up and over as the taxi spun crookedly. Sab regained his position behind the wheel and instantly loosed two short bursts into the jungle. He roared with wild laughter. "How'd you like that, fuckface? Didn't expect that, did you?"

The old Plymouth was wobbling forward, mortally wounded. Steam began pouring out from under the hood. Fifty yards down the road, Sab stopped.

Fa'uza was firing, through the rear window as Sab swung around. Two men were crouching beside the overturned Land Rover, firing back at them. Spangenberg shoved his door open and tumbled out. Coming to his knees, he opened up. The men beside the Rover ducked for cover. Sab's bullets pounded into the vehicle, several whining off into the jungle. A moment later, the men leapt up and darted into the brush.

Sab looked over the rear window. "Jacob, you okay?"

"Yes, Colonel." His broad brown face was sweating, his eyes sparkling with excitement. He opened the door and stepped out, bent.

"Take the downslope," Sab said. The taxi was hissing loudly. "They're gonna try to come past us."

Fa'uza handed him two loaded clips. Still bending forward, he sprinted across the road and melted into the underbrush.

Spangenberg shoved the spare clips into his belt and crawled around the front of the taxi. He paused, checking the jungle. He lurched for the edge of it and plunged through the low shrubbery.

Now squatting, the M-16 braced across his knees, he looked around, then rose. He set his feet cautiously and moved forward, turning his shoulder into the leaves, shifting his hips, his body bent, easing branches away soundlessly. His boots went down toe-first, holding the weight, easing to heel.

Softly, softly . . .

He had gone ten yards when he heard a twig break. He froze, his head swiveling back and forth, homing on the direction. To the left. Absolutely motionless, he waited, feeling his heart joyously pounding through his chest.

Several yards to his left a face peered through the brush. An ugly face filled with a strange tranquillity. Sab had seen such calm before. In hard-time combat men, who had seen so much of death, its terror no longer lurked in their eyes.

He slowly uncoiled his legs, coming erect. Leaves brushed across his face. Just as slowly, he brought up the muzzle of the M16.

"Hey, shithead," he called softly.

The man swung around and dropped at the same moment. Sab's first burst blew into him, threw him back with a loud crashing of shattered boughs. Instantly Spangenberg darted forward. As he came up, the man rose to meet him. Thick arms wrapped around Sab's shoulders. Both men went down. He heard the man's gasping breath, felt his teeth clamp onto his shoulder. Over and over they rolled. Sab's free hand flailed out, searching for the man's eye sockets. He felt hair, teeth, then the gelatinous give of eye tissue. He rammed his fingers into it and felt blood spew like hot urine over the back of his hand. The man screamed.

Sab rolled free and leapt to his feet. The man was hunched over, his hands gripping his face. Sab pushed the muzzle of the M16 into his throat and fired. He could feel the counterrecoil come up through the barrel. Tissue burst over the leaves and the man pitched backward, rolling over and over like a snake gut-shot.

Spangenberg dived into the brush, his ears ringing. He heard the man take one last rattling breath. Then there was silence.

The first sonobuoy jammed in the firing chamber. The second came up the conveyer trough and slid off onto the bay deck, cracking the rotor cap. Kitchens' voice snapped through the intercom. "What's the problem, Mathias?"

"We got a jam in the chamber, sir. And number two's busted its SR cap."

"How long?"

"I don't know how bad the jam is. Give me five minutes."

"Get on with it."

They came around on a long reach. In the console room, Bonner and Chaffee were braced behind the operators, swaying as the Orion banked, and banked again. Chaffee kept brushing his hand across his eyes as if wiping sweat.

Bonner walked back to the galley and lit a cigarette. The smoke tasted stale and dry in his throat. He peered out the porthole. The sunlight slanted across the surface, giving the swells a solidity. He felt a malignancy come off the water. No, he corrected himself. The ocean was never malignant. It was forever the ocean. Only what man put into it was malignant.

The second run went smoothly and they pulled away, the screens coming up with light slowly. This time the buoy probes were traveling all the way to the bottom of the Trench. When the bounce came, it made weak tracings on the screens, like the white smoke trails from descending flares. Nothing showed in the trace path.

The next buoy went without a hitch too, and they made another long reach while Mathias set up the Torpex canisters. Napah and Buchanan held a conference. It was decided that single explosive drops would be best: the confusion of overlapping rebound from the Trench wall would be cut down.

Kitchens brought them around again and dropped close to the surface. The intercom clicked off seconds and Mathias sent out the first Torpex canister. Everyone's eyes were glued to the number-one screen as they pulled up and away. Then *wham*! Lights blared all over the place as counterfeed blew trace rebound into the side scan. The other screens were glowing too, with a lesser light, like a sunrise seen from different angles. To the right, the VDI panel clicked as rapidly as a typewriter. A few seconds later the high-resolution analyzer fed visual readout. In the clear water of the Trench the visuals were crystalline.

Nothing.

Number-two canister made funny, wavy lines and blobs of shimmering light. "What's that?" Chaffee blurted.

Napah and Buchanan both shook their heads. "A plankton swarm," Gilchrist said.

Chaffee screwed up his face and scratched viciously at his neck. Napah suddenly leaned forward. She mumbled something to Buchanan and with the eraser of her pencil made an invisible circle on the screen.

"What is it?" Cas asked.

"There's something on the eastern edge of the charge," Buchanan said. "We can't quite make it yet. But it looks solid and ferrous."

He relayed to Kitchens. The answer came right back. "Where do you want the drop?"

Hurriedly Buchanan figured heading and time setup, and called them forward.

The number-three Torpex seemed to take forever. Everybody was tense. Kitchens and Mathias laid it in right on the button.

The second screen went crazy with lights. Flying scatter everywhere. A thick blob of light near the center came up high, held a moment, then faded into an afterglow.

Amid the chatter of the VDI, the enhancement came up. The blob of light sat squarely in the center of the screen. Buchanan stared and stared. Beside him, Napah pulled slowly away from the console and eased into the back of her seat. "There she is," she said softly.

Ten

46 Hours, 28 minutes

Marshal Sergei Petrov kept Admiral Kruchevsky waiting until nearly nine o'clock in the morning before he was ushered into his office on the top floor of the General Staff Building located at the north end of Red Square. It was a vast office with a huge window that overlooked the Lenin Mausoleum. Done in gold-leaf furnishings of the Imperial period, the office had an air of intimidating stateliness about it. This atmosphere befitted the office of the most powerful military man in Russia.

The marshal was seated behind a massive, ornate desk that had once belonged to Catherine the Great's vizier. He did not look up when Kruchevsky came in. The admiral stood at rigid attention, outwardly expressionless. Yet inwardly he was seething at Petrov's failure to acknowledge his presence. He despised the marshal. Before the rise of the new Party Secretary, Petrov had been only a minor general in the Ukraine. Personal friendship with several members of the Politburo had lifted him over the heads of the far abler men on the committee list of officers.

Finally Petrov laid down his pen and smiled languidly at Kruchevsky. Recently returned from a Rumanian skiing trip, he wore a healthy tan. At fifty-one, he was the youngest member of the General Staff and an ardent supporter of the new Secretary's program of *perestroika*.

In accordance with it, he had surrounded himself with youthful staff personnel.

"Well, Admiral," he said quietly. "What is so urgent this morning?"

Kruchevsky recounted his conversation with Tsander and briefly outlined Lubentsov's analogue projection. He and his staff had been evaluating its implications throughout most of the morning, he explained, and they had all agreed that it warranted serious consideration.

Petrov listened, his eyes aloof. When Kruchevsky finished, he asked, "Who is this Lubentsov?"

"One of our leading computer scientists from Moscow University. He has been working with the Levenev Institute on weather predictions. He is extremely highly thought of in his field."

"And how did he manage to obtain so much classified information?"

Kruchevsky faltered for a moment. "Admiral Tsander gave him full use of his section files."

"I see. And Admiral Tsander will, of course, be severely reprimanded for this breach of security?"

"Of course, Comrade Marshal."

Petrov's gaze wandered lazily up and down the admiral's tunic. "So, you and your staff find this analogue thesis credible."

"We find it highly provocative."

"Why? Our own analysts have already considered this Pacific situation and have found no such projections."

"That's just it, sir. I think we've all failed to see these moves as part of an overall strategy. When looked at in conjunction with other moves by the Americans and their allies throughout the world, the conclusions are foreboding."

Petrov pressed a button on his desk. Instantly the wall paneling to his right slid back, exposing a huge electronic map of the world. Its holographic lighting gave the landmasses a three-dimensional solidity. He nodded to it.

"Show me."

Kruchevsky moved around the desk and stood before

the map. "To begin with, Comrade Marshal, a concentration of Allied seapower has formed in the southwestern quadrant of the Pacific within the last forty-eight hours. The United States Seventh Fleet out of Subic Bay, a Royal Navy task force, and a French nuclear armada from French Polynesia." He pointed out each of the naval positions, then moved across the map to the Atlantic Ocean.

"For the last three days our satellite reconnaissance has been tracking a large American carrier battle group operating off the Azores in coordinated exercises with the British Mediterranean fleet. Such exercises are not particularly unusual. But there are two aspects of this one that are.

"First, the battle group has a large number of antisubmarine contingents. More than forty of the new Spruance-class destroyers and two squadrons of ASW Orion P-3C's. KGB reports state these squadrons were recently moved from the southern United States and Spain to a base at Isla Fayal in the Azores.

"Second, the deployment of these ASW forces is different. Normally the Americans use the traditional phalanx formation at sea, with the destroyers and Orions working convoy duty. But here both destroyers and aircraft are strung out in a wide arc on the battle group's northern flank. They form a solid antisubmarine barrier of a thousand miles from south of the Azores to Newfoundland. In other words, the Americans have very neatly arrayed themselves and the British to control both oceans."

For the first time, Petrov's eyes flickered with interest. He studied the map carefully, then reached out and keyed his intercom. "Project updated position reports of NATO forces and NORAD movements. Red-overlay those areas where movements have taken place over the last seventy-two hours."

Lights immediately began appearing across the eastern face of Europe. On the other side of the map a few blinked on in the U.S., Canada, and Alaska, indicating

NORAD bases. Petrov rose and walked to the map. He and Kruchevsky stood silently watching.

The red overlays were scattered from Norway to the eastern borders of Turkey, showing recent deployments of division strength within NATO's Allied Command Europe. The NORAD reds were only two, one at Dutch Harbor in the Aleutians and Cartwright AFB in Labrador.

Kruchevsky shook his head. "There is extreme movement in Europe."

"Current NATO exercises. They refer to it as Operation Spearfish."

Kruchevsky's head snapped around.

"Yes," Petrov said. "It is a rather odd name for a ground operation, isn't it?" He turned. "So, Admiral, what does all this say to you?"

"It confirms what I said, sir. This Lubentsov projection has somehow uncovered something in the American strategy."

"But why the Pacific?"

"Tactically it's the perfect point for battle from the American position. It's the only place on earth where they are stronger than we are. With allied forces added, we wouldn't stand a chance."

Petrov shot him a hard-eyed look.

"Forgive me, Comrade Marshal, but it's true. In a nonnuclear engagement there, we would be outnumbered five to one."

Slowly Petrov returned his gaze to the map.

Kruchevsky pressed on. "Think of it, sir. If such a confrontation were initiated, it would practically eliminate our one major offensive option, the preemptive strike. American defense systems would be ready for us. Their counterstrikes would cripple us, probably prevent any launch-under-attack capability we might mount. In either case, we would be on the defensive. As you know, sir, our entire military structure is geared to offensive action."

Petrov remained silent.

"I realize, Comrade Marshal, this Lubentsov theory is

just that, a theory. It does contain certain untenable components. But it's the essence of it that intrigues and concerns me. However inadvertently, this man has discovered a key thread in these American moves."

Petrov did not say anything. For a full minute he looked at the map, his eyes narrowed. At last he turned abruptly, returned to his seat, and began writing.

"Thank you for coming, Admiral," he said curtly. "I will consider your recommendations."

Kruchevsky's face flushed. "Do you have any orders for me, sir?" he barked.

"You'll be notified."

"Comrade Marshal." Kruchevsky snapped to attention, whirled, and strode from the room.

After he was gone, Petrov put down his pen and once more stood. He studied the map. After a while, he moved to the other side of the room and studied it some more.

He returned to his desk, punched the intercom. "Get me GRU headquarters."

Napah was having a hard time with the parachute's harness buckle. It kept half locking and then going out again the moment she straightened. Under the harness her Mae West scratched her throat. She'd never jumped out of a plane before.

The *Vorhees* had arrived on site ten minutes before. It was holding a sonar fix on the *Panjang* and waiting for the submersible crew to join up. Bonner stepped through the forward hatch, all cinched up in his chute. He was barefoot, in shorts, with a huge sea knife strapped to his right calf. He stopped short when he saw her.

"What the hell do you think you're doing?"

"What does it look like?"

"Forget it. This is where we part company."

"Bullshit."

"Look, Napah—"

"Will you come off it, Bonner?" She fumbled angrily with the buckle. "This macho protectiveness makes my ass ache."

Cas glowered at her. She glared right back.

Chaffee poked his head through the floor hatch down into the launch bay. "Hurry it up," he snapped. "We're almost over the drop site."

Bonner confronted him. "Did you tell this dippy broad she could come?"

"Yes, why?"

"What for?"

"I want her on the _Voorhees'_ sonar. She's too damned valuable to leave up here."

Cas didn't say anything, but he looked as if he were about to bite off the strap of his harness. Napah gave him a smug look.

Chaffee glanced at her. "You _do_ know how to jump, don't you?"

"Sure," she lied.

"All right, let's move it." He disappeared down the hatch.

Bonner gave her one searing look, moved around her, and followed Chaffee down. Napah waited until he was out of sight, then went to the forward hatch and called Buchanan. He came back grinning.

"You look like a Screaming Eagle."

"I feel like a turd. Here, will you buckle this damned thing?"

He did.

"Now tell me how to do it," she said.

"Do what?"

"Jump out of this SOB."

"What? You've never jumped before?"

"No."

"Hey, honey, you better think about this. They're going in low, without static lines."

She stared at him. "Bobby, just tell me, okay?"

He shook his head, but went on to explain jump procedure. It all sounded complicated and dangerous. Napah could feel her heart getting wound up. He finished with a strong caution: "Remember, estimate your height from the water. When you're about twenty-five feet above it, bang that release. You'll drop out of the harness."

"Right."

"I mean it, Napah. Don't screw around. You don't want that chute coming down on top of you."

"Right, right." She smiled nervously. "Listen, thanks for everything. Anytime you want to quit playing sailor, I'll get you a job with Sutter." She touched his cheek and went down the bay hatch.

The ocean looked as if it were just below the aircraft. The bay was open, formed a big square through which a heavy rush of air came, filled with engine noise. Chaffee touched her shoulder. "Cas will go out first," he shouted. "Then you. Try to land as near to him as you can."

She nodded.

Across the bay, Mathias was kneeling with his head tilted, listening to Kitchens through his helmet earphones. Bonner had moved around to the after side of the bay. He squatted with his back to the open door, watching Mathias.

The chief held up a clenched fist. A second later, he pointed at Bonner, who immediately fell backward, his head tucked, arms folded across his chest. In a flash he was gone.

Chaffee shoved her. "Move it," he yelled in her ear. "Move it."

She took up the position where Bonner had been. Her blood was pounding in her temples. She looked at Mathias. He pointed at her.

"Oh, shit," she mumbled to herself, and shoved backward.

The slipstream hit her like a hurricane. She was whisked away, tumbling. For a millisecond she saw the tail section of the Orion flash past her toes.

One-one-thousand . . .

Her tumble slowed. She lifted her head. The horizon lay all around her, a vast, motionless demarcation of blue on blue. She had no sensation of falling.

Two-one-thousand . . .

She could hear the turbulence in the air. It soughed and *whomped* like a wind rushing over sand dunes. Deep in it was the sound of the aircraft's engines, fading.

Three-one-thousand . . .

The ripcord came easily away from her harness. She clung to the ring. A moment later the straps jolted hard against her legs and armpits. The chute made a huge, opaque umbrella above her, the shroud lines trembling with her weight.

Napah let out a whoop of relief and exhilaration. She glanced down. The *Voorhees* was off to her right, drawing a curved wake on the surface as she came about. Bonner's chute was just going into the ocean, and Cas was swimming away from it as the billows of fabric collapsed like a deflating balloon.

She glanced back at the *Voorhees* and started: its angle to her had changed rapidly. Directly below her the surface was coming up fast. She stared at it, trying to estimate its distance. She couldn't.

Frantically she looked for the *Voorhees* again. It was behind her now. Faster and faster the surface rushed at her. She could see the sunlight on the swells, could even pick out little etchings caused by the breeze.

In panic she hit the release. Instantly the harness flew apart and she plummeted into the water.

Her momentum drove her down in a burst of bubbles. She opened her eyes. The water was clear, shimmering fuzzily with dappled light. She let her plunge dissipate, then somersaulted and began stroking back to the surface.

The color of the water turned suddenly white with streaks of yellow through it. Thin strands of something caught her arms, slowly descended, entangling her upper body.

The shroud lines.

She popped through the surface, her face full of wet nylon. It was all around her, sinking gently like thick billows of milk. She gasped for air, felt the fabric suck in against her mouth. She managed to pull it away, took a gulp of air. The chute was taking on water now, and the increasing weight of it was pulling her down. She kept sculling her legs, twisting back and forth, trying to find the edge of the canopy.

It seemed as if she did this for a long time. Then something jerked her powerfully to the side. The force of it was strong enough to actually drag her and the chute through the water. A knife ripped through the nylon, letting in a patch of sky. Into the patch loomed Bonner's face, grimacing.

"Oh, God, Cas," she gasped.

He dragged her free of the shrouds, his arm around her waist. She could feel his panting breath against her neck.

"You dumb bitch," he yelled. "Why didn't you inflate your Mae West?"

"I forgot I had it."

"Jesus!"

She let herself relax against his thick, knotty arm. After a moment he released her. She turned in the water to face him. His face was red from exertion. He had covered a lot of distance in a short time. They bobbed up and down on the swell.

"Don't say it, Bonner," she croaked. "God help you, don't say it."

Behind him she caught sight of the prow of the *Voorhees* looming toward them.

The Saran sat on a pedestal at the stern of the *Voorhees*. Alone, Cas climbed up onto it. He peered down through the open capsule hatch. Below him, the launching crew hustled about, preparing the submersible for the dive. He slipped down the hatch ladder and squatted in the dim interior. The capsule was about six feet wide, crammed with electronic and radio gear. The pilot's couch lay on the starboard side with a swing-out control panel. Forward was an observer's seat that faced twin view ports. A console of instruments formed an arc below the ports.

The air smelled of instrument oil and electric wire. And enclosure. Bonner was taken with a powerful sense of returning. This particular submersible was very different from the others he'd been in, yet it was the same too. It bore the same sensation of a suspended cocoon.

After the pickup he, Napah, and Chaffee had taken quick showers. Then, dressed in blue navy flight suits, they held an update briefing with Hillar on the bridge. The *Panjang*, he told them, was unstable. She was slowly dropping deeper; she had already lost twelve hundred feet since the Orion's fix. And there was no way of telling her position in the water from the sonar reads.

The dive was scheduled for just after sunset. Chaffee explained to Hillar that Gilchrist would be assisting his sonar operators on the hull scan. While he and Napah went over procedure, Bonner had gone aft to meet the Saran.

Now, as he ran his fingers over the instruments, he could feel the high-tech power of her coming through. "You're something else, baby," he said softly.

He was still in the capsule fifteen minutes later when Napah appeared in the hatchway. "Cas?"

"Yeah."

She came down the ladder and knelt beside him. "What do you think?"

"Well, she's sure as hell not the old Diver. Have you been down in her?"

She nodded. "A couple of shallow run-throughs off Midway. She's a good, solid vehicle."

Someone started tapping on the hull. There was the heavy metal clank of chains as the harness bit was hooked on.

She touched his shoulder. "Cas?"

He turned to her.

She had pulled her wet hair back from her face. Her features were stark and clean. "Good luck down there."

"Thanks."

She climbed out. A moment later, Chaffee came down. His flight suit was soaked with sweat. His face was stiff, like that of a man at a funeral. He settled into the pilot's couch without a word.

For the next thirty minutes he and Bonner ran through

systems. The Saran was still hooked into the *Voorhees'* power supply, so all instruments were active. It came back to Cas swiftly. The essential components of the submersible were like the Diver's, only boosted with new power grids and electronic components that made operation easier and more tightly monitored.

At last Hillar called down final instructions for the launch. Costello came down for a few last words, then climbed out and locked the hatch. They could hear the crane winch sighing. The Saran jerked and then she was lifted up and out. Very gently they were dropped into the water.

They floated for a few minutes, the tether hook still attached. Cas caught sight of the stern of the ship, rolling gently on the long swell. Radio bursts crackled. Three divers in wet suits were in the water with them, running a final exterior inspection of the battery racks and thrust motors.

Everything was go. Chaffee radioed Hillar. One of the divers climbed onto the hatch apron and unbuckled the crane line.

Almost immediately the submersible began to sink slowly, pulled down by the six hundred pounds of iron ingots fixed under her battery racks. Cas watched the surface pass slowly across the upper view ports. The water was dark, dappled with the ship's stern lights. This quickly faded and they were in blue-black darkness.

They were dropping in a deadfall. Cas took his eyes from the ports to scan his instruments. They were nearing the hundred-foot depth. He could hear tiny creaks and pops as the outside pressure built across the hull and exterior struts. The overhead speaker of the acoustic phone crackled. "Saran, how do you read?" Hillar's voice sounded tinny, quavering.

Chaffee keyed. "Receiving clear and true. How do you read?"

"Clean. What is your descent rate?"

"One hundred forty feet per minute."

"We've got you on sonar now. You're drifting slightly

off fall line, two degrees southeast. Correct to heading
three-five-eight, three-second thrust."

Chaffee flicked several switches near his right arm.
There was a soft hum as the stern thrust motors kicked
in. They moved forward.

"That's good," Hillar called down. "Adjust again at
fifteen hundred feet."

"Roger."

Chaffee twisted around and threw a switch on an overhead panel. Instantly the forward strobe light came on. It
punched a glaring round hole into the darkness that
faded about forty yards out. Flecks of floating material
made tiny flashes of reflected light in the beam.

Cas squinted at the outer edge of the light. A remembered illusion of motion, as if giant things were slipping
past just beyond the light.

Chaffee's voice droned behind him. He was recording
the dive log onto tape. He switched off the forward
strobe and turned on the flare strobe on the bottom of
the Saran's undercarriage. This threw a wide pattern of
light that went out only twenty feet directly below. Along
the carriage struts the light formed eerie halos of blue.

At fifteen hundred feet they made their forward ad-
justment. With the lights off, they seemed to be motionless in the water. Hillar continuously fed parameter fixes.
The *Voorhees* was now tracking them from three points:
the ship itself, the *Panjang*, and the Murchison wall.
Readout was apparently coming up clean.

At three thousand feet things went off the track. Hillar's
voice suddenly became distorted, cutting in and out:
"—you on one—inter-discon—."

Chaffee switched on the strobes. The water was thick
with microscopic animals. It looked like a boiling soup.
They had entered a plankton cloud. A slimy film formed
on the port windows. Through it the strobes looked orange.

Two minutes passed. They continued down through
the plankton. Slowly it began to thin, the film peeling off
the windows. The water cleared until there were only

trailing curls of organic matter sucked downward by the drop of the vehicle.

Hillar's voice was still sporadic. Chaffee worked a small dial on his panel that turned the exterior acoustic phone disks. He began picking up the sound impulses off the Trench wall. He keyed his mike. "We have you clean. Are you reading?"

"Affirmative. We'll hold that angle. You'd better make another correction."

Chaffee complied with the motors.

At five thousand feet something struck the capsule. The impact was soft, as if someone had lightly slapped it with the palm of his hand. There was another and then a sudden crescendo of collisions. Chaffee's hand shot to the strobe switch. The beam was filled with a compacted, roiling mass of foot-long red squid. The water was solid with their entwined tentacles and eyes glowing like droplets of electrified gelatin.

Cas leaned forward, chuckling. "It's a *Histioeuthis* school. Look at the little buggers. They're trying to figure out how to eat this damned thing."

He glanced back at Chaffee. Steve's face was coated with sweat, despite the fact the inside temperature had dropped to forty degrees. Cas watched him a moment, then turned back to the window. He felt the hairs of his neck rise.

At six thousand feet Hillar came on. "You have seven hundred feet separation from target. Advise you slow your descent."

Chaffee activated the ballast pump and partially blew out ballast tank three. There was a gurgling rush. The Saran trembled slightly. Cas checked his descent monitor. They had dropped to eighty feet per minute.

"Good," Hillar called. "Hold that for four hundred feet and blow again."

"Call out depth," Chaffee barked.

"Six-three-five-five."

"You're a hundred yards northeast of target," Hillar

crackled. "Adjust for sixty-seven hundred feet and you'll be able to pick her up with your side scan."

"Six-seven-zero-zero."

Chaffee wiped sweat from his eyes and blew number-one ballast tank. Descent rate dropped to ten feet per minute.

"Activate side scan," he snapped.

Cas could see his reflection in the port glass. It was distorted, his features squeezed as if they were being pressed between the sides of a vise. He snapped on the sonar switches. The display screen to his right flashed into brightness. It was filled with scurrying lines, picking up the *Voorhees*' probes. Their pings filled the capsule with tiny blips of sound, like the gentle striking of glass balls on a stretched sheet of steel.

Bonner glanced at the depth gauge. "Seven thousand."

Chaffee blew more ballast. Now they were nearly stationary in the water.

Hillar said, "You're just about level with target. Heading one-five-zero degrees. Stabilize."

With a sudden burst of rage Chaffee screamed into his mike. "Shut down your fucking sonar. We can't read."

Hillar came back calm and clean. "Roger that."

A few seconds later the scurrying lines disappeared off the monitor. Now there was only a single large flare of light in the lower-right-hand corner of the screen. It was drifting upward.

"Depth, goddammit."

"Seven-thousand-one-zero-zero."

Chaffee blew ballast. The blob of light shifted position on the screen. Alternately blowing and drawing, he fixed it in the lower center. Sweat streamed off his face.

"We've got her," Bonner called over his shoulder. "We're in her drift."

Chaffee activated the thrusters. The Saran slowly swung around until Cas's magnetic compass fixed on one-five-zero.

"That's it," he yelled. "Hold that heading."

Chaffee threw on the strobes and the Saran moved slowly toward target.

The *Panjang* appeared in the outer fringes of the strobe like a ship emerging from a nightmare. She seemed to drift toward them, suspended in the clear space of the ocean, the strobes sparkling softly off the polished metal struts of her bow deck.

They were slightly above her, off the starboard bow. Her king posts appeared, then the dark mass of her midship housing. Twenty-five yards from her, Chaffee neutralized the thrusters. They drifted with the freighter, holding position in the current. They could clearly see her Plimsoll markings on the forward hull, the rust streaks from her drain ports. The entire hull had a glossy appearance, the illusion created by a thin coating of microscopic oxygen bubbles, the by-product of iron-eating bacteria that had already begun decomposing her metal surfaces.

Chaffee keyed. "We have her visual."

Hillar came right back. "Bingo, gentlemen."

"She's stable upright but listing several degrees to starboard. Settle rate approximately ten feet per minute. Stand by for interior sonar scan. We'll make one inspection circuit and then start scan of holds two and three."

"Standing by."

The *Panjang* had dropped slightly below them. Bonner could see most of the forward deck, the hatch coamings, and deck gear. The cargo booms were locked fore and aft beside the number-two hold hatches. From this angle he spotted the shattered bridge window, and stiffened. Bullet holes ran like stitch marks above and below the window frames.

"Look at that, Steve," he said quietly.

"What is it?"

"She was attacked. There are bullet holes all over her forward bridge bulkhead."

Chaffee ducked his head to look through the lower viewing port and swore. The ship was dropping steadily away from them. Chaffee worked the ballast controls, letting more water into the after tanks until they were again synchronized to the *Panjang*'s rate of descent. He

powered the thrusters and they went gliding slowly above
her bow deck forward number-one king post.

Cas gave a gasp. "Jesus Christ!"

"What?"

Bonner pressed close to the Plexiglas port, staring directly below the Saran. Then he turned and looked at
Chaffee, his face stark, jolted. "It's the crew."

"What!"

"Their bodies are netted on a deck pallet."

Chaffee slipped from his couch and squatted beside
Cas, gazing down. The bottom strobe illuminated the
forward deck like white sunshine. The corpses under the
netting were already bloated with internal decomposition
gases. Clothes and exposed flesh were pressed tightly
against the net. Deeper in the mass, heads lolled in the
current. Now and then an open eye glistened in the light.

"My God!" Chaffee breathed. He lunged back to his
couch. For a full minute the Saran drifted slowly away,
both men silent and stunned into inactivity.

Finally Chaffee came out of it. He hurriedly adjusted
his thrusters and brought them above the port bow. He
keyed his mike and notified the *Voorhees* of their
discovery.

There was a long silence. "Acknowledge your transmission." Another long silence. "Get on with it, gentlemen."

It took them fifteen minutes to circle the *Panjang*,
hugging close to get as much light on her as possible.
They counted eight ruptures in her hull, all along seam
lines. The metal was warped outward, curled with the
force of explosions. It was discolored a powdery white
where the heat had tempered the plating.

Neither man spoke during the entire circuit. Chaffee
had forgotten the log tape. Bonner squatted near his
port, his insides knotted, taking in the devastation. He
thought: God, let the sonar pick up the Tridents. I don't
want to go down in that ship. But he would if it came to
that, and knowing it made it worse.

He could feel the tension in the capsule. An odor
stronger than the smell of working circuitry and flex oil

seemed to drift in the cold air. He glanced at Chaffee and was shocked at how much his face had changed in the last few minutes. It looked like that of a man straining beneath some terrible weight. The smell in the air was Chaffee's fear.

He shifted his cramped legs and thought: Come on, come on, let's do it.

Chaffee aligned them on a position forward of the freighter's starboard beam, abreast her number-three hold. He keyed: "We're ready for internal scan. Turn off your sonar."

"Roger."

Steve boosted the frequency of the Saran's sonar probes. The audible pings immediately tuned up into a higher, sharper range. On the display screen a distorted picture of light dots formed, wavered, formed again. The submersible's high-frequency pings were penetrating the metal of the outer hull plating, infusing it with its modulation. This in turn was being carried through the metal to interior structures and back again along the bounce line. The Saran's VDI analyzers automatically separated them into density levels that were then projected onto the display in light patterns of different intensities.

Images of interior stanchions appeared, then cross girders, their weight-adjustment punch holes showing up as dark ovals. They were looking at the overhead of the hold.

Chaffee adjusted ballast slightly and they dropped to the *Panjang*'s waterline. The display screen instantly distorted as the pings rebounded quickly off the hull plating. The signal probes had hit an air discontinuity inboard the hull.

The *Pangjang*'s hull tanks were empty.

Bonner blinked slowly, once, twice.

A warning buzzer went off. Confused for a moment, Cas swung back to scan his instrument panel. A red light was blinking on and off on the battery sector.

"Run a check," Chaffee yelled.

One at a time, Bonner activated his battery trace lines.

Number-four packet was shorting out. Obviously it had
sprung a leak and seawater was seeping into the oil
packing. If enough water got in, the entire battery would
eat itself up and short out the whole electrical system.

"Cut off number four."

Cas shut it down. The strobes and inside lights dimmed
slightly. The warning buzzer and red light went off. He
quickly checked his other battery indicators. They were
showing a drop. Even with the number-four packet bypassed, eventual power loss could come as the other
batteries weakened.

Chaffee powered the stern thrusters slightly and the
Saran moved forward to hover abreast hold number two.
Again the display screen showed the probes coming right
off the hull: number-two hull tank was also empty. They
couldn't see into the holds at cargo level. Undoubtedly
the port-side tanks were empty too, since the ship was
riding stable.

Suddenly Chaffee shut down the sonar. There was a
short, rushing burst of air as he blew ballast. The Saran
lifted sharply, rose along the hull sheer, and cleared the
bulwark.

Chaffee keyed: "*Voorhees*, the ship's hull tanks are
empty. Air discontinuity prevents interior scan. Track us.
We're going to breach her."

Bonner swung around, shocked.

Chaffee played the ballast knobs, edged the thrusters.
They rose higher, skimming past the second king post,
lifted still higher, and went over the bridge deck.

"You crazy bastard," Cas shouted. "We can't breach
her now. We'd blow power before we even cut first
plate."

Chaffee ignored him. He was staring through the upper ports, eyes wild.

"Goddammit, will you listen to me?" Cas yelled. "We
can't breach."

Outside the windows the huge mass of the *Panjang*'s
stack moved by to starboard. Cas twisted and crawled
across the capsule deck. He grabbed Chaffee by the front

of his flight suit and pulled him off the couch. "Listen to me, you insane son of a bitch. You've got to pull the plug before we lose our systems."

Chaffee shook his head. "No, there isn't time. We have to go into her now."

Bonner shook him. "Pull the fucking plug." He reached out with his other hand and began prying Chaffee's fingers from the thruster controls. For a moment they struggled in the cold, compacted air.

A high, whistling sound burst into the sonar's audible loudspeaker. It was so high and powerful it rode over the Saran's own signal. Both men froze, their eyes seeking the display screen. Extremely bright flashes of pinpointed light were scattering over it like tiny bursting stars.

Hillar's quavering voice cut through the whistle. "Saran, stand by, stand by. We're getting intercepting probe signals."

Bonner let Chaffee drop and leapt back to his seat. He could feel intense pulses of sound striking the titanium hull, impregnating the air. His hair follicles seemed to vibrate, tingling down into his scalp. His eyes darted to the view port. *Something was out there.*

Hillar announced, "We've got a fix. It's a submarine, at your depth, bearing one-one-zero your position, range twelve hundred yards. Stand by, we're trying for ident."

The submersible's lights flickered, brightened, then settled. But they were dimmer now. The warning buzzer went off and the red panel light began blinking rapidly. Cas ran a quick battery trace. His hands were tingling from adrenaline. He found that number-one packet was shorting out.

By now they had drifted out of sight of the *Panjang*. Both men were sitting silent, listening to the noise inside the capsule.

Hillar came back: "We've got ident. Delta-class, Russian. He's moving toward you."

What the hell? Bonner thought.

"Steve, get us down beside the freighter again," he

barked. "If that son of a bitch comes in close, he's liable to overrun us in open water."

Chaffee stared at him.

"Get us down!"

Chaffee's head jerked up as if from sleep and he turned to his control panel. They began taking on ballast water. They dropped. Once more the *Panjang* fused out of the blackness. The Saran was above her afterdeck housing. Chaffee kept taking on water. The Saran continued dropping and the after king posts appeared on the edge of the strobe.

"That's enough," Cas shouted. "Steady her, steady her."

Chaffee fine-tuned the ballast and they hovered.

Hillar reported, "They're closing. Separation distance eight hundred yards. Get the hell out of there. If he passes close, his turbulence will catch you."

Beneath the shrill whistle Bonner's senses began picking up another sound. A slow, shushing whirl: the sub's prop cavitation. On the display screen a solid object was emerging through the flashing pinpoints of light as the Saran's probes picked up the submarine's blip. It grew steadily and the cavitation noise increased to a ponderous whoosh—whoosh—whoosh.

"Separation distance five hundred yards. He'll pass north your position."

Chaffee started fumbling with the control panel. Bonner reached out and clamped his hand over Steve's wrist. "Hold it. Not yet."

The cavitation noise filled the capsule. Tiny objects on the control panels began tinkling as they responded to the vibration. The outside strut wires were trembling.

Several seconds passed. Hillar's voice came on. "They're on you. North your position, range one hundred fifty yards."

Cas turned and peered through the view ports. He couldn't see anything beyond the strobe, but he could feel the submarine moving past in the blackness. Huge, sliding through the water, her props churning hard. The cavitation noise reached a powerful level, then began to slowly fade off.

"Now!" he cried out. "Drop the ingots and blow full ballast."

Chaffee hesitated.

"Do it!"

Steve's hand moved to the right of the panel. An instant later the six hundred pounds of iron dropped away and landed on the *Panjang*'s after house. He blew ballast. For a moment they were enveloped in a cloud of bubbles. Then the Saran seemed to leap upward.

Bonner shut down the strobes and closed off all unnecessary electrical systems. The sonar screen went black, the warning buzzer stopped, and all interior lights went out.

There was a sudden rolling lurch as the sub's turbulence hit the Saran. Bonner was flung against the sonar panel. The submersible yawed and pitched crazily. He found a bulkhead strut and held on.

Gradually the Saran began to settle, leveling out. Cas turned and looked through the darkness, alleviated only by the tiny instrument lights. He heard Chaffee make a sound. A soft, animal sound.

Steve was weeping.

Eleven

41 hours, 56 minutes

Defense Secretary Glayshod stood on the rain-shiny departure ramp of the Andrews AFB depot and watched as *Air Force One* lifted into a windy, overcast sky. The President's departure had been seven minutes late, due to a minor foul-up with his helicopter, *Marine One*, from the White House. Glayshod had ridden across with the President and Paul Lirette. Lirette was accompanying the President to Guadalcanal. They had gone over last-minute details. Glayshod updated the President on the latest reports from the Pentagon concerning the unusual Russian naval moves in the Pacific. In addition, he notified him that their bypass network for dealing with the *Panjang* situation was now in operation.

At last he turned and walked back through the slowly dissipating cluster of reporters and military personnel who had gathered for the President's departure. A few reporters scurried after him, shooting questions. He waved them off curtly. They persisted until he climbed into his limo parked in the small executive lot beside the depot.

Forty-five minutes later, at his desk in the Pentagon, his intercom buzzed. He tapped the button. "Yes?"

"Sir, there's a call from the Russian ambassador's office. He requests an immediate meeting with you."

"Immediate?"

"Yes, sir. They say it's quite urgent."

The Secretary frowned. "All right, I'll see him in fifteen minutes."

He sat back in his chair, musing. With the President already gone and Secretary of State Aldrich still in London, Ambassador Paranov had obviously been working his way down through the Cabinet officers. Why?

In precisely fifteen minutes Anatole Paranov was ushered into his office. He rose to greet him and offered a chair. He returned to his own and put his elbows on the table. "Would you care for some coffee, Ambassador?"

"No, thank you, Mr. Secretary." Paranov was a short Slavic man with wisps of white hair and horn-rimmed glasses. He was known to be quite charming and erudite, with a pleasant, quick smile. He was not smiling now.

"So, Ambassador," Glayshod began. "What can I do for you?"

Paranov adjusted himself into his chair and clasped his stubby hands together in his lap. "Frankly, I had hoped to speak directly with the President. Unfortunately, that is not possible."

"Unfortunately." Glayshod leaned back in his chair and crossed his arms.

"This morning I received a most urgent message from Supreme Soviet Headquarters. They request an explanation for recent unusual deployments of your military forces in various sectors of the world."

"Oh?"

"These movements have caused some disquiet in Moscow."

"What specific sectors are they referring to?"

"The South Pacific, in the main. Particularly around Guadalcanal."

Glayshod shook his head slowly. "Why is that of so much concern? You know the Pan-Pacific Conference is about to convene. Our Commander in Chief will be in attendance. An increase of our security in the area is certainly understandable."

Paranov's eyes were studied. "Yes, that would seem reasonable. However, there are also sizable contingents of French and British naval armament in the area also."

The Secretary shrugged that off. "Mere coincidence."

"I see. Well, perhaps the other sectors cannot be explained away so easily."

"Such as?"

Paranov sat forward. "You presently have a large carrier battle group operating in the mid-Atlantic."

"That's true. It's a power projection exercise to test existing tactical procedure. All quite normal."

"There has also been an extensive upsurge of activity throughout the NATO divisions of ACE. I believe you refer to it as Operation Spearfish?"

Glayshod nodded. "Yes, Spearfish. Again, normal operational and maintenance maneuvers."

Paranov settled back into his chair. "Nevertheless, these deployments have caused disquiet in Moscow. The Supreme Command was hoping for the President's assurances that such concentrations do not signal, shall we say, provocative intentions."

Glayshod's eyes narrowed. "Provocative intentions? How easily you Russians utilize that phrase. Isn't that being a bit paranoid?"

Paranov's thick features hardened instantly. "I find that particular expression rather insulting, Mr. Secretary."

"As I find yours, Mr. Ambassador."

There was an awkward moment. Paranov finally sighed and readjusted himself in his chair. "Nevertheless, my government insists on assurances."

"Will mine do?" Glayshod shot back.

"They will help."

"Then you most assuredly have them. This is nothing more than coincidence and normal exercise activity."

Paranov nodded with a jerk of his head. "I will convey your answer to my government."

"Splendid." Glayshod stared at the ambassador, his fingers tapping lightly against his arm. "Now, perhaps, you will answer *my* question."

"Ah?"

"Why have you stepped up your undersea deployments in the South Pacific?"

Paranov's dark eyebrows arched. "I was not aware of any unusual deployments."

"Then I would suggest you request more updating from your Supreme Command."

For a fleeting moment, fire sparked in Paranov's eyes. It was instantly quelled. "Indeed, I will request confirmation on that point. In the meantime, if such a situation does exist, I would assume it is, as you have said, coincidental."

Neat, Glayshod thought. He had to admire the ambassador's adroit riposte. It in turn inspired a tiny barb he couldn't resist. "Suspicions pinch the suspicious foot, don't they?"

Paranov looked puzzled. "Sir?"

Glayshod waved it away. "Merely a figure of speech, Mr. Ambassador. So, is there anything else you wish to discuss?"

Paranov rose stiffly. "Not at the moment, Mr. Secretary."

"I'll notify the President of your concerns at the first opportunity."

"Thank you." The ambassador bowed formally and withdrew.

Glayshod stared at the closed door for a long time. So that was the reason for the increased activity. The Russkies were worried. Well, let the bastards stew a bit. It'd keep them occupied. Maybe they'd keep their noses away from the *Panjang*.

Dureau was running. Although he moved slowly through the jungle, the Ingram in one hand, the other sweeping tangled limbs aside, in his mind he was sprinting. Desperate gasps came out of his lungs.

He had been twenty yards away when Villachio was killed. He froze, listening to the thrashing, hard grunts of fighting men. Then the final burst of gunfire. And he knew Pellegrino was dead, felt it in his heart.

Now he was far away from that place. Going upward, climbing the mossy boulders and fern-covered ravines, like a blind man always moves upward. He yearned for the wisps of sunlight that filtered through the high foliage. Up there somewhere was sky and the long, easy run to Marau.

He heard the cracks of the axes before the voices. They made sharp pops, followed by sucking squishes as the blades pulled free. Then the voices came, chattering unintelligibly.

Three Tikapi Indians were in a small grove of jungle oak. The trunks of the trees were dark with moisture except where the axes had pounded in, exposing gashes of blue-white wood. The men wore leather gauntlets around their arms to protect against the flying wood chips. One man was squatting beside a rusty jerrican. He unwrapped a white bandanna from his head, tilted the can, wetting it, then rubbed it over his dark face and shoulders.

Dureau hid, watching. His mouth was parched. He eyed the water, hungering for it. He slipped the clip from his Ingram and lightly tapped it against the back of his hand, listening to the sound it made. It had ten rounds left. He couldn't waste them on the Indians. Still holding the clip, he crawled away.

Thirty minutes later he came to a thinning of jungle. He could feel concentrated heat washing back through the brush. The jungle opened into savanna. *Kunai* grass eight feet tall. Over the tops he could see mountain ridges that made dark green contours against the brilliant blue of the sky. The nearer cliffs were already deepening into shadow as the sun neared the ridgeline. Night would fall in a few hours.

With a little groan of fear he stood upright and plowed into the *Kunai* grass. Its sharp blades sliced at his arms and neck. A hundred yards in, his lungs gave out and he sank heavily to the ground. It was littered with dry grass blades, papery and crisp as autumn leaves. The air was heavy with heat that sucked the water from his pores.

He forced himself to his feet and plodded ahead. The heat was overpowering. He stopped again.

Dureau froze at a soft rustle nearby. He peered through

the grass. He could see no more than four or five feet in any direction.

Another rustle.

Six feet to his right he saw grass blades tremble like a wave. An instant later the head of a large snake appeared out of the floor litter. It was chocolate brown, the plates of its head like tawny, polished tiles. Alain gave an involuntary gasp and leapt backward, his hand fumbling to insert the clip. Instantly the snake lifted half of its body and struck at him.

Whimpering, Dureau leapt up and down like a man on white-hot coals. Once more the snake drew back and struck. Its mouth locked onto the front part of Dureau's boot. As Alain leapt into the air again, his momentum pulled the snake up fully out of the grass. It was five feet long and as thick as a man's bicep.

His fingers clawed the trigger. The sound of the Ingram slammed and rumbled through the grass. The bullets caught the snake in the center of the body. In a frenzied convulsion of coils, it balled up, trashing over and over in the litter. Gradually it stilled, quivering, the bullet gashes pumping blood.

Dureau ran blindly away from it, unmindful of the slicing blades. He ran until he couldn't run anymore, and then he stopped, staring with horrified disbelief at the crushed alley through the grass. He'd gone in a circle. He was lost in the savanna.

He sank to the ground and drew in lungfuls of heat-saturated air. He looked at the Ingram. After a while he pulled the trigger. It was empty. He laid it on the ground and sat there looking numbly at it.

Then smoke drifted through the grass like faint wisps of fog. Then it thickened, forming little billows that washed over him. Dureau smelled it. His head jerked up. For a few seconds he sat there confused. The smoke smelled like the straw fires off the barley fields of Touraine. Somewhere off to his right came a soft crackling.

Alain's heart threw a full load of adrenaline into his veins. *The savanna was on fire!* He scrambled to his feet and ran from the sound of it.

Again and again he stumbled and fell, only to leap up and continue. Going beyond endurance, fear driving his muscles, he went on and on. Suddenly he saw trees loom above the tops of the grass. Close to weeping, he stumbled on, broke through the final strands of *kunai*, and emerged in the dappled shade of eucalyptus.

He stopped short, his chest heaving.

Thirty yards ahead of him, a man in Marine fatigues was leaning against a tree. He had an M16 assault rifle in his right hand, the muzzle resting on the tip of his boot. He was grinning devilishly at him.

He slowly lifted the rifle to his hip and fired.

Dureau felt himself catapulted into the air. The entire upper part of his body went numb. The tops of the eucalyptus trees leapt across his vision and he smashed against the ground.

He stared at the sky. Its blueness seemed to come down at him in shifting layers of different shades. Lights burst on the edges. He moved his buttocks, felt a stone boring into his back. All of his shattered senses focused for an instant on that insignificant stone.

The last sound he heard was the fading screech of a parrot somewhere in the trees.

At 10:06 A.M., as Admiral Tsander stepped out of Kruchevsky's office, he was placed under arrest by two officers of the GRU, the military counterpart of the KGB. He was briefly allowed to return to his office in the Analysis Section to retrieve a few personal belongings. He was then taken to temporary quarters in the Lutserov Naval Barracks. There he would remain until an investigative board convened to consider his flagrant breach of security.

At almost the same instant, two other GRU men appeared at Lubentsov's laboratory. They ordered Nikolai's assistants into one corner, and demanded Lubentsov turn over all documents he had received from Admiral Tsander. Nikolai trembled with panic. Although he had intellectually known this might happen, now that it was actually taking place, he could not control the fear that violently took hold of him.

He hurriedly assembled the documents, including his series of projection printouts. He placed everything into Tsander's attaché case and handed it over. The assistants huddled across the room, silent and pale. One of the agents ordered Nikolai to get his coat. The other instructed the assistants to remain in the lab until further notice. As they left, with Lubentsov between them, two soldiers with automatic weapons stepped into the room and closed the door.

They walked two blocks to a shuttered gray house on an alley. Nikolai was put in a room with drab green walls, a table, and a single chair. It was cold in the room. The men left. Ten minutes later a third man came in and began interrogating him.

He was tall and spare and wore an expensive sheepskin jacket. He smoked long cigarettes the color of tar, and walked back and forth in front of the table as he asked questions. Lubentsov told him the truth. Admiral Tsander was an old friend. He had come to him for help, for his knowledge and equipment to formulate analogue projections pertaining to American intentions in the South Pacific.

Had these projections been made? the agent asked.

Yes. They were, of course, purely theoretical.

The officer nodded and paused long enough to light another cigarette. Once more he began to pace, asking further questions in his slow, methodical manner.

This went on for an hour. Again and again Nikolai was forced to go over the same ground, answering slightly altered questions. The room filled with smoke. Lubentsov's throat became parched. He asked if he might have a glass of water. The man ignored the request as if he had not heard it.

Lubentsov's nerves were now wire-taut. He was becoming confused. He would hesitate before answering. He found himself contradicting himself and scrambled back, trying to recover. The GRU man showed no change of expression or pace. Just the same monotonous tone, the same quiet questions.

In another part of his mind, Nikolai thought of his wife, his son, a junior Army officer stationed in East Germany, and felt their lives, like his, precariously balanced on the edge of a terrifying abyss. Sudden nausea gripped him. For a frightening moment he thought he was going to vomit onto the table. Instead he clamped his hands together, fought it, swaying from side to side with the effort.

There was a knock on the door. The GRU man opened it, then stepped out and closed it again. In a moment he was back. He crooked a finger at Lubentsov, indicating that he follow him.

Ten minutes later, they entered the General Staff Building in Red Square. A muscular Army major rose behind his desk in a waiting room with ornate leather furniture. He spoke briefly to the GRU man, then touched Nikolai's shoulder. The major summoned him to follow as he approached a heavy wooden door. He lightly tapped on it, then stepped back, indicating that Lubentsov should enter.

Marshal Petrov was eating lunch at his desk. He continued eating for a few seconds, then dabbed his mouth with a napkin. He pointed to a chair beside the desk.

Nikolai sat down.

Petrov studied him for a full minute before speaking. "Well, Professor, it seems we find ourselves in a rather unique situation. Would you agree?"

"Comrade Marshal," Lubentsov stammered. "I don't know what to say."

Petrov snorted. "Then why don't you tell me about these analogue projections of yours."

Nikolai obeyed. He was aware that his voice was higher than usual; it seemed to belong to someone else. He repeated what he had told the GRU man. Petrov began eating again, seeming to pay no attention. His eyes were far away. Lubentsov finished and fell silent.

"And you believe the Americans are actually planning a major confrontation in the Pacific?" Petrov snapped.

"Yes, Comrade Marshal. That is, within certain parameters."

"What parameters?"

"There is always percentage of blue area in analogue concentration. Organic variables which simply cannot be programmed."

"How is it your projections vary so widely from ours?"

"I don't know, sir."

Petrov's gaze lifted, held on Nikolai's face. "Perhaps you know something of American strategy we do not?"

The question, insidious with undertones, flustered Lubentsov. "Well, sir—you see . . . over the years, I've made a study of the American character."

"Ah! And how exactly did you do that?"

"By studying their music, their movies, and reading their novels. Such things portray a nation's cultural soul much more accurately than its historians."

A flicker of mockery touched Petrov's eyes. "Indeed?" Those same eyes went opaque. "I find your conclusions so much hog shit."

The obscenity struck Nikolai like a slap in the face. He recoiled, gripped his chair for support.

"It contains glaring weaknesses," Petrov went on. "It lacks a central theme of purpose, a pivotal goal that must always be consistent with any strategic thrust."

"Yes, sir," Lubentsov blurted. "I agree. The projection is fallible." He looked at the marshal pleadingly. "But, sir, you must understand, my purpose was—"

"Better you should agree that you are a pretentious old fool."

Nikolai felt the panic rising again, like molten lead through his blood. He nodded numbly, staring at his hands. "Yes, Comrade Marshal."

The echo of Petrov's sharpness along with Lubentsov's utter humility hung in the air. The marshal pushed away from his desk and walked around to stand very close to Nikolai's chair.

"Nevertheless," he said slowly, "sometimes even a fool can see things others can't."

Lubentsov lifted his eyes.

Petrov was smiling with cold relish. "I want you to

repeat your projection runs. With one bit of added data."
He picked up a sheet of paper from the desk and held it
out.

Nikolai took it. It was a naval communiqué. He stared
at it, a forlorn sense of hope beginning in his heart. The
communiqué read:

```
113200Z—TS-ABS 1500
TRANS/NC:YUROVNI—DELINEATION PREP ONE
210100Z RECEIVED ELF: SS 189 PUP

MESSAGE FOLLOWS:
MADE CONTACT WITH PARTIALLY SUBMERGED FREIGHT-
ER LIBERTY CLASS 252 KM SSE GUADALCANAL . . .
FREE-FLOATING 5000 METERS BELOW SURFACE . . . SUB-
MERSIBLE SERVICING FREIGHTER . . . REPEAT: SUB-
MERSIBLE SERVICING FREIGHTER . . . SINGLE MOTHER
SHIP ON STATIONARY BEARING FIX . . . ADVISE ACTION
END TRANSMISSION
TS-ANS:1500
223200 Z
```

Nikolai read it twice before glancing up. "I don't understand, sir."

"The Americans have deliberately sunk a freighter off
Guadalcanal. They are servicing it with a submersible. I
want you and your machines to tell me why."

The sense of hope flushed through him like a warm
light. "Yes, Comrade Marshal," he blurted. "I'll do it
immediately." He started to rise, but paused. *Dared he
ask?* "Perhaps, sir—this would exonerate the cir—"

"Perhaps."

Nikolai came to his feet. "I will do my best, sir."

"Do it quickly."

"Yes, Comrade Marshal." He fled from the room.

Bonner couldn't get the image of the bloated bodies
aboard the *Panjang* out of his mind. There was something terribly bizarre about all those men drifting down

there in the darkness. It wasn't the fact of their dying. He'd seen lots of death in Nam.

There was more to it. Beyond the fear was a dark moral objection. All the stakes were on the table now. No choice left. Someone had wanted those Tridents. What other reason would they have had to kill two dozen men? He didn't think the missiles were still aboard, but there was always the hope. Either way, it had to be checked. And to do that, he had to go back down there.

The long ride from the *Panjang* had been slow and silent. Chaffee turned on the overhead lights soon after they left the freighter. His eyes were filled with tears. He didn't seem to care if Bonner saw. He sat perfectly motionless. Wouldn't talk, not even to answer Hillar's frantic calls.

Finally Cas took the mike. "*Voorhees*, go ahead."

"Christ Almighty," Hillar came back. "You had us shitting O rings. Have you taken damage?"

"Two battery packs are leaking. We've shut down all systems."

"Roger, we'll track you up."

Bonner switched off the radiotelephone and turned off the panel lights. He absently reached up and flicked off the overhead.

Chaffee let out a gasp.

Cas started to turn the light on again, but stopped, wanting to see what Chaffee would do. A second later he felt Steve's fingers claw the back of his hand. He cupped his hand over the switch. Chaffee tried to force it away. He groaned, a wrenching sound of terror. "Please, not the darkness."

Cas turned the light on. Chaffee's face streamed with sweat. His eyes shivered and he dropped his head and stared at his trembling hands.

At 12:03 the Saran popped through the surface, rolling in the swell. Bonner climbed over Chaffee and cracked the hatch. The *Voorhees* was hove to a hundred yards away, her decks ablaze with lights. Divers were already in the water. One scampered onto the submersible. He grinned at Cas.

"How you doing, man?" he shouted up. "Must have been one hairy mother down there."

Cas put his head back and inhaled the sweetness of the ocean.

Twenty minutes later, Hillar held a debriefing in the wardroom. It was a somber affair. Chaffee seemed to be under control again. He recounted the dive, episode by episode, his voice even. He didn't mention the confrontation with Bonner. Neither did Cas.

Hillar informed them he had notified Midway of the discovery of the bodies. There had been some confusion. Naval Intelligence was handling all relay calls now, using different frequencies and a whole new code book. Costello came in to tell them the divemaster projected a twelve-hour repair time on the Saran. The leaking battery packets had blown interior circuits and they had to be completely changed.

Hillar finished his coffee and stood up. He suggested they get some sleep while the submersible was under repair. Before leaving, he mentioned that the *Panjang* was nearing the eight-thousand-foot level and still dropping.

Shortly after one, Bonner wandered out onto the forward deck. The *Voorhees* was holding station, riding her sea anchors. The sliver moon lay on the other side of the amidships house. All around the ship the dark sea seemed to breathe in ponderous rhythm.

Someone came up beside him. It was Napah. She silently put her elbows on the railing and looked out.

"What's going on here, Cas?" she asked quietly.

"You know what's going on."

"No, I don't. There's something about that ship down there nobody's telling me."

"It's not important for you to know."

"I want to."

"She's carrying nuclear missiles," he said flatly.

"Oh, wow!"

A winch started up somewhere astern. The sound drifted like a man humming softly.

Cas looked at her. "What do you know about Chaffee?"

"Nothing except the fact he's the best in submersibles."

"What happened to his copilot?"

"Eckhart? They said he got sick."

"He ever say anything to you about Steve?"

She thought a moment. "Once. He took me to dinner one night at the officers' mess on Midway. He got a little tight and began going on about how Chaffee was pushing too hard."

"How pushing hard?"

"He said Chaffee was getting freaky and that he would kill somebody else and he sure as hell didn't want it to be him."

Cas stiffened. "Somebody else?"

She was quiet for a moment. "He's popping pills. You know that, don't you?"

"Yeah."

"My God, Cas, you can't go down again with that man."

"I have to."

"Why? There has to be somebody else on this ship qualified to take his place."

"What does that matter? It has to be Chaffee."

"I just don't want anything happening to you, okay?"

He chuckled. "Nobody'd be around to keep your butt out of trouble, right?"

She shook her head. "Bonner, you're a real asshole."

For the first time since she'd come up, he felt her presence. His nostrils sniffed the bouquet of her hair. He wanted to taste the sweetness of her skin, to probe the essence of her hair.

He put his left arm around her waist and pulled her against him. He kissed her full on the mouth. There was a slight hesitation in her lips, then she melded against him and her mouth opened, her tongue darting against his lips.

At last they broke apart. Napah's eyes darted over his face. "Well," she said huskily, "I wondered."

"You wondered what?"

In answer she took his hand. They moved aft the deckline, down a companionway. A crewman passed them in a corridor, smiling pleasantly. Bonner felt foolish being led. He gazed at Napah's hair in front of him, the lift of her haunches, and followed.

She had been assigned Costello's cabin. It was small and crammed with books from the seamen's service library: Genet and Proust and Aristotle. Costello was obviously a deep thinker.

Napah closed the door and looked at him. Her deep green eyes were alive and smoldering. She flicked off the light. A soft moonlight glow came through the porthole. She took off her flight suit. Hurriedly, fumbling slightly, Cas did likewise.

The bunk was small and cramped. His elbow cracked the bulkhead, but against him was Napah's nakedness on fire. Nothing was said. Not a word. He kissed her neck, felt her arms enfold him, felt her breath scorch his cheek. Napah moaned deeply when he entered her, and raked his back. The room was filled with the creak of bunk springs. On and on he plunged. Finally he shuddered in orgasm and she, sobbing, followed.

They lay whispering softly. Cas, still within her, regained his erection. Again they coupled, back and forth, Napah gyrating her pelvis in furious ecstasy.

Afterward he shifted and fell off the bunk. Napah giggled and reached out to curl a wisp of his hair around her finger. "God you're clumsy," she said with soft affection.

He lay on his back on the rug, feeling the heat in his body dissipating. He stared at the dark overhead. Above him Napah, satiated, ran her finger along his chest.

Please not the darkness.

He pulled himself to his feet and began feeling for his clothes. Napah turned on the bunk lamp. She was sitting cross-legged, looking sexy and disheveled. "Boy, you're not big on after-sex conversation, are you?"

"I've got to talk to Hillar."

When she saw the look on his face, she didn't say anything else. She slid off the bunk and dressed.

Lieutenant Philpotts was OOD. His face was sunburned and there was a smear of white ointment on his nose. Bonner asked for Hillar.

"He's catching some Z's."

"Get him on the horn."

Philpotts looked anxious. "He said not to disturb him until middle watch."

"It's important."

The lieutenant sighed. "Okay, but he's gonna chew ass."

"I'll let him chew mine."

Hillar finally came on, his voice thick. "Yeah, what is it?"

"Bonner wants to talk to you, sir."

There was a pause. "All right, send him aft."

Philpotts nodded toward the port doorway. "Second on the port side."

Hillar was sitting on his bunk in skivvies, smoking a half-finished cigar. He was thick-chested, his belly just beginning to go to fat. He nodded Bonner to a seat beside his desk.

"Chaffee, right?" he said.

"Yeah."

Hillar rubbed his face. "I figured. What happened between you two down there?"

"That's not important. How long have you been with him?"

"Three months. Orientation at Norfolk and Pearl and then the Midway trials."

Cas stared at his hands for a moment. "What do you know about him?"

"Not much. He's the whiz kid of submersibles, that's about it."

"Did he have any recent accidents?"

Hillar nodded. "Yeah, one off Bermuda. About a year and a half ago, I think. His copilot was killed on that one."

"How?"

"I don't know details. Everything went into heavy classification right afterward."

Bonner swore. Blue cigar smoke wafted around the room and then drifted up toward the air ducts. "What about this Eckhart? Can I talk to him?"

"No way. The kid's in the Midway brig."

"What the hell's he doing in the brig? I thought he got sick."

"Apparently that was a cover story. Scuttlebutt has it he and Chaffee got into it. He tried to pop him. He's up for court-martial."

"Look, I have to talk to him."

Hillar's stare was studied. "That bad?"

"That bad."

Hillar shifted his legs tiredly and punched his intercom. "Philly, get a priority through to Midway requesting contact with Lieutenant Eckhart. Use the old frequency and go through Midway Comm. Code it seven-up."

"I think Eckhart's in the brig, Coach."

"I know he's in the goddamned brig, goddammit. Just do it."

"Yes, sir."

Hillar squashed out his cigar. "God, I hate these fucking things. My wife says they make me smell like a latrine." He rubbed his eyes, then stood up and began dressing.

It took forty minutes to raise Eckhart. Midway Comm wanted to know why the *Voorhees* needed to speak with a prisoner. Hillar asked for clearance through Captain Karo, reminding the operators of the *Voorhees'* override authority.

Everything was being handled through radiotelephone code. The outgoing messages were automatically encoded by the ship's TEL-18A gear, using a designated scramble base. Incoming answers were decided instantly and fed out on a strip of yellow paper.

Eckhart's first question: "WHAT DO YOU WANT?"

Bonner dictated to the radio operator: "WANT INFORMATION CONCERNING CHAFFEE ACCIDENT."

A minute later the tape clicked out. "MUST HAVE LEGAL RELEASE FIRST."

Hillar swore and started to dictate something. Cas held up his hand. To the operator he dictated: "I AM COPILOT. WILL SOON SCALE EVEREST WITH CHAFFEE." To scale Everest was slang among submersible men for a deep dive. "MUST KNOW DETAILS. PILOT EXTREMELY UNSTABLE. PLEASE."

There was a long pause before the next tape came in. "BERMUDA TRENCH. EIGHTEEN MONTHS AGO. COPILOT KILLED DURING BREACH. CHAFFEE TRAPPED FOR SIX HOURS."

Bonner closed his eyes. *Please not the darkness.*

The tape clicked again. "OBSERVE EXTREME CAUTION. GOOD LUCK."

Now he knew. Steve was fighting the one thing a submersible man could not tolerate. Claustrophobia.

Twelve

37 hours, 25 minutes

Admiral Charles Hawkins was late for his first Joint Chiefs of Staff meeting. Ever since ten-thirty the night before, when he had learned of Admiral Smith's death, he had had staff meetings, one-on-one briefings with key men in Naval Operations, mountains of reports and updates, trying to get a handle on things. The realization that he was now Chief of Naval Operations hadn't caught up with him yet. He had always jokingly referred to the CNO as Cookie Nut One. Now the Cookie was him.

By dawn Hawkins still hadn't managed to pin it all down. He was floating on a sea of caffeine. At 9:45 he gathered his latest sea-deployment figures and headed for the Joint Chiefs conference room. Four officers were already seated around a large oval table. The chairman, General Mark Turner, paused in the middle of a sentence. The other men turned as Hawkins, flushing with embarrassment, took his seat. They were General Hawley McComas of the Army, General Leland Decker of the Air Force, and General Brockfield McCandless of the Marine Corps.

Turner put his elbows on the table and tented his fingers. "To bring you up, we were discussing this alarming increase in Russian military activity over the last twelve hours. I assume you have latest updates of their naval deployments?"

"Yes, sir."

"All right, let's start with NORAD and SAC reports." He turned to General Decker. "Air Force."

Decker launched into his most recent reconnaissance reports. He was a tall, dignified officer who spoke in clipped, precise bursts. The reports indicated an upsurge of Russian military units all over the world. ICBM crews on alert status at Yedrovo on the Baltic Sea, at Pervomaysk in east Poland, at the missile center of Ryuratam, and at Olovyannaya on the Manchurian border. The APVO air defense around Moscow was also on alert. At eastern air bases such as Megadan, Khabarovsk, and Vladivostok, scramble status was in effect for squadrons of Mig-23 Flogger and Su-27 Flanker fighter-interceptors. Overflies of Cam Ranh Bay were not yet available, but communiqués from Subic seemed to suggest there was movement there too.

General McComas of the Army was next. Most of his report centered around NATO recon observations. Border surveillance showed an increase of activity of division magnitude all along the AEC frontier. Particular upsurge seemed to be around East Germany and Czechoslovakia.

Marine Commandant McCandless was bypassed in the go-round. Not usually included in JCS meetings, he had been called in primarily for contingency update as several of his Marine amphibious forces were presently operating with the carrier battle group in the Azores and a smaller TLA in the northern Philippines.

It was Hawkins' turn. He reported numerous at-sea sightings of unusual submarine and surface activity, particularly in the southern quadrants of the Pacific. Sub crews and underwater acoustic arrays were picking up deployment of Russian attack submarines all over, out of their normal station positions. Several reports had clearly identified land-attack cruise-missile carriers, Typhoons and Yankees, making position moves. He concluded with a Pearl Harbor issuance and the latest SOPAC-13 satellite scans, which showed a sizable cruiser force preparing to move into the South China Sea from Cam Ranh Bay.

All five officers were momentarily silent, digesting the information. The men looked like travelers huddled around a tundra fire.

Finally Turner spoke. "Well, gentlemen, let's have comments."

"Overall," Decker put in immediately, "it seems predominantly defensive in nature."

McComas nodded. "I agree. I was with the Eighty-second in Belgium when Kennedy had his crisis in Cuba. The Russian sectors there thought sure as hell we were going to attack them. Their deployments were quite similar."

"Hawkins?"

"At this point, it's hard to tag their naval intentions. There's just a helluva lot of movement out there. Except for the repositioning of the Typhoons and Yankees, it doesn't seem aggressive."

Turner glanced at General McCandless. "Brock, what do you think?"

"The way I look at it, you have to interpret any movement this massive as aggressive. Or at least provocative. The question is, why are they doing it so suddenly?"

"I might have a partial answer on that," Turner said. "The Russian ambassador visited the Secretary of Defense this morning. He claimed his government was quite concerned over unusual concentrations of naval armament in the South Pacific and around the Azores."

"That would explain my Pacific reports," Hawkins suggested. "But why the movement in Europe?"

"Obviously the Soviets see our deployments as aggressive," Turner said.

"But none of our moves are strategically offensive," Hawkins replied.

"Apparently their perceptions of the situation are different from yours, Admiral."

Hawkins smiled good-naturedly. "Yes, I guess you could say that was fairly accurate."

The others chuckled quietly, even Turner.

The discussion continued for another thirty minutes.

Finally Turner called a halt. "I suggest we adjourn for now. I want your option summaries and recommendations in two hours."

Hawkins' first JCS meeting was over.

It had rained just before dawn, leaving the higher ridges of the Maragud Ride clothed in mist. When the sun came up, the jungle slopes smoked and the trees wore a deep virescence.

It had taken Spangenberg and Fa'uza till sunrise to bring in the bodies of Dureau, Dominique, and the Italian to the Honiara infirmary. Although he had been drinking all night—a bottle of Japanese *sho-ju* from Pickens—Sab insisted on driving the infirmary hearse, going at breakneck speed along the narrow coast road while the corpses tumbled crazily in back.

Dr. Sakai was waiting for them. He was indignant as he watched the corpses being unloaded. "What the matter, you?" he barked at Sab. "Every time I see you, more bodies."

Fa'uza came around the corner of the rear entrance. "Colonel, a newsman is here. What should I say to him?"

"Tell him to go fuck himself," Sab growled. "Where's your jeep? I need it to get home."

"In the driveway, Colonel." He went away shaking his head.

Spangenberg headed unsteadily down the drive. A man was standing near Fa'uza's jeep.

"Colonel," he called. "Might I have a moment?"

Sab stopped, swaying.

The man came up. He was tall, dressed in a khaki safari jacket. "I'm Hal Worthington of the BBC. I understand there have been some rather messy killings."

"Who the hell told you that?"

"Oh, I was sniffing about, local color, that sort of thing. One of the constabulary boys mentioned there had been a clash near Tumai. Is that true?"

Sab looked Worthington up and down slowly. "Get the fuck out of my way."

The newsman recoiled at the tone in Sab's voice, the cold, drunken look of his eyes. He held up his hands. "As you will, Colonel. As you will."

Spangenberg continued across the grass to Fa'uza's battered jeep. He climbed in, started the engine, and gunned away.

His cabana was silent, the lights still on in the front room. The Melanesian woman was asleep on the *punee*, completely naked. There was an empty bottle of brandy on the floor. Lying on her stomach, she was snoring softly.

He took off his fatigue jacket and flung it onto a rattan chair, walked over to the liquor cabinet, and took out a fresh bottle of gin. He cracked the seal and tilted it up for a long pull.

He returned to the *punee* and stood looking down at the woman. Her heavy hip was lifted slightly, the round, dark contour of her buttocks accentuated by the position. Her pudenda was just visible, looking sealed, shut down, like the steel grille across a saloon door at dawn.

He took another deep drink and put the bottle on the table. He stripped off his boots and trousers, balancing unsteadily from foot to foot. He stood there with only his green undershirt on and a strident erection.

He moved lower along the *punee*, braced his right leg. Gently he lifted the woman's hips, his middle fingers pulling the lips of her vagina open. She moaned quietly, still asleep.

As he probed into her, there was a moment of mucal dryness. He kept shoving until he was fully engulfed in her. Slowly, then faster and faster, he drove himself into her. She was awake now, grunting, shifting her body to meet his thrusts, her head buried in the cushion.

Sab closed his eyes. He was nearing it. He felt his groin bunch, grip down hard. The ecstasy shivered through his thighs. Somewhere in the ecstasy his mind heard the cracking chatter of his M16.

An hour later, someone was pounding on his door. He was in bed, down deep in sleep. He catapulted out of bed, his body coiled. His hands reached for weapons, found only coverlet.

The pounding continued.

"Who the hell is it?"

"Colonel Spangenberg," a man's voice called faintly.

He staggered to his feet. His head exploded with needle points of pain. He wandered around for a moment, confused, trying to find his clothes. Then, remembering, he went out into the front room. The woman was sitting up on the *punee*, holding his fatigue jacket over her breasts. He jerked his head at her, and she rose and scurried into the bedroom.

Wearing only his trousers and undershirt, he wrenched the front door open. "What the hell do you want?" he demanded.

A navy lieutenant in summer tans stood with his hands in his pockets. His blue eyes took in Sab's unkempt appearance.

"You Colonel Spangenberg?"

"Yeah. Who are you?"

The lieutenant held up a plastic card. It was a Naval Intelligence ID. His name was Lieutenant Otis Aspen. "I'd like a word with you, sir."

Sab looked him up and down, then nodded and stepped aside. "All right."

Lieutenant Aspen walked in and stood by the coffee table, his hands back in his pockets. Sab sank onto the *punee* and rubbed his throbbing temples. "Get on with it," he snapped.

"As I understand it, sir, you killed some men west of Tumai last night."

"Right."

"I'd appreciate some details, sir."

"How come NI's in on this?"

"The local medical examiner, a Dr. Sakai, reported the incident to the governor-general's office and it got sent up to us. NI's responsible for on-site security during the conference."

"What do you know about it?"

Aspen shrugged. "Not much at this point. We've taken prints off the bodies and will be running FBI and CIA checks. From what I got, they were involved in some murders?"

"Right."

"And they had Ingram machine pistols?"

Sab nodded. He leaned over and poked around in an ashtray for a half-smoked cigarette. Aspen lit it for him.

"Weapons like that," the lieutenant said, "indicate terrorist connections. I was hoping you could shed some light, sir. It could be critical."

Blowing a cloud of smoke, Sab began recounting the events leading up to the confrontation in the jungle. Aspen listened intently, never interrupting. When Sab finished, he shook his head admiringly. "That was a helluva job of tracking, Colonel. Still, I wish you'd contacted us earlier."

Sab snorted.

Aspen pulled something from his pocket. He held it up. "You ever see this?" It was a dog tag on a gold chain.

Spangenberg turned it over a couple of times. Six sets of numbers were stamped into the metal. Along one edge was a dark smear of dried blood. He handed it back. "I never saw it before. Where'd you get it?"

"Off one of the men you killed."

"Yeah? What do the numbers mean?"

"I don't know, Colonel. I've been thinking about that. Before I was assigned to NI, I was with Pearl's Division Eight Submarine Attack Force." His blue eyes seemed to deepen. "Every time I look at those number sets, I get a bad feeling."

"Why?"

"Sometimes on the WestPac cruises, we'd conduct mock sabotage exercises. Three or four of the crew would run drills to see if we could break into the sub's SLBM-C4 fire-control system. We were good. Sometimes we'd get all the way to the missile heads before they'd discover the break-in." He held up the dog tag. "We used number sets just like these to enter the missile computer banks for reprogram."

Spangenberg's back came up off the *punee* as if somebody had just kicked the other side of it. His eyes were quivering with intensity. "Are you telling me one of those scumbags had number codes to break into a missile?"

"I don't know, Colonel."

"Well, you sure as hell better find out."

"I intend to," Lieutenant Aspen said.

Air Force One landed on Ford Island in Pearl Harbor at 11:04 A.M. Hawaiian time. The President was taken by limo to the Arizona Memorial. On the windswept platform of the boomerang-shaped war memorial dedicated to the dead of December 1941, the President stood with his hand over his heart. A twenty-one-gun salute exploded across the water. A cruiser skimmed by. She dipped her ensign as she passed, her bow cutting through the water. The President returned the salute, then waved at the braced columns of seamen on her afterdeck.

When the ceremony was over, the commandant's gig conveyed him to a brief meeting with Admiral Prudoe and his staff for updating and recommendations pertaining to the conference. His itinerary included many stops and had been worked out with split-second timing. Takeoff time was scheduled for 6:30 A.M., which would put him on the Canal at nine their time.

His meeting with Prudoe was grim. The admiral brought him up-to-date on the latest reports from the South Pacific, along with the Joint Chiefs of Staff MSOP relayed from the Pentagon.

Admiral Prudoe then outlined his own countermeasures for his sector of command. He would have a memorandum covering contingency adjustments within the hour. As to the Joint Chiefs' recommendations for stepped-up reconnaissance and diplomatic probes, he concurred completely. He particularly stressed their last recommendation, strongly advising the President to postpone his appearance on the Canal.

The President approved all the items of the advisory except the last. He explained to Prudoe that it would be impossible to postpone the conference at this point. That would mean loss of face in the area and a capitulation to Soviet pressure. He would carry out his schedule as planned.

Ten minutes after the meeting with Prudoe, he got the second blast of bad news. It was carried by CIA Chief Rebbeck, who had just been contacted by Secretary of Defense Glayshod. Rebbeck had been on his way to Guadalcanal to oversee security when the call came. Using a makeshift patois, Glayshod told him that Naval Intelligence reported that the *Panjang* had been located sunk and that all her crewmen were still aboard, murdered.

The President was shaken, as was Lirette, who was also present. Ashen-faced, the President walked to the window and gazed out at the vast panorama of Pearl Harbor, drenched in brilliant tropical sunlight.

Rebbeck was the first to break the silence. "Mr. President, in view of this terrible turn of events, you must cancel the conference."

"He's right," Lirette put in. "This time he's right. It's too goddamned dangerous for you on that island now."

Still at the window, the President asked, "What is NI's view of the situation?"

"Glayshod didn't say. I would certainly imagine that since the freighter was obviously attacked, the probability that the missiles were stolen has increased."

"It could still have been pirates."

"Yes, that's true. We won't know for sure until that submersible crew can verify the cargo." He paused. "There seems to be a problem there, however."

The President swung around. "What kind of problem?"

"I couldn't make out all of it from Glayshod's conversation. It was something about the crew being unable to scan the ship from the outside. Something about a double hull."

"Then they'll have to breach the ship."

"Yes, sir, apparently."

"When?"

"I'm not sure. It seems the submersible took some damage during the first dive."

The President cursed softly.

"One other thing, sir," Rebbeck added. "A Russian submarine was detected in the vicinity of the *Panjang*."

"Oh, terrific," Lirette cried.

The President paced back and forth in front of the window for a few seconds, then paused. "What is your assessment, Rebbeck?"

The CIA chief didn't answer for a moment. "Are you asking me as an American citizen, sir, or as director of my agency?"

"What the hell kind of answer is that?" Lirette boomed.

"Paul." To Rebbeck the President said, "Both."

"As a citizen concerned for my President's safety, I would unequivocally recommend you stay away from the Canal."

"And?"

"As director of the CIA, I would stake my life on the fact those Tridents are still aboard the *Panjang* and constitute no danger to you."

"Good God!" Lirette was furious. "What if this . . . this pompous ass is wrong? What if one of those godawful things is sitting somewhere on that godforsaken island just waiting for you?"

The President studied Rebbeck's face. "Director?"

"That is not possible, sir. My field agents have saturated the entire southern Pacific area with intelligence probes for months. No such operation could have been mounted without being picked up. Absolutely nothing *has* been picked up. The attack on the *Panjang* was committed by some roving band of raiders and is nothing more than coincidence."

Lirette pointed an accusing finger at Rebbeck. "You're sure goddamned cavalier with this man's life."

"Dammit, Paul," the President snapped. Lirette, still fuming, sat down and stared daggers out the window.

The President leaned against the windowsill and crossed

his arms. Speaking to both men, he said, "I intend to go to the Canal. First, because I don't have much choice in the matter. Second, because I *do* have total confidence in my security people."

Rebbeck nodded curtly. "Thank you, Mr. President."

"Do you have any further bad news?"

"No, sir."

"Then that'll be all."

"Yes, sir." Rebbeck withdrew, closing the door softly.

The President glanced over his shoulder. A ship was coming up the long outer channel to Lock 2. He watched it for a moment, then turned back.

"Paul, if you would prefer to remain here, I'll understand."

Lirette's head jerked around, his eyes blazing. "By God, that's the most insulting thing you've ever said to me."

The President grinned. "That's what I thought you'd say." He pushed away from the sill. "Well, come on. We've got an Air Wing to look at."

Jimbo Gillespie was dreading his first midmorning press briefing. He'd spent most of last night in his room, getting tight on two six-packs of beer. It had been a wearying, frustrating day for him. There was still nothing concrete on the missing ship. Around three in the afternoon, he'd even gone to the Naval Intelligence office. They stone-faced him out the door. Finally, after the worst hamburger he'd ever eaten in his life, he went back to his room and sat bare-ass naked on his bed and cracked beers. The phone kept ringing but he ignored it. "Screw it," he said, cracking open the second six-pack.

At eight o'clock the next morning, with his head throwing shafts of incandescent pain, he trudged across the wet quad to the delegation compound. There was a curt little memo from Wilcox on his desk. "Tried to call you this morning. *No* answer. Report from NI: several killings on island last night. Automatic weapons used. Possible terrorist implications. Suggest you investigate *immediately*."

Jimbo's eyes fixed on *Possible terrorist implications.*
Frantically he glanced at his watch. The briefing was only
ninety minutes away. There wasn't time to go helter-
skelter around Honiara, asking questions. *Shit!*

He began making calls. First to the governor-general's
office, then constabulary headquarters, the Marine barracks, the Australian delegation liaison, and finally the
NI office. He'd managed to glean a few skimpy facts.
Yes, there had been killings. Three, two men and a
woman. The identifications were incomplete on all except the woman. She had been the wife of a local copra-
plantation owner. Name: Dominique Mott-Smith. The
investigations were continuing through proper channels.

He looked at what he had and felt sweat pepper his
brow. It was zilch. The press hawks would have ten times
this much.

At seven minutes to ten, he forced himself out of his
chair and up the corridor to the briefing room. He was
hailed, mockingly, like a returning hero: "Hey, Jimbo,
where the hell you been?" "The prodigal warrior returns." That sort of shit. He took it all with a lopsided
grin and began with the usual agenda clutter. Updates on
arrival times for the dignitaries, time changes, interview
procedures, and schedules. Threw in a few outdated items
just to punch up the content.

He paused before touching on the hot stuff. "There's
one last thing. I've just been informed that there were
some killings on the island last night. Apparently two
men and a women were involved. That's all I have for
the moment." There was a rustle of chairs as the assem-
blage leaned in. "There *is* one ominous note to this,
however. Automatic weapons were used."

The questions exploded.

He held up his hands. "Just hang on a moment. We're
running ident checks. If anything of significance turns up,
I'll let you know."

The reporters were flinging hands and questions at him
before he finished. Nat Cruickshank of NIE called above
the chorus: "I have it the woman was the wife of a
big-shot copra grower. True?"

"Yes."

"What's her name and involvement?"

"I don't know that yet."

Martha Camarillo, looking pert in white slacks and blouse, shouted, "Reports from local constabulary personnel claim there were two other killings connected with these. One was the copra grower. Are we looking at some sort of conspiracy here?"

"I have no confirmation on that."

"What about a terrorist plot?"

"No substantial facts about that." He scanned the thrusting faces and spotted Worthington. "Hal?"

"Are you aware that Marine hero Colonel Sabbath Spangenberg was personally involved in the killings last night?"

Gillespie went cold. Spangenberg the wild man? He hadn't even known he was on the island. Apparently some of the reporters were caught off guard too. They turned and stared at Worthington.

Hal continued, "I spoke with him myself this morning. He admitted involvement. Does this indicate the U.S. Military is in it too?" The flood of questions erupted again. Above it, Hal pressed a final point. "Is this another CIA adventure?"

Jimbo felt sweat begin to trickle out of his armpits. He tried to still the noise. "I have . . . I have no information concerning Colonel Spangenberg. I repeat, we are conducting identification searches to pinpoint just who *was* involved. As far as I know, that is the extent of our government's involvement at this point."

The questions went on, rapid-fire. Gillespie tried to field what he could, mostly falling back on non-confirmation. He sounded helplessly evasive even to his own ears.

They were getting nowhere. Even the reporters sensed it, and the clamor began to wind down. It was at that point that Cliff Cartelli of *Newstime* made a ninety-degree turn. Before he was done, the rest of the pack veered with him. "Gillespie, why is it we haven't had more details on this ship incident south of the island?"

Jimbo thought: What the hell? It couldn't get any worse.

"As I've told you before, the facts are that a ship got into some sort of minor trouble in the Coral Sea. That's it. I don't have anything more on that item."

"Why the blackout?" "What's the name of the ship?" "What was her cargo?"

"No comment," Jimbo said.

"Was it military?"

"No."

"It *was* American, right?"

"To my knowledge, yes."

"Then why have her sailing documents been sealed in San Diego and Pearl?"

"I wasn't aware they were."

"Is the damned ship lost?"

"I have no confirmation on that."

Martha Camarillo was standing, giving Jimbo coy looks. "Come on, honey, what's going down here?"

He clung tenaciously to his position. "I have no further information on this ship other than what I've already told you. Frankly, I think you all are making a big thing out of nothing." There was a chorus of boos. "The damned ship had a minor malfunction. What do you want from me?"

That set off another crescendo of accusatory queries. Jimbo adamantly stood his ground. He could feel his rage in the pit of his stomach, feel it tingling in his fingertips, through his temples. He went on for a few more minutes, then he'd had enough. He quietly folded his notebook, waved his arms indicating the briefing was over, and headed for the door. Questions tugged at his coat, followed him out.

He didn't lessen his pace. He headed straight for Wilcox's office and flung the door open.

Wilcox's secretary, a plump redhead from Texas, glanced up.

"Is that prick in?" Jimbo boomed.

"Yeah, but he's— *Hey!*"

Gillespie went charging through the door and slammed it behind him. "God damn you," he yelled.

Wilcox's head jerked up. "Gillespie, what the hell do you—"

"You left me out there with my thumb up my ass."

"What?"

"Why wasn't I told about these killings sooner?"

Wilcox's lean face went stiff. "I tried to call you this morning. Obviously you were otherwise occupied."

"Big deal. One lousy hour. What good would that have been? They fucking massacred me out there."

"I was only notified myself at six this morning."

Jimbo couldn't contain his rage. He dissipated it by pacing back and forth. "You listen, buddy. Something's going on here. Something's going *on* here. You people are stonewalling me."

"You people?"

"Why haven't I been getting updated reports?"

"You're getting what I'm getting."

"Bullshit."

Wilcox lunged forward. "Now, you listen here, Gillespie. I won't tolerate you coming in here raving like a . . . a maniac."

"Why wasn't I told Colonel Spangenberg was involved in these killings?"

Wilcox drew back. "What are you talking about?"

"Colonel Sabbath Gung-ho Spangenberg, you son of a bitch. The guy with decorations down to his dick. He was *in* on it."

"I don't know anything about that."

"I'll bet you don't. Just like you don't know the whole story on that goddamned ship out there."

"What ship?"

"You know what ship. The one you and Washington have been playing tight asshole with for two days."

"That's absurd."

"Is it? Then how come I don't have names and details?"

"You have what I have."

"Which is nothing."

"If it's nothing, then I have nothing. Look, what possible reason would I have for holding anything back?"

Damn, Jimbo thought. If that was the truth, the stonewall had been built higher up. "Is that straight, Wilcox?"

"Yes."

Gillespie looked at the floor, feeling suddenly washed out. His mind shuffled through new implications. "Look, I'm sorry," he said. "The briefing was hellish."

Wilcox looked away, deployed objects about his desk. "Well," he said.

Jimbo grinned. "We're all under pressure, right?"

In the corridor he ran into Christine. She came scurrying at him in a heady cloud of gardenia-scented perfume. "Jimbo, honey, where you been? I tried to call you."

For a moment Gillespie thought of fleeing. Christine came up, pressed her hip against his, ran a scarlet fingernail down his necktie. "Are you avoiding me?"

"No, Chris, really, I've been busy as hell."

"I have something for you. Something on that old ship of yours."

"What!"

"One of the girls in Records said—"

Before she could go on, Jimbo grabbed her arm and dragged her up the hall, searching for an empty room. He found one, hauled her inside, and slammed the door.

"What did you find out?"

"Hey," she said coyly, pressing her body against his. He felt her grope his crotch. "We gonna have a quickie?"

Judas Priest, he thought. The woman's a screwing machine.

He eased his crotch out of range. "Chris, please, tell me. What about the ship?"

"Boy, sometimes you're bo-o-oring." She sighed and slid up onto the corner of one of the desks in the room. "All right." She looked at him sideways. "It's kinda gross."

"Gross? What gross?"

"All the crew members are dead."

Gillespie gasped. "Dead? How dead?"

"Dead dead. Some ship coded Mama Bear apparently located this lost ship and radioed through special-frequency dispatch that the bodies of the crew were on the forward deck." She shivered.

"Jesus." Jimbo wandered around the room, dumbstruck. "What else? What's this special-frequency-dispatch stuff?"

"About twenty-four hours ago, Communications got an SO from the Defense Department telling them to set up a priority DL with this Mama Bear ship to go through Naval Intelligence network."

"The Defense Department?"

Christine nodded. "It's got a whole separate code reference and all. Bypasses transmission through Midway and Pearl Communications."

"Why?"

"I don't know. Our CR office just passes it through to NI headquarters and they take it from there."

Gillespie stared off into space. He had the crazy feeling he was handling dynamite.

"Chris," he said tensely, "get back to that chick in Records. Pump her, get everything you can on this. Will you do that for me?"

The sly, heavy-lidded look again. "You gonna be nice to me if I do?"

"God, yes. All over the place."

"I like that thought."

"Do it. I'll get back to you."

Lubentsov's anxiety had reached an acute pitch. For hours he had been toiling alone in his lab. It was freezing cold, and he wore a tattered Irish sweater he'd purchased many years before in Rome. The printouts remained incomplete, giving only what had been given before. The added data of the sunken freighter had not altered anything.

Nikolai instinctively knew what was wrong. He had not been able to break down that data into a significant code input. The freighter was just sitting on the surface of his run, superfluous and nonlinked. The piece was not fitting into the puzzle.

Soon Marshal Petrov's men would come for his results. Without them he would be helpless to save himself, his family. He began pacing aimlessly around the lab. For a moment he stopped at the window, looked out, absorbed nothing, moved on. He paused beside the tea table where his assistants took their breaks. The table was cluttered with math books, notepads, a small portable chess set with a thin paperback book lying open on it: *Famous Chess Games.*

He chuckled in the midst of his anxiety. Apparently one of the assistants had been mimicking game strategies. He had done that himself many times. He looked at the page the book had been opened to. It was the final game for the World Championship between Andrei Soyka and Christian Kolta in Vienna, 1924.

Yes, he remembered that one. Soyka's brilliant, shocking maneuver had become known as *Der Verlust du Vienna*: the Viennese Sacrifice. At the perfectly timed moment, Soyka had sacrificed his Queen, thereby throwing Kolta's prime tactical array into confusion. With two lightning moves, Soyka had checkmated the Black King.

Caught up for a moment in his beloved game, Nikolai fingered the tiny board pieces, moved them through Soyka's attack. Then with a growl of disgust he scattered the pieces and headed off for another circuit of the room.

He was clear to the door when it struck him. He stopped short, turned slowly to stare across at the tea table. He felt his scalp tingling with a crazy sense of sudden discovery. His heart pounded.

Could that be the key?

Unable to contain his soaring excitement, he scurried to his main computer. With flying fingers he began to enter data. It came pouring out of him as if it had been waiting in the recesses of his mind for the light. Figures and instructional phrases leapt onto the computer screen. Faster he went. Transpositional baselines, definitions of premise and evolved parameters, specification codes, integrated arc entries, final projection gradient, and key-on process.

He was trembling when he finished. He leapt to his feet and circled about, wringing his hands, afraid to begin. He stared at the expressionless, mechanical faces of his machines for almost a minute.

He punched the start key.

Seven minutes later he gazed, stunned, at the printout. The structure of it was perfect, utterly logical. Premise, exposition of prime tactical factor, timing, lightning resolution. It was all there. He had boxed the American strategy.

The key was the *Verlust*. Just like Soyka's Queen, the concentration of the heads of state on Guadalcanal was a ploy. They were to be sacrificed! Their deaths, instantly attributed to the Soviets, would galvanize the world against this barbaric act. All nations would stand against Mother Russia.

But how would they die? What would be the killing instrument?

The projection defined the only logical answer. A catastrophic incident. A nuclear detonation.

The printout also pinpointed the source: the sunken freighter. A weather expert, Lubentsov knew what a blast at that position in the Coral Sea would create: a tidal wave of enormous proportions that would sweep across Guadalcanal and engulf everything on it.

There was a sharp knock on the door.

Nikolai, deep in the horror of his projection, cried out. He glanced at the door. Petrov's men.

Another booming knock.

He shook himself. "Yes," he called, his voice shaky. "Yes, I'm coming."

Thirteen

26 hours, 53 minutes

The quarter-moon softly gilded the pine trees north of Bluepine, Tennessee. A small honky-tonk named Kenny's stood among the trees. The dirt road that ran in front of it was lined with several dozen cars and pick-ups, their headlights turned on. People were sitting on their fenders, drinking beers.

Near the entrance to Kenny's, two horsemen were trying to quiet their mounts. The animals swerved and stamped their hooves, nervous from the lights and noise. One of the horses was an Arabian, its hide glistening like polished ebony. The rider was Lew Langenscheidt, director for research at the Bluepine missile complex.

A flashlight a half-mile up the road signaled. A man standing a few yards from the horses shouted, "Ready 'em up, boys." He had a Winchester carbine.

"Set?"

He fired the rifle.

Leaning his wiry six-foot-four frame forward, Langenscheidt drove his heels into the Arabian's flanks. The horse exploded under him. They went pounding up the road amid squeals and bellows from the spectators.

The cold night air rushed into Lew's face. The Arabian's broad back pounded against his buttocks as his long legs gripped the animal's rib cage. Lew kept his eyes on the flashlight and loosened his hands on the reins, letting the Arabian run free. Fifty yards from the light he let out a howl of pure joy. Beside him, it was answered by his opponent. They flew through the moon-dappled night.

The light zipped past. Lew put all his strength down into his legs, hauled back on the reins, twisting to the side. He saw the other horse thunder past, its rider cursing, trying to turn.

The car lights formed a glistening necklace far down the road. Langenscheidt loosened the reins again. With one hand he rubbed the thick spine muscle of the Arabian, bent forward, cooing softly into its laid-back ear.

The man with the rifle fired two shots as Lew flashed past Kenny's. Four seconds later, the buckskin came pounding up beside him as both horses slowed, trotting. The rider grinned over at him.

"God *damn*, Lew," he shouted. "You're right. That horse of yours flat *flies*."

They shook hands and cantered back to the café amid cheers. While the spectators reparked their cars and straggled back into Kenny's, the riders walked back up the road with their mounts. The flashlight man came walking by. "Helluva race, boys," he called. "Helluva race."

At thirty-one, Langenscheidt was considered something special in the field of aeronautical physics. A graduate of MIT at twenty, he had garnered numerous honors along with two directorships with NASA before coming to Bluepine, the largest missile research and coordinating center in the U.S. A specialist in missile propellants and reentry phenomena, he had been instrumental in programming several Challenger shots. Now he was occupied with streamlining tracking and deployment procedures for the American defense system.

Before returning to the café, he rubbed and brushed down the Arabian until it quit steaming, then ran it up into the trailer connected to his Ford pickup. He blanketed the animal, locked the trailer, and walked around to the entrance of Kenny's. There were seventeen setups waiting for him, along with ten twenties the other rider had left on the bar in payment for their bet.

Fifteen minutes later, a long-necked Bud in one hand, he was two-stepping with a girl named Marge when one of the waitresses signaled him.

"Telephone, Lew honey. It's the complex."

With his arm around Marge's waist, he took the call at the end of the bar. It was Ray Salter, deputy director.

"I hate like hell bothering you, Lew. But we got a little problem. We just got a high-priority request from the Navy for an S-and-P on one of their Trident 3A's. Apparently the silly bastards have lost it."

"You're kidding."

"I wish I was. But this is red-code shit. They want a pinpoint location track, posthaste." Each nuclear-warheaded missile—from the smallest, single-man-carried Stinger to the top-of-the-line Trident 3A—was track-filed within Bluepine's computer bank.

"That's no problem. Just trace the tag numbers."

"That's the problem. They only sent us break-in numbers."

"Jesus Christ."

"They want us to span-run the entire inventory to see if there *is* such a missile."

Lew made a disgusted sound and took a pull of his Bud. "Okay, I'll be up in about an hour."

For the last seven hours, ever since dawn, Chaffee had worked silently on the Saran. He neither spoke nor answered questions directed at him. During that time, though no one noticed, he periodically turned his gaze to the eastern horizon. He saw a balloon as large as a stadium dome hanging about sixty feet above the line of the sea. It was diaphanous, like the rounded, transparent body of a gigantic jellyfish.

No one mentioned it, yet he knew they saw it too. Oh, yes. He'd caught the sly looks that passed among the crew. And Bonner. Well, let them play their little game of keeping secrets, the rotten bastards. They were good at that sort of thing.

Each time he had to go down into the submersible, he

would always glance at the balloon. And it was always there.

The Saran was giving them a hard time. The low power from the leaking battery packets had fouled main circuits throughout the vehicle. Everything was being pulled, repaired, then replaced. An additional ballast tank had to be installed. Also, since the *Panjang* was now nearly twelve thousand feet down, the breach-chamber suction locks would need more pressure to secure the lock base onto the freighter's deck. This meant reaming new rings.

Chaffee approached each new problem with calm deliberateness while the others cursed and fretted. Each time he glanced eastward and beheld the balloon, it seemed to replenish his sense of cunning knowledge. He'd tried to sleep last night. He and Bonner had been assigned the sick bay. He lay on his bunk feeling the perspiration coating his body, intermittently thinking of what lay ahead. It was as if he peered down dark corridors.

Sometime in the night he began to hear a sound. At first he thought it was the ship, but it grew louder. He listened and listened, and at last figured out what it was. The axle of the earth. He was hearing the earth revolving, ponderous and booming. Finally, unable to bear the sounds any longer, he rose, fumbled through his flight suit, and took several pills. He returned to the bunk and watched Bonner's sleeping form across the dark room.

His eyes blazed. He'd seen Bonner watching him, narrow-eyed, suspicious. He was one of them, probably had been all along. They wanted to destroy him. But they never would. He knew what he was doing. When he found those missiles and told the President, *then* they'd know.

The pills were hitting hard now. His heart leapt, sending surges of energy through his body. It was as if he were made of thousands of tiny wires, each vibrating with energy. He stealthily went out and up to the port deck. It was nearly dawn. Long swells from the south gently lifted and lowered the *Voorhees*. The water was very dark beside the ship, but Chaffee was not frightened now. He felt powerful, invincible.

The horizon began to fuse with light. Indigo crept upward, drawing brighter washes of red and purple with it. It was then he saw the balloon for the first time, drifting out there on the ocean. He could see the light through it, distorted slightly by the thin, gelatinous tissue of it. As the sun rose directly behind it, the balloon was filled with a bursting kaleidoscope of color.

The Orion rendezvoused with the *Voorhees* at 1430 hours. Last night had been frustrating for Kitchens. During the Saran's dive he'd circled the *Voorhees*, ready to relay analysis of the submersible's scan. They'd just been sitting up there and the Russian Delta had snuck right up on them. It was Hillar who told them they'd made a submarine contact.

Afterward they'd tracked the Russian for about forty-five minutes, until their fuel forced them to turn back to the Canal. He had gone off on a southwestern heading, just moving slowly, as if he didn't care that he was being tracked.

Rather than attempt a night landing at Kukum, Kitchens took them into Henderson International. They refueled and stayed there till dawn and then flew to Kukum to wait for Hillar's call notifying them the Saran was ready for another dive.

While at Henderson, he'd tried to code-report the encounter with the Delta to his SVR-4 command unit on Midway, but they refused to receive the report. They told him to switch to other frequencies and file directly to the Naval Intelligence unit on Midway. He couldn't figure it out, especially since they said he had to transmit on special code. He didn't have the book on it and finally had to relay through the *Voorhees*, which encoded for him and sent it on.

Everybody was shocked at the news that the Saran had discovered the *Panjang*'s crew. They talked about it over cards. They were sure it had been raiders. Nellie Carpenter said he'd read Aussie CW reports that claimed the waters around New Guinea were infested with pirates. They used to hijack whole ships and run them into points in the Tanimbar Islands. Probably had a complete friggin' navy by now.

At noon Kitchens raised the *Voorhees* again. Hillar said the submersible was taking longer than expected. Dive time was moved up to sunset. He told Kitchens that from now on they would have to use new code names. The Saran would be referred to as Baby Bear, the *Voorhees* as Mama Bear, and the Orion as Goldilocks.

Kitchens gave Klinch a nauseated look. "Goldilocks? Jesus H. Christ."

By two in the afternoon he couldn't stand waiting around any longer. They cranked up the Orion's engines, and soon reached the *Voorhees*, sitting on the placid ocean like a toy boat. Kitchens called down. "Mama Bear, this is Goldilocks. What is Baby Bear status?"

"Goldilocks, thought you were holding."

"We got bored."

"Baby Bear still sleeping. DL moved to twenty-one hundred hours."

Kitchens cursed before keying: "Roger that. Think we'll take a walk in the woods for a while."

"Roger, Goldilocks. Keep in touch. Out."

He keyed the intercom: "Bobby, standby. We'll make some MAD passes, see if we can pick up Ivan again."

"Right, Skipper. You want a buoy on load and lock?"

"Might as well, just in case. How many Torpex we got left?"

"Fifteen."

"Okay, lay up four. If we find the prick, let's make his ears ring."

The rear garden of the Royal Crest Hotel was decorated as if for a wedding. There was a striped canopy backed against the veranda, and flags of all the nations in attendance at the conference were posted along the garden walks and around the pool. Security people were everywhere, stolidly mingling with the gathered dignitaries or out skulking among the shrubbery.

At the edge of the canopy, Rose Treleven stood talking with the French President, Pierre Vasselon. A tall, regal man, he had a habit of gazing over her head as she talked, as if her words were contained in little balloons that he studied diligently. Rose caught herself gazing at Vasselon's skin, astounded to find not the slightest trace of perspiration. In this heat it seemed inconceivable.

On the veranda a small delegation of Japanese men in blue business suits and dark ties huddled in a clot. Scotty Cox began talking animatedly with the shortest of the group, the Japanese Prime Minister, Yasio Higame. After a moment he led Higame down the rest of the steps and over to Rose and Vasselon, his thick arm around the Japanese PM's shoulders. Higame's entourage followed at a respectful distance, hands clasped in front of them like so many preteen boys waiting self-consciously onstage at awards night.

Cox was intercepted by an extremely tall Australian with a scar on his nose. "Excuse me, Prime Minister," he said softly, nodding apologies to the others.

Scotty, in the middle of a joke, swung around. "What is it, Parkes?"

"Might I have a word with you, sir?"

Scotty made a face. "I'm afraid the punch line will have to wait. Excuse me a moment, please." He and Parkes walked off into the garden. They paused beside a flaming hibiscus bush, away from everyone.

Rose watched them from the corner of her eye. Parkes was talking rapidly. Scotty seemed stunned. She could see his face get red. At last he nodded and headed back toward the veranda. On the first step he paused, as if considering a return to the group under the canopy, then shook his head and stormed up the stairs into the hotel.

Four minutes later, a waiter came up to Rose. "Excuse, please," he said humbly. "I have a message for the Madam Prime Minister." He held out a small gold dish with a white card on it.

Rose read it. It said, "Must speak with you at once. Scotty."

Cox was pacing furiously in a small sitting room behind the hotel's front desk. He stopped long enough to glare as she came in. He waited until the waiter closed the door before letting loose.

"Those bastards," he hissed. "Those bleeding stupid bastards."

Rose gently rested her drink on an ornate Victorian table. "What's wrong, Scotty?"

"Those Yanks. They've bloody well lost one of their ruddy ships."

Rose frowned. "A ship? I don't understand."

"A ship, a freighter." He shook his head with utter disbelief. "I just got an intelligence report. My people picked up a leak that an American cargo vessel is down in the Coral Sea."

"I still don't understand your outrage."

He stopped pacing, stared at her. "The bloody thing was carrying nuclear missiles for Tamarand."

"Oh, my," she said. She turned and walked to the window, looked out on a shower of plumeria blossoms. "Oh, my, my."

"Damn the clumsy bungos."

"Have they located it yet?"

"No."

"Was it lost or sunk?"

"They don't bloody know."

"What does Washington say?"

"Oh, they're playing it belt-up, they are. My people couldn't find a chink."

"Is there any danger from these missiles?"

"No, of course not. If the damned thing's on the bottom, it'll just sit there till it rots." He made a growling sound in his throat. "That's not the bloody problem. Davis is. If he gets wind of this freighter and its cargo, he'll put it all together. The man would have to be a blithering idiot not to see how the pieces fit." He thrust a thick forefinger at the ceiling as if calling down damnation. "If that mongrel knows about the Tamarand, Rosy, if he knows, he'll bloody well blow us out of the water with it."

Treleven didn't say anything for a long moment. Then she turned resolutely. "Not if we all stand steadfast and deny it."

Cox paused in his mad pacing to study her. "*We* deny it? Ah, Rosy, you're a staunch one, you are. But you can't afford to be a part of this. No, you stand clear."

She dismissed that with a wave of her hand. "We've already agreed that American dominance in this region of the world is absolutely essential." Then she picked up her drink and sipped it thoughtfully. "How effective is Davis's intelligence?"

"Shabby. Hell, remember the French were able to blow up a Greenpeace ship right in this bleeding harbor."

"Then chances are he might never learn of this freighter sinking or the Tamarand operation."

"That's true."

"Besides, everyone knows his stance concerning the ANZAC agreements. He would be *expected* to interject something at this conference which would discredit both the U.S. and Australia. Isn't that so?"

"Oh, you can bet a tick on it."

She stared into Cox's eyes. "Then I suggest you do something to prevent him from doing that. Immediately."

"How?"

"By utilizing his own tactic before he does."

Scotty looked puzzled for a moment. Then a slow grin began to creep across his face. "By God, Rosy, of course! We plant a rumor among the delegates that Davis is *planning* some absurd accusation. We discredit the bloody bib before he says a word. Then if he does make claims, they'll carry no weight."

"Precisely. They'll be perceived as hollow challenges. Denials by you and the President, along with votes of confidence from me, Japan, and, I assume, France, will easily defuse the whole affair."

"Lord!" Scotty said, awed by her cunning logic.

She gave him a cold smile. "You remember one thing, Scotty. Sometime very soon I expect a detailed explanation of this Tamarand affair."

*   *   *

Hillar held a conference in the wardroom just before seven in the evening. Bonner, Chaffee, the divemaster—a CPO named Carough—and Napah. Everyone looked haggard.

Hillar lit a fresh cigar and turned to Steve. "What's your dive estimate, Commander?"

Chaffee was looking hard at the table. He was calm, his fingers entwined in front of him. "Two hours," he answered without looking up. "Two more circuit reconnects and she's ready."

Hillar's eyes lingered on Chaffee for a moment, then turned on Carough. "The new tank functioning all right?"

"Yeah, Coach. We got the breach lock shaft chambered up to fourteen thousand feet and she's holding." He scratched his long, narrow nose. "I'm a little worried about them lock seals, though. They're holding all right now, but we've gauged a little warpage in the seat. She might go below fourteen."

"How about milling 'em?"

"Yeah, I think we might manage that."

"Do it."

Chaffee said, still staring at the table, "Pull the bottom chamber bolts and replace them. I saw some fracture. And countersink the seats deeper. There's burr on them now."

Carough's eyes flickered to Hillar, then back to Chaffee. "Yeah, Commander, that's a good thought."

"Make sure you run an extra brace on the deadweight rack," Chaffee went on tonelessly. "And see it's perfectly centered."

"Yes, sir."

Hillar tapped his cigar ash into his coffee cup. He seemed to be turning something over in his mind. Finally he looked at Carough. "All right, Chief. You better get on with it."

"Aye, sir." Carough left.

Hillar blew a cloud of smoke and sighed. "Okay, let's get to the nitty-gritty." He stared stonily at Chaffee.

"Commander, I want a straight answer. Are you fit to make another dive?"

Chaffee's eyes revolved slowly upward and he gazed at Hillar from beneath his brows. There seemed to be some dark laughter in his eyes. "What is the reason for that question?"

"I think that's fairly obvious."

"I disagree. Despite what others might think."

The skin around Hillar's eye sockets was beginning to bunch up, as if he were staring into a bright light. "That's not a goddamned straight answer, Commander."

"The straight answer is that I *am* fit for another dive."

"This time it will be a breach."

"Of course."

Bonner interrupted. "What's the *Panjang*'s depth now?"

Hillar shot him a surprised glance. The interchange with Chaffee had wired their gazes together, and he broke it reluctantly. "Twelve thousand, five hundred. She's still sinking, but descent has steadied up. Rate's about five feet per minute now."

"She's stabilizing again," Bonner said. "Maybe we're in luck and she'll go into free-float neutrality."

Hillar leaned back and crossed his arms. His forefinger tickled the red hairs of his forearms. "A half-hour ago I got a DM from *Air Force One*. A personal message from the President. He wants that cargo verified. No more bullshit."

Chaffee, still watching him, said, "It *will* be verified."

Hillar glanced at Cas. "What do you say?"

"I want a third man on the dive."

Chaffee's gaze swung slowly to Bonner. Head still down, the same cunning laughter in his eyes, he stared, saying nothing.

"I agree," Hillar snapped. "The only problem is, nobody on this ship's qualified for deep work."

"How about Carough?" Bonner asked.

"He's never been down. He might go. I'll ask him, but I won't order him."

For the first time Napah spoke up. "You won't have to do that, Hillar. I'll go."

All three men looked at her. Even Chaffee was momentarily surprised.

Cas shook his head with finality. "No way."

"Why?" Napah shot back. "I'm a qualified submersible operator. And I've been down in the Saran twice." Her eyes fumed green fire. "There's no reason why I shouldn't go. Except that damned chauvinistic BS of yours."

Bonner's head snapped around. "Get off that shit," he cracked. He glared at her, then looked away. When he spoke again, the voice was softer. "There's one other reason. We might not come up again."

Napah had been startled by his vehement retort. In reflex she had drawn back. Then, realizing fully what he had said and why he said it, the green fires banked and she reached out and touched his wrist. "I know that, Cas. But I still want to go with you."

They looked at each other. For a heady moment they were alone, just staring.

Hillar broke it. "You're a civilian, Gilchrist. I won't intervene in your choice. If you want to go, it's up to Bonner and Chaffee."

Chaffee said, "Let her go." Just like that. And the laughter in his eyes touched the edges of his lips.

"Bonner?"

Cas had swung around at Steve's words, startled. But Chaffee kept gazing at the table. He seemed again lost in some inner joke.

"Well?" Hillar pressed. "Does she go or not?"

Napah said, "Please."

Bonner studied the air in front of him. He sighed. "All right, she goes."

The Krylov Military Hospital was located a hundred kilometers west of Moscow, on a bluff overlooking the Volga River. In a small doctors' lounge in the south wing, an emergency meeting was about to be convened. Called by Marshal Petrov, it included six of the eleven members of the Presidium of the Supreme Soviet and

Council of Ministers. They were now awaiting the appearance of General Secretary Yuri Markisov.

The day before, Markisov had been stricken with a violent attack of acute cholecystitis. He had been returning from an inspection tour of missile silos in Toropets when the attack came. He was rushed to Krylov and immediately went into surgery. He had not been scheduled to return to Moscow for another three days.

Now there was a murmur of voices outside the lounge door. It swung open and an Army major quickstepped in and snapped to attention. Out in the hall, Markisov was in a wheelchair, a coterie of nurses fussing about him.

He waved them off and, grimacing, pulled himself to his feet. He was unsteady for a moment, then straightened and came into the lounge. He wore a white hospital robe and a thick red scarf around his neck. His slippers *thacked* on the concrete floor.

Petrov and the ministers instantly came to their feet. Markisov settled slowly into the chair at the head of the table. Ordinarily a robust man of fifty-six, he looked pale now and there was a thin veneer of perspiration across his forehead.

Petrov glanced at the Army major. "Leave us, and see that no one comes near this room."

"Yes, sir." The major withdrew.

Petrov turned back to Markisov. "Comrade Secretary, I apologize for calling this meeting in this manner. Unfortunately, it is of an extremely urgent nature."

"Get on with it."

Petrov opened his briefcase and withdrew a sheaf of papers made up of several clipped sections. He placed the top one in front of Markisov, then one before each of the ministers, who began scanning their sections. "What you have there, comrades, is the summary of one of the most diabolical strategy moves in the history of the world. And one that is about to place our nation in extreme jeopardy."

Puzzled looks shot up at him. Only Markisov continued to page slowly through his copy. Finally he snapped at Petrov, "What does this mean?"

"As you know, sir, over the last two days there have been significant relocations of American and allied military units throughout the world. Because of that, we found it necessary to place ourselves in a state of Level Two alert."

Everyone nodded.

"As I was studying these movements, I was struck by the fact that they all seemed part of an overall purpose. They were elements of a single strategic thrust. I ordered the Defense Ministry's Division of Strategic Coordination to run a computer analysis of these movements in an effort to isolate that single thread." He pointed dramatically at Markisov's brief. "That is their finding. It shows that the Americans and their allies will strike our naval forces in the South Pacific sometime over the next thirty-six to forty-eight hours."

Everyone at the table stiffened, their faces white with shock.

"Their opening salvo," Petrov went on, "will be a nuclear detonation in the Coral Sea. The detonation will kill every head of state attending the Pan-Pacific Conference, including the President of the United States." A clamor of voices erupted in the ensuing shock. Markisov looked as if he had been struck. Finally, gathering himself, he rapped sharply against the table with his knuckles. "That is madness."

"Yes, Comrade Secretary, that *is* madness. And it's also quite brilliant."

"No, your analysts have miscalculated somewhere. This can't be."

"But it is, sir. See for yourself. It is all beautifully logical and strategically balanced. By this move the Americans would instantly achieve three prime objectives. First, their naval forces would defeat us within a time frame of twelve hours. Second, the explosion of a nuclear device there would immediately be attributed to *us* by the entire world. It would be perceived as so barbaric an act, every nation would stand against us. And third, the Americans would hold the offensive initiative."

The power of his points swept around the table like a wild wind.

Markisov's eyes bore into the marshal's face. "I can't believe American strategy would call for the destruction of its own leader."

"That's the key," Petrov cried triumphantly. "This is undoubtedly the *coup de maître*, the masterstroke of a military takeover of the United States."

He straightened, watching the faces around the table. He could see the effect of *that* statement; these men understood the concept of a military coup. Even Markisov seemed shaken.

Gradually the noise quieted. Everyone was watching Markisov. The General Secretary stared down at the papers beneath his hand. Slowly he glanced at the man on his right, a minister named Koldunov.

"Give me your opinions."

Koldunov launched into a tirade about American duplicity. Next came Tretyak, ex-KGB chief of the infamous Palyavich Detention Center. His condemnation was savage, delivered in a low, slow voice. On his right was Petrov, then Brulov, whose face showed more agony than outrage. Only forty-seven, a strong advocate of Markisov's plan of *glasnost*, he was often attacked by the more strident elements of the Old Guard for his ideas of peaceful coexistence with the U.S. In a faltering voice he tried to reestablish rationality in the discussions. He suggested Markisov personally contact the President. This was met with loud scorn by several of the other ministers.

Besides Markisov, only Rynbinin, to Brulov's right, remained silent during the outburst. A small man with impeccable manners and bearing, he was also a proponent of the new regime's *perestroika*, an internationalist who fancied his opinions expansive. But here he was intimidated by the powerful rush of emotions. At first he equivocated but finally acceded to the condemnation of America.

The next man was Bardeshevsky, the Nazi conquerer, one of the most powerful of the Old Guard and still as

fiercely aggressive as when he fought the winter war
outside Leningrad. Without hesitation he demanded immediate all-out war against the United States. He drove
the point home, pounding his fist on the table. Finished,
he sat scowling like a thunderhead.

The final man was Aliev, a huge man with a coarse
Mongolian face. He had recently suffered a stroke that
had left his body untouched, but had taken the fire from
his soul. In a quiet voice he said he would go along with
whatever the others decided.

Markisov had listened to all this in grim silence. Now
and then an eye would flicker as if in pain. His face had
turned gray and a droplet of sweat trickled slowly down
the curve of his cheek. For two full minutes he remained
this way. Then he focused on Petrov.

"Is the entire General Staff in agreement with your
perception of this situation?"

"Yes, Comrade Secretary. They are equally shocked
and outraged at the Americans' audacity."

"Have they contained their emotions long enough to
formulate options?" Markisov snapped bitterly.

"At this early point, they propose three general options. One: immediate preemptive nuclear strikes against
the United States and designated points in NATO."

There was a sharp intake of breath from several ministers. Only Bardeshevsky boomed approval.

"Two: immediate nonnuclear invasion of NATO fron-
tiers. This option is open as to whether we strike China
at the same time. She may remain neutral. But then she
could attack us, sensing we might be vulnerable.

"Three: a delay of either strike option until the Americans have fully committed themselves in the South Pacific."

Bardeshevsky's fist instantly hit the table. "The last
option is unacceptable," he roared. "To wait for the
enemy to strike us first is insanity."

Brulov stared across the table at him "Surely you can't
mean we should utilize either of the first two options on
the basis of a mere theoretical prediction?"

"That is precisely what I mean."

"We are speaking of nuclear war."

"So be it. It has always been an inevitability. The one who waits to be struck first is the one who will be destroyed."

"We'll *all* be destroyed."

"If that is our fate, so be it."

"Good God!" Brulov shouted in utter frustration.

Koldunov shoved his porcine face forward. "I think we should move against NATO at once. We could destroy AEC completely within three days. We would own Europe. Then let the Americans play their little games in the Pacific."

Brulov swung on him. "And if it escalates into nuclear exchange?"

"I agree with Comrade Bardeshevsky. If fate dictates that we are to die in a nuclear holocaust, better to go fighting than like slaughtered sheep."

Markisov called a halt to this. Begrudgingly everyone quieted. He looked at Petrov. "Which option do you and the General Staff favor?"

"The third, Comrade Secretary." Petrov ignored the hard glance he got from Bardeshevsky. "But first we *must* go into OB Red Alert status immediately. Including ICBM prefiring standby. Actual full commitment of our forces will then be contingent on a nuclear detonation in the Coral Sea."

The General Secretary sat silent again for a long time. When he did finally speak, there was no hesitation. His orders came out swiftly and precisely. "I want full ministry contingency and recommendative reports on my desk in Moscow within the next four hours. Petrov, you are to begin the implementation of full OB Red Alert immediately. You will supply me with continual updates as to progress. I also want personal assessments from each of the sixteen Military District, Air Army, and Fleet commanders as to their individual readiness."

Petrov nodded. "Yes, sir."

"I want a concentrated monitoring of all reconnaissance from our satellite and overfly sources. And internal

KGB station reports sent to me with ministry staff recommendations on content. There is to be an immediate survey of our consulate staffs around the world as to the military and political status in their areas. I myself will speak with our ambassador to the United States." He turned to Petrov. "Do you have a definite time when the President is to arrive at Guadalcanal?"

"A KGB report says he is presently in Hawaii and is scheduled to arrive at the conference site at nine o'clock tomorrow morning, Guadalcanal time. That's roughly eighteen hours."

Markisov nodded. "If this projection of yours is correct, we can assume nothing will occur until the President is there. We then have eighteen hours to explore and prepare." He paused. "One thing further. Where is this submarine your brief states sighted the derelict in the Coral Sea?"

"Her last position fix was two hundred and fifty miles southeast of the sighting."

"Very well. You are to send its captain my direct order. He is to return to the derelict and destroy it."

Fourteen

18 hours, 14 minutes

Commander Glen Harnie, skipper of the Sturgeon-class attack submarine USS *Plymouth*, was just biting into a fresh Hershey bar when the intercom in the attack center activated.

"Conn, I have a contact, bearing three-five-zero."

"I'll be right in."

The *Plymouth* was on watch detail at the southernmost end of her triangular patrol run that normally took her from the coast of Peru to the south polar icepack, then up to Tahiti and back to Peru. With the increase of Russian undersea traffic, however, she'd been ordered to linger in the Antarctic's Ross Sea to monitor submarines transitting that quadrant. She was now drifting twenty miles from the fringes of the pack in Discovery Inlet at the center of the Ross.

Chief Sonarman Eddie Vilchek was standing sonar watch. "He's still on the outer range, sir," he said as Harnie stepped into the small sonar room. "About ten miles. But he's coming fast and straight, at least forty knots."

"You make him yet?"

"The analyzer's scanning tape now. We're getting a lot of ice-shift interference."

Because it was summer in the Antarctic, the sea was filled with breakaway icebergs that had come off the heavy pack which covered the inlet. Deeper in, the pack remained permanent.

"Let's hear him," Harnie ordered.

Vilchek switched on the overhead speaker. There was a low, intermittent rumbling occasionally broken by sharp cracks. The rumble came from new chunks of ice which were breaking off the front of the pack. The cracking sound was from shrinkage deep within bergs that had drifted out into warmer water.

Beneath the sounds was a softer, steadier sonant. As the *Plymouth*'s analyzer computer began feeding back filter tape, the bottom sound became clearer, a throbbing *whoosh*.

Harnie squinted, trying to signature the cavitation. "Sounds like a Typhoon to me. How do you make it?"

"I think you're right, sir. But ain't this way off regular Typhoon track?"

Harnie nodded. "He's sure cutting water. How deep is he?"

"Eight hundred feet. If he holds to this bearing, he'll pass us fifteen hundred yards, down and away to starboard."

"Track him past and let me know when he's forty-five degrees astern."

"Aye, sir."

Harnie returned to the attack center. "Rig for silence," he called out. "We've got a big sucker coming in."

The watch officer echoed the command. Everything unnecessary aboard the *Plymouth* was shut down, and crewmen throughout the ship settled in where they were. A submarine's sonar capability diminished in inverse proportion to her speed. Normal procedure for a sub working an area was to run-and-drift, alternately firing up and then riding the current, listening with her passive sonar.

Within six minutes the men in the attack center could hear the fixed regularity of the Typhoon's nuclear reactor and the whirl of its props. The watch officer, Lieutenant Brullard, said, "He's really moving."

The Russian bored through the water, throwing all kinds of noise. It reached a peak and then faded gradually as the Typhoon passed. Harnie waited. Ninety seconds later, the intercom crackled. "Conn, target forty-five degrees astern, still holding bearing and speed."

"All right, let's get on this tail," Harnie barked. "Give me twenty degrees right rudder and go to a third. Fix on new course of bearing one-seven-zero and go to full."

On a small chart table, an electronic screen built into a four-by-four cabinet, tracking grids made thin lines across the screen. Harnie called for Ross Sea Q-TAC display and track. Instantly the outlines of the Ross Sea came on. They were green, the estimated ice front blue. A tiny white blip showed the *Plymouth*'s position, a red blip the Typhoon's.

For the next half-hour the *Plymouth* stayed on the Russian's tail, slowly losing ground. Only capable of thirty-three knots full out, she was giving away nearly ten knots to the Typhoon. That was not what was bothering Harnie. As the Russian drew closer to the ice pack, he wasn't attempting any hard turns to ping his backtrack. A submarine moving forward created a sonar blackout area directly astern. A careful commander usually made periodic turns to ping that area, watching for a trailing opponent.

But this commander didn't seem to give a damn if anybody was following him. Worse, he wasn't slowing a bit as he neared the ice pack. Harnie couldn't understand that foolishness. To go under ice at flank speed was extremely dangerous. The underside of the pack was a treacherous area of inverted peaks, some reaching hundreds of feet below the upper shelf.

As Harnie watched the red blip on the chart screen, it crossed the blue line of the pack's front. He was under ice. A few seconds later, Sonar verified the fact.

Harnie's stomach was knotting. Should he follow the Russian? Why was the Typhoon going under ice in the first place? And at such speed? It was obvious to him the whole thing was not a normal operational move.

"Distance to ice?" he called out.

"Fifteen thousand yards, sir."

"Conn, I'm losing him. Our probes are getting lost in rebound off the ice."

"What's the bottom depth?"

"Twelve hundred feet with slow upgrade south."

Harnie felt his excitement mounting. He had to find

out what the Russian was doing. Was the bastard simply challenging him? In effect saying, "Come on, Yank, we fly under the ice. Do you have the testicles to do likewise?"

Anger flushed through him. Yeah? he thought. Well, screw you, Ivan.

"Rig for ice run," he shouted. "Maintain bearing and speed."

The order went cracking across the attack center. Lieutenant Brullard threw a questioning look at his skipper. Harnie's eyes were fixed on the chart table.

"Conn," Sonar called, "cavitation indicates he's slowing."

Now what?

"Range to target?"

"We're getting a blurred fix. Estimate range at five miles, holding same bearing."

"Give me Ulcer read."

A panelman from his left barked: "Water temperature thirty-eight degrees, drift one-eight-seven degrees, five knots."

The *Plymouth*'s blip was two inches from the blue line.

"Sonar, can you filter exact fix?"

"Negative, sir. Cavitation indicates he's slowed to twelve knots, same bearing."

"What the hell is he trying to do?" Brullard asked softly. "He'll ram that damned boat right into permanent ice."

"Bottom depth?"

"One thousand, sixty feet, rising."

Thirty seconds later they passed under the edge of the pack.

"Distance to underside of ice?"

"Underside, seven hundred feet, lowering."

"Conn, target has dropped to seven knots. He's pinging now. I'm getting heavy rebound signal off the pack."

"Underside?"

"Distance to underside, five hundred feet, lowering."

Harnie felt his heart beating rapidly. The pack was getting thicker. Well, he thought defiantly, you got through, Ivan asshole. So can we.

"Give me underside distance in fifteen-second intervals. Now."

"Distance to underside, four hundred thirty feet, lowering."

"Bottom?"

"Bottom, eight hundred fifty feet, rising."

Harnie had a terrible vision. It was all a hallucination. There was no Russian sub out there. He was tracking a chunk of ice and soon the *Plymouth* would drive itself into a solid wall of ice.

"Conn, target making turn to port."

The vision vanished.

"Range?"

"Four miles, closing."

"Go to six knots."

The *Plymouth*'s speed dropped quickly. Harnie took a breath and tried to figure. Was the Russian going to come right back out again? Soon he would be bow-on to the *Plymouth*. Harnie cursed his stupidity. He had been suckered into an extremely dangerous position, he now realized. Bow-on to a Typhoon with no maneuvering room under the ice.

The Ulcer man continued giving his fifteen-second soundings. Harnie snapped at him, "Belay that. Drop to sixty-second intervals. Sonar, target position."

"Target has completed turn. He's four degrees off starboard bow, speed approximately three knots."

Harnie felt cold scatter up his spine. He couldn't just sit there with a Russian sub staring down his throat.

"Fire control, stand by for firing sequence. Tubes one and three. Begin TA lock-on now."

Brullard's head jerked around.

"Range to target?"

"Fourteen thousand, eight hundred yards."

They were right on the edge of their own Mark 48 torpedoes' running distance. Harnie frantically tried to recall the nomenclature of the Typhoon's torpedo run.

"Conn, fire control set up and standing by. Tubes one and three. Still holding for TA lock-on." A pause. "We have lock-on."

"Conn, underside ice distance six hundred feet, rising."

"Sonar, what the hell's he doing?"

"All cavitation has ceased. He's drifting, sir."

Harnie's thoughts were, like his sonar, pinging. Was the Russian commander at this very moment arming his own torpedoes? Taking still, deadly aim?

Another minute had elasped. The Ulcer man came on: "Conn, ice underside has disappeared off scope. We are now under open water."

"All stop." The *Plymouth*'s power seeped away and they went dead in the water.

Harnie turned slightly to his right. An involuntary movement to release his pent-up energy. Muscles in his body flexed. He stared forward, as if he could see all the way to the torpedo room, where grim men waited for his order that would kill men, perhaps themselves. Suddenly his head snapped around the other way. He glared at the panelman sitting directly ahead. "Ulcer, say again."

"The ice shelf has disappeared, sir. We're now under open water."

It hit him with the force of a blow to the stomach. This was the reason for the Russian's unusual behavior. He had been searching for a skylight, an open patch of water within the ice pack. *A fixed, safe platform to launch his SSN-N-20 ICBM's.*

At that moment his ears picked up another sound that came clearly through the *Plymouth*'s hull. A harsh, expulsive hiss.

The intercom crackled: "He's flooding his tubes, sir."

Harnie's blood froze. Somehow his voice found its way out of his mouth. "Fire control, flood your tubes. Stand by for firing. Sonar, stand by to blow DD scatter."

The acknowledgments were echoed. Everyone in the attack center shifted on his seat, sought each other's eyes. Harnie scanned the instruments. They were primed. He could almost feel the menace of the Russian sub facing him like a snake in shadow ready to strike.

Rules of engagement prevented him from taking the first, irreversible step. He must wait, must respond. His ears strained for the first tell-tale rush of compressed air that would signal a Russian torpedo inbound.

Or was the Russian now preparing ICBM launch? Maybe

the holocaust had already started up there in the rest of the world. Were missiles already arcing across the skies?

A minute as long as a year passed. The air in the attack center seemed heated from the tension.

"Sonar, what's he doing?"

"Just sitting out there, sir. He's even stopped pinging."

Standoff.

Five more minutes dragged by. The two subs continued facing each other, each holding the same fixed position. Harnie thought: Fuck this!

"All back full," he barked. "Fire control, maintain maximum ready status. Sonar, scan us out."

The *Plymouth*'s power plant made the hull tremble slightly as it came up into full astern. They backed, rocking gently. For the next few minutes Harnie was busy holding the *Plymouth* steady as she backtracked. He couldn't chance a turn now. That would present his broadside to the Russian.

They cleared the outer fringe of the ice pack. He kept backing until his own probes became lost in the pack rebound and the Typhoon's fix was no longer accurate.

"All stop."

They drifted. They were beyond any possible range of the Russian's torpedoes.

"Give me twenty degrees right rudder, ahead two-thirds. Maintain for sixty seconds and bring us to periscope depth."

The commands were relayed and answered. The *Plymouth* picked up speed and her deck tilted as she came about, climbing through the water.

"Helm, coming up to two-six-zero degrees."

"Running depth approaching three hundred feet."

The sub skimmed now, running smoother in the lighter water near the surface.

"Helm, coming up to three-zero-zero degrees."

"Depth?"

"We are at periscope depth."

"Stand by, antennas. Deploy."

A few seconds later came the reply: "ESM deployed and reading."

Harnie turned to Brullard. He saw in his eyes an odd
mixture of relief and disappointment, and knew they
were reflected in his own. "Hold her for two minutes, then
bring her around to one-seven-zero degrees and drift."

"Aye, sir," Brullard said.

Harnie stepped from the conn platform and headed for
the radio room.

Langenscheidt was tired and disgusted. He had a headache and the coffee he'd been pouring in since midnight
had made his stomach sour. Running Trident-3A traces
was a frustrating job. The first production models of the
T-3A's had come off the assembly lines in early 1986.
Now there were 563 scattered all over hell. Without
specific ident serial numbers, using only the break-in
sequences from the Navy, the job was proving to be one
big scramble. Added to that was the Navy's requirement
that each T-3A—whether in transit, depot storage, or
deployment—must have its break-in sequences changed
every fifteen days.

The purpose of the break-in subsystem was sound
enough. It primarily allowed a submarine commander to
force-enter a firing sequence because of malfunction or
sabotage and abort the launch, at least up to the final
flight stage. Moreover, it gave a tighter security watch on
every missile in storage, and afforded periodic test runs
to show the efficiency of handling personnel and sub
crews.

But this requirement was forcing Lew and Salter to
obtain access to the computer records of thousands of
break-in sets from bases and depots all over the world.
Getting clearance to access these records was eating time.
They had to go through the endless security procedures
again and again, bypassing, back-verifying for entry permission. Some of the depots and base record units were
carrying backlogged entries, leaving blanks in their run
tapes that had to be extrapolated from known data. Key
personnel were not always present and had to be rousted.
And those missiles already at sea could not be positively
verified, so their traces had to stop at point of loading.

Still, they'd held to it through the long, dark hours. By dawn, through some slick computer sleight of hand, they managed to filter the whole mess down to four probables.

Langenscheidt called a break. He wandered over to the window to watch the sun come up. The missile complex was composed of dozens of drab, squat buildings and towers scattered across three thousand treeless acres atop a plateau. To Lew it all seemed suddenly stark and artificial, an intrusion in the green wilderness. As Salter went out to round up some breakfast from the complex cafeteria, Lew remained at the window.

Something in all this kept nagging him. Where had the Navy gotten this particular break-in sequence? Why didn't they have more information? There obviously had been some sort of security breakdown somewhere.

Salter returned with two plates of soggy ham and eggs, and they sat at the consoles and wolfed it down. By seven o'clock they were back at work, running traces on the four probables.

The first was resolved with surprising speed. Identical sequence numbers had been used four months before. The particular missile was now in a storage depot in Price, Utah. They made verification of position.

Scratch one.

The second was a little harder. They tracked it from Seattle, Washington, to Anchorage, Alaska, and then to the Scammon Bay Naval Base. The base commander, irascible as hell, gave them a definite verification that his missile had been loaded aboard USS *Miami*, which was presently at sea.

Scratch two.

The third one took them all the way to the Mediterranean and into an international brick wall. Data indicated this particular missile was part of a British/American interchange of operational material. Lew had to resort to the Navy Department. It was nearly eleven in the morning before they got a verify. The missile was in a British munitions depot on the island of Mallorca.

Scratch three.

Number four created a mystery. They managed to

trace it from Norfolk, Virginia, where it had been part of an armament load aboard USS *Houston* until four months ago. At that time it had been unloaded in Norfolk, went into maintenance, was transshipped across the country to San Diego, and then sent to Pearl Harbor.

At Pearl headquarters they ran into a heavy security shield. All their access attempts kept getting diverted to Naval Intelligence. NI played it very tight, refusing any information except on direct order of the Secretary of Defense. Lew glanced over his terminal at Ray. "Something's screwed here," Lew said. "We're getting smoked. Why in hell is NI taking orders from Defense?"

Salter shrugged.

"Get the Navy again. I'll find this damned missile or know why."

The Navy finally got some pressure put on and managed to bypass directly to Pearl Logistics. They told them the missile in question had been loaded aboard an MST freighter named *Panjang*, her destination Rockhampton, Australia. Cargo manifest indicated transfer of missile to USS *Greensboro* at that point. Break-in sequences had been dutifully changed to the precise sets Lew had twenty-four hours before loading aboard the *Panjang*.

Lew frowned. "Why in hell would they transfer a nuclear missile at Rockhampton?"

"That does sound strange, doesn't it?"

Lew shoved to his feet and walked to the coffeepot. He poured himself a cup and sat on the edge of Salter's terminal, staring at him. "This is the one, Ray. I know it, I can feel it. But why the bullshit from Pearl?"

Salter made a face. "God only knows."

"Run a trace on the *Greensboro*."

It was an easy access into Norfolk's ship-registry bank. Response came back in two minutes. No USS *Greensboro* registered.

"Goddammit," Lew shouted. "Request nonregister trace."

Salter tapped it into his console.

Langenscheidt was standing near the window again when the trace came back. Ray glanced at it, then looked at him with a strange expression.

"What does it say?"

"The damned *Greensboro* hasn't been commissioned yet. She's still under construction."

A low-pressure area had been forming in the Tasmanian Sea over the past six hours. Now it began moving toward the northeast, crossing the tip of Fiji, and the *Voorhees* started catching its western edge. Nothing big, but enough to make things touchy during the launch of the Saran. Wind was running about twenty-five knots and the sea was whipping up lots of chop and whitecaps.

The storm only added to Hillar's already nervous state. He couldn't remember having slept for more than two hours. The President's message had honed his trepidation to a fine edge. It wasn't every day a ship's skipper got a direct order from the Commander in Chief. An officer's career could be made or broken on how he handled that order.

Hillar's restlessness continually sent him back and forth between the bridge and the after ramp as the launch crew prepared the Saran. It was now 11:15, an hour and a half beyond the projected launch time. Now he stood in the rain watching the prelaunch run-through. Bonner, Chaffee, and Gilchrist were already inside the submersible, checking systems. Divemaster Carough, his clothes soaking wet, hustled around shouting orders through a portable blow horn.

The rain blowing into Hillar's face was warm. He studied the ocean off the stern of the ship. The arc lights flooded the surface for about fifty yards out. In daylight a launch in such a sea would have been easily controllable, but the lights distorted the ocean surface. Swells feathered with scud seemed to loom out of the darkness beyond the lights without discernible pattern.

At last everything was go. Bonner appeared in the Saran's hatchway and said something to the diver already standing on the submersible's capsule. They exchanged a single high-five, and Cas dropped down, pulling the hatch shut.

Carough was at the edge of the ramp, standing on
tiptoes to see out beyond the near chop. Hillar started to
call an order to turn on the afterdeck railing spots, but
Carough was already doing so. A few seconds later, three
sharp beams of light jabbed through the rain into the
darkness beyond the outer limit of the arcs. The beams
bounced and flashed across wave tops as the *Voorhees*
rolled against her sea anchors.

The Saran's holding beams and chains were unlatched,
and slowly the crane lifted her off her pedestal. For a
moment she swung wildly at the end of the cable. Then
the crane man got her out over the ramp and then water,
expertly countering her swing with his controls. Back on
the ramp, Carough was stretching again, trying to read
the sea. Finally he lifted his right arm and signaled the
crane to lower.

When the Saran was about four feet from the water,
Carough halted the drop. Again he studied the ocean for
several seconds, then held up his fist and moved it in a
counterclockwise motion, easing the submersible down
slowly. As the vehicle's bottom racks became awash,
Carough dropped his hand sharply. Instantly the cable
went slack on the tip block, and the Saran dropped
heavily into the sea. The divers aboard her began scurrying toward the hatch and started unbuckling the lock
hook. The submersible suddenly rolled hard to the right,
and one of the divers fell off.

Up on the deck, Hillar saw a big swell loom up into the
lights. It was about twenty feet high, the spot beams
sparkling across its deep sloping front. He screamed a
warning. At the same moment the remaining diver got
the cable free. On the ramp, Carough finally saw the
wave and bellowed at the diver through the blow horn.
The man turned, realized what was coming, and frantically grabbed the hatch ring just as the Saran was lifted
by the wave.

Crewmen were scattering to get off the ramp. A sudden gust of wind hurled rain at them, and two slipped
and went down. Carough stared openmouthed at the

wave-driven Saran, then dived to the port side of the ramp and slid into the scupper groove.

Slightly tilted back, the submersible slammed into the ramp. The undercarriage crumpled in a furious screel of clashing metal. The six hundred pounds of iron ingots was torn off, flung across the ramp, and then slid off into the water. A forward camera housing was hurled against the bank of the ramp, and then followed the ingots into the sea.

Hillar, his heart exploding, vaulted down through deck debris to the foot of the ramp. The Saran was sliding slowly down the slope on its side. He caught sight of a face in the starboard viewing port. Then the vehicle gently rolled off the end of the ramp and back into the water.

Hillar found one of the crew lying on the ramp. His thigh had been sliced open from just below the groin to his knee. Blood pumped steadily out of the wound, and sharp slivers of bone were visible. He knelt and put his palm against the sailor's chest to keep him from getting up. The young man gazed at him, pain squinting his eyes. "Oh, shit!" he moaned. "Oh, damn shit!"

"Get over here, goddammit!" Hillar bellowed. "Give me a hand!"

Crewmen stumbled and slid down to help. Their faces were ashen in the rain. Carough had come out of the scupper groove, still on his hands and knees. "Get that cable on," he kept yelling through the horn. "Get that fucking cable on."

When the Saran had struck the ramp, the diver on her hatch had been thrown onto the ship. He was now lying near the scuppers where Carough had been, trying to get up. Two crewmen skidded down to him.

The other diver was now climbing onto the submersible. The crane man had lowered his cable, and it was sweeping back and forth in the water about twenty yards from the vehicle. The diver waved frantically for him to bring it over.

Carough, still yelling, finally flung his blow horn aside and dove off the ramp. For a moment he was lost in the

chop. Then his head and shoulders appeared, and he
wildly swam after the cable. He reached it and, tugging
and backing, took it to the Saran. Grappling with its
weight, sliding and slipping on the capsule hull, he and
the diver got it cinched up. The cable went taut.

Five crewmen carried the injured sailor up the afterdeck and below to sick bay. Hillar, still kneeling, watched
as the Saran was hoisted out of the water and back to her
pedestal. The blood all over his trousers seeped into the
soaking-wet cloth. As the vehicle was slowly reseated and
chained, he climbed up the ramp and squatted beside it,
surveying the damage. Carough slid down off the Saran
and hunkered down beside him.

"Jesus, skipper," he blurted, gasping for breath, "I'm
sorry. I didn't see that bastard coming in, I just flat didn't
see it."

"It couldn't be helped, Chief. I didn't see it either."

"One of my boys get it?"

"Yeah, a broken leg."

"What about the diver, sir?"

"He's all right." He studied the twisted remains of the
undercarriage and swore.

Carough was shaking his head forlornly. "She took one
helluva crack on that ramp, Coach. Her internal systems
must have been damaged."

Above them, Bonner was now sitting on the rim of the
hatch, trying to see around the curve of the vehicle's hull.

Hillar called up, "How's everybody aboard?"

Cas made the okay sign with his thumb and forefinger.

"All right," Hillar said, standing. "Get a damage report to me as soon as possible."

Jimbo lay quietly in Christine's bed and listened to the
rain and the whispering snore of his companion. He
couldn't remember when the rain had started. The sky
had still held a few stars when he dutifully entered the
rear entrance of the dormitory wing and tapped lightly on
Christine's door. She had opened it stark naked.

While he undressed, he pumped her about any new

developments from the girl in Comm Records. She said there was nothing, but the girl was getting antsy.

"What'd you tell her?"

"Just that I had a stud who liked to be on the inside." She giggled. "In more ways than one."

"Does she know it's me?"

"I think she's got an idea."

"Oh, no."

"Look, you better be glad. If she figured it was some-body on the outside, she wouldn't give me anything."

"Yeah, but pretty soon the whole damned delegation'll know."

"Don't worry about it, hon. Angie likes her side nookie with the best of us. She won't tell anybody."

"Yeah, well—"

"Hurry up, for God's sake."

Chris had bought some coke off a sailor that afternoon and they did a couple lines. Jimbo had done coke a few times at parties. It was all around nowadays, but he hadn't really gotten with it. It always made his heart beat too rapidly and didn't last.

But tonight he was thankful for it. It stoked the fires of his stamina, made him feel like King Kong. He actually stayed up with Christine. In an absurd sort of turnaround he felt pride in that. As he labored, he thought that maybe he'd get his wife to snort a line or two before they had sex. He didn't even feel guilty thinking about her while Christine was beneath him, breathlessly driving him on.

He listened to the rain and felt melancholy. The down slide of the coke was leaving him depressed. That after-noon he had bypassed the late press briefing. He couldn't hack another one, and one of the delegation flunkies had passed out prepared releases. Besides, he had to track down anything he could get his hands on about the freighter's dead crew. He knew that when that bit of news leaked, as it eventually would, the shit was really going to hit the fan. This time he wasn't going be in the dark.

He had turned up very little. The only thing he managed was a verify on the new code assignment concerning Naval Intelligence. He got that from Midway Communications, but Wilcox did the actual radio work. He didn't mention the dead bodies to Wilcox. That would have compromised Christine's girlfriend in Records. Wilcox looked troubled after the conversation with Midway. In fact, he actually got a little pushy with them.

Jimbo watched him. "See, you're starting to pick up on it too, aren't you?"

Wilcox frowned. "Well, they certainly are being awfully evasive here."

"Bingo," Jimbo said.

He glanced over at the luminous hands of Christine's bedside clock. It was 2:34 in the morning. In less than seven hours the President would arrive.

Captain Lapshin, seated in the *Sabir*'s control center, slowly reread the decoded emergency ELF from Cam Ranh Bay. He had been holding his sub in a slow double-eight pattern three hundred miles southeast of the freighter, awaiting orders. Now he had them: SINK IT. Frankly, that puzzled him. The fact that it was directly from General Secretary Markisov astonished him. Yet neither of these emotions showed on his face.

Lapshin turned to Lieutenant Chernov, who was now OOD. "Bring quadrant fifteen up and focus on northwest sector. Stand by to change course."

The control screen flashed on. Lapshin studied it for a few seconds, then snapped orders for a starboard turn and set up for a new bearing of three-five-zero. The *Sabir* heeled slowly.

"Bring up data on derelict."

Statistics began printing across the screen: E-class:5, design-type C-1, 600 gross tons, Liberty designate:::: position coordinates: 160 E/015 S:::: observed depth: 3300 meters:::: drift factor: 2 knots SSW:::: settle rate: 8 meters per minute.

"Calculate present depth."

More numbers riffled. Time 224800Z: EDC: 4500 meters.

Lapshin had a major problem here. The pressure hull of his submarine was stressed red limit of 2,800 meters. The derelict would be nearly 5,000 meters below his maximum stress limit. Moreover, his Mark C 533 wire-guided torpedoes were functional only up to and including a forty-five-degree angle off his sonar hub. Since their running distance was 4,300 meters, the span angle would be beyond maximum hub angle. If he launched far enough from the derelict to lessen that angle to acceptable limits, the distance would be too great and his torpedoes would dissipate their runs before reaching the target.

There was only one thing he could do: send the torpedoes to target using their internal guidance systems. But since the derelict had no heat source for the infrared sensors in the torpedo heads, guidance would have to depend on their tiny sonar units that activated 1,500 meters from the target. These were highly susceptible to interfering signals.

Well, he'd just have to minimize any external sonar disturbance, and give the torpedoes a steady firing position so they would shoot well within the 1,500-meter pickup range.

"Chernov, bring us to a hundred fifty meters. Full ahead, maintaining bearing three-five-zero. Torpedo room, pull torpedoes one and three and rig for internal sonar guidance. Call up when complete."

He settled back into his chair. . . .

Three hours later, the *Sabir* crossed the hundred-kilometer point from the derelict's estimated position. Lapshin had remained in the control center since the course change.

"Give me maximum magnification of quadrant fifteen and northwest sector."

The screen jumped through magnifications until the screen showed 1:10,000 reading. The computer estimate, he saw, placed the derelict now well within the Murchison Trench.

"Superimpose Murchison topography."

A few seconds elapsed and then the bottom contour lines came on beneath the quadrant-fifteen picture. The Trench formed a six hundred-kilometer curve in the bottom of the Coral Sea. Its width varied from two kilometers at the uppermost end to nearly a hundred kilometers at the southern tip. The derelict's blip showed her at a point sixty kilometers wide, nearly midway between the Trench walls.

The *Sabir* herself was already over the Trench along the southern curve. Lapshin mentally projected his maneuvers. They would soon be within range of the surface ship's sonar, and the ASW aircraft that had tracked them earlier could still be in the area. To play it safe, he decided to go deep into the Trench now, then come in slowly until he had a hard fix on the derelict. With the Trench walls and possible thermoclines disturbing sonar probes from the surface, he might slip in without being detected.

"Come to bearing two-nine-five."

Chernov repeated.

"Helm coming to bearing two-nine-five . . . fix."

"Down planes fifteen degrees and go to two-thirds."

"Planes down fifteen degrees, holding."

"Two-thirds."

The *Sabir* tilted slightly forward. A few seconds later, soft pops began through her hull.

"Stabilize and maintain rate of descent. Give me depth increments of fifty meters."

In the right-hand corner of the main screen a blinking set of numbers appeared: DRO-15DD: 200 ms. Lapshin's gaze fixed on the sets as they changed. He listened to the creaks and pops of his submarine's hull as she dived into the Murchison Trench, going in for the kill.

Fifteen

11 hours, 59 minutes

At 4:50 A.M., Hawaiian time, the President reached over to turn off his traveling alarm clock. It was set for five sharp, but it was his habit to awaken before it chimed. In the ten years he had owned it, he'd never heard the chime.

He lay for a moment, inhaling the unfamiliar scent of tropical flowers and ocean that wafted through the open bedroom window. There was a soft knock on the door.

"Five A.M., Mr. President."

"Yes, thank you."

At 5:23 he walked downstairs, accompanied by his two security men. As he ate, Admiral Prudoe, in starched whites, gave him updates on the Russian situation.

"It's beginning to look quite ominous, sir. Russian mobilization is increasing rapidly."

"Has its nature changed?"

"Joint Chiefs still maintains no." He frowned. "Except for one incident. One of our attack subs tracked a Russian Typhoon under the Antarctic ice pack. A standoff developed, which our boys finally broke off. Apparently it was very close for a while. Our sub commander believes the Russian was searching for an open stretch of water within the pack. These are excellent sites for ICBM launch."

The President looked at him. "What do you think?"

"Well, the Russians do have regular under-ice runs, much more often than we do. The only thing about this one was the Russian commander's aggressiveness and the fact that the Ross Sea is not a normal Typhoon patrol zone." He paused for a moment before delivering his recommendation. "Sir, I must again suggest that you postpone this trip. Things are becoming unpredictable and, frankly, potentially quite hazardous to you. We consider the— "

The President held up his hand. "My decision on that is irreversible, Admiral. Please continue with your report."

"Yes, sir," Prudoe said.

At 6:23 *Air Force One* took off. Below, the green ridges of the Koolau Range dropped away, and then they were over ocean. In less than six hours the President would arrive on Guadalcanal.

Napah stood in the rain and wind, looking with disbelief at the damaged undercarriage of the Saran. *Wow, a close one.* She'd been horrified when the submersible was lifted by the huge wave and slammed against the ramp. She had been lying near the port window, and the ramp had just come up at her. They hit with the jarring finality of a car accident. When she felt the Saran heeling and sliding backward, she thought for sure they were going down into the Trench. Six miles of straight-down blackness.

The lights flickered but stayed on. She shot a look at Bonner. He was gripping a panel bracket, cursing steadily. She looked at Chaffee. He sat there, not even holding on, just this diabolic grin on his face.

When the Saran was safely mounted on her pedestal, Napah relaxed. The sense of relief was so intense it was as if she had finally peed after a long, agonizing wait. Then it occurred to her she'd have to go through the whole thing again soon. She lashed out with a few choice obscenities of her own, and was surprised at her vehemence. Her voice was quavering with fear.

The after loudspeaker blared above the wind. "Will the captain please come to the sonar room."

Hillar hissed, "Now what?" He started forward, then stopped and looked back at Napah. He jerked his head for her to follow.

The young sonarman, a skinny kid with a ripe pimple on his chin, was studying his screens when they came in. "Coach, I can't figure this out. I was scanning and I picked up what looks like a deep target. But it's all diffused, lots of wash."

On the screen, the light arm was picking up confused, bouncing flares off something south of the *Voorhees*. Cross threads of light flicked and ran crazy. Hillar studied the screen for several seconds, then glanced at Napah. "What do you think?"

She lifted her eyebrows. "Your Russky submarine's back."

"Damn!" Hillar said hotly. The sonarman stared openmouthed at her.

"What's your probe range?" she asked him.

"Ten miles normal."

"He's much farther out. You're getting bounce off the Trench walls and they're merging with his probes."

"Is he coming in?" Hillar asked.

Napah didn't answer immediately. She watched the light arm go through four revolutions and noted the slight movement across the grid lines.

"Yeah, and he's real deep, down under a thermocline." To the sonarman she said, "How tight can you beam your probe?"

"Down to four degrees aperture."

"Tighten it all the way and put on full power."

The young sailor looked at Hillar.

"Do it," he snapped.

The sonarman threw two switches, tuned a dial. The light arm came around. The flare was gone.

"Bring up your TPO map."

The sonarman did it. Napah examined it, taking particular note of the *Voorhees'* position in relation to the summit of the northwest wall of the Trench. "Okay, throw your probe beam at about forty degrees. Then walk it down the wall at five-degree increments."

The sailor complied.

The light arm swung around once, twice, showing nothing. The third time around, it picked up the edge of the flare. By the fifth time the flare had coalesced into solid light. "Hold it at that angle," Napah said. She turned to Hillar. "In that position, your probe impulses are bouncing off the wall, striking the sub, and coming right back along the outgoing impulse angle. It's like a cushion shot in billiards. As long as you adjust laterally and he doesn't make any sudden depth changes, you'll be able to bypass the thermocline zone and hold him."

Hillar stared at her, impressed. Then he tapped the sonarman's head. "Get a range bearing and depth fix."

"Aye, sir."

He leaned around the edge of the door. "Radio, raise the Orion."

"Aye, sir." Thirty seconds later, he reported: "I've got him, Skipper."

Hillar walked back to the bridge. "Put him on overhead." He picked up his mike. "Goldilocks, Mama Bear. We have the wolf again. What is your position?"

Kitchens' voice spluttered through the loudspeaker. "Mama Bear, we are twenty miles northwest your position. We're coming around, over."

"Suggest you patch through our probe signal. We have him locked in. Heavy thermocline interfering with normal pings. We are using Trench wall for cushion shot."

"Roger that. Will begin receiving in sixty seconds. Out."

Kitchens received the news of the returning Delta with a touch of ice prickling up his spine. This Russky dude was getting *too* nosy. Why did they give a flying fuck about a half-sunken freighter?

For the last thirteen boring hours the Orion had been running dog loops, using the *Voorhees* as their hub. When Hillar's call came, Kitchens had been working out estimates of remaining flight time. At present consumption rate he had a little less than two hours left, including the forty-minute trip back to the Canal. He keyed the intercom. "Bobby, you get that?"

"Right, Skipper." Buchanan laughed. "I'll bet old Napah's showing them swabbies how to do it."

"Let me know when you're reading."

"Right."

"Mathias, stand by buoy and Torpex."

"Aye, sir."

Kitchens adjusted his bank slightly until they were level again. The wind shook and rocked the aircraft.

"I've locked Mama bear's signal, Skipper."

"Give me a vector."

"Hold one-six-five degrees. Range to target approximately five-two miles."

"I have it."

He brought the Orion up to the new course.

Deep below them, Captain Lapshin paused in the doorway of the sonar room. "How bad is the scatter off the walls?"

The sonarman lifted one earphone. "The probe signals are collapsing, Comrade Captain. And there's a water anomaly above us. We're getting scatter there too."

Lapshin nodded and continued to the CC. He climbed into his pedestal seat. "Range to target?"

"Range, eleven thousand meters, stationary."

"Hold present speed for two minutes, then go to a third."

"Present speed for one-two-zero seconds, then go to third, aye."

"Depth?"

'Two thousand, five hundred meters."

They were nearing the edge of the *Sabir*'s red-line limit. Well, Lapshin thought, let's push her a little. He knew his ship, knew she could stand more pressure than the engineers with their slide rules called for.

"Dive planes, down six degrees."

The call was echoed.

"Six degrees, holding."

The *Sabir* moved into deeper water. Once again her hull began popping.

"Call out depth."

"Depth, two thousand, six hundred meters."

"Coming up on one-two-zero seconds," another voice called out. "Steadying . . . fix. Going to one-third."

"Depth, two thousand, eight hundred meters."

Gently the *Sabir* slowed.

"Range to target?"

"Range, ten thousand, three hundred meters."

"Fire control, set torpedo guidance for fifteen-hundred-meter click-on. Stand by to launch."

"Fifteen-hundred-meter click-on, standing by."

"Depth, two thousand, nine hundred meters."

The hull pops were sharp now, echoing through the compartments.

"Level out and maintain one-third." Lapshin's eyes narrowed as he watched the blips on his screen. "Range to target?"

"Range, eight thousand, nine hundred meters."

"Fire control, enter firing data for resolution lock-on. Range to target?"

"Range, eight thousand, four hundred meters."

"All stop."

The OOD called the order. The *Sabir* went dead in the water.

"Conn," Fire Control called. "Range eight thousand, three hundred meters, elevation angle at maximum depression. We have lock-on."

"Prepare to fire."

"Flooding tubes." A moment later: "Outer doors open, tubes flooded and set."

"Fire one."

"Firing one." The *Sabir* trembled slightly as the first torpedo was hurled out of her in an explosion of compressed air.

"Fire two."

"Firing two."

Again the submarine shook as her second torpedo rocketed into the waters of the Murchison Trench.

Kitchens and Klinch had just picked up the misty lights of the *Voorhees* in the darkness when their earphones crackled with Buchanan's startled bellow.

"Holy shit! The bastard's flooding his tubes!"

Kitchens' blood coagulated. He and Klinch shot each other stunned looks.

"He's going after the freighter," Buchanan yelled again.

Kitchens keyed his radio. *I knew it*, he kept thinking, *I knew it*. "Mama Bear, do you read?"

Hillar's voice came back clean. "Goldilocks, go ahead."

"Wolf is baring his teeth and about to bite. I repeat, Wolf going after the freighter."

Hillar was stunned into silence. Finally he said, "You must prevent."

"Negative, he's too deep."

"I repeat, you *must* prevent. We are riding blue lightning by Kleenex. Do you understand? Blue lightning by Kleenex. The freighter must not be touched."

Kitchens blinked, twice. He swiveled and looked into the startled eyes of Wally Klinch. Hillar had just used Navy slang: riding blue lightning meant a nuclear-armed vessel. Kleenex referred to a white-paper directive, a direct order from the President of the United States.

He keyed: "Are you, for chrissake, saying what I think you're saying?"

"You must stop attack. Blue lightning by Kleenex."

Buchanan cut in. "Skipper, he's launched. One fish in the water and running."

Hillar said, "Goldilocks, do—you—understand?"

"Second fish in water and running."

Through the windshield the *Voorhees*' lights were closing rapidly.

Kitchens clicked off the radio and went to intercom. "Bobby, give me range to target." Kitchens' brain was running at high throttle. The freighter was down deep, too deep for a straight run from Ivan. That meant he'd have to go to torpedo internal guidance.

"Mathias, stand by to deploy fuzz ball." The fuzz ball was a compact but powerful sonar transducer that threw out a constant stream of violent acoustic bursts which automatically ranged through a fan of frequencies. It was designed to smear a torpedo's probes to target.

"Crack bay door," he barked.

"Running down." A second later. "Bay open."

"I have him, Skipper," Buchanan called up. "He's deep as hell and we're running into a thermocline."

"Take over launch."

"Got it. Maintain same heading."

Kitchens gripped the control wheel with both hands. The night blew rain onto his windshield as he listened to Buchanan's relays to Mathias.

"Set vane trigger to six thousand feet." That setting would allow the fuzz ball to drop straight through the water and below the thermocline before deploying its deceleration vanes and activating the transducer.

"Trigger set, bay open and clear."

"Steady. Counting: twenty seconds . . . fifteen . . . Skipper, drop fifty feet."

Kitchens adjusted the power levers.

"That's it. Eight seconds . . ."

Kitchens was furiously calculating again. The fuzz ball might stop Ivan's torpedoes this time. Then what? He knew what the Russian commander would do on the second try. Move in close enough and deep enough so he could use his wire guidance on the next two torpedoes. His ship's computer filters would wash out the acoustic fan from another fuzz ball.

White-paper directive . . .

That left him only one option. The thought of it turned Kitchens' insides to a boiling caldron.

White-paper directive . . .

"Son of a *bitch*," he cried.

Buchanan: ". . . three, two, one. Let her go."

"Fuzz ball away."

Kitchens pulled back hard on the control wheel and poured on the power. The Orion lifted away from the ocean.

Napah could feel the air conditioner blowing icily across her wet flight suit. The cold went into her bones. The only sound in the sonar room was the soft pinging of the audible panel. The tiny bursts of sound were wrapped in wavering impulses. Deeper down was a slighter, hissing sound.

Hillar was standing just outside the door, still on the bridge. His mike cord was stretched all the way from the radio console on the starboard panel. His head was cocked to listen.

For a moment of razor-sharp terror she envisioned the *Panjang*'s missiles going up when the torpedoes hit. One mind-boggling explosion. Everything, herself somewhere in the center of it all, vaporizing in the blink of an eye.

"Oh, man," the young sonarman cried excitedly. "I'm getting high-speed screws now, skipper. That sucker's really gone and done it."

"Can you follow range?" Hillar yelled.

"It's real faint, sir."

Napah was staring at the visual readout screen. The fix on the Russian sub was still coming in clear and defined. But the torpedoes were lost, creating furry smears under the swinging arm. Suddenly the screen went crazy with lines and vivid bursts of light. The sonarman gave a pained yelp and tore off his earphones. A violent fusillade of static blew through the audio.

Napah jumped and Hillar thrust his head around the door.

"What the hell is that?" he cried.

The rush of static slowly faded, then came up again powerfully. Then down, up, down. The sonarman turned down the volume and gingerly replaced his earphones.

"The Orion's dropped something," Napah said. "Probably some sort of high-intensity acoustic unit. It's ranging through frequencies."

"Yeah, that's it. He's trying to disorient the torpedoes' sonar." Hillar put his chin on his chest, breathing softly: "Come on, do it. *Do* it."

Napah stood very still. All her senses had suddenly come alive, like the first time she had done acid: she had thought she could hear the wash of a butterfly's wing. Over the softened static of the audio she could hear the rain still lashing the bridge window, the clank and sizzle of acetylene torches working aft, the soft creak of the *Voorhees'* hull.

Hillar's voice broke into it. "Anybody here know the speed of a Russian torpedo?"

Someone from the bridge said, "Our Mark Forty-eights run forty-five knots, I think."

Napah tried to mentally figure the running time, starting from the sub's fix point and using the Mark Forty-eight's speed. She came up with an approximate four and a half minutes. She glanced at the chronometer over the console panel. How long had it been since launch? Two minutes? Three? She couldn't tell. In any case, the torpedoes were no more than two minutes from the *Panjang*.

She glanced around. Everybody was frozen in place. Unconsciously her hand gripped a panel stanchion.

One minute clicked off the chronometer.

Napah had a completely illogical memory surge. Once on a flight from Fairbanks a young girl had gone into violent labor in the lounge of the Vancouver airport. Everybody freaked. Finally two men got the girl down on a couch and Napah timed contractions. She remembered staring at the girl's distended belly and thinking with horror that any minute the baby would come out. Was that like now?

She came to and found herself staring at the chronometer. Another minute had gone by.

Beside her Hillar relaxed a little. He looked at her ~efully.

Two seconds later the bridge loudspeaker blared: "Mama Bear, Goldilocks. Cancel two fish."

Lapshin had seen the effect of the fuzz balls on his monitors three seconds before Sonar called up. "Conn, we are picking up high-intensity acoustic bursts. Source believed to be electron-magnetic interference canister."

The captain's face showed nothing, but inwardly he smiled quietly. So, the American ASW aircraft *was* there. He marveled at how accurately the canister had been placed. Good flight crew. They had undoubtedly just robbed him of two torpedoes.

He felt an unmistakable lift that came from the challenge of the aircraft's presence. Until now he had felt cheated in sinking a ship that was already sunk. No resistance, no counterreaction. Now that was changed. Now he had an opponent.

For the next three minutes he listened to the fire-control officer calling out the torpedo runs. They headed straight and clean until they passed the fifteen-hundred-meter boundary and went to internal guidance. Divergence from the zero-line trajectory started almost instantly in number-one torpedo. It began falling off to the right. By the time it reached the target, it was two hundred meters to starboard.

Number two seemed to be holding to the trajectory line, but apparently that was not true. At this distance the return pings from the *Sabir*'s probes were too close to show a minute drop angle. It eventually crossed directly beneath the derelict. Like the first, it went harmlessly past and out into open water until the run dissipated and it sank to the bottom.

The OOD swore softly.

Lapshin sat forward. "Go to a third. Five degrees down planes."

"Going to a third, five degrees down planes, aye."

The *Sabir* once more began a slow dive. Soft, riffling pops started.

"Call depth."

"Depth, three thousand, one hundred meters."

'Give me five more degrees down plane."

"Five degrees down plane, aye."

The popping increased sharply as the submarine's outer hull responded to the rapidly increasing pressure. Lapshin sat motionless. The solution was simple. And dangerous. He would dive far enough to come within the limits of his sonar hub angle. From that position he could utilize normal torpedo-wire guidance. They would be homed directly through the *Sabir's* fire-control computer.

"Fire control, prepare torpedoes four and six for firing. Normal wire-guidance run."

The order was acknowledged.

"Depth, three thousand, five hundred meters."

A sly thought entered Lapshin's mind. Why not show the American precisely what he was going to do? Let him see how helpless he would be in stopping the next run.

"Flood tubes," he said.

Crewmen in the center exchanged puzzled glances. Their captain was deliberately altering normal firing sequence. Flooding of the tubes usually came after platform position had been reached and there was a lock-on solution to target.

"Flooding tubes." There was a rushing sound. "Outer doors open, tubes flooded and set."

"Depth, three thousand, seven hundred meters." The popping was now like small-arms fire throughout the ship.

"Range to target?"

"Range, seven thousand, eight hundred meters."

"Angle of maximum trajectory?"

"ATT coming up on four-six degrees."

Just a little deeper, Lapshin thought.

When Buchanan heard the Russian flooding his tubes again, he was puzzled. His tactical plot of the submarine showed that it was still in dive configuration. Like Kitchens, he was sure the Russian commander would put his next shot at the *Panjang* from a stable platform deep enough to use wire guidance. Then why was he breaking firing sequence?

"Skipper, he's flooding tubes again. I can't figure it, he's not into firing position yet."

Kitchens acknowledged the news with a nod. It was as if he had already heard Buchanan saying it minutes ago. From the moment they pulled away from the ocean after deploying the acoustic canister, he had been warring with himself, looking at hard decisions he would have to make. It was one bad-ass situation, no doubt about it. And he was right in the center of it. He could almost feel himself up to his armpits in its quicksand.

Under the rules of engagement, he could not fire at an enemy until fired upon. Philosophically, he had always considered it a posture that garnered enormous liability. In a dark alley, the dude who waited to get hit usually got the crap beat out of him.

Had the Russians fired on American property? No, the *Panjang* was not really American property anymore. It was a sunken ship in international waters. In the act of sinking, it had defaced itself, had become a chunk of metal.

But there was the override: Blue lightning by Kleenex.

With that clipped on, everything else went out the door. A direct order from the President: "*Protect that ship.*"

There was nothing else he could do.

"Mathias, rig a Mark Forty-eight and stand by for launch instructions." He spoke it quickly lest the words catch in his throat.

There was stone silence through the intercom.

"Goddammit, Mathias. Acknowledge."

"Aye, sir, rigging torpedo for launch."

"Sonar, give me bearing and range. Prepare for firing solution."

"Yes, sir," Buchanan came right back.

He was aware of Klinch's stare. "Heads up, Lieutenant," he snapped without turning.

"Yes, sir."

The rain had stopped momentarily, but the Orion was now flying through air that was moist and heavy. Wind shear jolted them periodically. Slowly he brought them back to the sea.

Buchanan called, "Maintain bearing one-nine-seven. Bring us to launch altitude of sixty feet."

"Roger that."

The crew was slowly coming out of shock. Their responses were automatic, instilled during a thousand dry runs.

Mathias called, "Skipper, torpedo off-locked, wired, and armed."

"Go to automatic-carriage set."

"Automatic-carriage set, aye."

Kitchens flicked on his landing lights. The ocean ahead instantly leapt into view. It was roiling with whitecaps that reflected the light and distorted his perception of height.

"RTT?"

"Coming up to nine miles."

"Solution?"

"Negative, Skipper. I'm still extrapolating off *Voorhees*."

They were receiving a lot of ground effect now. The aircraft leapt and pitched. Yet through the turbulence Kitchens could feel the airflow across the bottom of the fuselage change as Mathias brought down the torpedo carriage just aft the main bay, and he corrected for it, easing on slight power.

"I've got lock-on," Buchanan barked. "Entering data.'

Bobby was now feeding from his computer into the Mark 48's guidance unit located just below the 500-pound warhead of high explosives. Once deployed, the control unit activated, igniting battery-powered motors and adjusting deflection fins to a programmed trajectory line. When the torpedo came within a thousand-yard perimeter of the target, its highly calibrated infrared sensor would take over guidance, steering it directly into the heat created by the submarine's power units.

"Program entered. Torpedo in lock-on, holding."

"Time to launch?"

"Coming up on fifteen seconds. Now."

"I'll take it," Kitchens said. Ordinarily the tactical sonar officer initiated the actual launch, but this time, he knew, the responsibility must be his alone.

His eyes held on the illuminated chronometer directly ahead of him. "Counting: nine, eight . . ."

In his peripheral vision he could see the lights of the *Voorhees* drifting in the darkness. It moved in a slow-motion arc toward his right.

". . . four, three, two, launch."

He felt the torpedo go and the Orion lift as the weight of it was cast off. He shoved full power to the engines, and they soared into the air, the twin beams of the landing lights jabbing into open space. The roar of the engines swept back over him as his heart roared with the realization that he had just committed his country to an act of war.

The Russian sonarman's voice cracked with shock. "Conn, I have high-speed screws, range five thousand meters, bearing zero-one-eight degrees."

Every head in the control center except the captain's jerked up. Someone muttered something. Lapshin stared at the console screen, outwardly unmoved. In his heart he was stunned.

In a calm voice he said, "Give me DID analysis."

"DID identifies signature as Mark Forty-eight torpedo. Angle from surface forty-seven degrees, speed approximately forty-one knots."

In a tiny space of his brain Lapshin thought: The Americans have torpedoes that can deflect beyond our angle range. But the rest of his mind was whirling. "Maximum down on diving planes," he snapped.

The OOD echoed the command. A second later the planes operator shouted, "Planes at maximum, holding."

The *Sabir*'s deck tilted sharply. Lapshin felt his buttocks slide on the pedestal seat. Around him standing crewmen were leaning away from the slant, holding on to stanchions.

"Go to full."

"Going to full, aye."

"Depth?"

"Four thousand, four hundred meters."

The sub's outer pressure hull was groaning audibly amid the scattered poppings of stressed metal as the *Sabir* streaked into deeper water.

"Torpedo range?"

"Four thousand, one hundred meters, holding constant."

"Outside pressure reading."

"Hull pressure eleven thousand pounds per square inch."

Lapshin shuddered inwardly. The only sign of it was a double blink. The *Sabir* was being compressed beneath a pressure of four thousand pounds per square inch beyond her red limit. Every thousand meters doubled it.

Like a billion fingers across her hull surfaces, the pressure searched out weak points: weld lines, butt shears, surface curves and links. It probed her exit hatches, the torpedo ports and deck door for her five SSN-N-9A antiship nonnuclear cruise missiles.

It found one, a tiny strip of metal fatigue in the carbon-steel seal in number-three missile door. As the *Sabir* drove deeper, microscopic air bubbles began to form around the fatigue strip, forced from the metal by the tremendous pressure. Heat buildup by the transference of energy rose rapidly to an explosive level.

At precisely five thousand, two hundred meters, the surrounding steel melted, causing an instantaneous expansion that shattered a portion of the seal as if it were glass. Seawater driven by the pressure blew into the missile-firing chamber, first as a single ribbon, then, as half of the seal ring gave, a massive spray of violently propelled water that instantly sliced through polyethylene stabilizing rings around the seated missile.

The missile was slammed out of its moorings and up against the chamber wall. Water flooded onto the firing block at the base of the chamber, shorting circuits. Three seconds later the explosive propellant charge ignited, and number-three SSN-N-9A lifted off its firing block and into the closed hatch door.

There was a violent explosion as her three hundred pounds of high explosives detonated. A huge portion of the *Sabir*'s forward deck was torn apart. White-hot explosive debris was flung out into the waters of the Murchison.

The first hint Lapshin had that something was extremely wrong was the sound of the water coming through the shattered seal. It was a sound so precise that he knew instantly something on his ship had cracked open. For a millisecond he froze. Someone, his voice seeming far away, yelled. A solid jolt came up through the deck, followed almost instantly by a violent shudder that went through the submarine like a clap of thunder.

Lapshin was thrown from his seat. He landed on the control-center deck on all fours. Directly ahead of his face was the shoe of a crewman. He could actually see the stitches on the sole.

The *Sabir*'s bow had been shoved away from the explosion and this deepened her angle of dive. She was now nearly vertical in the water, her screw still driving. As her forward compartments flooded, she became a weighted missile plunging with full-engine power toward the bottom.

A thousand yards above her, the Mark 48's heat sensor activated. It scanned the water in front of it. The closest heat source was a chunk of bow decking whirling slowly in the water. The sensor fixed on it, activating the screw rudder sharply to the left. Forty-three seconds later it slammed into the chunk and exploded.

In the control center, Lapshin could not regain his feet. The angle of the deck was too severe. He grabbed for a stanchion, missed, and slammed into one of the sonar screens. His face shattered the glass. Blood stung his eyes. Bodies, loose gear, were falling on him. He clawed for something solid, struggling to gain equilibrium. Men were screaming all around him. As more

water flooded into the after compartments, bulkheads
were blowing open with shuddering cracks.

He found a panel bar and pulled himself upright. The
lights went out, plunging the control center into a darkness broken only by the blue lightning of shorting circuits. For one stultifying moment Lapshin knew he and
his ship were going to die. A thought punched into his
mind: a moment of sunshine and green grass and dappled
shade trees near his home on the Reclavich River.

An instant later a wall of water hit him in the chest and
flung him with terrifying force against the after bulkhead.

At twenty-six thousand, two hundred feet the water
broke through the insulated housing of the nuclear reactor and flooded across the superheated coils of the return
system. There was a tremendous explosion and the *E.R.
Sabir* disintegrated in the darkness.

Sixteen

9 hours, 3 minutes

Langenscheidt was now running on pure determination. He hadn't slept for thirty-two hours, yet his body was not tired. The *Greensboro* had gotten to him. It stunk of clandestine operations. He despised clandestine operations.

He and Salter had been burning up telephone lines, trying to find an explanation for the *Greensboro*'s assignment of armament before even leaving the ways. Lew was sure that once they found the link, they'd find the missing Trident. But so far they'd hit walls of ignorance, or at least what sounded like dummy-up ignorance.

In exasperation he finally flung his telephone at the wall. "I tell you, it's gotta be covert," he blurted. "This whole thing stinks of CIA shit."

"I think you're right," Salter agreed. "But what the hell can we do about it?"

"Go to the source. Where in hell's that DO directory?"

Five minutes later he was on the line to CIA headquarters in Langley, Virginia. He asked to speak to the director.

"Director Rebbeck is in Honolulu," a young woman said. "What is the nature of your business?"

"Who's the next-highest man there?"

"Deputy Director Holbrook. What is the nature of your business, please?"

"I'll take that up with him, honey."

"Do you have a security-clearance number?"

"Yeah, I got one." He gave it to her.

"One moment, please." She went off the line. In a moment she returned. "Would you hold, Mr. Langenscheidt?"

Lew glanced at Ray and moved his fist up and down like a man masturbating.

A minute later a man came on the line. His voice was sharp and snappy. "Mr. Langenscheidt. You're with the Bluepine Missile Center, right?"

"Right. Who's this?"

"DDI Holbrook. What is it you want?"

"Information. What do you know about the *Greensboro*?"

"What in hell's the *Greensboro*?"

"A ship that hasn't been launched yet."

"Look, Langenscheidt, I don't know what you're talking about."

"I'm talking about a missing Trident missile assigned to a ship that hasn't even been launched yet."

Holbrook grunted. "What makes you think *we'd* know anything about a Trident missile?"

"Because I'm getting stone walls in tracing it. When I get stone walls, I naturally think of you."

"Bullshit."

"Bullshit it may be, but think about this, Holbrook. Somewhere out there is a nuclear missile and somebody's got the break-in numbers to detonate it."

"What! How do you know that?"

"Because I've got the numbers."

"From where?"

"The Navy."

"And *they* don't know where this missile is?"

"No."

"Jesus Christ!" There was a long pause. "I don't know anything about this."

"Come on, Holbrook, let's stop playing footsy. Do you or don't you have an operation involving this *Greensboro*?"

"Definitely not," Holbrook snapped.

Lew sighed.

"Look, where are you now?"

"Bluepine."

"All right, let me explore this thing. I'll get back to you."

"Do that." He hung up, sat looking out at the cold winter sky. A dark premonition was forming. He could feel it in his belly along with the coffee and the acid.

Twenty minutes later Holbrook called back. "I've got something for you. The *Greensboro* is scheduled to be launched and begin sea trials in sixty days. Her station assignment has already been posted. It's Australia."

"Australia? You mean that will be her patrol area?"

"From what I gather, it's to be her permanent base station."

"I didn't think we had bases in Australia."

"We don't."

"Then what the hell is going on?"

"I don't know."

There was a link here. After a second Lew grabbed it. The *Panjang*, the MSC ship at the end of the missile trace, had been logged to transfer cargo at Rockhampton, Australia. "You know anything about a ship called the *Panjang*?" he asked.

"No, doesn't ring a bell. What's the involvement?"

Lew explained.

Holbrook sucked his tongue thoughtfully. "You know what this sounds like to me?"

"What?"

"You're running into a double command channel. Apparently the Navy's using separate command channels, and neither one knows about the other."

Lew swore.

Holbrook chuckled. "It happens all the time."

"So what do I do?"

"I suggest you trace out one of the lines. All the way. Then establish the tie-in and trace up the other line."

"Yeah, that makes sense."

"Good luck."

"Thanks."

Lew punched down the phone button and swung around.

"Ray, I've got a hunch. Run a trace on the whole consignment of 3A's logged for shipment aboard the *Panjang*. There had to be more than one in the load."

"Will do."

"And who was the one from ND that gave you the trace order last night?"

"Commander Phil Bellwood." Salter checked his telephone log. "Here's his number."

Lew dialed it. On the second ring a man answered.

"Navy Department, Section Fifteen, CPO Fisher."

"Chief, my name's Lew Langenscheidt." He gave his code and security numbers. "Let me talk with Commander Bellwood."

"Would you hold a moment, sir?"

Langenscheidt had to hold for five full minutes. At last the phone clicked. "Commander Bellwood."

Lew identified himself.

"Oh, right," Bellwood said. He had a high, smiling voice. "How's the trace coming? My DH asked me about it this morning."

"It isn't. I need your help."

"Oh? What's the problem now?"

"Where did the original request to locate the 3A come from?"

"We got it through Pearl Harbor Comm. That's all I know."

"Can you trace it to the source?"

"Yeah, I suppose so. I could have something for you in a half-hour or so."

"Good."

Bellwood didn't call back for an hour. In the meantime Lew and Salter tracked down the *Panjang*'s other eleven missiles and their eventual destinations. They were broken into three groups of four missiles each. The first group, including the trace missile, was assigned to the *Greensboro*. The second group was to go to an Ohio-class submarine, USS *Portland*. A check with Norfolk Ships Registry revealed that the *Portland*, like the *Greensboro*, was still under construction.

Lew called Holbrook again. The CIA man dug up the *Portland*'s future duty station. Australia.

Things were beginning to fall into place. The trace on the third missile group clinched it. These 3A's were earmarked for USS *Tempe*, a Poseidon SSBN. Norfolk Registry verified commission date. She was presently on duty station in the North Atlantic, but was scheduled to come into the Norfolk shipyards for refitting in two weeks. Her eventual patrol reassignment was Quadrant Westpac/ designate: Tamarand.

Lew searched through an atlas and, sure enough, there was a Tamarand Estuary in northern Queensland. "We nailed it, baby," he cried triumphantly. "You know what we're looking at here, don't you?"

"Secret base?"

"You better know it."

When Bellwood's call finally came, his news made Lew's chest go hollow.

"I got the trace, Langenscheidt. Request for missile locate was originated by an NI man. A Lieutenant Otis Aspen. He's assigned to security duty for the Guadalcanal Conference."

"What conference?"

"Jesus, don't you read newspapers? There's a summit conference being held at Honiara on the Canal. Heads of state from all over. I think the President's already there."

Lew shot Ray a hot, crazy glance.

Bellwood had more. "Apparently this Lieutenant Aspen found a dog tag with the number sets we gave you. It was on a dead body."

"A what?"

"A corpse. There was some kind of shoot-out on the Canal. Aspen saw this tag on this dead guy and got scared as hell. He's ex-submarine and remembered that they used to use sets like those to run break-in drills aboard ship."

Lew distractedly touched the reverse key on Salter's computer panel. The premonition that had been flitting like a shadow loomed suddenly into the light.

"Who was the dead man?"

"NI's still checking. They're running CIA and FBI files now. They suspect he's a Mideastern terrorist."

"Oh, sweet mother," Langenscheidt whispered.

Markisov's sutures were bleeding again. He could feel the wetness seeping through the bandages and the tiny pinpoints of pain where his skin had been punctured. They had bled a little earlier when he first had arrived at Yoshkar-One, the main underground ABM deployment site located a few hundred yards south of the Kremlin.

One of four such underground complexes ringing Moscow, it contained siloed Galosh ABM-1B's that worked in conjunction with the Try Add guidance and engagement radar systems to protect the military command authorities during a nuclear crisis. It was now Markisov's command post.

For the last hour he had been deluged with incoming reports from field stations, Air Army, Fleet, and TVD commanders coming on line with alert readiness. Throughout the complex there was the heady, heated atmosphere of war fever. Rumors were flying through the corridors.

He probed the soggy dressings. The touch sent a shiver of pain up into his chest. He quietly withdrew to his private bathroom. He laboriously took off his coat and shirt. Blood was already running down into his trousers. He washed himself, closing his eyes tightly as he pressed against the ugly, yellowed puckering of his wound until the blood coagulated and ceased flowing. Then he rebound the wound, dressed, and returned to the command room.

During his time in the bathroom, he reached a decision on a question that had been nagging him ever since Petrov's conference. Brulov had voiced it at the expense of the other ministers' contempt. But Brulov was right: he *must* speak with the President of the United States.

It was an extremely dangerous choice, he knew. The Old Guard would pounce on this like a pack of hunting dogs, accusing him of pleading, even betrayal. Still, it had to be done. The alternative, which he saw rushing headlong all around him, was total disaster.

He punched his intercom. "Erien, come in here, please."

An instant later his chief aide stepped through the door and hurried to his desk. "Sir?"

"I wish to speak personally to the American President," he said slowly. "There is no need for an interpreter or a scramble line. And I want no one else monitoring this conversation."

Erien Trofimov showed no sign of surprise. He nodded. "Yes, Comrade Secretary."

It took seventeen minutes to establish the connection. There was a splay of static and then the President's voice came through, even and clear.

"Hello, General Secretary."

"Mr. President. How are you?"

"Fine. And you?"

"I am fine."

There was a pause, and a wash of static riffled through the phone.

"I am frankly not surprised at your call," the President said. "And I am pleased with it."

"Mr. President, as you must be aware, we are in a very dangerous situation."

"Yes."

"I am hopeful that we can defuse it."

"I deeply share that hope."

"Why have you and your allies concentrated such a large armed force in the Pacific?"

"I assure you it is not deliberate."

"We perceive it as aggressive."

"Forgive me, but your perceptions are incorrect. There is no aggression intended."

"You have a multilateral force also in the mid-Atlantic, and NATO contingents are massing on our satellites' borders."

"Again, let me assure you, General Secretary, these are normal movements. They are totally without aggressive intentions."

Unconsciously Markisov touched his side, instantly sending a shaft of pain down into his stomach. He clenched his teeth. "Perhaps, Mr. President, you are not aware of your military establishment's intentions."

"I do not understand the meaning of that statement."

"Is it possible that you are soon to be a victim of a military coup by your commanders?"

"No, that is not possible," the President came back instantly.

"Anything is possible."

'Not under *our* system of government."

Markisov shifted gently in his chair. The phone felt sticky against his ear. "Are you aware that there is a partially sunken ship off the coast of your destination?"

There was a slight pause. "Yes, I am aware of that."

"Why is it there?"

"The ship was disabled and sank."

"What does it carry?"

"General cargo."

"For your secret base in the Tamarand Estuary?" Markisov asked coldly.

Another pause. "Yes."

Again he shifted. The pain was becoming more powerful. "I find such subterfuge counterproductive to relations between our countries."

"And what of yours in Nicaragua?"

"We are speaking of the Pacific now."

"Yes, yes, we are." The President was silent for a few moments. When he spoke again, his voice was steady. "General Secretary, tell *me* why you have increased your military deployments throughout the world."

"I have already told you. We perceive a general aggressive stance by you and your allies."

"What can I say to you to assure you that we are not formulating aggressive moves against the Soviet nation?"

"Your assurances are very gratifying. Nevertheless, we must act for our own protection."

"But, dear God, think of the possible consequences."

The pain in Markisov's chest and stomach was becoming unbearable. "Yes, Mr. President," he said tightly. "Think of the consequences. And beware."

He hung up.

He sat motionless for a long time, afraid to move. Finally he punched the intercom. "Erien, get the doctor."

Napah, Hillar, and the young sonarman listened to the Russian go to the bottom. They heard the monitor recording the explosions, saw the imprint of the same explosions bursting across the screens. At last Hillar, his face hard, moved out onto the bridge and called the Orion.

Kitchens' voice was subdued. He explained the sequence of the sub's destruction as monitored by the more sophisticated analysis gear aboard the P-3C. The Mark 48 had not struck the Russian. There had been a violent explosion within the submarine while the torpedo was still a thousand yards from her. Apparently its heat sensor had homed on hot debris in the water. The second explosion aboard the sub occurred at twenty-six thousand feet, and the air crew figured the sea had finally reached the reactor's exchange system.

Kitchens went on to say that he was now running infrared scans to see if the sub's nuclear core had gone into meltdown. They were picking up a few scattered hot spots near the bottom from drifting debris, but no drastic change in the radioactive profile. Apparently the nuclear reactor had been blown completely apart.

The Orion continued tracking for the next forty minutes until fuel requirements forced Kitchens to turn back for Guadalcanal. He called down for an update on the Saran and was told diving operations were now tentatively set for 0700 hours. He said he would be back in two and a half hours.

He clicked off, then came right back. "Mama Bear, what do you advise on report procedure?"

Hillar put his head down and rubbed the edge of the mike across his forehead. Finally he keyed: "Suggest keep radio reports to minimum. I will say we observed

Russian submarine in difficulty. In-depth reports can sub-
sequently be filed at end of mission."

Dawn threw a diffused light through the cloud cover,
making the sea look like liquid gray metal. The submersible was almost ready. Carough and his men had rebuilt
the weight rack, torn off the camera-housing brackets,
and reinforced the long scar across the pressure capsule
where it had slammed into the ramp. Onboard, Cas and
Chaffee were nearing the end of circuit and systems
checks.

Hillar came aft with Gilchrist. He stood on the upper
ramp, his hands plunged into the pockets of his windbreaker. Napah had changed into a dry flight suit. She
climbed up onto the Saran and went down the hatchway.
She nodded to the men, her eyes dark and haunted, like
a prisoner staring through barbed wire.

Inside the capsule, the once neat operational state of
her control and monitoring panels was now torn up.
Console boards were exposed, cables had been rerouted
along the overhead, and jerry-rigged wire conduits were
taped together and ran across the deck.

The ocean had calmed somewhat, but Hillar was waiting for full daylight before ordering the launch. To the
southwest the high cloud cover was breaking up into
scud, and beyond it was the deep purple of open sky. It
was seven o'clock before final checks and position fixes
were done. The *Panjang*, which had stabilized earlier,
was now dropping again. Her descent rate was approximately four feet a minute. She was now beyond the
fourteen-thousand-foot level.

Finally Hillar ordered prelaunch operations to begin.
The Saran was sealed. Her holding chains and stay bars
were unhooked, the crane cable affixed. Slowly she was
lifted and swung out beyond the ramp. Everything went
smoothly this time. At 7:58, the submersible slipped below the surface, leaving a lone diver bobbing on the
swell. She began her two-and-a-half-mile fall to the
Panjang.

* * *

Under a steaming shower, Langenscheidt closed his eyes and tried to lay things out. He had four points of reference. One: the missing 3A's last fix was the *Panjang*. Two (assumption): a secret submarine base existed somewhere in the Tamarand Estuary of Australia, to which the *Panjang* was hauling a cargo of missiles. Three: a break-in set that precisely fit the Trident's last entry set had been found on a dead man who was a suspected terrorist. Four: no one seemed to know, or want to tell, where the *Panjang* was.

Solution: find the *Panjang*.

When he returned to Wing Two, in a clean sweatsuit, Salter was making a new pot of coffee. He looked haggard, his eyes bloodshot.

Lew's first act was to call Bellwood. "We've got to find the *Panjang*," he said simply.

"I'll do what I can," Bellwood said. "There's a lot of hush-hush connected with that ship."

"Just do it."

"Right."

His next call was to Holbrook. He quickly summarized Bellwood's news. "Look, your people are supposed to be running ident trace on this dead man. What do you have so far?"

"Hold on a minute." Holbrook was back quickly. "Yeah, he's in the track system now. The FBI has nothing on him. But Interpol thinks there's a chance he could be a Frenchman named Dureau. The other guy they made right off, an Italian named Pellegrino Villachio, a small-time mercenary. Reports indicate he was seen several times with a Frenchman. This Dureau is a jackal, a gun for hire, very elusive. The last sighting of him was in Beirut. Interpol suspects he had some connection with the Black September movement."

Both men fell silent. At last Lew said, "All right, Holbrook, you guys have the moves. Get your people to find the *Panjang*. She's the key."

Holbrook's mind was still ranging. "Lord God, Langenscheidt," he said quietly, terribly awed, "are we looking at an armed Trident on Guadalcanal?"

"I don't know."

"The President's there. Half the world's leaders are there."

"Look, I don't know. We've got to find the *Panjang* to be certain."

Bellwood called sixteen minutes later. "I've found her. She's down in the Coral Sea."

"Down? What do you mean down?"

"She sank."

"How?"

"I don't know. A submersible crew out of Midway has located her and they're diving now to see if they can verify that all her Tridents are still aboard."

So, he thought, somebody else is onto this. Somebody high up.

"When will they know?"

"I'm not sure. For some reason, the reports on the *Panjang* were being channeled through Naval Intelligence. That's why we've been getting so much blackout crap. Hell, I'm still having trouble getting specific details."

"Stay with it."

Lew put the phone down slowly and started pacing around the room. If the submersible crew could verify that all the missiles were aboard, that would be the end of it. Or would it? His instincts told him no.

Bellwood's next call blew the lid off. "This time I've got some bad shit," he said slowly. "The *Panjang*'s entire crew was murdered before the ship went down."

The possibilities in Lew's mind scattered like rats breaking out of a cage. If the crew was murdered, then the killers had access to the Tridents. And if one of those killers had been this Frenchman, Dureau, then he could conceivably have broken into the missile's guidance pod. *And armed her on a time-lapse detonate sequence.*

For a full thirty seconds he was pinioned into voicelessness by the realization of it. Bellwood was saying something. Lew came to and cut him off sharply: "What's the precise position of the *Panjang* relative to the Canal?"

"What?"

"Goddammit, how far from the island is she?"

"I . . . Wait, here it is. Two hundred miles southeast."

"How deep is she?"

"Nobody's sure. One report said she's in some sort of ocean trench at about ten thousand feet."

Lew swung around to Salter. "Ray, run a surface-surge displacement for a 3A detonate in ten thousand feet of seawater, inside a nonspecific chasm configuration."

Salter instantly began inputing data.

"Bellwood, I have to talk directly with this submersible crew. Now."

"That'll be a little rough."

"Can I do it?"

Bellwood was thinking. "Do you have an airfield at Bluepine?"

"Only a heliport."

"The closest heavy-power communications center is Pensacola. That's over two hundred miles from you. A helicopter'd take you a couple of hours."

"Can Pensacola patch through to here?"

"Yeah, I guess they could. But security clearance would take forever."

"Dammit," Lew bellowed. "Goddammit."

"What's the nearest field to you that'll take a jet?"

"I don't know." Frantically Langenscheidt tried to think. "Chattanooga."

"Get there as soon as you can. I'll requisition a TR-4F to pick you up. And I'll start clearing the way at Pensacola."

"Lew?" Salter called over.

"Hold on."

Ray began reeling off energy-displacement figures. "At ten-thousand-foot detonate position, surface disruption would create outsurge displacement somewhere in the neighborhood of sixty meters in height. Depending on the width of the chasm, ranging from one mile to two hundred miles, funneling effect would increase surface outsurge to between two hundred and five hundred meters, with lateral velocity about one hundred ninety knots."

Lord!

Into the phone Lew said, "Get that plane here." A pause. "And, Bellwood, you better start getting people off that goddamned island."

Seventeen

5 hours, 58 minutes

At 9:02 A.M., Guadalcanal time, *Air Force One* entered the downwind leg of Henderson International's traffic pattern. The copilot poked his head in the AC center. "Excuse me, Mr. President. We're approaching the Canal."

"All right, thank you."

The President swung his chair around and clipped on the safety belt. Then he slid the blocking panel over his viewing window and glanced out. Far below was Malaita Island, Guadalcanal's twin. It was covered with spiny mountains clothed in lush, smoky jungle. He watched for a moment, then closed his eyes. Once more he replayed Markisov's conversation in his head.

The call had alarmed him. The fact of it alone was reason for concern, but it was more than that. The tenor of it, Markisov's grimness. A crisis stature.

But what crisis?

The President had been baffled by Markisov's question about a military takeover of the U.S. Surely the Russians knew that in an open society like America's, a clandestine plan of that magnitude could *never* be mounted without detection.

The aircraft began its descent. A faint tremor vibrated up into the President's seat. The tiny movement deflected his concentration from the concrete to the conceptual. Two men, ten thousand miles apart in both space and philosophy, had talked on a phone while millions upon millions of lives depended on what they said. A slight misunderstanding, perhaps a moment of spite, and the world could be launched into conflagration.

Henderson International was a mess. The embargo had created a massive tie-up of commercial and civilian aircraft. Only those with the highest priorities, cleared through the flagship of the American naval force, were being allowed out. Since the embargo had been put into effect, numerous aircraft had landed, most because of ignorance of the restrictions and low fuel. The result was aircraft parked along taxiways, on perimeter roads, even far across the field at abandoned World War Two fighter bunkers. The terminal was packed with crews and passengers, some sleeping on the floors or out in shady spots near the jungle. Others were camping on the beach across Highway 62. Many had gone into Honiara, hoping to find accommodations.

The huge crowd in the terminal had come out at the announcement of the President's arrival. Hundred of people milled along the wooden barriers of the main ramp. Many hooted and booed as the glistening silvery Boeing 747 touched down. A group of dignitaries, including Treleven and Cox, waited at the edge of the ramp. A Navy band in dress whites with leggings and black boots tood beside a Maori dance troupe, the men in loincloths, the women in sarongs and *maile* leis in their hair. Darting, nervous security people were all over. Stretched along the entire southern side of the field were marines in jungle battle dress.

A tall passenger ramp was wheeled up, and the President stepped out, smiling and waving amid the chants and cheers and catcalls, all of which were instantly drowned out by the Navy band, which broke into "Hail to the Chief."

Far across the field, the Navy Orion was parked near an old storage revetment. Kitchens and some of the crew were sitting on the wings, looking through binoculars at the ceremonies. Like everyone else, they had not been able to get clearance and were now shunted into the general lineup. Kitchens had tried getting some pressure put on the tower by Midway. It was useless. The Henderson controllers didn't give a shit who was out on the field. Everybody was going to stay in line and that was that.

Kitchens watched the President step into his Cadillac. For a moment he felt a strange, powerful surge fill him, an inexplicable wash of love and awe. But then the feeling vanished, left only sour, petulant anger. All morning he'd been sunk in silent brooding. His wife called it his "honky mood," since they were always engendered by the small, inevitable collisions between his blackness and the white world in which he lived. The subtle indignities, the snide asides overheard.

From the instant his torpedo had dropped from his aircraft, Kitchens had felt disrupted inside. Although technically he had not killed, he knew he *had* killed. Men had died trying to avoid his thrust. Through the glasses he watched the Cadillac reach the highway. Man, you know what I just did for you? he cried out silently. The only answer he got back was the diamond-sharp glint of sunlight off black metal.

Bellwood was running into frustrating dead ends and clearance verifies all along his chain of command. It was now after six in the evening in Washington. Staff offices had already changed to night-duty personnel. Anticipating the horrendous boondoggle he would have getting evacuation orders cut for the Canal, he opted to shoot for Langenscheidt's jet first.

From his ND RecCon 14 bank he pulled up a list of air bases within an hour's flight time from Chattanooga. The closest was the Naval Reserve Station at Decatur, Alabama. All he found there was a cadre chief and a lieutenant of armaments standing night OD. All pilots were reservists, couldn't get one for at least two hours. The lieutenant suggested he try the Sanference Point Naval

Air Station at Anderson, South Carolina. His RecCon 14 showed a fighter squadron of SF-180's there.

The Sanference Point duty officer said, "Sure, we've got free aircraft. What do you want one for?"

Bellwood explained.

"A civilian ride? Whoa! What's your clearance priority?"

Bellwood gave his department code number.

"Not high enough. We gotta have ND Division O-level to release aircraft. Can you hustle that?"

"I'll try."

Bellwood's tension was reaching the red zone. He had a blistering headache. He knew now he had to divert to the evacuation order, at least get the ball rolling.

Division O, the separate, upper echelon of the Navy, was located in the Pentagon. There he ran into a seemingly endless succession of pass-offs. Over and over he had to explain his purpose. Finally he ended up with a Captain Webster, one of the lower-section officers on the CNO staff.

Bellwood didn't hesitate an instant: "Captain, we've got information that an armed Trident missile might be in or near Guadalcanal."

Webster's voice cracked in reply. "What the hell are you saying?"

"We've traced a nuclear missile to a freighter in the—"

"We?" Webster cut him off. "Who's we?"

"The Bluepine Missile Tracking Center, sir."

"Bluepine? Never heard of it."

"It's a research-and-tracking complex in Tennessee. For God's sake, Captain, we've got to initiate an evacuation of that area."

"Wait a minute. Do you, for Chrissake, know what you're talking about?"

"Yes, I do, sir," Bellwood snapped hotly. "And I also need an O-level authorization for a jet vectored to Chattanooga."

"Why?"

"To get the Bluepine director to Pensacola NAS immediately."

"You're losing me, Commander," Webster said impatiently.

"This man *must* establish radio contact with a submersible crew in the Coral Sea. Pensacola's the nearest high-power communications center."

"Evacuations? Submersible crew? This is absurd. What the hell is your name again?"

"Commander Philip Bellwood. Look," he said slowly, "at this very moment there could be an armed missile within arm's reach of the President. Now, what the hell do you want to do about that?"

He could almost feel the weight of that statement through the phone line. Webster bellowed someone's name. Instantly the phone clicked and another voice came on.

"Sir?"

"Bellwood, you're on taping conference line now. I want you to repeat everything you just told me. Including your service number and security-status code."

Bellwood did. He finished, waited.

"All right, Commander," Webster said. "I'm running a check on this. I'll get back to you. What's your extension?"

He gave it, added, "Sir, what about the aircraft?"

"I'll get back to you." Webster hung up.

While he waited, Bellwood paced around his office, constantly glancing at the clock on the wall. It had now been over an hour since he'd talked with Langenscheidt. Suddenly his desk station computer kicked into life. A trace request was coming through from the Pentagon, checking his credentials and those of the Bluepine complex.

Webster called back in eight minutes. "All right, Bellwood, you check out. I'm going to authorize an aircraft for you. What's your nearest connection?"

"Sanference Point NAS in South Carolina, sir. The duty officer there is holding for me on Green Line."

Webster spoke to someone with him.

"Sir?" Bellwood said. "Can you clear for Langenscheidt into Pensacola?"

"I'll issue a Division Communications priority to Pensacola. That'll get this Langenscheidt access. Now, understand this. From now on, everything is to be transcribed and cleared through us."

"Yes, sir." He paused. "Will you handle the evacuation alert from this point, sir?"

"That's going to take some heavy authority, Bellwood," Webster said. "A damned sight heavier than mine. I'm tracing the CNO now and have already initiated a Status Alert to the Defense Department." Webster was thoughtful for a moment. "I'm going to keep your division in the link-up on this since you've been dealing directly with Bluepine. But everything is now on top-security red level. Clear your division of everyone not on M5 status. Is that understood?"

"Yes, sir."

There was another thoughtful pause. When Webster spoke again, his voice was low and very precise. "You had better be goddamned sure of what you've been saying, Bellwood. Because I'll have your fucking head if you're wrong."

Langenscheidt had flown the Bluepine helicopter, a tiny Schumann 110, from the complex himself. It was now parked on the Chattanooga terminal hangar line. If some screwup developed on Bellwood's jet, Lew intended to take a quick charter to Pensacola.

In the terminal he located the airport manager's office and went in. A pretty blond in a red sweater was sitting at a desk in the outer room talking with a flight steward. Coy smiles, heavy flirting. Lew barged up to the desk.

"I want to see the manager," he snapped.

As the steward looked him up and down, the girl said, "I'm sorry, sir. He's not here at the moment."

"Let me talk with the tower chief."

"For what reason, sir?"

"It's an emergency. A Navy jet is supposed to pick me up here at any moment. I want the tower to clear him in and out without any delays. Override commercial flights if necessary."

"Well, sir, I don't know if—"

Lew leaned across the desk. "Listen, honey, I'm not going to argue with you. Now, get that tower chief on the phone."

The steward laid a hand on Lew's arm. "Hey, pal, let's take it easy."

Lew whirled and viciously knocked his hand away. He shoved a finger into the man's face. "Back off."

The steward blinked. He backed off.

The girl stared daggers at Lew a moment, then snapped up her telephone receiver. She punched a button. "George, this is Sandy. Look, I've got a guy here says a Navy plane's supposed to pick him up. Some kind of emergency." She listened. "That's what he claims." She listened again, then looked at Lew.

"Langenscheidt," he said, anticipating her question.

"Langenscheidt," she said into the phone. She nodded. "Yeah, right." She hung up and said icily, "They'll call you on the PA when your plane gets here. You can wait in the lobby."

He made a circuit of the large terminal, deep in thought, his hands shoved into the pockets of his sheepskin jacket. Under it he still wore his sweatsuit. As he started the second round, he paused at the Southeastern Airlines counter. The plump clerk came over, smiling.

"Yes, sir? May I help you?"

"I want to use your phone."

"The public phones are right along that—"

"Your phone."

The clerk's smile snapped off. She looked at him, then shrugged. "All right."

"I'm at Chattanooga," he said the instant Salter answered. "I'll keep this line open. Things are coming at me and I'll need you to run traces. Any word from Bellwood?"

"Not yet."

He glanced at his watch. "I'll give the jet another fifteen minutes. If it doesn't show by then, I'll go charter or fly the damned Schumann down."

"Right."

"I want you to dig up some hold and frame schematics on this *Panjang*. Or at least a ship of the same class. Interior bulkhead arrangements, hold configurations, all that shit. Try the Library of Congress info line and also the Maritime Museum archives."

"Okay. Shouldn't be too hard. She was a Liberty class."

"And I want a trace on Navy personnel who served on Liberties. Anybody living in or around Pensacola. Go through Bellwood, he'll have faster access to service records."

"Will do."

On his second terminal circuit he stopped at a hot-drink machine, chose cocoa. Holding the cup in both hands, he sat on a bench beside a man dressed in coveralls and a straw hat. He was snoring, his breath heavy with the sour odor of whiskey. Lew stared down into the thick, dark chocolate, and his mind brought up the image of the Trident's circuitry. It all came full-blown. Once more he ran through the unit, following each step of the staging sequences. For each he formulated an intercept action. And with each successive step, the window of disarming it grew narrower, the option range tighter. He reached the final stage, the launch firing. From that point on, for the full eighteen-minute flight time of the missile, it would be on its own, arcing in the sky, its computer free of everything on earth.

"Will Mr. Langenscheidt please go to departure gate 3L immediately," the PA system blared. "Mr. Langenscheidt, please report to departure gate 3L. Your aircraft is now on approach."

At 11:03 P.M., Moscow time, Yuri Markisov again underwent emergency surgery. This time the surgeon was Dr. Dimitri Makaroff, the General Secretary's personal physician. The operation took place in a small dispensary in Yoshkar-One.

The Secretary's internal sutures had worked loose. He was hemorrhaging through the drain tube. His temperature was 105 degrees and his count was loaded with white blood cells, indicating the bacterial infection of the cholecystitis had spread into the abdominal cavity. Makaroff performed a mesentery-wedge resection, then closed off a small ulceration that had perforated the intestinal wall. Closure was completed by 1:13 A.M.

One of Petrov's aides was waiting for the doctor in the corridor. He informed him the marshal wanted to speak to him as soon as the operation was over. Still in his operating gown, Makaroff followed the aide to Markisov's office.

Petrov waited till the aide had closed the door, then turned to Makaroff. "How did it go?"

"The operation was successful," the doctor answered.

"Is he conscious?"

"Of course not."

"When will he be?"

"Not for at least two, three hours."

"Will he be lucid then?"

"Perhaps groggy, but lucid enough." Makaroff studied him closely. "What's going on here? I see things rushing, soldiers running. Why?"

Petrov didn't answer right away. He moved around the desk and sat down. He looked at Makaroff. "We are on the brink of war, Doctor."

Makaroff blanched. His little ferret face seemed to quiver. Then he blurted, "I must get home."

Petrov shook his head slowly. "You'll remain here."

"The other physician can monitor Markisov temporarily. I'll be back in an hour."

"You'll remain here," Petrov repeated.

"But my wife, my—"

Petrov cut him off with a burst of anger. "I don't give a damn about your wife. You—will—remain—here. Now, get the hell out and do your duty."

This time Makaroff could not hold the marshal's eyes. Resignedly he turned and went out. Petrov stared at the door until he had quieted. He punched the intercom.

"Trofimov, in."

A moment later Markisov's aide came in. "Yes, Comrade Marshal?"

"Place a guard on Dr. Makaroff. He's not to leave this area."

Trofimov frowned. "Yes, sir."

"Tell all entrance guards *no* one is to enter or leave this facility without my direct order. All outgoing communications are to be channeled through me."

Trofimov looked anxious. The marshal was usurping authority.

Petrov scrutinized him narrowly. "Trofimov, the General Secretary will come out of anesthesia in an hour. At that time he will be able to command again. For now it is critical that no one outside this facility, *no* one, finds out he is incapacitated."

The young man still looked disturbed, but he nodded. "Yes, Comrade Marshal. I understand."

Petrov glared down at the papers and reports scattered all over the desk, then rose and went into the private bathroom. He found several spots of dried blood on the basin, a bloody tissue under the toilet bowl. He washed his hands slowly, drank some water, and returned to the desk. The small respite had calmed him. He held up his hands. They were steady. He picked up a communiqué from Legnica Army Headquarters and began to read.

Supreme Marshal Sergei Petrov was now in the command seat of the Union of Soviet Socialist Republics.

Eighteen

4 hours, 54 minutes

Inexorably the Saran sank into darkness.

Napah, squeezed between Chaffee's command couch and a bank of bare wires and conduits, felt the ocean enveloping her with a premonitory sense of isolation. She'd never been down this far before. Outside was pressure and blackness so profound it made her think the core of night had overtaken her and would never let her go.

She worked the radio link to the *Voorhees*. Hillar's voice warbled through the layers of water, filled with harmonic distortion. Now and then Napah shot a glance at Chaffee. Shivering in the increasing cold, she was astounded to see him sweating. Droplets like bullets slid down his cheeks and soaked his suit. Yet his orders were clear and curt. He seemed to be in control of himself.

Slightly forward of her, Bonner hunched over his control panel. Once he turned and winked back at her. No smile, no word, just a wink. His face looked grainy in the artificial light, and she grinned nervously at him.

Nearing twelve thousand feet, Chaffee ordered Bonner to run the breach-chamber check. Cas slid his observer's seat aside and moved some gear to get to the hatch. It was a heavy, domed plate sixty inches in diameter, located in the deck forward of the command couch. It had a recessed main dog wheel in the center and six spring

locks fitted to jaw releases around the perimeter. Back
on Midway, Eckart had given Napah her orientation of
the submersible. He had explained the breach chamber
at great length, since it constituted the main mission
purpose of the Saran.

The chamber was part of the vehicle's hull, located
slightly forward of the Saran's vertical center line. It was
three feet deep, double-walled, and made of high-stress
titanium. Embedded within the wall were twenty laser
tubes spaced three inches apart around the circumfer-
ence. Each laser tube, called a klystron, contained a ruby
rod, beveled at both ends. Around the rod was wrapped
a flash tube that, when activated by its own magnesium/
lithium battery pack, saturated the rod with high-frequency
light bursts. The chromium atoms in the ruby's oxide
crystal lattice instantly released photons in phase, forming a needle-thin beam of intense light capable of burning
through several inches of carbon steel.

The entire rod system was angulated on a curved pendulum armature that allowed each klystron beam a three-
inch slice area slightly overriding adjacent beam cuts. It
could thus cut a continuous bead sixty inches around,
with edges as neat as if they had been bore-stamped.

The only glitch to the system, discovered during tank
trials in San Diego, was that a breach could not be made
on a surface tilted more than twenty degrees from horizontal. Beyond that, the pendulum armatures jammed to
the side of the klystron tubes, creating a stitch cut in the
target metal.

Bonner cracked the deck-spring locks, swung the main
dog wheel, and lifted the hatch open. Napah leaned out
to look into the chamber. The sides were brightly polished, resembling the inside shaft of a huge engine cylinder. The acetate smell of seal packing drifted up into the
capsule.

Chaffee started reading his checklist, and Cas inspected
and cleared each item.

"Pressure flooding vents?"

Bonner ran his finger into each of the eight vents

located just below the hatch rim. Through these vents ocean water could be flooded or blown.

"All clean," Cas called.

Chaffee slid a small control panel on an arm swing beside his couch. "I'm activating laser-tube doors." A soft whir came from the chamber as the protective door ring on the bottom of the laser tubes slid back, exposing the beam channels. "Stand clear, blowing."

Two quick bursts of compressed air *shushed* through the laser tubes, clearing them of accumulated dust and condensation. The whir of the door ring sounded again.

"Door locked and clean?"

Cas bent into the chamber. "Locked and clean."

"Bottom plate bolts?"

"Bolts clean, no warpage."

"Disengage ring charges?"

Using a small Phillips screwdriver, Cas unscrewed each of the six explosive-charge locks spaced around the bottom of the chamber and examined them. He then withdrew the out-end shield ring and inspected it for warpage. During the disengage operation these shields would direct the blast energy of the small charges of Nitramon WW outward into the main silicon holding seal, which was the actual cement that held the submersible to the ship's breach point. The small explosions blowing through the seal would destroy its integrity. Outside water pressure would instantly shatter the seal, allowing the Saran to drift free of the breach site.

"Disengage ring charges clean," Cas yelled, his voice made hollow by the chamber. "Connections cohesive, shield rings clear."

Hillar came in with a drop status. "Baby Bear, you've drifted southeast two degrees. Correct with thirty-second thrust to heading three-five-eight."

"Roger that," Napah answered. "Heading three-five-eight degrees, thirty-second thrust."

Chaffee complied, then returned to the checklist. "Main hatch seal?"

Bonner ran his fingers slowly around the rim of the hatch. "Main hatch seal clean."

"Close hatch."

Bonner obeyed.

"Dog down and check main wheel and spring locks."

The hatch made a heavy, soughing sound followed by the chunk of metal on metal. Bonner swung the dog wheel, engaged and locked the springs.

"Hatch dogged and secure."

Chaffee ran a quick panel-circuit check. There were rows of tiny lights on the panel, the upper set for the laser circuit, the lower for the explosive-charge ring. All lights were orange, indicating clear linkage to the M/L battery.

The breach chamber was ready.

Napah hunkered down in her cubbyhole among the wires and conduit lines. She stared, fascinated, at the chamber hatch with its red dog wheel and domed surface. Through it Bonner and Chaffee would enter the *Panjang.* The death ship.

Hillar came back, calling separation distances. They were now at thirteen thousand feet. The *Panjang* lay directly below them, two thousand feet away.

Chaffee hit the strobes. Sharply defined cylinders of luminescence punched out into the darkness. The bottom strobe threw a strut shadow against Bonner's view window. Napah felt her arms erupt with gooseflesh as they continued to drop.

Hillar called, "You're right on top of her. Separation distance eight hundred feet. Advise you slow descent to fifty feet per minute. Correct one degree northwest."

"Roger that."

Chaffee blew ballast. The thruster motor made a tiny hum.

Hillar called, "Separation distance one hundred fifty feet. Adjust descent. You should get visual any minute."

At 10:41 the *Panjang* came into the outer glow of the bottom strobe like the slow fade-in on an outdoor movie screen. It was shockingly huge drifting up out of the solid darkness.

"I've got her visual," Bonner snapped.

Napah fumbled with the mike key. "Mama Bear, we have visual." Her voice betrayed the pounding of her heart. She peered over Bonner's shoulder. They were right on top of the amidship house of the *Panjang*. The glow off her decks intensified as they neared, washing over struts and bulkhead plates like a white rain. The shadow of the boat-deck railing made a checkerboard shimmer off the bridge housing.

Chaffee stabilized ballast, and they hovered ten feet above the main stack. It looked like a cavernous hole that bisected the ship. Napah's temples were throbbing with energy. Her eyes flitted here and there, absorbing every bit of deck gear, stanchion beam, every rivet with its accompanying domed shadow.

"She's listing to starboard slightly," Bonner said. "Looks about ten degrees."

Chaffee worked the stern thrusters. They glided slowly toward the stern. The strobes danced along the after main deck and leapt up as they struck the forward bulkhead of the stern house. Lowering slightly, he brought them ten feet over the after-house deck.

Bonner cursed suddenly. "There's a goddamned chain across the deck."

"Is it fast?" Chaffee barked.

"Wait a minute. No, I don't think so."

"Tell that damned Hillar to shut down his sonar," Chaffee blurted sharply to Napah. "We're going to interior probe."

She relayed. Almost instantly she felt the *Voorhees'* probes disappear inside the capsule. They had been so constant, she hadn't noticed their soft vibrations before.

Bonner clicked on his sonar screen. There was open wash for a moment, then a flare of trembling lights as the *Saran's* rebounds flashed on. The pings bounced around inside the capsule like tiny balls of sound. Napah cocked her ears, reading. The probes were hitting the solid metal of the *Panjang*'s hull.

Chaffee turned up the power. Instantly the pings grew sharper in pitch and closer together. The light dots formed a single thick blob on Bonner's screen. Images began to appear. The probes were following the line of a stanchion within the after house. The readout was as sharp as a negative of a photograph.

"The compartment's clean," Napah shouted. "No flooding." She heard Bonner sigh, and couldn't tell if it was from relief or constituted the first step he was taking to psych himself for what lay ahead.

He glanced at Chaffee. "How the hell do we move that chain?"

"We'll move it."

For the next eight minutes Chaffee maneuvered the Saran with astounding dexterity. His face was pallid, feverish. The strain cut stark lines from his nostrils to the end of his mouth.

Since the Saran had no manipulator arm, the only way he could dislodge the chain was by tilting the submersible enough to scoop it up with one of the forward struts. It was a dangerous maneuver. If the bottom chamber plate collided with the deck too solidly, it could damage the flange and silicon seal. On the other hand, if the tilt was too sharp, the strut might impact hard enough to tear it and the main battery packs away.

Chaffee worked his starboard ballast until the tip of the starboard strut was only a foot from the after-house deck.

Bonner kept calling out directions. "You're eight, seven inches from the chain. Easy, easy . . . You got it," Cas yelled. "Right there. Bring her down."

Chaffee fingered the ballast switch. Too much! The Saran dropped heavily. Metal screeched as the strut struck and then slid along the deck.

"Blow her!" Bonner yelped. "Blow her!"

Chaffee frantically released compressed air into the

ballast tanks. The submersible jettisoned away from the *Panjang*'s deck, pitching crazily.

"Shit," Bonner mumbled, pressed against the view window. A moment later he put his hand up in the air. "It looks okay, no damage on the strut." He glanced over his shoulder at Napah. His eyes were quivering and he was sweating now too.

They drifted in watery space. Chaffee closed his eyes tight and rested his dripping chin on his chest. He remained like that for three, four heartbeats, as if he were summoning something from his intestines. Then he jerked his head back and began working controls again.

They made another run on the chain. They came in slow and easy this time.

Hillar's voice made everybody jump. "Baby Bear, what the hell is your status?"

Angrily Napah keyed: "Not now, dammit."

They closed.

"Okay, you're looking good," Bonner called softly. "Down, down. Go easy. There!"

The soft nudge of strut on decking.

"You've hooked it," Bonner said.

The Saran leapt upward in a burst of ballast. Napah caught a glimpse of the chain looped over the strut arm. In the next moment they collided with the outside vent horn with a crunching thud. The Saran snapped sharply over and Napah let out a squeal. Bonner cursed. Chaffee threw heavy ballast air.

The submersible lifted sluggishly and the vent horn scraped loudly along the bottom of the battery rack and cleared. They went up and away.

Bonner was darting back and forth in front of the viewing window like Ray Charles bobbing to the blues. "It's all right," he said. "No damage and the chain's off."

Hillar came in, "Baby Bear, what the hell is your status? Come back."

Napah looked dumbly at the overhead speaker, the mike forgotten in her hand. She shook herself and keyed: "Mama, we're all right. We've cleared deck for breach."

"Goddammit, keep us advised."

"Yes, yes."

Napah's palms were moist. She shifted her legs, suddenly aware of how cramped her muscles were, and blood tingled in her thighs and calves. She felt exhilarated suddenly, as if she had hooked a fifty-pound salmon. She glanced at Chaffee. The muscle tone in his face was flaccid. The deep reserves he'd been drawing from seemed finally sucked up out of him.

Hillar's voice snapped her head around. "Baby Bear, are you go for breach?"

She looked at Bonner, uncertain. He was staring at Chaffee, his eyes slitted. Chaffee cried in a stifled voice, "Yes. Yes, we're go for breach."

As Cas studied Chaffee, his lips were drawn inward against his teeth. He came to a decision. He swiveled slightly toward Napah and nodded.

She keyed: "Affirmative. We are go for breach."

"Roger that. Keep us tight."

The Saran had drifted off the *Panjang*'s stern and hung over darkness.

"Pull bottom plate bolts," Chaffee croaked.

Bonner swiftly opened the hatch. He bent into the chamber and began unbolting the plate nuts. These bolts held the bottom plate to the underside of the chamber. Before the Saran could settle into a breach position, the plate had to be dropped, done by flooding the chamber with seawater until the internal pressure equaled that of the surrounding water. At that moment the weight of the plate would pull it away, opening the chamber to the sea. Once the submersible settled onto the deck, this water would be pumped out, creating a vacuum. The tremendous outside pressure would then seal the silicon ring to the deck plating.

Cas panted from the exertion of loosening the bolts. As he got each one free, he tossed it over his shoulder up onto the capsule deck. At last they were all out. "Plate bolts all cracked and out."

"Close and dog the hatch."

"Hatched dogged and secure."

There was a hissing inside the chamber as Chaffee let in the seawater. Slowly the rumbling lessened to a soft gurgle as the trapped chamber air fed off through the ballast blow lines. Then even that sound faded. Bonner squinted through the viewing window. "All right, bottom plate's away."

Chaffee's tortured eyes scanned his chamber panel. All indicator lights were now white. He slowly brought the vehicle around. The *Panjang*'s stern, slightly below, came into the lights again. Napah caught a glimpse of the fantail pennant mast. Shreds of the small flag willowed in the drift current. They drifted to within three feet above the after-house deck.

"We've got clear space," Bonner called out. "Hold that vertical position. Ease her down. Slow—slow."

They trembled, slipping downward. The soft hiss of intake valves made tiny bursts of sound as Chaffee delicately fed in water. There was a gentle nudge, and the faint scrape of metal on metal.

The Saran was sitting squarely on the *Panjang*'s after-house deck.

Seen from above, the main conference hall resembled a gigantic wheel set in a ring of lawn. Slightly domed, it had long glass strips radiating from its center that supplied light during daylight sessions and fluorescent illumination at night. The architects had thought to project the feeling of a huge flower opening to the sun. They had instead created a rather large circular bunker.

Inside the vast hall the opening ceremonies had already been gaveled to order by the designated chairman, Tumalai Tataa'wafa, Prime Minister for Fiji. At a long U-shaped table were seated the twenty-four delegates from the island nations and trust territories. At the open end of the U were the heads of the major nations attending the conference. On the south side of the hall was a large glassed-in booth for journalists and television cameras. On the next level up were spectator seats behind bulletproof glass.

CIA Director Rebbeck was standing near the hall's east entrance with the agency's on-site supervisor, Wilt McCoy. They had already made six circuits of the inside of the building, and Rebbeck was pleased. Security seemed tight and well-oiled. Glancing across the parking area and adjacent lawns, he noted groups of plainclothesmen making their rounds. Beyond, marines patrolled.

McCoy's walkie-talkie buzzed. He slipped it from his belt and keyed: "Yes?"

It was his secretary. "There's an overseas SC call for Director Rebbeck, sir."

"What's the PO?"

"D2 at Langley, sir. They've been trying to locate the director for the last hour."

Rebbeck frowned. "What the hell does Holbrook want?"

"You want me to take it, sir?"

Rebbeck thought a moment. "No, you stay here."

Six minutes later he entered McCoy's office. The secretary was waiting for him at the door. "It seems quite urgent, sir," she said. "I've transferred to scramble line already." She led him into a small soundproof room with a desk and a couch. On the desk was a Telcom 7 scramble unit with a phone seat and a key panel below a computer screen.

A red light blinked. Rebbeck picked up the phone. A female voice, hollow and metallic, said: "Overseas unit, SR line, code reference: Brisbane key 19008. Go ahead, please."

There was a pause. Nothing came through the telephone, but the computer screen lit up. Four seconds later words began to flash on it:

HOLBROOK/TT: 6:13 EST/PO LANGLEY, VIR—EO:D1
MESSAGE URGENT REPEAT MESSAGE URGENT
AS FOLLOWS:
HAVE RECEIVED FROM DIRECTOR BLUEPINE MISSILE TRACK-
ING CENTER (CLEAR CHECK) POSSIBILITY ARMED TRIDENT MIS-

SILE ONBOARD SUNKEN FREIGHTER DESIGNATED PANJANG IN
CORAL SEA

Rebbeck's bowels went to mush.

NAVY DEPARTMENT INVOLVED (SPACE) POSSIBLE LINK WITH
INTERNATIONAL ASSASSIN DESIGNATED VIPER AND ASSASSIN
13 IDENT: DUREAU (SPACE) KILLED ON CANAL (SPACE) NAVAL
INTELLIGENCE SUSPECTS LINK TO BREAK-IN OF MISSILE GUI-
DANCE
ADVISE
MESSAGE PAUSE

Rebbeck's mind was whirling like a set of grinding
gears. He stared at the screen. The phone in his hand
suddenly seemed to weigh a great deal. At last he managed to find his voice: "Verification," he cried. "What
the hell verification do you have?"
The screen went blank. A few seconds elapsed.

NAVAL INTELLIGENCE REQUESTED IDENT RUN OF DUREAU
THROUGH LANGLEY FILES (SPACE) ALL INDICATIONS VIA BLUE-
PINE AND NAVY ACCURATE
MESSAGE PAUSE

His heart pounding, Rebbeck began to gather control
of his panic. He pinched the skin of his forehead until it
sent pain into his skull. "There has been no alert here.
Why?"

CANNOT EXPLAIN (SPACE) RECEIVED BLUEPINE INFORMATION
AT 1200 HOURS EST (SPACE) ASSUMED NAVY ALSO NOTIFIED AT
SAME TIME
MESSAGE PAUSE

Questions assailed him. Why hadn't Navy reacted?
Had they retraced and found the situation unfounded?
For a moment he felt a sliver of hope. *Yet they knew of
the* Panjang *and its cargo.*

He pinched his forehead again and closed his eyes. The President, he must get him away. But how? Should he simply barge into the conference and hustle him out? No, that could be disastrous. What if it turned out to be a hoax? But he had to tell the President. Yes, that's it. Let him decide.

"Holbrook, I'm going to tell the President. I can't act on this information alone. The decision for action must be his."

UNDERSTAND AND CONCUR
MESSAGE PAUSE

"Retrack through Navy and find why they haven't reacted. Relay what you find out immediately."

UNDERSTOOD AND WILL COMPLY
MESSAGE END

Rebbeck hung up the phone and stared at it. Then he leapt to the door and flung it open. In the outer office the secretary jerked back, startled.

"Get that goddamned McCoy in here."

Four minutes later McCoy came into the smaller room. Rebbeck whirled on him. "You fucking idiot."

McCoy blanched.

"Was there a murder on this island in the last twenty-four hours?"

McCoy, confused, mumbled, "Yes—yes, sir, there was. Something to do with drugs."

"Drugs!" Rebbeck cried. "Drugs!" Enraged, he paced to the couch and turned. He stared with contempt at McCoy, then seemed to gather himself sufficiently to speak. "Has the President begun his keynote address yet?"

"Yes, sir. About seven minutes ago."

Rebbeck hissed. "Get your men in here."

McCoy went to the door. He spoke quietly to the secretary and came back looking stricken. The three staff agents were there in four minutes. Rebbeck informed them of what Holbrook had said. Everybody looked stunned.

Rebbeck looked at McCoy. "Give me your walkie-talkie." The supervisor handed it over. "You stay here. Holbrook's going to call back on a check with the Navy. I want to know as soon as he does."

"Yes, sir."

"You," he said, pointing at the agents. "I want everything you can find out about this dead Frenchman. His name's Dureau. I want *everything*, here, in thirty minutes."

They nodded grimly and headed for the door.

With one final searing look at McCoy, Rebbeck followed them out and sprinted down the circling corridor.

Pensacola NAS looked like a carnival perched on the dark edge of the ocean. Langenscheidt felt the inertial lift of his intestines as the Navy Corsair dropped out of the sky. He watched the runway come up, luminescent lines converging on a dark horizon. Then there was a jolt, the sharp screech of tires, and they were down.

No one was waiting for him.

The Communications building was perched on the edge of the beach. There were stunted coconut palms and rocks painted white along the entry walk. Inside, a duty chief was sitting behind a counter watching a portable television set. He glanced up as Lew hurried in.

"I'm Lew Langenscheidt," he said. "Somebody's supposed to meet me."

The chief narrowed his eyes. He was dressed in creased whites. "Who?"

"I don't know. *Some*body."

The chief swiveled around and picked up a phone. He scrutinized Lew while he talked. "Jocko, D1 Desk. I got a Lew Langenscheidt here. Says somebody's supposed to meet him."

The chief listened for a moment and put the phone down. "Lieutenant Caravalli's coming down." He turned back to his television.

Lieutenant Caravalli showed up five minutes later, whistling up the corridor. He had a deep tan and sun-bleached hair. He smiled at Lew like a salesman meeting a new client. "Langenscheidt? We been waiting on you," the lieutenant said. "Up here."

Walking back up the corridor, Caravalli asked, "What the hell's all this? We got all kinds of heavy-priority interject on you."

"Have you raised the submersible yet?"

The lieutenant looked at him from under bleached eyebrows. "The what?"

"Never mind," Lew said, and thought: *Oh, shit.* He glanced at his watch. It was 7:31.

They came out into a room as large as a warehouse. Communication units and console banks were scattered around. Dozens of sailors and officers in tropical tans were working. Caravalli led him through a maze of equipment to a side office. Three officers were sitting drinking coffee, watching another television set. One of the officers, a tall, angular commander, lifted his eyes as they came in.

"Sir," Caravalli said, "here's Langenscheidt."

The commander rose and, holding his coffee mug by the bottom, walked around his desk. He didn't offer his hand. "What the hell is going on?" he asked.

"It's too complicated to explain," Lew answered. "It's an emergency. Believe me, it's an emergency."

The other two officers swung around and looked at him. The commander said, "I figured that much." He continued looking at Lew, didn't seem to want to do anything.

"Have you gotten through to the submersible crew?"

"No."

"Why not?"

The commander lowered his eyebrows. It was obvious he didn't like civilians, especially ones who came with heavy priorities to screw up his operation. "First, because we haven't obtained priority overrides for use-access relay through San Diego." He sipped his coffee before going on. "Second, because there's a blanket blackout in the Coral Sea area."

"Can I speak with you in private?"

One of the other officers chuckled and turned back to his television set.

The commander looked annoyed. He put his coffee mug down. "Out here."

They went into another office. The commander leaned against a desk and folded his arms, waiting.

"Commander—" Lew began. He glanced at the name plate on the desk. "Commander Craig, we have—"

"Carr."

"What?"

"My name's Carr. This isn't my office."

"All right, Commander Carr. We've got a potential disaster of horrendous proportions here." Lew explained as quickly as he could.

Carr's expression passed from stolid to frowning to jolted. He unfolded his arms and gripped the desk.

"Now you understand why I have to raise that submersible crew," Lew said.

Carr gritted his teeth. "Why the fuck didn't Navy detail?"

Lew shook his head helplessly.

Carr lunged from the desk. "Come with me."

As they passed the other office, Carr slammed his palm against the door sill. "Lay out here, on the double."

The two officers sprang out of their chairs as if someone had slammed a baseball bat against their backs. All four men sprinted down the lines of consoles, drawing puzzled looks from the working operators. Carr took them to a secondary room filled with radio gear. Five seamen were seated in front of panels, wearing headsets. Carr thumped the nearest one on the head. "What's status at San Diego on the Coral Sea relay?"

"They're still evaluating request, sir."

Carr swung around to one of the officers. "Frank, get on the mainframe line to SD commander. Tell him this is

U5 priority clearance request. Kleenex is involved. We want that southern line opened now!"

Heads jerked up at the mention of Kleenex. Frank hurried off.

Carr went down the line of operators, barking instructions: "You, see if you can pass into the southern line through Panama. You, go through Seattle Section Three. You, link in with satellite through Corpus Christi for vector through Phoenix Station." He turned to the remaining officer. "Jim, get clearance from Norfolk for satellite transmission. U5 priority."

"Right."

Carr pointed to the last two operators. "You both take over traffic transmissions and pass them to Bradenton and Fort Lauderdale. When you're clear, let me know."

The men nodded.

Carr gripped Lew's arm and propelled him out the door and back up the line of consoles. He jostled in close, talking quietly. "Look, if we can make this submersible crew, are you going to be able to defuse that damned thing out there?"

"I think so."

Carr sucked air through his teeth. "Jesus!"

Langenscheidt glanced at his watch. It was 8:31 P.M.

On the Canal, it was now 11:31 A.M.

Twelve minutes before, Chief of Naval Operations Hawkins had pulled his wife's Pontiac onto a quiet residential street in Chrittenden Woods, then up the driveway to his house. Hawkins and his wife, Bernice, had deliberately dawdled through dinner and taken a circuitous route along the Potomac. It was the first time they'd been alone since the notice of his appointment.

Two men stepped from the shadows of the garage, startling Bernice. They were naval officers. Hawkins recognized one as a commander from Captain Webster's staff.

"Admiral Hawkins, sir," the commander said. Both men braced and saluted. "I'm terribly sorry for the intrusion, sir. But Captain Webster wishes to see you. It's extremely urgent."

"What is it, Commander?" Hawkins asked.

"I don't know, sir. But Captain Webster was quite agitated."

"Where is he now?"

"At NO Headquarters, sir."

He sighed. "All right, let me call him."

A minute later he was speaking to Webster. "What the hell's going on, John?" he demanded.

"Sir, we have a very bad situation on our hands. There's a distinct possibility an armed Trident missile is on or near Guadalcanal."

"Good God!" Hawkins's outburst leapt from his mouth. His wife glanced over in alarm. "What the hell are you telling me? Where? How?"

Webster explained. Hawkins listened in staggered silence. Finally there was a pause on the other end. Webster was waiting. Coming out of the tumult of his thoughts, Hawkins managed to say, "Have you put out a code alert to the Canal?"

"Not yet, sir."

"Goddammit, man, why not?"

"Sir, I didn't know what to do. This could be some horrible hoax."

"Have you notified the Joint Chiefs?"

"Yes, a status alert to the Pentagon. No response yet."

"Hit them again. Get Aldrich, Glayshod—roust every goddamned son of a bitch who can make decisions."

"Yes, sir."

"I want whoever you can get on clean conference line when I get there."

"Yes, sir."

Hawkins slammed down the phone and shuddered. "My God, my God."

"Are you all right?" his wife asked.

"What?"

"Are you—"

Hawkins cut her off. "I've got to go to Headquarters."

*   *   *

For the last three hours Marshal Petrov had been drowning in a flood of incoming information: ministry staff reports, reconnaissance updates, air, naval, and army readiness statistics, KGB and GRU communiqués from around the world, including confirmation of the President's arrival on Guadalcanal. Markisov's continued state of sedation had forced Petrov to field all command decisions that couldn't wait. Using the force of the Secretary's office had been heady and exhilarating at first, but soon it grew oppressive. As the hours passed, Petrov's sense of burden increased. He felt more and more hemmed in.

Two section reports that had crossed the desk had been ominous. The first, from Cam Ranh, said no radio contact had been received from the *Sabir* since her acknowledgment of Markisov's order to sink the derelict freighter. ATF 8 headquarters was concerned. Captain Lapshin was known to be extremely meticulous in observing CAE communication transmissions on schedule.

The second report came from a KGB operative planted in the Pentagon. It stated that over the last two hours a sudden increase of activity within the Navy had been noted. All low-security personnel had been shunted to other on-site areas. Also, the Chief of Naval Operations had been called in from his house.

Why the sudden movement within the Navy command? Had something gone awry with the American timetable? Perhaps the detection of the *Sabir* had forced the military conspirators to step up their schedule.

While he was still weighing that, Trofimov came in with a new report from the KGB agent chief in Washington. The staff offices of the Joint Chiefs were showing activity of a frenetic nature. And the Secretary of Defense had just chartered an aircraft in Boston to return to Washington.

The buzzer of his phone sounded and Trofimov picked it up. "Yes?" He listened a moment and glanced up. "The General Secretary has awakened, sir." Without a word Petrov darted through the door and headed down the corridor.

Markisov was lying on a bed in a small room of the dispensary. Dr. Makaroff was standing beside Markisov's bed, talking softly. The Secretary looked pale and drawn. A rubber tube protruded from one nostril. There was an intravenous needle in the wrist leading up to a bottle suspended on a hook. The sheet over his chest looked bulky because of the drain pack.

Makaroff swung around as Petrov came in and gave him a sour look. He said something else to Markisov, then strode past Petrov. "Five minutes," he snapped over his shoulder. "No more."

Petrov nodded and approached the bed. "How do you feel, Comrade Secretary?" he asked.

"I've felt better." Markisov's voice sounded strained, as if it took great effort to pull it from his throat. "How long have I been unconscious?"

"Three hours."

"What has happened?"

Petrov summarized the situation. When he was told about the increased activity in Washington, Markisov's eyes narrowed, but he said nothing. Petrov finished, fell silent.

"Do you think the submarine accomplished its mission?" Markisov asked.

"I don't know, sir. Perhaps. That could explain the activity in the American Navy command."

Markisov rested his head back into the pillow and stared at the ceiling. From somewhere up the corridor the sound of boots came as a squad of seamen who guarded the Yoshkar-One complex marched past on their way to post changes. The Secretary seemed to be listening to the crack of the boots until they faded. Still looking at the ceiling, he said quickly, "We are in a bad place, eh, Petrov?"

"Yes, sir."

"Have one of the corpsmen fetch my uniform."

Petrov's face opened with shock. "Comrade Secretary, you can't leave your bed."

"Call him."

Petrov hesitated, then turned and started for the door. At that moment Makaroff came in. "Good God!" he cried as he saw Markisov trying to rise, pulling the tubes attached to him. He rushed past Petrov and began trying to restrain the Secretary.

"Get out, Dimitri," Markisov growled.

"No! You can't do this."

"I said, get out." His eyes blazed at the physician. After a moment Makaroff backed away helplessly.

Petrov came forward. "Comrade, this is too dangerous for you. We can convene here."

Markisov viciously pulled the tube from his nostril. It must have been painful. He grimaced for a moment, then blinked several times and looked up at Petrov. "Would you have me send my country into war lying flat on my back?" he asked quietly.

Petrov felt the words go into him like pellets of ice. He shook his head. "No, Comrade Secretary."

"Then get the corpsman."

"Yes, sir."

Nineteen

2 hours, 43 minutes

The Saran's lasers cut through the *Panjang*'s deck plating in thirteen seconds. As the first blow-through cleared, there was a high-pitched hiss from the chamber as the vacuum began sucking air from the after house through the bead cut. As the cut was completed, the lasers shut down automatically. Bonner pressed his ear against the hatch. The hissing sound was deepening. Cas swung around and yelled at Chaffee. "Blow pressure, dammit. The cut will jam up in the chamber."

Chaffee moved as if in a trance. His thumb threw the ballast-intake switch. There was a countering whoosh as air began feeding into the chamber. Three seconds later the cut plate fell into the deckhouse with a slamming jolt that echoed through the capsule.

"Switch off," Cas said, and began whirling the dog wheel one-handed, the other flipping claws off the spring locks. "Napah, bring up the welding pack."

This pack contained oxygen and acetylene cylinders, each with a pressure regulator attached. A welding kit was strapped to the pack harness, and in it were goggles, gloves, a fire striker, torch handle and cutting nozzles, and the coiled siamese feed hoses. A flashlight and a small walkie-talkie were stuck to the oxygen tank with magnetized strips.

Napah laid it on the capsule deck as Cas threw the last

spring lock. He lifted the hatch. There was a soft sucking as the ring seal parted. The acrid stink of scorched metal fumed up out of the breach chamber. Just behind it came the fetid smell of the *Panjang*, of damp rust and cold steel.

Bonner flashed a light down through the hatch. The deck of the after house was about seven feet below. The cut plate lay on the deck, its edges smoking in the frigid air.

As Chaffee grunted, they glanced back at him. He was unbuckling his couch harness, staring straight ahead. He looked like a man straining to see a bullet rushing to kill him.

"No," Bonner hissed. "I do this alone."

Chaffee stopped working on the buckle. He peered out beneath his eyebrows like a horned animal about to hook. Slowly he sank back onto the couch.

Bonner gripped Napah's arm. He didn't say anything, just stared hard at her. The stony stare conveyed a silent warning.

Then he lifted himself and in one smooth, pivoting motion put his legs down into the chamber and dropped through. His jogging shoes slapped on the deck. Napah looked down and then lowered the welding pack.

An instant later Bonner disappeared into the dark catacombs of the *Panjang*.

The instant Rebbeck saw the naval officer charge through the front entrance of the hall, he knew the whole thing had broken open. The man ran in like a bull entering a ring.

Rebbeck had been halfway around the perimeter walkway, his eyes fixed on the President, when he heard the slight commotion near the door. At this point he hadn't even thought about his own death, only his disgrace and failure.

He stopped instantly and turned back toward the entrance. He must stop the officer. No one could tell the President but himself. In that act lay the vague promise of expiation, perhaps even forgiveness.

As the Navy man started down the long stairway to the conference area, he was intercepted by three security men. He began talking earnestly to them. They kept shaking their heads and were firmly moving him back toward the entrance.

A big, slope-shouldered man suddenly swept past Rebbeck. He recognized him as the President's chief of security. He leapt after him and they went racing to the door. By the time they reached it, the three security men had worked the officer out on the landing. He was a husky blond man. His face was very red and excited. He glanced up and saw them coming.

"Jesus, Rice," he yelled. "Will you tell these fools who I am?"

The security chief, huge hands on hips, stopped as he reached the little clot of men. "What's the problem here?" he said slowly.

The three men looked at him. One said, "Who the 'ell are you, mate?"

Rice flipped out a small wallet. The Aussie glared at it, then jerked his head at the officer. "You know this bloke?"

"Yes. He's U.S. Naval Intelligence."

"Well, I don't like the bleedin' way he come in, Rice."

"I'll handle it."

The Aussie looked back at the officer. "You lucky you didn't get your bloody head blown off, mate." He and the other two men went back into the hall.

Rice took hold of the officer's arm and they walked down the stairs. "What the hell's this all about, Aspen?" Rice said.

Aspen began to speak, but saw Rebbeck following. "Who the hell is this man?"

Rice swung his head around. "Stay out of this, Rebbeck,"

He came up, pleading. "You mustn't listen to this officer, Rice. I tell you, I know what he's going to try to do."

"Who the hell *is* this asshole?" Aspen cried.

"CIA," Rice said.

With a growl of disgust Aspen placed his palms against Rebbeck's chest and shoved him viciously. "Get the fuck out of here."

Rebbeck hesitated.

"Go on," Aspen yelled.

Rebbeck backed up the stairs, then moved to the door and stood watching.

Rice and Aspen talked quietly, the officer making feverish gestures. Rice asked him something. Aspen nodded vigorously. A second later they came up the stairs and started for the entrance.

Rebbeck tried to block them. "Not this way," he cried out. "You can't do it this way."

Rice quietly moved him aside and continued on through. Rebbeck stood for a moment, grimacing with anxiety, then hurried after them.

Jimbo Gillespie, standing with Wilcox, had also noticed the sudden entrance of the naval officer. He recognized the blond hair and athletic build of Lieutenant Otis Aspen, one of the NI men attached to the delegation. He watched as the security guards stopped him and then hustled him back out of the hall. He glanced up at the journalists' booth. Several of the correspondents were observing the encounter with binoculars.

As Jimbo turned back, he caught sight of John Rice hurrying around the opposite side of the hall. Without a word to Wilcox, he slipped away and mounted the stairs that led to the booth. The upper landing was blocked with television cables and lights, so he moved up into the spectators' area. Above him the President's voice boomed through loudspeakers bolted to the arch rafters.

By the time he reached the entrance, Rice and Aspen were coming back into the hall with the CIA chief, Rebbeck, right behind them.

Oh, shit, Jimbo thought. Something's up.

He fell in a few yards behind as the three men started around the perimeter walkway. They were stopped for a few seconds by stair guards, then allowed to pass. When Jimbo got to the guards, one held up his hand.

"Let's see your credentials, mate," he said.

Jimbo flipped the lapel of his jacket up, showing his press liaison badge. The Aussie peered at it and he shook his head.

"No newsies up 'ere."

"I'm not a reporter," Jimbo said. "I'm liaison with the American delegation. Look at the seal, for Chrissake."

The Aussie grinned at him. "You got a newsie badge, you're a bleedin' newsie. Now bugger off."

Disgusted, he returned to the inner entrance landing. He paused beside a skinny little man furiously taking pictures of the proceedings. His camera went click—zzzzz, click—zzzz.

The President's voice said, "There is always a point when destiny begins. For the South Pacific, this conference is that point."

Good line, Jimbo thought absently. He glanced at his watch. It was 12:13. The President's speech still had another hour to go.

Suddenly he heard the voice of Christine Shumbacher shouting outside on the landing. "God damn you," she shrieked. "Let me go!" She was struggling to get free of a security guard as Gillespie came out onto the landing.

"You better settle down, sweet thing," the guard said.

"Oh, please."

"Hey, what the hell you doing?"

Christine twisted her head. "Oh, Jimbo. Oh, God, Jimbo."

The second guard stepped in front of him. "Hey, I know this woman," Jimbo said. "She's with the American delegation."

The man holding Christine let her go, shoved her away from him. She stumbled, then hurled herself into Jimbo's arms. He glared over her shoulder at the guard who had been holding her.

"You know her, pal," the man said. "You better get her out of here."

Half-carrying her, he led her down the steps. "Calm down, honey. Hey, it's okay."

She pulled away, looked beseechingly up into his face. "You gotta get me out of here. Oh, please, you gotta get me out of here."

"Calm down, Chris. Jesus, what the hell's the matter?"

"We're going to die. We're all going to die."

The intensity of her hysteria splayed chilling tendrils across his back. "That's crazy talk."

Christine stopped her sobbing long enough to drag in a lungful of air. "There was—there was a red-code alert. They're going to evacuate the President."

Jimbo stiffened. "What?"

"It's true. A Trident missile, it's out there in the ocean."

He gripped her shoulders and shook her violently. "What in Christ are you talking about?"

"It's true. A freighter—it has a missile. Oh, God, it's going to blow up."

Gillespie gasped. The blood drained from his upper body and left an empty hole in his stomach. "Sweet Jesus!" he whispered as he gazed out onto the lawn. The bastards, he thought. That's why the cover-up, the high stone walls. They were hauling nuclear weapons and something went wrong. *Something went wrong.*

Christine was clawing his jacket. "You gotta get me off this island," she whimpered. "You can do it. A plane, you can get me on a plane."

He didn't feel her hands or hear her pleadings. His thoughts were coalescing. The filthy, sneaking, rotten bastards. He whirled around and broke into a run back toward the stairs.

Instantly Christine started after him. "Where are you going?" she screeched. "Where the hell are you going, you son of a bitch?"

Jimbo was vaulting up the steps four at a time.

"Come back, you bastard. What about me?" Christine stopped, crumpled to the ground, sobbing plaintively. "Oh, you goddamned son of a bitch."

Rice paused at the landing behind the curtain and flicked his finger. Instantly four men converged on him.

He snapped whispered orders. The men dispersed; two ran past Aspen, their coats flapping, exposing Uzis in long black holsters.

Rice started around the curtain. Rebbeck stepped in front of him.

"Look," he said desperately. "I know what this is all about. You can't handle it this way. Let *me* speak to the President."

Rice's big hand came up, grabbed Rebbeck's jacket, and literally lifted him aside. He nodded to a man near the lectern platform. "Get this asshole out of here."

The man took Rebbeck's arm and hauled him away, protesting helplessly.

Rice stepped around the edge of the curtain and went up the three steps to the lectern platform. Heads turned as he started across the small space that separated him from the speaker's podium. In the middle of a sentence, the President caught a glimpse of Rice's movement and paused. Everyone at the chairman's table turned about.

"John," the President said, frowning. "What the hell are—"

Rice gripped his arm. "Come with me, sir. Don't ask questions, just move."

"But I—"

"Please, sir. Do as I say." He firmly pulled the President from the podium. Instantly security men from the other end of the curtain stepped up onto the platform, their faces alert, eyes scanning. Treleven and Vasselon had moved forward in their chairs, looking incredulous. Tataa'wafa reached for his gavel. Scotty Cox lunged to his feet.

"What the bloody hell is going on here?" he boomed.

Down in the lower conference area, delegates and aides were gawking. In the silence caused by the sudden cessation of the President's speech, a scattered, confused murmuring was beginning.

Rice and the President reached the edge of the curtain and went down the platform steps. Instantly three men fell in behind. The swiftly moving group crossed the landing and disappeared into the lower corridor.

*   *   *

Gillespie furiously made his way for the journalists'
booth. People were starting to stand, pointing down toward
the conference section. Suddenly the loudspeakers in the
high rafters went silent. Bodies appeared in his peripheral vision, trying to get out of his way. Somebody cursed
at him. He burst into the booth. All the correspondents
were lined in front of the window, gazing fixedly down at
the lectern platform. One of the newsmen glanced back
at him. "Hey, Jimbo, what the hell's happening down
there?"

He planted himself in the center of the booth beside a
taping television camera. The operator jerked his head
from the viewfinder. "Hey, watch it, buddy," he growled.
One of the network commentators whirled away from the
huge glass panel and scooped up a telephone. He stopped
when he saw Gillespie's face.

"You want to know?" Jimbo cried, panting from his run.
Heads snapped around. "You really want to know? Well,
I'm going to tell you. Surprise! You're all going to die."

Correspondents edged back from the window as if a
crazed gunman had just dropped from the ceiling. Somebody said, half joking, "Gillespie's finally freaked."

He ignored him. "You want to know why you're going
to die? Because they lied to you." He jerked his head
toward the south. "Out there, in the ocean. That freighter?
You know what's on that bitch?" His rage had peaked.
He was almost laughing. "A Trident missile out of control. Any second now, that motherfucker's going to blow
us to hell."

Frank Evern wrenched him up and rammed his face
into his. "You're lying, you son of a bitch."

"You think so?" He pulled his arm free, jabbed it in
the direction of the lectern platform. "Then where the
hell is your President?"

Heads swiveled around. There was a sudden stampede
for the door. Jimbo was flung to the side, struck the sill,
and went down. The television camera shunted aside by
the press of bodies rolled across the booth and crashed

through the plate-glass window. A light stand went over, the bulb popping like a pistol shot.

Gillespie, slightly stunned, started to get up. A woman's high heel plunged into his crotch and sent a fiery surge of pain up into his groin. Eyes watering, Jimbo rolled over, clutching himself. A crumpled candy wrapper lay on the floor an inch from his nose. It still held the rich scent of chocolate.

"Oh, shit," he moaned.

Outside in the conference hall, pandemonium erupted.

Rose Treleven had been looking at the journalists' booth when the camera smashed through the viewing window, blowing shards of glass down onto the conference pit. She watched its slow-motion journey in dismay. There was the sharp crack of something exploding. The hall was coming alive with people yelling, chairs falling over, feet echoing hollowly on the platform. What were they saying? Something about a missile.

At that instant an arm encircled her waist and bodily lifted her out of the chair.

"Oh!" she cried softly.

Lips pressed close to her neck. "Sorry, Madam Prime Minister," they said. Very precise, very English. She felt herself being carried across the platform, down stairs and more stairs, and along a corridor smelling of cement. People darted by her, grim faces flashing. The tips of her shoes touched the floor, flew, touched again. A heavy steel door was flung open in front of her. Sunshine and heat battered her with such suddenness after the dark corridor that she saw tiny dancing needles of light for a few seconds. Her bearer took her up an incline of concrete and across a road. She could hear him panting hotly behind her head.

"For God's sake, man," she said quietly. "I can certainly run myself."

"Sorry, Madam Prime Minister."

Out on the lawn behind the hall, her Royal Navy honor guard had formed. Their lieutenant barked an

order as she came up. The seamen instantly enclosed her
in a square, their boots quickstepping heavily on the
grass.

There was a sudden burst of rushing sound. A helicopter's shadow raced across the lawn and hovered. She
glanced up. The flashing blades fanned across the sun. It
settled swiftly onto the grass, and the sailors formed a
circle around it. In the open after bay a seaman in a blue
flight suit reached for her. Her bearer started to lift her
up to the bay.

Above the slow *whomp* of the blades, she heard Scotty's
voice. She turned and saw him plunge through the cor-
don of seaman. She struggled against the lifting arm.
"Put me down," she commanded. "Damn you, man, put
me down."

The man put her gently onto the ground as Cox rushed
up. His forehead was bloody. He gripped her shoulders
and shouted above the sound and rush of wind. "I had to
see you were safe, luv."

"Scotty, what's happening?"

He shook his head in a kind of confused submission.
"It's an American missile. Out there in the ocean somewhere. God, something went horribly wrong. The bloody
thing's armed, could go off any minute."

"Oh, my," she gasped, and felt her skin flush with
cold.

With a powerful sweeping motion Cox lifted her, de-
posited her gently onto the aircraft's deck. He squeezed
her hand. "Good-bye, Rosy, luv."

She refused to release his hand. "What are you saying?
You're coming with me."

"No, Rosy, I'm staying. God forgive me, this is my
fault."

Her protest was cut off by a barked command from the
Navy lieutenant. "Steady, lads, steady. Close ranks and
fore. Don't let them through."

Treleven glanced up, and was jolted to see a mass of
people wildly running from the hall toward the helicopter. She felt Cox's hand pulling away.

"Scotty, please."

He made the thumbs-up sign to the copter crewman. "Get her the bloody hell out of here."

The deck under her trembled violently as the copter's engine roared. The struts started to lift off the grass. The mass of people struck the seamen. The circle buckled but held. A furious, fist-swinging melee broke out.

A huge Melanesian lunged through. In a desperate leap he vaulted into the air. One huge hand clamped onto the starboard strut of the copter.

The small aircraft tilted over sharply, the pilot frantically trying to correct for the sudden off-balance weight. Treleven started to slide out the door. A hand grabbed the collar of her jacket and wrenched her back.

The copter kept pitching and rolling, the movements deepening. Pressed flat to the floor, Rose saw Scotty hurl himself at the man on the strut. He threw his arms around the man's thighs. There was a violent tremble, and then Cox's momentum tore the man's hand from the strut. Down they dropped onto the struggling seamen.

Freed, the helicopter bolted into the air.

In the Marine liaison Quonset, Spangenberg had just returned from lunch with a Portuguese whore in the Slot when he heard the quick *zzzzump* of an Uzi, followed almost instantly by the more solid rap of a .38 Special. With a single lunge he was out of his chair and at the window. From the Quonset's position up the hill Sab saw people fleeing the conference hall.

"Burke."

The sergeant poked his head around the door. "Sir?"

"Call barracks. Somebody's taking fire."

Sab watched the people a moment longer, then dived back to his desk. He wrenched the lower drawer open and took out a holstered Colt .45 on a web belt. He slapped it around his waist, scooped up four extra clips, and jammed them into a leg pocket. He paused in the outer office long enough to ask Burke, "What do they say?"

"The operator said he heard gunfire, but he doesn't know what it is."

"Grab your piece."

He and Burke sprinted around the Quonset and down into a field where heavy construction equipment had been parked. A huge D-8 bulldozer had been moving telephone poles near the fence. It was stopped now, the Melanesian driver up on his cab, looking toward the hall.

They reached the road that circled the outer edge of the complex and crossed it. They could hear people yelling, the screech of automobile tires. A French delegation staff car parked near the rear entrance was the object of a cluster of men and women tearing hysterically at each other.

"Holy shit," Burke panted.

They moved out into one of the quads. A woman in a pretty summer dress lay crumpled at the edge of one of the small access alleys. Sab ran over to her and knelt down. Her chest was crushed; blood seeped through the flower print. She was dead.

Three marines suddenly appeared from around the corner of a building, running hard. The butts of their M16's were braced into the crooks of their arms, and their field gear clinked with the impact of their boots.

"Stand fast there," Spangenberg hollered.

The three troopers halted. They waited, shifting from foot to foot, fuming with energy. One of them was a tall black corporal.

"What the fuck is going on here?" Spangenberg demanded.

"Oh, Jesus, Colonel," the corporal said. "They's a Big T-Waster out in the ocean set to blow."

Big T-Waster. Marine jargon for a Trident nuclear missile. Sab's eyes narrowed. Behind him Burke sucked air. "Where's Captain Carls?"

"I don' know, sir. Lieutenant Newberg said we should see we can find the President and guard him."

"Do it."

"Yes, sir." The three marines ran off.

He watched them go, then turned to Burke. "Go help them, Sergeant."

Burke stared at him. The sergeant's face was blotched from the exertion of their run.

"Go ahead, Burke," he said quietly. "It'll be all right."

"Yes, sir." The sergeant lumbered away.

Spangenberg walked slowly across the quad into an area of fountains and concrete benches under plumeria trees. The blossoms on the grass looked like red and pink confetti. He stopped beside a small pool with *Koi* fish nibbling at the surface. The sounds of panic were distant.

Saigon. During the big pullout, when the forward elements of the NVA were still on the outskirts of the city, Sab had walked alone, in the heart of it. Everything had been locked in the same tense, expectant silence. He'd peered into empty villas, their rooms still reeking of joss sticks and tempura. He wandered the back streets, the *bao* vendors' carts bereft of wares, the tiny wooden benches under the banyans deserted, the alley doors empty where whores had hissed at passersby.

He spotted the padded door of one of the complex lounges and went in. The jukebox was still playing. Merle Haggard. From the back of the bar he chose an unopened quart of Beefeaters gin. He cracked the seal and took a long drink.

Once more outside, he walked through the office complex, drinking as he went. At random he picked a building and went up its elevator. It opened onto a roof terrace with picnic tables and umbrellas. He put his feet up on a table.

He had a panoramic view of Leadbottom Sound. He caught the faint wailing of boatswains' whistles, the deep churn of props. Some of the corvairs and destroyers were already cutting wakes, incongruously huge and white beyond the palms as they skimmed close to the shore. He lit a cigarette and lifted the Beefeaters in grinning salutation. "Well, you terrorist scumbag, you did it."

Twenty

1 hour, 44 minutes

The damp, frigid air turned Bonner's breath to frost, little eddies that drifted through the beam of his light. Two decks below the after house was a large compartment whose curved hull plating formed the stern of the *Panjang*. A huge steel box nearly filled the bottom of the compartment. Cas climbed down on top of it. Thick weld beads ran along the counter seams of the structure's plating. It, like the rest of the compartment, was painted with red lead.

Bonner figured this was the after-shaft bearing housing. He tapped the butt of the flashlight on the housing. It sounded hollow, which meant it wasn't flooded. If he could get into the housing, there would have to be inspection hatches from it into the main shaft tunnel. That would take him all the way to the engine room.

Shaking his hands, which were numb from the cold, he took the walkie-talkie from the oxygen tank and keyed: "Napah, I'm directly below you. I'm going to try to get into the main shaft tunnel."

"All right. Be careful."

He searched all over the bearing house for an inspection door. Shining his light all around, he saw a slight bulge in the forward bulkhead. It went from the housing plate all the way to the ceiling. He picked up the welding pack and went back up the ladder to the tween deck.

Sure enough, there was a small hatch on the forward bulkhead, waist-high, with a dog wheel: an escape trunk.

He swung the dog wheel and pulled the hatch open. A surge of icy air drifted out, smelling of shaft oil. He flashed the light down. The trunk entered the shaft tunnel.

Feeling with his shoes for the grimy rungs of the ladder, he went down. He threw his light beam up the tunnel. It faded out about sixty feet ahead. The tunnel was coated with rust grime and condensation. A cable ran dead center along the top, which Bonner assumed was for an inspection dolly. Unfortunately, the dolly was at the other end of the shaft.

He blew on his hands for a moment, then shouldered into the pack harness and cinched it. Bracing with his hands, he eased his body down until he was straddling the main shaft. The cold oil grime instantly soaked through his flight suit. Hunched over, he started pulling himself forward by planting his palms, then sliding his buttocks up.

It took him sixteen minutes to traverse the one hundred and thirty feet of shaft. His hands and the bottom side of his suit were filthy, and his skin was numb. He reached the inspection dolly, on little canted metal wheels. He climbed onto the dolly and examined the forward bulkhead. Like the after-bearing housing, it had a huge seal on shank posts. There were two inspection hatches, port and starboard. He got the starboard one open and climbed through. The recess was painted with white lead that smelled like fingernail polish. The recess contained four forward inspection hatches, two topside, two below. Cas crawled over and tapped his flashlight on the inside starboard hatch. The rebound was hollow.

He quickly swung the dog and pulled it open. It led into the turbine's foundation space. Directly overhead were the floor plates of the starboard turbine pit. Cas pulled off the weld pack and put it through the hatch, then crawled after it. The space was cramped with conduits and he had to work his way forward slowly.

He reached a grate across a break in the overhead

plating. He ran his fingers along the edge until he found
a hand grip. Bracing, he pushed it up. It was heavy, but
it must have been on counterweights because a foot or so
up, it opened easily and fell back against the side of the
pit with a loud, hollow clank.

Bonner wriggled out and stood on the floor plates.
He'd made the *Panjang*'s engine room.

For the last hour Pensacola Communications had been
frantically trying to punch a patch line through to the
Canal. Yet, despite priority-code pass-throughs, they were
still running into security and regulation stalls. The bot-
tleneck was San Diego, where heavy security meant complicated and time-consuming clearance procedures.

Langenscheidt and Carr haunted the main communications room. Carr's face grew darker and darker. Lew
kept moving about, trying to keep the frustration from
clouding his mind. Carr had, on Lew's request, ordered
one of the computer terminals moved near the door of
the main comm room. Salter had managed to track down
complete blueprints of a Liberty-class ship, and was now
feeding them into the computer's memory bank. He'd
also come up with the identification on the submersible's
mother ship, USS *Claude Voorhees*.

A chief suddenly appeared at Carr's shoulder. "Sir,
there's a couple shore patrolmen at D1 desk. They got an
ex-swabbie says he was told by CNO headquarters to
report to you."

Langenscheidt swung around. "That must be the Liberty man. Get him up here."

Two minutes later a middle-aged man in cutoffs and a
yellow windbreaker boasting LA CHAND AVENUE LANES
came into the main comm room. He was short, beer-
bellied, balding.

Lew met him halfway. "You served on Liberties, right?"

"Yes, sir. Second engineer on sixteen cruises."

"Good, good." Lew pumped his hand furiously. "What's
your name?"

"Jack Shattuck, sir."

"Call me Lew. We're going to be working together for a while." When he introduced him to Carr, Shattuck braced. "Sir."

Carr put his hand on Shattuck's shoulder. "Forget the formalities. We appreciate your coming in."

Langenscheidt pointed to the computer terminal near the door. "Jack, I want you to sit there and study Liberty blueprints. Refamiliarize yourself with every aspect of the ship. Everything. Do it fast, there isn't much time."

Carr turned to the terminal operator. "Get him a chair and stay with him. Bring up whatever he wants."

"Aye, sir."

"Commander Carr," one of the radiomen called from inside, "SD Comm's finally cleared us. They're putting us through."

"About fucking time," Carr mumbled. He and Langenscheidt hurried into the room. "What's the route?"

"Through Pearl and via Midway to the Canal, sir."

"Put it on overhead when you make the Canal."

"Aye, sir."

Another operator leaned away from his radio console. "Commander, Corpus Christi just got verbal command from the CNO himself to clear satellite reposition." He grinned. "I guess the CNO chewed some ass. They're all go."

Carr thought a moment, then shrugged. "What the hell, let's shoot from two directions. All right, go for reposition. Advise CC to focus on Phoenix Station on full TPR status."

"Aye, sir."

They waited, listening intently to the one-sided conversations of the operators. "Commander," the second operator barked. "I'm getting the Phoenix Station signal. Very faint but coming up."

Carr nodded. "All right, when you're on verbal, advise them to stand by."

"Yes, sir."

A minute went by. The first operator said, "I've got NI detachment on the Canal, sir." He flicked a switch.

A speaker blared: "—Bear on special DD Yellow Frequency. Request verification of user clearance for transmission, over."

Carr put his head down, then glanced at Langenscheidt. "Can you believe this shit?" He stood there, thinking.

There was a sudden burst of static from the speaker. Everyone glanced expectantly at it. A guttural cry was followed by a violent expletive, both clothed in circuit feed. Then, clear and agonized, the voice screamed: "Mayday, mayday, Nuclear missile has—"

Silence.

Carr jerked around and stared at Langensheidt. "Jesus Christ, has the thing blown?"

"Oh, my God," Lew said softly.

Everyone froze.

Carr was the first to move. He grabbed the interoffice phone and rammed in the button. "Jim, raise SAC Headquarters in Colorado Springs." His voice was quavering. "Request seismograph verify of nuclear explosion in the Coral Sea."

Cross-talk suddenly erupted through the loudspeaker as operators along the link line were breaking into the transmission:

"This is Midway Comm CVR-3, we have experienced abrupt disconnect from NI unit on Guadalcanal with Mayday call. Running locate, ranging on frequency one-two-zero-point-one."

"CVR-3, CVR-3, this is Compac Comm G1. Do we understand Mayday call has been declared? Explain and advise, over."

San Diego came on: "Compac G1, this is SD CC on M and B status. Do we understand Mayday call has been issued? Designate point of issuance and procedure follow-up. Repeat, designate point of issuance and procedure follow-up, over."

"All stations, CVR-3. We are ranging for reconnect on emergency frequency one-two-zero-point-one. Stand by."

Langenscheidt touched Carr's shoulder. "This naval satellite, is it capable of picking up radiation or flash signals?"

"I don't know." He barked an order to the next panelman in line. "Raise Corpus Christi. Find out if the CorComm can receive radiation or flash signals."

"Yes, sir."

To the operator holding Phoenix Station: "Tell Phoenix to stand by. We are now on emergency red status."

"Aye, sir."

The phone buzzed. Carr wrenched it to his ear. "Go."

"No explosion."

"Are they certain?"

"Affirmative. They've got seismographic stations in the Philippines and Sydney computer-linked with their own machines. Nothing's coming in."

Carr slumped and glanced at Lew. "No detonation."

Lew sucked air through his teeth. Everybody relaxed.

"John?" Jim said. "Listen, we might be in luck here. Have you made the Canal yet?"

"Yes, but something's wrong. We got an abrupt disconnect and a Mayday call came in just before."

"What? What the hell's going on down there?"

"I don't know."

"Look, I explained to Colorado Springs that we've been trying to raise a ship in the Coral Sea. They said we could go through them."

"How?"

"Apparently there's a British meteorological survey satellite in sync orbit over Borneo. They've got a direct link to it through the Aleutians and a seismic tracking station on Mindanao in the Philippines. They said we can use it."

Carr gave a joyous bellow. "What's procedure?"

"They've already alerted the Aleutians and are raising Mindanao."

"All *right*! Tell them to contact the *Voorhees*. If they can't raise, advise them to use code reference Bear."

"Got it."

"Patch through to panel three."

"Right." He was gone.

Carr yelled at the operator who had been calling Corpus Christi: "Belay on CC. Hold open line for transmission from Colorado Springs coming through."

He hung up the phone, grinning at Langenscheidt. "I think we finally got *this* sucker by the short hairs."

Six minutes later the panel-three loudspeaker came on: "Pensacola NAS Comm, this is Colorado Springs MM Division. We have established contact with USS *Voorhees*. You are cleared to full IDO transmission relay now. Stand by."

A second passed, then Hillar's voice came through the speaker. "This is USS *Voorhees*. Receiving clean. Go ahead, over."

With just the slightest tremor in his hand, Langenscheidt took up the jack mike. "*Voorhees*, my name is Lew Langenscheidt. I'm director of the Bluepine Missile Tracking Center in Tennessee. I want you to listen very carefully."

General Secretary Markisov entered the small conference room in Yoshkar-One at 5:06 A.M., Moscow time. He was dressed in the uniform of a field marshal, which was his right as commander-in-chief of all armed forces of the Soviet Union. He moved slowly but with dignity and control. Only his face, terribly pale and drawn, betrayed the pain he was feeling.

The five men seated around the table rose silently. This group composed the inner sanctum of the Soviet nation. In wartime it would be the personal council of the General Secretary on every decision he would have to make.

Markisov settled himself stiffly into his chair and waited for the others to do likewise. Without preamble he began a concise summary of the situation. It included American activity over the last seventy-two hours; the computer analysis of Petrov's staff; status of Soviet readiness; options for action; and closed with the latest reports of intensive activity in the Pentagon.

As a conclusive adjunct he told them that the submarine *Sabir* had not been heard from for over seven hours.

The Americans must have sunk her. This, he went on, constituted both an act of war and an indication that the militarists in America intended to carry through on their plans.

He paused. The others were silent and grim. Markisov's tone had clearly indicated that no comment was expected. He put his hands gently on the table. He stared at them a moment, then began speaking. "As supreme commander of this nation, I am hereby declaring a state of war shall exist between the peoples of the USSR and those of the United States of America."

There was no motion in the room, not even a breath.

"I further order," Markisov went on, "total mobilization of the Soviet nation to conduct this war. Conventional offensive invasion will begin against NATO forces on dawn of this day. All nuclear transoceanic ballistic missiles will be placed on strategic alert, and shall be launched the instant a nuclear detonation is registered in the South Pacific."

The two secretaries had stopped writing and were staring open mouthed at Markisov. Trofimov gently touched their arms. They instantly bent forward and began writing again. Around the table, eyes stared into space or were fixed on fingers or tablets.

The General Secretary resumed. Without notes he went through the entire process of mobilization. Call-up of nine million reservists, to be operational in three days. Implementational orders for increased industrial and agricultural production. Rationing of food supplies and power. The rounding up and imprisonment of all suspected dissidents. He was well into the overall war strategy and force deployments when there was a soft knock on the door. Trofimov instantly leapt to his feet and hurried across the room.

A young major stood in the outer office. He spoke quietly to Trofimov and handed him a sheet of paper. Trofimov closed the door and came quickly to Markisov's side. "Excuse me, General Secretary," he said. "An urgent communiqué has just come in from one of our KGB agents in the Solomons."

The Secretary scanned it. A frown formed on his forehead. He read it again more slowly.

```
URGENT/URGENT
KGB/OPER:TARTAR . . . SITE TT 12:53 (TRANS INDIA)
RE: GUADALCANAL CONFERENCE
MESSAGE FOLLOWS
TOTAL CHAOS IN HONIARA (STOP) NUCLEAR BOMB
DETONATION IN CORAL SEA RUMORED IMMINENT
(STOP) MANY CONFERENCE LEADERS BELIEVED DEAD
OR INJURED (STOP) WHEREABOUTS OF US PRESIDENT
UNKNOWN (DOT)
    WILL SEND FURTHER DETAILS WHEN AVAILABLE
(DOT)
    END OF MESSAGE
```

Markisov lifted his eyes and stared across the table at Marshal Petrov. Then he handed the sheet of paper to the man on his right, Minister of Defense Shukhov. It was read and passed on around the table.

When it completed the circuit, Markisov studied it for a few more seconds, then laid it on the table. "Petrov," he snapped. "You're the military man here. What's your analysis of this development?"

The marshal's eyes glinted. "It would seem that the American plan has misfired. At least temporarily. News of the missile obviously leaked out."

"What is your projection?"

"There could conceivably be an abort to the entire operation. The element of surprise is no longer with them. The President's whereabouts are uncertain. He could be alive. Moreover, the element in their plan which designated that we be blamed for the detonation has been seriously jeopardized."

For the first time one of the other men spoke, Defense Minister Shukhov. "You are assuming that, Comrade Marshal. Our agent did not specify that it was known to be an American nuclear device. Besides, if the American President is alive, he could be powerless."

"All of that is true," Petrov conceded. "But from a strategic standpoint, I think their continuing with the plan would be extremely risky for them."

"But how can we be sure *what* they intend?" Shukhov cried.

"By the detonation," Petrov shot back. "If the nuclear device goes off, it will be the clearest indication that the American militarists feel they have committed themselves too far to pull back."

Heads turned to Markisov. "I agree with Comrade Petrov. The signal of American intentions will be the nuclear detonation. I feel we should continue our mobilization. But the initiation of any hostilities must be contingent on that detonation."

"Won't any delay," Shukhov put in, "lessen our offensive impact?"

"I don't believe it will make any difference," Markisov answered. "No, whatever the Americans decide to do, they will do quickly. They have to." He scanned the faces around the table.

No one said anything.

"Very well. Trofimov, begin implementing my mobilization orders immediately. Notify all field commanders of TVD rank, and all deputy and ministerial staff. I want status reports as soon as possible."

Markisov eased back in his chair. His face was still gaunt, yet his eyes seemed to sparkle for the first time since he'd come into the room. "Comrades," he said, "make yourselves comfortable. I don't think we'll have long to wait."

Napah couldn't sit still. Nervous energy kept springing her from place to place inside the capsule. She peered down the breach chamber, studied deck markings. She keyed and unkeyed the radio mike. She gazed through the viewing window, watching the drift of scum the Saran had stirred up.

She tried not to look at Chaffee.

A grotesque sense of unreality kept assailing her. She

wanted to scream, if only to do *some*thing. She almost climbed down into the after house to wander around, to touch the icy metal of the *Panjang* to prove here was here.

But she didn't. Cas's final look had made it clear he wanted her inside the capsule. When she dared look at Chaffee, her eyes skimmed off him. It was dangerous to look directly into the gaze of a mad dog. He lay motionless on the command couch and stared at the open hatch with an intense expression. Sweat poured off him like a man in a malarial attack.

The walkie-talkie crackled. "I'm in the engine room," Bonner said in a hollow voice from a thousand bulkheads away.

"Is it all right? Are you all right?"

"So far, so good."

"Can you move forward?"

"I don't know. I'm gonna look. I'll be off radio for a few minutes."

She sighed, hugged her knees.

Two minutes later Hillar came down. "Saran, stand by."

She keyed: "Go ahead."

"Stand by."

She frowned. Had she detected a change in Hillar's voice? No, she must have imagined it. Sixteen thousand feet of water made crazy inflections.

He came back: "Where is Bonner now?"

"He's reached the engine room. He said he was trying to find a way forward of it."

"Is Commander Chaffee functional?"

His eyes were closed now. She reached out, hesitated, poked his arm. No response. She could see his eyeballs moving beneath his lids like a dreamer flying over far landscapes.

"Negative," she said.

"Then it's up to you, Napah. I want you to rig the walkie-talkie so we can speak directly with Bonner."

"I don't understand."

"Disconnect the lead wires to the mike and hook them to the on-off terminals of the walkie-talkie. White to white. Then depress-lock both transmit and receiver keys. Do you follow?"

They wanted her to bypass the capsule's radio! She'd be out of touch with the *Vorhees*. Total isolation. "I don't understand. Why do you want that?"

Hillar's voice crackled, "Goddammit, Gilchrist, don't ask questions. Just rig the fucking walkie-talkie."

The desperation in his voice sent ice across her back. "What's wrong?" she demanded. "What's happened?"

There was another pause. Long, dragged-out seconds. She was about to key when Hillar came back. "All right, Napah. Just don't come apart on me. Christ, don't come apart."

"What? What?"

"One of the Trident missiles aboard the *Panjang* is armed and may be set on a time-detonation sequence."

For a shattered second she felt nothing. Just a void. Then an explosion of nerve charges blew through her entire body.

"Gilchrist?" Hillar called. "Listen to me, it's going to be all right. Do you hear me? We're going to try to defuse the missile."

She stared at the mike and saw every tiny portion of it. Could almost see molecules whirling.

"Gilchrist? Goddammit to hell, come back."

She heard Chaffee moan long and deep, as if something had reached into his chest to draw out his heart. She looked at him. His eyes were wide, his facial skin quivered.

"Gilchrist? Gilchrist?" Hillar yelled. "Acknowledge."

Somehow her finger keyed: "Yes. God!"

"Gilchrist, you must rig the walkie-talkie," Hillar's voice slewed through the frozen air. "You—must—rig—the—walkie-talkie. It's our only hope."

She finally came to. "Yes," she blurted. "Yes, yes."

She began frantically fumbling with the back of the mike housing. She tried to work the set screw out with her fingernail, but couldn't. Cursing wildly, she searched for a screwdriver, found one, and viciously attacked the screw.

Chaffee screamed. It impregnated the capsule with raw sound.

Oh, sweet Mother.

"The light!" He cowered back against the bulkhead, staring at the hatch with an insane terror. "The blue light. It burns."

"Gilchrist, acknowledge your status."

Suddenly Chaffee's expression changed. The terror-stricken eyes slitted. She could see them glinting between the lids. With a quick, monkeylike movement he went to the capsule deck. She watched, mesmerized, unable to look away. He crept toward the open hatch. His head was tucked onto his chest. He touched the hatch rim slowly with one finger, and then another. Shading his eyes with the other hand, he leaned forward and looked down. With a howl of pain he recoiled.

Napah let loose with an accompanying scream that came out of her like an orgasm.

Hillar called, "Please, Napah, come back to us."

Chaffee huddled against the observer's seat. He seemed to be studying his fingers. He whimpered a petulant singsong.

"Gilchrist!" Hillar bellowed.

She keyed: "He's freaking." Voice hushed, whispering secrets.

"What? What?"

"Chaffee's gone crazy." *Oh, God, hear me. Do something.*

At that instant Chaffee lunged forward, his body uncoiling. He shoved his hands against the hatch and threw it up and over. It slammed shut with the hard crack of metal. Groaning in little bursts, he began whirling the dog wheel.

"No!" Napah screamed. "What are you doing?"

She leapt onto his back, clawing at his shoulders. He flung her away with inhuman strength. She came at him again, grabbing hair, punching at the back of his head. Again he flung her back. She slammed into the observer's seat and felt a jolt of pain shoot up her arm. With it came an explosion of rage. "You bastard," she screamed. "You're killing Bonner!"

Chaffee had the hatch dogged, the spring locks engaged. With the same monkey movements he skittered to the command couch and wrenched the breach control panel around on its swivel. He punched buttons. A line of tiny lights came on.

Oh, God, he's going to blow the seal charges.

She drove at him again. He cast her aside onto the hatch. She twisted over and desperately began undogging the wheel. It spun in her hands, coming up.

With a bellow of anger Chaffee hauled her away from the wheel and redogged it. He growled at her, baring teeth, then returned to the couch.

The second line of panel lights came on.

"Gilchrist, are you all right?" Hillar's voice came, unheard. "For the love of God, are you all right?"

Napah dragged herself up and started on the dog wheel again. Worked at it with blind, crazy determination. Up it whirled. She began disengaging spring locks.

The little warning buzzer of the detonation circuit sounded, a soft chirp that gently ricocheted off bulkheads. She got the last spring lock free. Bracing her legs, she hauled back on the hatch. It came up and cracked into its bar hinge.

Chaffee was on her, his weight knocking her to the deck. She felt his fingers clamped onto her throat. His face, inches away, was contorted, monstrous. She struggled helplessly. Terror hurled adrenaline through her system with the power of a thousand volts.

She found the screwdriver.

Her thrust came up at an angle, past her head, and speared the left side of Chaffee's throat. She felt the point strike his jawbone and veer. She drove it deeper. His mouth blew open. In it she saw the shaft of the screwdriver tear up through tongue, gum, into the roof of his mouth. Blood vomited over her hand.

He reared back onto his knees, screaming. His hands clawed at the screwdriver's shaft. It was jammed. With a powerful wrench, he pulled it free, but the backward momentum threw him across the open hatch. His shoulder went down, then his head, and he disappeared into the chamber.

A second later Napah heard the thud of his body as it struck the after-house deck. She sobbed. Her right hand seemed to burn where the blood covered it. Revolted, she wiped it onto her pant leg, as if scorpions were stinging her flesh.

She tried to force herself to look down into the hatch. She couldn't. She listened, senses ranging with incredible clarity.

There was the soft tang of metal on metal. A short, grunting *whuff* of air. And Chaffee's hands shot through the hatchway.

Unconscious of moving, she scrambled to the hatch cover. Chaffee's head and shoulders filled the chamber. He was trying to pull himself through. His face was covered with blood.

The hatch wouldn't move. The back-fall had locked it into the bar hinge. Whimpering hysterically, she put all her weight against it. Still it wouldn't move.

Chaffee's arm cleared the rim.

Her fingers fluttered along the bar hinge. She found the lock key, flipped it, then hurled her weight against the hatch again. It went up, became fully vertical—

Chaffee's head popped through the chamber.

Down.

The hatch struck him on the head and slammed against his arm. The arm pivoted, fingers clawed, reaching to lift the hatch.

She leapt onto it, screaming, pounding down with her knees. The arm swung, fingers gripped the cloth of her flight suit.

Then there was a soft jolt and the arm was snatched

out from under the hatch. The hatch came down and its rim seals whooshed. She bent over the dog, whirling it.

"Gilchrist," the radio called. "Gilchrist."

She slumped. Time was a march of pounding heartbeats. She listened, but heard only the sound of her own body. Below, there was silence.

Then a faint whimpering started, the crying of a child abandoned in a dark attic. Inexorably it rose, gathering terror. It burst into an open howling.

Her skin crawled.

"Gilchrist, Gilchrist." Hillar's voice was plaintive, resigned. "For God's sake, acknowledge."

She crept over the capsule deck. Her body trembling, she encountered a seat bracket and went around instead of over it. She reached the radio mike and keyed: "I stabbed him." She began to sob again, quietly. "I stabbed him."

"Dear God! Is he dead?"

"No. He's in the ship."

Pause.

"All right, Napah. Never mind Chaffee now. You must rig the walkie-talkie."

"Yes."

Vaguely puzzled, she looked at the mike housing. What was she doing? Oh, yes. She crept back across the deck. Felt around for the screwdriver. When she found it, she gazed at the shaft. The blood looked blue-gray in the artificial light.

She retrieved the mike. Concentrating, she began to unscrew the back.

At 2:07 the pass-through was complete.

Bonner was frustrated. For the past few minutes he'd been fruitlessly searching the forward bulkheads of the engine room for a point through which he could cut. Everything gave back heavy rebound to his tapping, indicating flooded compartments.

When he had first entered the engine room, he'd wandered around out of morbid curiosity, just to see what had happenned. His tiny light bounced off polished brass valves, over turbine and machine housings, forming star rainbows. Oil and steam lines crisscrossed over the main turbine, a Curtis 105 B, and went up overhead. He noticed one of the steam lines had mattress packing jammed into a break. A large hatchway was athwart the control panel, and the hatch was ajar. The dogs had been blown off, and the metal was twisted and scarred with explosion burn.

He stared at the blown hatch, reading what it said. Then he pushed it open and went through into a long, curving alleyway. There was more mattress material there, and the deck was littered with burnt ticking. He kept tapping with a crowbar he'd found, but the sound came back heavy.

The alleyway ended with a heavy bulkhead. Just forward of it on the starboard side was a small hatch with a jack ladder leading to it.

He tested it. It rang hollow. Quickly he slipped the dogs, opened the hatch, and crawled through. He was in a twenty-by-twenty-foot compartment containing a small power generator and a two-thousand-gallon steam boiler. He assumed it was an auxiliary power source used to operate the deck gear when the main boilers were down. He tested the forward and starboard plating and got back flooded sound. Disgusted, he opened a hatch on the after bulkhead and climbed onto a small metal grate. A ladder led from it down into the main stoke pit. He went down into it. The stern ends of the huge main boilers protruded through the facing, and below were several fire doors. He crossed the pit and went up the port ladder, which brought him back to the blown hatch.

It was then he heard the screaming. It was faint, yet it bore the sound of naked terror. Bonner's hackles rose on the back of his neck.

"Napah!" he yelled, and hurled himself back toward the turbine pit, where he'd left the welding pack and walkie-talkie. He plunged down the ladder and ran to the pack. The radio wasn't there.

For a moment he stood there confused. Where in hell had he left it? Cursing, he began flashing his light here, there. Then he remembered. He'd laid it on the main control-panel desk.

He raced forward, found it, keyed: "Napah? Can you hear me?"

No answer.

"Napah? Do you read?"

Still no answer.

He whirled around and started back for the turbine pit. As his foot hit the pit grating, there was a splurge of static through the radio's speaker. He stopped.

"Bonner," Hillar's voice burst out. "This—" It faded out and became lost in a hum. Suddenly it came again: "—mitting direct. Can you read?"

Hillar? He keyed: "Your signal's intermittent. What the hell's happened?"

There was a pause. "Bonner, can you read now?"

"Yes. I heard a scream from the stern. Is Gilchrist all right?"

"Chaffee went berserk, tried to kill her. She had to stab him. He's somewhere in the ship."

Cas closed his eyes and opened them. He felt a sudden terrible wash of sadness.

Hillar's voice shattered it. "Bonner, listen very carefully. There is a horrible problem. But you must keep control when I tell you. Everything depends on you. Do you understand?"

"What is it?"

Hillar spoke slowly, as if instructing an obstreperous child on chores. "One of the *Panjang*'s missiles is armed and possibly set on a time-detonation sequence. You must locate and disarm it. Do—you—understand?"

The words went into him and came out again. Hillar was still talking. Cas glanced around. Within feet of him chaos was softly ticking away the seconds of his existence.

His legs felt weak. As he sat on the bottom rung of the pit ladder, panic blew into him like an arctic wind. His temples throbbed with pressure. His whole body wanted to leap up and run away.

He heard Hillar talking once more. The words were gushing out now, hurtling down through three miles of water in an effort to keep the fragile link.

Bonner pressed the transmit button and shut him off.

He sat very still, felt his self-control come, fly off, come back. He flashed his light onto the turbine and stared at it. It looked so huge and solid and real. He swung the light to the coiling steam lines overhead and studied them, noting each valve, each polished shunt wheel. Then he looked at his hand.

At last he lifted the radio. "I read and understand," he said softly. "What do you want me to do?"

Then he sat in the dark silence and waited for instructions.

Langenscheidt couldn't believe it. He, along with everyone else in the communications center, had been listening to the cross-talk between Hillar and Bonner. He found it eerie. He would soon be speaking to a man who was sitting on the top of devastation.

Hillar said, "Pensacola, I've explained to Bonner and am patching you through." After a long pause he continued, "You're on line now, over."

Lew keyed his mike. "Bonner, this is Lew Langenscheidt. Can you read?"

"I read."

Lew swung around and motioned to Shattuck to sit beside him. "Bonner, I'm turning you over to a man named Jack Shattuck. He knows Liberties. He'll tell you how to get to the forward hold. Understood?"

"Yes."

Shattuck was very nervous. His sweaty fingers trembled on the transmit button. "Where are you in the engine room, Bonner?"

"The starboard turbine pit."

"Have you checked all forward bulkheads for upside flooding?"

"Yes, everything's flooded."

"Even the alleyway overhead?"

"The alleyway is clear, but everything forward and overhead is flooded."

Shattuck shook his head, his brow furrowed with thought. "What about the donkey boiler room?"

"If you mean the auxiliary power unit, yes, I checked it. Compartments forward are flooded."

"It's no use," Shattuck cried. "He's trapped. There's no way he can move forward of the engine room."

"Dammit, there's gotta be a way," Lew snapped. "Think, Jack, *think*."

Shattuck put his dead down, eyes clamped shut with concentration.

Bonner's voice rasped into the air. "Come on, Shattuck. Hurry it up."

Carr glanced at Lew. "He's running close to the edge. Come on, Jack, tell him something. Anything. Christ, we don't want to lose him now."

Shattuck's eyes suddenly flew open. "Does this ship have a double hull?"

"I don't know," Langenscheidt answered. "Why?"

"If it does, he could go through the settling tank into the hull recess. That'd get him abreast the forward holds."

"Tell him."

"Bonner, on the starboard side—the right side—there's a big fuel tank channel-beamed to the main engine-room deck. Can you see it?"

"Yes."

"Check the depth gauge beside the jack ladder."

A minute later Bonner reported, "The settling tank's full."

"Oh, no," Shattuck groaned.

"What?"

"He'll have to go into the fuel in order to crack the sump drain."

"Will he be able to do that?"

"Sure, if he's got enough breath. But when he cracks that drain, the weight of the tank fuel could jam him against the grating. He'd drown before the tank emptied."

"Do it, tell him."

"But he could die in that tank."

"Tell him!"

Shattuck inhaled deeply, then keyed: "Bonner, crack the tank inspection hatch."

A few seconds later Bonner said, "She's cracked."

"Strip naked. Down to bare balls. You have to go into the fuel. At the bottom of the forward side of the tank is a sump drain. It'll have a recessed swing wheel that opens *counter*clockwise. You got that?"

"Yes."

"As soon as the wheel gets near open, the weight of the fuel will blow it out. Watch out! Don't get jammed against the sump grating."

Silence.

"Bonner?"

More silence.

"Oh, shit," someone said softly.

Bonner said, "I'm going into the tank now."

They waited. Nobody spoke. Sweat ran off Shattuck's face and dripped onto the panel desk. A telephone suddenly rang somewhere. A seaman sprinted off to get it.

Two minutes passed.

Shattuck looked at Langenscheidt. Lew stared at the overhead speaker. A sailor said, "Oh, man."

Another minute.

The speaker crackled. It was Bonner's voice, breathless. "I got her open. She's draining into the hull recesses."

There was a general exhalation of relief. Somebody said, "Give me a fucking cigarette." Shattuck drew a finger across his forehead, slashing the finger on his cutoffs. "Bonner, you'll have to get the oil off your body. If you flame the cutting torch, the fumes from your body heat will ignite. Do you understand?"

"Yeah."

"You'll also need a tarp. There's a storage chest abaft the log desk. It's on the starboard—the right side—of the turbine."

Bonner's voice came back violently. "Quit telling me

right side for starboard, goddammit. I'm not a fucking moron. God*dammit*!"

"Easy, easy," Carr said. He put a hand on Shattuck's shoulder.

"Christ, I'm sorry, Bonner," Shattuck blurted. "Hey, listen, I'm sorry."

"All right, all right. Stand by."

Carr shook his head and glanced at Lew. "That boy's close to cracking. You hear it in his voice?"

"I couldn't have lasted this far," Lew said.

Bonner came on. "All right, I've got the tarp. Now what?"

"As soon as the settling tank is drained, go back in and take the sump grating off. It lifts out. You'll be able to crawl through into the number-four starboard hull recess. There's a small catwalk in it. Okay?"

"Right."

"In the recess, every ten feet will be a frame strut. After the fourth one will be a bulkhead. It'll have an inspection door that goes into the next hull recess. As soon as you go through, dog the hatch immediately to keep the settling fuel fumes out." He paused, scratching furiously at his forehead. His finger was still on the transmit button.

"Unkey," Carr yelled. He lunged forward and slapped Shattuck's hand from the mike.

The speaker instantly blared the tail end of something Bonner was saying: "—the hell is number-two hold?"

Shattuck's hand crept back to the mike. "Number-three starboard recess is abreast the number-two hold. Do you understand?"

"Yeah, right, yeah."

"Test for flooding. If the hold's clean, you'll be able to cut anywhere along the inner hull plate."

Silence.

They launched into another agonizing wait.

Suddenly a red light began blinking on the panel in front of Shattuck. He jerked back as if touched by fire. "What the hell is that?"

Carr leapt forward, scooped up the mike and keyed: "Bonner?"

Nothing.

"Damn, we've got dead air. He's gone."

Eyes lifted to the overhead.

"Wait a minute, sir," one of the panel operators shouted. "We're still picking up signal. We've been shunted into an intercept."

A female voice with a thick English accent came through the loudspeaker. "You are on sixty-second transition mode. Vanguard DD unit is readjusting to trajectory alignment. Please hold."

Shattuck stared at Carr, his eyes saying: What? What?

"It's all right," Carr said. "The satellite's swinging disks."

A heavy blow of static came through the speaker. They waited. Another burst. Then the female voice came on again. "The alignment is completed. Affix to new AFD position of fifty-degree span. Normal transmitting frequencies are from five-zero-zero to three-zero-zero-zero kilohertz. Thank you."

Carr threw switches and adjusted dials. The overhead crackled with Bonner's faint voice: "—hell are you? Pensacola, where the hell are you?"

"Bonner, can you read?" Carr shouted into the mike.

"Yes, very faint."

The riffle of static in the speaker faded off as the Mindanao and Aleutian operators adjusted. "Do you read clean now?"

"Yes."

The tension in the compacted air inside the radio room lifted like steam seeking the ceiling. "Where are you now?" Carr asked.

"Goddammit, I told you. Weren't you listening? In number-three starboard recess."

"Have you tested for flooding in number-two hold?"

"She's clean."

Carr slid the mike back to Shattuck and gripped his shoulder. Shattuck clenched and unclenched his fists for a few seconds like a safecracker about to listen for tumblers. He keyed: "All right, Bonner. You're halfway home. Tap the bulkhead till you find free cargo space. Then cut through there. What's your nozzle tip?"

"Number three."

"Good, good. She'll cut through four-inch steel. What's the ambient temperature?"

"How the fuck do I know? I don't have a fucking thermometer. It's cold."

"It'd be near freezing at that depth," someone said from the doorway.

"Bonner, wrap the nozzle in something to prevent frost clog. Understood?"

"Yeah."

"And wuff the cutting surface before you flame. Cover yourself with the tarp."

"What?"

"Wuff the . . ." Shattuck paused. "Clear the cutting surface of fumes and drape the tarp over you."

"All right."

They waited again. The seconds, little sparks of eternity, ticked off. At last the overhead speaker came on. Bonner's voice was clothed in a soft, warbling whoosh. "Torch on and blue." There was a pause, then the sharp clatter of metal. "Starting cut now."

Lew glanced at the panel chronometer. It was 11:33 P.M. *On Guadalcanal it was 2:33 in the afternoon.*

The acetylene torch made a hissing blue needle of light under the tarp. Bonner could feel its heat fuming off the bulkhead plating. The metal was slick with oil scum that shimmered off, making tiny wisps of flame. He slipped on the welding goggles and adjusted them over his eyes.

They plunged him into an amber darkness in which only the blue needle of flame was visible. He ran his fingers across the metal, then put the tip of the needle against it. A shower of sparks erupted, sizzling. The pressure of the torch soughed loudly under the tarp, throwing orange flicks of flame to the side. He held the blue tip steady and began the cut.

The air grew smoky and acrid with the odor of burning metal and oil. The spot ahead of the cutting flame began to glow, first orange, then red, then white. Sparks began blowing back onto his gloves. Slowly the plating began to curl. There was a sharp hiss as a slit formed, scattering tiny white dots of molten metal.

Bonner fixed his eyes on the cutting point. He focused his thoughts directly to it. Other parts of his mind kept springing images at him: what lay on the other side of the bulkhead? He couldn't block out the images completely. They slid over the cutting flame. He saw the Trident with such precision that he could actually see the metal grain, the polish. The images grew chaotic, replicating with stunning velocity. His hand started to tremble, and the blue flame lost its fix.

He took several seconds to recover himself. The amber isolation of his goggles offered the blue needle, and he homed to it. He stared at it with hypnotic concentration.

The torch began to sputter.

The regulator, unable to automatically adjust to the decreasing pressure in the tanks, was beginning to starve the acetylene line. The flame turned orange as too much oxygen blew through the nozzle. It popped and snapped like tiny firecrackers held under a tin can.

Bonner quickly adjusted the intake knob on the acetylene feed, then knocked his fist against the regulator screwhead to loosen any frost buildup on the baffles. The flame turned blue again, the blowing hiss of the nozzle steady.

He cut another six inches, then had to stop. His legs were cramping and the smoke under the tarp was almost unbearable. He lifted the edge of the tarp and took a deep breath of the fetid recess air. He pushed the goggles up onto his forehead and studied the cut he'd made. It formed a half-moon to the right, three feet long. Smoke curled off the cut line, and the metal glowed, throbbing.

He ran the tip of his gloved finger down the left side,

imprinting in his mind the bead for the second cut. Behind him on the outer hull plating, his shadow flickered and danced.

He flipped down the goggles, pulled the tarp, and began the second cut.

In number-two hold, the sound of the cutting torch made a soft, sibilant echo through the cavernous compartment. As Cas made his first blow-through, a rat frightened by the small rushing explosion burst from under a cargo skid and hurtled up along an arch strut to an overhead crossbeam. There it paused, looking back, its eyes glistening in the tiny bursts of light coming through the blow hole.

The cut was between two stacks of cargo, bags of cement on the forward side, machine parts across the alleyway. As it deepened, showers of sparks started blowing through and scattering out onto the hold deck. The tiny glowing filaments bounced like metallic rain.

But this wasn't the only light in the hold. Across the center line and far back against the after bulkhead was a little square of green light with numbers flashing on it. Dureau's computer.

As Bonner started his second cut, the numbers read: 963.

He had to stop again halfway through the second cut. This time he shouldered out of the weld harness, braced it and the nozzle into the strut wedge with his light, and climbed down to the catwalk. He moved about, stamping his numbed legs.

For a moment he thought about keying to Pensacola, but didn't. Oddly, his total isolation seemed to strengthen him in some inexplicable way. Slowly the blood was coming back into his legs.

Suddenly, from somewhere forward, came a quick, sharp explosion like the blast of a shotgun. It was followed instantly by the furious, whistling blow of water under high pressure. Cas went stiff. He could feel the tiny reverberations of the explosion trembling through the hull plates. The *Panjang* groaned softly, the protest of a giant in sleep. Then she settled again, and the sound of seething water diminished. The explosion had shattered his fragile control.

No, he told himself. *No, not yet*.

He touched the other hull plating. Icy cold seeped into his fingers. He inhaled again and again. The fume-tainted air oxygenated him. Slowly his self-control returned. He moved back to the welding pack and retrieved his gear. Without the tarp, he began cutting again.

It took him eight minutes to finish a ragged circle in the plating. He rammed his foot in the center. Once more. It pulled loose and clattered noisily into the hold.

He reached for the walkie-talkie. "The cut's complete. I'm going into the hold. Where is the missile?"

Pensacola came right back. It was Langenscheidt's voice. "Bonner, we don't know specific location. There will be more than one. Probably in some sort of scaffolding. Silver casings, fifteen feet high, over."

"How will I tell which one is armed?"

"You'll be able to hear the click of the timer."

Timer. The word skewered through his chest. He focused his attention on the edges of the hole. He ran one ungloved hand over the metal. It was still very hot. He hung the walkie-talkie around his neck and clamped the flashlight between his teeth. Climbing through, he dropped to the hold deck.

He moved swiftly along the alleyway, flashing the light on the stacks of cargo. He reached the line of stanchions that bisected the hold along the keel and threw his light forward, looking for metallic reflections. He swung around, looked aft.

There!

Far back against the after bulkhead, twelve shafts of metal faintly reflected in the very edge of the beam. As he stared at them, he felt gooseflesh crawl up his arms. He started forward and keyed the radio: "I've got 'em."

"Bravo, Bonner," Langenscheidt yelped, his excitement ringing across all the miles.

"What will I—" Bonner stopped. His eye had caught a tiny glint of light near the edge of the missile pod. He flicked off the flash. There it was: a square green light, like a tiny television set someone had carelessly left on. A computer screen.

"There's a computer on the scaffold," he snapped into the radio.

"That's the one, Bonner. Get to it. You've got to override its command."

He started ahead again, running. Suddenly the tiny computer brightened. Words began flashing on the screen, throwing more light. Bonner's heartbeat accelerated, spiraling upward into ominous speed. "It's alive," he screamed into the walkie-talkie. "The computer, it's coming alive."

"Oh, God," Langenscheidt came back. "Bonner, you've got to get to that computer."

The countdown on Dureau's computer screen had reached ninety seconds. Words flashed below the numbers: PRE-IGNITION SEQUENCE PHASE ONE CLICK ON NOW . . . Things began to happen inside the Trident. Soft hums, electronic burble drifted up through the titanium casing. In the upper shaft, heat shields of filament-wound fiberglass enclosed the entire command-control computer unit. Navigation gyros were uncaged and spun. The flight-control computer, inert until this moment, activated. The completion of each step was acknowledged on the screen.

Seventy-eight seconds . . .

In the after steering vents, the engine gimbal bearings were unlocked. Turbulence vanes revolved to flare position while anti-radar-chaff packet switches clicked on. The network of external sensors along the apex of the nose cone were circuited.

Sixty seconds . . .

New words flashed: PRE-IGNITION SEQUENCE PHASE TWO CLICK ON NOW . . . The first-stage rocket's propellant line valves were turned to the vertical preparatory to feeding the nitrocellulose, nitroglycerine, and ammonium perchlorate fuels into the LR87-AJ-5 engine. Although there were no propellants aboard, this system, like all the others, continued on automatic function.

Thirty-five seconds . . .

PRE-IGNITION SEQUENCE PHASE THREE CLICK ON NOW . . .

The guidance computer cleared its circuits to receive trajectory and plot-to-target data from the fire-control system of the carrier submarine. Since there was no data input, the missile's computer accepted the preset X-moment of coordinates 0000 NS/0000 EW as a command fix and fed this target point to the on-board inertial navigational system to home on. Instantly the missile's accelerometers began scanning.

Fifteen seconds . . .

Quick blasts of compressed air cleared the engine-thrust chambers of both stage engines. The second-stage propellant line valves turned to the vertical.

Ten seconds . . .

The base buffer-plate locks were disengaged so as to prevent travel of the shock wave from the submarine's gas-generated launcher.

Four seconds . . .

Circular nipple rings around the stage and median section seams were activated to spray water on the seam seals to prevent expansion release during the launch.

Two seconds . . .

One second . . .

The computer screen went blank. Then a single word flashed across the center: LAUNCH . . . LAUNCH . . . LAUNCH.

Twenty-one

zero

TIME: 1080 MINUS 0001 SECONDS.

Langenscheidt watched with horror as the second hand on the chronometer passed ninety seconds. It was over. Now nothing on earth could stop the Trident.

The moment Bonner screamed that the computer had come alive, Lew's eyes had shot to the clock. He kept frantically trying to raise Bonner with the desperate hope that he might still disarm the missile. But only silence came back.

It was ironic. Dureau had been temporarily cheated of his big moment. His computer command had brought the Trident to launch, not detonation. Maybe he'd known and it hadn't mattered. It was a meaningless difference. In precisely eighteen minutes minus one second, the missile would detonate itself.

At this moment its guidance system was arching across a programmed sky. For eighteen minutes it would wander through its electronic universe, discarding all coordinates as its target until at last it returned to its starting point. Then it would explode.

Carr, seeing Lew's face, gripped his shoulder. "What is it? What happened?"

Langenscheidt could only shake his head. His insides were roiling yet his instincts, honed by scientific training to. challenge everything were beginning to reassert themselves. There must be a way. There was always a way.

His thoughts, freed, cut through his brain, searching, scanning the billions of bits of stored data. Neurons flashed, sent probes up option channels, hit dead ends, backed, raced up new channels. They drove down deep, below conscious level into unthought thoughts.

And he found it. It was a slim chance, but a chance. It had been there all the time, formed whole in the first instant he fully understood the true situation.

With it came a movement that literally hurled him out of the chair. "Carr," he bellowed. "Get Bonner back. Do anything, beg, scream, lie, if you have to. Just get him back."

He raced through the door to the computer terminal. The operator slid out of the way. Lew bent forward and his fingers raced over the keyboard:

SALTER: TRIDENT IN PTF STAGE. NEED QUANTUM ANALYSIS OF EXPLOSIVE FORCE SUFFICIENT FOR PHOTON-GENERATION SPECTRUM FROM GROUND STATE TO SHATTER FREQUENCY OF TT ELECTRON-PHASE FLOW. CONSIDER PRESSURE DEPTH AND LIBERTY CONFIGURATION CONFINED.

He darted back into the radio room. The chronometer showed one minute after midnight.

TIME: 1080 MINUS 0062 SECONDS

Bonner's head had just cleared the scaffold when the missile went into launch. He stared into the computer screen, the successive orders driving into his brain. His own blast of adrenaline flung him off the scaffold. He hit the deck and, arms over his head, tried with hysterical desperation to merge with the steel. I'm going to die, I'm going to die.

Nothing happened.

Seconds hurtled past him. He waited. Still nothing.

He lifted his head and felt the force of the contracting muscles.

"Bonner, for the love of God, come back."

The walkie-talkie sent vibrations riffling up into his skull.

"Bonner, please come back."

He groaned, reached for the radio. "What the fuck is happening?" he croaked, whispery. "What the fuck is happening?"

"Bonner, listen to me. It's not too late. We can still stop the missile. Do you understand? The missile is in a temporary flight phase," Langenscheidt cried. "We can still stop it."

"What happens if I can't?"

"We—can—still—stop—it."

"Goddamn you son of a bitch. What will happen?"

A slight pause. "It will self-detonate."

"How long?"

"Seventeen minutes."

For a fraction of a second he was immobilized. Then, brutish, primeval life force exploded in him. The will to survive. "Tell me."

"You must get back to the engine room. Take your cutting gear. You'll need flame."

Before Langenscheidt had finished, Cas was on his feet. His flashlight had rolled across the stanchion way. He raced to it, scooped it up, then headed back through the hold, flying.

TIME: 1080 MINUS 0088 SECONDS

"I need an explosion in the engine room," Langenscheidt shouted at Shattuck. "Tell me how to make a confined explosion in the engine room."

Shattuck stared at him, shocked. He looked as if he had been on an eight-day drunk. "Christ, you'll kill him."

The statement was so absurd, Lew wanted to laugh. He grabbed Shattuck's shirt. "God damn you, tell me how to make a confined explosion in the engine room."

Carr poked his head through the door. "Salter's coming back with data."

Glaring, he pushed Shattuck back. "I want your answer when I get back." He ran through the door.

Salter was sending spectrum projections, straight off his mainframe:

HASPAN: ABSO AE/DEM 441 FT * 63 FT

PRESSURE: 8000 PSI

EXPLOSIVE SITE: MIDLINE

ACOUSTIC AREA: APP (KEEL STRAKE TO HULL DECK): 120,000 SQ FT

SINOSOIDAL FREQUENCY EFFECT: ENCLOSED/ABSORPTION OF ACOUSTIC ENERGY 98.101 PERCENT

FOURIER'S SERIES: EQUILIBRIUM POINT 0: PERIOD/AMPLITUDE/PHASE: CONJUNCTIVE

ELECTRON SHATTER POINT (CIRCUIT 115.07 ARC IN FLOW 0.999) 0.000012 NANOSECOND RANGE SPAN: 8000 TO 10000 KHERTZ// WAVELENGTH PROPAGATION 0.000189 APS: DISTRIBUTION SYM-METRICAL

Lew's eyes fixed on the next entry:

EXPLOSIVE FORCE (MINIMUM) RANGE: 9000 TO 12000 PFS/ ENCLOSED SPACE PROPAGATION OUTBURST NON-TRAVEL: 11000 PSF

He pushed in a request block:

GIVE ME EQUIVALENT NITRO

The screen went blank. Two seconds later it came back:

RED CROSS EXTRA: (SIXTY PERCENT) TEN STICKS

GELEX: BS (SIXTY-SEVEN PERCENT) SIX STICKS

NITROMEX: SS (EIGHTY PERCENT) FIVE STICKS

Shattuck was pacing the radio room in a little circle when Lew got back. He was sweating again, dazed by it all.

"We need an explosive force equal to at least six dynamite sticks," he yelled.

"Damn, I can't think," Shattuck cried. He held up his hands helplessly. Then something seemed to come to him. "How much time does he have?"

Lew shot a glance at the chronometer. "Fifteen minutes and forty-three seconds."

Shattuck's face grimaced. "No, that's not enough time."

"For what?"

"I was just thinking if he could fire the donkey boiler."

"And what?"

"If he drained the tank to red level and fired her, he could melt the crown sheets. She'd blow."

"That's it. Tell him."

"But I don't think there's enough time to build steam."

"Tell him."

Shattuck moved to the mike seat and dropped into it. His hands were shaking violently. "Bonner, come in."

Silence.

Shattuck turned and looked pleadingly at Langenscheidt. "Call him again."

Shattuck did.

Silence.

Three seconds later Bonner came on, breathless. "I'm in the engine room."

"Bonner, go to the auxiliary boiler room. You have to fire the donkey boiler."

"I don't understand."

"You have to fire the donkey boiler."

TIME: 1080 MINUS 0145 SECONDS

In the Trident's guidance unit, the timer scanner neared the end of the first rocket's two-and-a-half-minute burn. Since all the external sensors had indicated air-density environment at the moment of launch, the first-stage burn command had been activated immediately. Now new commands raced through circuits. Barrier seals in the second and inter-stages revolved forward. Flange locks went into click-off.

0148 seconds . . .

Main cam lifters shoved bolt rings forward, turned ninety degrees to the right by screw slots. Momentum seals snapped open along the inner casing joints of both stages.

0150 seconds . . .

Second-stage propellant line valves opened. Bevel locks disengaged.

The Trident entered its second-stage burn.

*   *   *

Bonner's light played across the two-thousand-gallon boiler drum. He keyed: "I'm here."

"There's a master valve on the port side of the boiler drum aft the generator housing." Shattuck's voice warbled hollowly in the small compartment. "Turn it counterclockwise. It'll drain the drum."

Bonner's fingers raced over the generator housing, felt along the side of the tank. He found the valve and swung it. Stale, oily water blew out of the drain cock, poured onto the deck.

"It's draining."

"Now open the grate door forward."

Bonner knelt and searched the boiler foundation pedestal. The grate door was two feet wide. The lock handle was worn, showing fire peel. He twisted it and pulled the door open. The nozzle rack extended across the bottom of the pedestal.

He was moving in continuous motion now, the voice in the radio activating him. Like a computerized robot, his mind absorbed the orders and his body carried them out. No thought lapse between command and action.

"On the starboard side of the boiler there's a manual pressure pump. Bring the pressure on the gauge up to sixty pounds."

Cas found it and began pumping: up, down, up, down, like a man furiously sawing a log. With his free hand he put the light on the gauge: twenty pounds.

"Check the water level."

He swung the light to a glass tube affixed to the forward side of the drum. The copper-colored water was gurgling loudly.

"Water's on orange band."

"You've gotta get it into the red."

He looked back at the pressure gauge: thirty pounds. The needle fluttered, rising slowly. Forty pounds. He could feel conduction heat coming up the pump shaft from the plunger casing. Sweat popped out on his forehead.

Fifty pounds . . .

Water was six inches deep in the compartment. It soaked through his jogging shoes.

"I've got sixty pounds." He locked the pump handle.

"Water level?"

"In the red."

"Where in the red?"

"Bottom."

"That's enough. Shut off the drain valve."

He did.

"All right, Bonner, now fire the spigots under the boiler rack. There's a panel beside the pressure pump. Upside is the main rack petcock switch, below is a smaller switch for the blow spigots. Open the spigot line and use your welding striker to ignite the fuel."

The welding pack had floated across the compartment. He retrieved it and took the striker off the hose clamp. He flipped the spigot switch and thrust his hand into the grate, rolling the striker. The spigots ignited with a little whuff of orange flame.

"Spigots fired."

"Good, Bonner, good. Now you're gonna have to speed up the heating of the main nozzle rack so the nipples will vaporize. The spigots are too slow. Use your torch. Unscrew the cutting tip and blow mixture into the grate."

Bonner stopped for the first time questioning the order. "You stupid son of a bitch, it'll blow."

"No, it won't. Just hold the nozzle inside the door. The mixture flame will help heat the nozzle rack."

The instant he shoved the torch in through the door, blowing raw mixture, there was a small explosion that threw droplets of flaming drip oil out the grate door and over the water. Slowly the flames died. He held the torch as far in as he could. Waves of heat washed over his hand. The hair on his wrist started burning. He clamped his teeth against the pain. The seconds streaking past him became sluggish, treacherous with pain. Stalled as the pain became unbearable.

He switched hands and swirled the first one in the icy

water. When he brought it up, it was steaming. He held on.

After two minutes he couldn't stand it anymore. He withdrew the torch. His hand couldn't hold it. It fell into the water, the flame snapping off, and huge bubbles of acetylene and oxygen began furiously churning the water. Groaning, he shut off the feed hoses.

"Bonner? Bonner?"

The little tinny voice suddenly enraged him. He keyed: "I'm here, you goddamn bastard, I'm here."

"Okay, Bonner, hey, okay. Let's go for the main nozzles now. Throw the petcock switch and fire 'em."

The room was full of smoke, and the beam of his light cut a foggy tube. He returned to the panel and threw the main switch.

There was a powerful sizzling blast inside the grate rack. Burning oil erupted through the door. It struck bulkheads and made pools of flame on the water. A large fire-ball was hurled through the hatchway onto the apron of the donkey room. It whirled apart as it hit, and flaming dribbles of oil seeped off the apron into the spoke pit.

Cas rammed his hand against the switch, shutting off the fuel flow to the nozzles. Popping and spluttering, the blow through the door stopped. He tried extinguishing the flames on the bulkheads, but it was useless. The metal, like the water surface, had a thin film of burning oil that kept spreading.

He keyed: "There's fire all over the place."

"You're getting blowback," Shattuck's voice echoed. "Shut down the main switch."

Bonner, panting with frenzy, stood helplessly watching the fires burn. Orange shadows leapt and danced in the small compartment. Gradually, as the film of fuel was exhausted, the flames began to go out.

"Bonner? Are you all right?"

"Yeah," he blurted. "Yeah."

"You've got to use the torch on the fuel-intake lines. The oil in the nipples isn't hot enough to vaporize. They're blowing back. Use your—"

Shattuck was cut off by a whomping explosion from the engine room. A brilliant bluish light flashed through the hatchway. Bonner felt the pressure of the concussion slamming against his eardrums.

Fumes from the settling tank had been accumulating up along the steam lines, flooding throughout the entire engine room. The fire on the donkey apron and down in the stoke pit had finally ignited them. An eight-foot column of fire was blowing out of the tank hatch with the sound of wind through a tunnel. Like a huge oil lamp, the fire was sucking fumes through the sump drain from the hull recess, throwing tremendous heat up along the overhead plates. Already steam-packing brackets were beginning to glow orange, and the air was thinning as the fire ate up huge amounts of oxygen.

Cursing maniacally, Bonner dived through the hatchway onto the apron and then leapt to the engine deck. He tried to approach the flame so as to shut the tank hatch, but he couldn't get close enough. He searched around on the brilliantly lit deck for something to use, and grabbed the crowbar he'd been tapping the bulkheads with. Shielding his face, he felt with the tip of the crowbar until he hooked the hatch. He braced his weight and brought it up and over. Instantly the flame went out.

Through the heat and smoke Cas made his way back to the donkey room. He could hear Shattuck calling. As he tried to climb through the hatch, it seemed suddenly that he moved in slow motion. A deep sense of utter dejection was beginning to take him over. Its stupor infiltrated his muscles, seeping through him. He fought it with all his will, commanded his arm to lift, his fingers to key the radio. "Time?" he croaked.

"Eleven minutes four seconds."

The lethargy was shattered. Seconds later he was heating the feed lines.

TIME: 1080 MINUS 0437 SECONDS

The Trident's main guidance computer ordered the predetonation phase. Deep within the warhead, the nuclear bomb assembly activated. In the center was the core support shaft called the cladding assembly. Within the assembly were two major components with their accompanying control gears, scram springs, and activating bar arms.

At the moment of detonation the upper component, the ram core, would be fired into a perfectly fitted cone slot in the second component, the coupling barrel, which held the U-235 fuel mass. Instantaneous fission reaction would occur, causing an atomic explosion.

Above the cladding assembly was a fusion sleeve, a hydrogenous mattrix composed of filament tubes containing deuterium. In the trillisecond of tremendous heat generated by the first explosion, the mattrix would go into fusion state, creating the secondary but more powerful hydrogen explosion.

Within the cladding assembly the ram cone's lock roller now pivoted, shifting aside to allow a tiny planet gear to engage a wedge tooth on the cone shaft. The scram springs of both the ram cone and coupling barrel were slightly depressed. Twin hydraulic pistons on the top of the fusion sleeve extended, fitting the sleeve down around the cladding assembly.

As these functions completed, the unit went on hold, awaiting the second predetonation command.

Shattuck furiously slammed the mike against the radio panel. "I can't do this no more," he bawled. "I've had enough." He shoved himself to his feet and headed for the door.

"Stop him!" Langenscheidt yelled, lunging for the mike.

Carr stepped in front of Shattuck. "Hold it." His eyes were hard pinpoints of intensity. "You ain't going nowhere, Jack."

"For God's sake, it's no use. Bonner'll never get pressure up in time." His face contorted. "That man's gonna get blown to hell and I'm gonna have to sit here and listen to it happen. No, I won't do it."

"You'll do it."

Bonner's voice suddenly burst through the speaker. "Why am I doing this?" A pause. "Tell me why I'm doing this. Where are we going with this insanity?"

The questions crackled through the radio room and drifted out into the main control area, echoing in the absolute stillness. Langenscheidt looked helplessly at Carr. "Christ, what do I say to him?"

"Tell him."

"He'll crack. He's so close, I can feel it."

"Tell him, goddammit. You have to, it's his right."

Lew turned back to the mike. His fingers hesitated, then pressed the transmit button. "All right, Bonner, listen to me. You have to create an explosion in the boiler." He spoke slowly, precisely. "I can't explain, but it's the only way. You don't have any other options. If you freeze now, you'll die. I can't promise this will work, but it's your only chance. The choice is yours."

There was dead silence. Every eye stared at the speaker. Lew's slid to the chronometer: nine minutes, fifty-one seconds.

Bonner's voice came back. "Main nipple grate fired. Boiler pressure coming up fast. What is explosion level?"

Lew swung around to look questioningly at Shattuck.

"Quarter-inch above red maximum," Shattuck yelled.

Langenscheidt relayed.

Bonner replied, "I'm torching the boiler drum. Pressure coming up very fast."

Cas could hear the water inside the boiler tank churning viciously. He kept sweeping the torch nozzle back and forth near the pedestal. Waves of heat came off the metal. White lead paint began peeling off and feathering. His panic was like an imprisoned animal raging. To hold it captive, he deliberately placed his palm against the hot metal for a second. Absorbed the pain, forced himself to focus on it.

Behind him in the engine room, the fire in the stoke pit had ignited ladder bindings. These in turn had crept up and fired oil rags near the control desk. In the dry, hot air, wooden panels were bursting into spontaneous combustion. The engine room was roiling with smoke.

"What is boiler pressure?" Langenscheidt demanded.

He ignored it.

The plates of the boiler were beginning to creak. Deep inside he could hear a crackling, sizzling sound like electrical wires shorting out.

"Bonner, what is boiler pressure?"

He leaned around the tank and squinted at the flickering face of the main pressure gauge. The needle had just entered the lower end of the red zone.

"Come on, you bitch," he growled at it.

He couldn't breath. It hit him suddenly that the fires had eaten too much oxygen in the small compartment. Gasping, his head whirling, he rammed the torch into the water, killing the flame. He closed off the acetylene hose line, allowing only the oxygen to feed through the torch's blow opening. He held it up to his mouth and sucked it in.

The pure oxygen hit him, jolted through his bloodstream. He kept hauling in more oxygen until his head started getting giddy.

"Bonner, please listen to me," Langenscheidt's voice kept bouncing around the room, sounding louder. "Once the pressure has reached the top of the red zone, you must get out and dog the hatch. Do you understand? The explosion must be confined."

He swung around and looked at the pressure gauge. The needle had climbed above the top of the red area.

He flung the torch away and headed for the hatch. The still-blowing oxygen fizzled and popped under the water, making bubbles that flared when they touched bits of floating fire. He crawled through the hatch, stumbled, fell onto the apron grate. He scrambled to his feet and grabbed the hatch door. He slammed it shut. His hand reached for the first dog.

There was a bloodcurdling scream below him. He whirled around. A figure loomed up out of the fiery stoke pit. Its face was monstrous, blood-drenched, its clothes afire. It came up shrieking, like a demon from hell.

Chaffee!

TIME: 1080 MINUS 0990 SECONDS

The Trident's guidance commanded the warhead to enter the second phase of predetonation. In the cladding assembly the ram cone's planet gear revolved, actuating the shaft wedge plate. The cone swung 180 degrees, bringing its tip to vertical-drop alignment to the coupling barrel's injector slot. Below it the barrel slid upward along screw grooves into perfect receptor position. Tension went onto the scram springs as pinion bolts came into contact with a bar-arm release shaft.

Bonner recoiled in horror as Chaffee cleared the top of the pit ladder and came at him. He was holding a crowbar double-handed. He swung it viciously at Cas's head.

Bonner threw himself back. The hook of the bar caught the walkie-talkie strap, tore it from his neck, and smashed it against the donkey hatch door. Cas darted to the left. Chaffee started a backswing. Moving on pure reflex, Bonner stepped forward and drove a fist into the side of Chaffee's face. The power of it hurled Chaffee back against the hatch.

Bonner's momentum carried him into Chaffee's chest. Frantically he tried to grab the man's arms and pin them. They struggled. Chaffee, tremendously strong, howled into his face, tried to bite his nose. Then Cas was lifted bodily off his feet and hurled back. He struck the apron railing and went down. Instantly Chaffee came at him again. Cas rolled to the right. The crowbar hit the railing, tanging metallically.

Before Chaffee could brace for another swing, Bonner came up off the grate, bellowing. He threw his arms around Chaffee's legs and drove him back against the hatch door. He straightened his knees and aimed another punch slicing down at Steve's face.

Before he could throw it, Chaffee brought the crowbar

up off the grate, slashing up and across. Cas saw it
coming and threw his left arm up to block it. He shuddered with pain as the bar struck. Hot flashes exploded
behind his eyes. His left arm and shoulder went numb.

Chaffee started another swing. Driven by rage and
instinct, Bonner hit him with his right fist. Drove it into
the cheek, felt bone crack. Blood spewed into his face
and Chaffee went down. Cas leapt onto him. Grunting
wildly, he smashed the man's face again and still again.
Then he grabbed the front of Chaffee's hair and began
pounding his head into the grate.

With an insane roar Chaffee lifted him and hurled him
back. He struck the apron railing. His vision blurred. He
blinked, trying to clear it.

Chaffee slowly got to his knees. The firelight made
coals in his eyes. He grabbed one of the hatch dogs and
pulled himself upright.

The donkey boiler blew.

The force of it tore the hatch door off its hinges and
into Chaffee's back. Trailing a column of smoke and
steam, it hurtled him across the engine room and up
against a bulkhead. The eruptive force pinned Bonner to
the apron railing. As the force passed, he dropped limply
to the grate and lay there panting. He could hear the
sound of the explosion traveling through the ship and
rebounding. It roared anew in the engine room, and met
the rebounding wave from the forward compartments.
There was a crescendo of clashing sound, like a new
explosion. And then these fled away to the ends of the
ship.

Again and again the sounds traveled back and forth,
locked in by the pressure barrier of the ocean. Cas lay
frozen, hearing the waves of sound echoing, crashing,
and echoing again.

The apron grate was vibrating violently in pulsing surges.
And under the fleeing and returning echoes came the
fainter chatter and hum of things in the engine room as
they picked up the resonance. Even the air seemed to be
vibrating. Down in the smoke pit the flames shimmered,

making curtains of fire like an aurora borealis that whistled and soughed.

TIME 1080 MINUS 1072 SECONDS

Within the guidance unit the tiny click of circuits was lost in a jolt of vibration hum. Oscillation waves rippled through the missile's outer casing, moving like radiation impulses into internal components.

The waves passed, came again, passed, came again. Each time they multiplied amplitude.

Seven seconds . . .

Command surges shot through the circuit lines. A tiny rotor arm in the cladding assembly activated, revolved, pressing a bar arm that released the pinion clip from the shaft that held the scram springs. In the upper cone shaft the CE trigger clicked into the second of three notches.

The *Panjang* was thrumming. Every bulkhead, plate, stanchion, cable, hummed violently. Glass objects in unflooded compartments shattered. Wooden panels cracked along density lines. In the holds the vast spaces acted like amplifiers as the sound climbed through the harmonic spectrum.

In the circuit lines of the guidance system, molecules and atoms in the wires were being excited by the vibration. They began to resonate in phase. Richer and richer the harmonic energy became, pumping them into a state known as "inverted population."

Five . . .

Photons began hurling off the wires.

Three . . .

In the cladding assembly the CE trigger clicked into the third and final notch. In the coupling barrel the scram-spring holding bolts revolved, unscrewing out of position.

Two . . .

Full excitation state was reached. Photon radiation fumed off the circuit lines of the entire guidance system. There was a sudden burst of coherent radiation as all atoms discharged overloaded energy. A rapid chain reaction followed and the electron flow through the lines shattered.

Without power, the rotor inside the cladding assembly flipped up, releasing both scram springs. The ram core was instantly swung 180 degrees back into original lock position. Below it the coupling barrel was also released and slid back down its screw guide and out of alignment with the ram path.

The Trident 3A had just gone inert.

Bonner stood in the reverberating madness of the *Panjang* and looked at Chaffee's body. It held no contours that were human. It was crumbled and structureless, like a pile of clothing thrown on a floor. He forced his fingers to touch it. There was nothing there. Its soul had fled.

A violent hissing echoed through the donkey room as high-pressure water began blowing through crumbling seams in the forward bulkhead. A wave of water erupted through the hatch and flooded down into the stoke pit. Sharp reports began cracking through the vibration noise. Old seams, driven at last beyond cohesion by the vibrations, were blowing out all over the ship. The *Panjang* lurched sharply to port, knocking Bonner to the engine deck.

He lay for only a moment before he hurled himself to his feet. Gripping his wounded arm, he headed for the turbine pit. He had only one thought now: get off this ship. The missile was forgotten, the continuing harmonics in the hull unheard. Like a drowning man in dark waters, there was only the hunger for air, escape.

He jammed himself down into the turbine foundation space. Unbelievably cold water was already cascading off the engine deck. His arm sent periodic shafts of electric pain into him. He ignored them and squirmed over tie plates and understruts. He reached the shaft tunnel hatch. Water poured down through the pit gratings. He crawled through the hatch and kicked it shut.

Darkness again. He felt along the shaft for the inspection dolly. He found it and heaved himself onto it. Lying on his back, he began pulling along the cable, skimming aft.

In the Saran, Napah Gilchrist was slowly going berserk. She sat in darkness. Something had blown all the operating circuits of the submersible soon after she'd heard the distant explosion. She could feel the *Panjang* rumbling like a volcano building up lava. Her first instinct was to get out, seek open air. How would she do that? Open air was three miles straight up.

Bonner.

Was he alive? She crawled along the deck, found the hatch wheel, and whirled it. Up it came. Dark iron stench fumed into the darkness.

"Bonner." Her voice echoed back. Slowly the echo died. Beyond was emptiness. Again her voice ricocheted off bulkheads. "Bonner, please, I know you're alive. Please answer me."

A single faint word, not hers, came back.

"Cas! Where are you?"

"Here."

"Where?"

She heard the soft tang of ladder bolts directly below. Then the clank of metal and a savage grunt. For a moment she drew back. Was it Chaffee? "Cas, is that you?"

"Yes, here," a voice replied, only feet away. "Grab my hand." His words came through clenched teeth. "You'll have to pull me up."

She bent into the chamber and flailed her arms until she found his hand. She gripped it with both hands, braced her knees, and began hauling back. She heard him let out a moan. Her back muscles strained as she felt him come off the deck, his weight dangling. Pulling, shifting her knees, she slowly brought him up.

His elbow cleared the rim of the chamber. He gripped it and his weight lightened. Quickly she freed one hand and grabbed his clothing. They struggled together and at last she felt him slide up and onto the capsule deck. He lay there panting, cursing softly.

Her hands scurried over him. "What's the matter? Are you hurt?" He was soaking wet and smelled of oil and fire.

"My arm," he gasped. "My arm's busted. But I think we killed the missile," he said. "It would have gone off by now." A pause. "Chaffee's dead."

She felt a shiver ripple through her.

"We've gotta get off this ship. She's going down. Turn on the lights."

"They're gone. Something blew the power out."

"Oh, no!"

They stared at each other through the darkness. Then Bonner barked, "Close the hatch. Dog and spring-lock it."

She obeyed without question. The hatch cracked down. She whirled the wheel and fumbled for the spring-lock jaws.

Bonner was testing switches around the capsule. They were now at a thirty-degree tilt. The ship was slowly twisting deeper and deeper to port. A tiny set of panel lights popped on near the command couch. "The camera panel's working," Bonner cried. He flicked more switches and the thruster lights came on. "I don't understand this. We've still got power, but the lights and the breach chamber panel's gone."

There was a sudden flurry of small explosions somewhere forward. Immediately a rumbling started as more compartments flooded. The sounds came rushing toward the Saran, rebounded, rushed away. New vibrations started.

The panel lights flickered. Instantly Bonner turned them off. "Was the breach chamber panel turned on when the vibrations came?"

"Yes, Chaffee tried to blow the disengage charges."

"That's it. The vibrations blew out only working circuits. We've still got power through any system that wasn't on."

"But without the breach panel, how can we blow the charges?"

"I don't know. Christ, I don't know."

"Can we feed off the main battery?"

"No, the breach circuit's on a separate battery unit."

The tilt of the capsule deck had reached forty degrees. The capsule was beginning to tremble from water colliding with it as the *Panjang*'s plunge picked up speed. Suddenly Bonner gave a yell. "Find me a light. Hurry."

Napah began searching crazily around the capsule, along conduit lines oddly out of position, along the deck that was a slanting bulkhead. Behind her a small orange flame flicked on. Bonner had lit his cigarette lighter. She swung around. In its tiny, flickering glow his face seemed ravished. "Hold this." She crawled to him and cupped the lighter. It went out. Frantically she relit it and held it forward.

Bonner was clawing at the back of the thruster panel. It held the main lead-in wires from the battery packs. With brute strength he ripped off the plastic backing.

"Hold up the light."

He squinted at the electrical board. His finger traced indicator leads, switch leads, and finally found the main lead-in. The cant of the deck reached forty-five degrees. Loose gear was falling off the upside bulkhead. Cas ripped out the lead-in wire and began pulling insulation packing off with his teeth. In a moment he had the twin wires bare.

"Look out," he cried, and rammed both raw wires against the side of the capsule. There was a crackling blue flash, and he was thrown back against Napah as the main battery circuit shorted out.

Simultaneously there was a muffled explosion on the bottom of the breach chamber as the disengage-ring charges blew through the holding seal. By shorting out the main circuit, Bonner had electrified the whole submersible, including the fuse casings of the Nitramon WW charges.

They moved gently sideward. Water blew up into the

breach chamber as the main seal disintegrated. The Saran floated free of the *Panjang*'s after-house deck.

But then it was violently slammed back onto the deck by the force of the water as the ship plunged. The submersible rolled over onto its side, scraped along the deck with the howling screech of metal. It struck an upright and slid off, twisting.

Napah had thrown her arms around Bonner and then clamped her fingers onto the cushion of the command couch, pinning him. They clung there, gravity pulling violently in crazy directions. At last the Saran cleared the after house, crashed across the stern railing, and went out into open water. But she was still caught in the *Panjang*'s suction. Down and down they hurtled.

Then a tremor shimmered through the submersible. She seemed to slow her insane streaking pirouette for a moment. In gradual increments the violent turbulence left her. Now she glided off at an angle to the ship's plunge line, a leaf flung out to the penumbral ripples of an eddying current.

They listened to the *Panjang* dropping. The soft scream of bulkheads ripped open, the distant thunder as the last of her air pockets were breached.

And then silence and she was gone.

Neither of them spoke. There was no need. Darkness enfolded them, suddenly sweet with life. At last Cas groped along the couch slot for the manual release of the ingot rack. There was a soft mechanical chunk as the weights fell away.

The Saran leapt upward like a newborn colt, and began her long journey to the surface.

Epilogue

Music from the Royal Hawaiian Hotel pavilion drifted into Napah's room like moonlit smoke: soft steel guitars playing "Sweet Mapuana." In her crumpled bed she swiveled her head and gazed out through the balcony door. Beside her, Bonner shifted, the cast on his left arm lightly banging the bedstand as he lit a cigarette. Far away, she could see the lights of a night excursion boat just clearing Kuhio Point at the southern end of Waikiki Beach.

She sighed and thought: Lord, I don't ever want to leave this . . .

It had taken the *Voorhees* seven days to reach Pearl Harbor, coming straight across the ocean with no refueling stops. Once docked at Ford Island, everybody went into a heavy security quarantine. Long debriefing sessions with Naval Intelligence men, intense and grim.

There was good reason. The reverberations of the incidents on the Canal were still thundering around the world. The whole Tamarand affair had come out into the light along with fragmented bits and pieces of the role the *Panjang* had played in it. American and Australian credibility was at zilch level. Even the British were taking heat for the panicky way their fleet elements had scurried out of Leadbottom Sound. The Pan-Pacific initiatives, with all their glorious promise, lay in the shambles of Honiara. Surprisingly, the human toll on the island was light, considering the horrific explosion of panic. Twenty-two dead, fourteen missing, and nearly three hundred injured.

But the curtain of secrecy which had dropped over the key elements of the scenario would keep the world from really knowing how close it had been during those tremulous hours before and after Honiara erupted. The Russians, psyched and ready to go, had prowled like Huns. In Yoshkar-One nerves were stretching to the breaking point. Too much time had elapsed without a nuclear detonation in the Coral Sea, and the meager reports coming in about the situation on the Canal seemed to indicate that the President was already dead. Would the American militarists continue on their insane scheme? Markisov, visibly near collapse, continued to hold his nation in check.

In Washington near-hysteria prevailed. As the sketchy reports of the Canal filtered in, the Pentagon was hurled into indecisiveness. Where was the President? Was he still alive? Their situation maps were now clearly showing an unbelievably massive deployment of Russian strength. Had it been a Soviet ploy all along? Would they strike now, when America was at its most vulnerable position? In reflex, Red War Alert orders were radioed to U.S. units around the globe.

The President remained out of contact for nearly an hour. Whisked from the convention hall, he had been driven behind a phalanx of marines to Henderson International. But the rumor of the Trident beat him there. As the phalanx approached up the airport entry road, hordes of panic-stricken people were pouring out of the terminal in a wild rush to board the lines of parked aircraft.

A small New Zealander twin engine in the fueling dock near *Air Force One* was overrun. In the confusion her fuel hoses were ripped out of the wings. There was a spark, then a small fire, and a powerful explosion as she and the fueling tanker went up. The entire tail section of the President's aircraft was engulfed.

The phalanx veered away, racing along the edge of the field toward a taxiing Qantas 727. Firing bursts ahead of the airliner, they brought it to a halt. Hurriedly the President, with two of his aides and four security men, was hoisted aboard. The 727 lifted off Henderson's tarmac and swung northeast toward Midway.

It took the pilot fourteen minutes to break through the frenzied chatter of radio traffic and raise Midway Communications. Seated at the navigator's console, the President was briefed on the situation, including the latest reports from Pensacola. He agreed to the Red War Alert, but ordered that a line be immediately established with Moscow.

It took forty-one minutes.

The ensuing conversation with the Soviet Premier was ominous. Although Markisov was relieved that the U.S. President was still alive, his voice quavered with outrage and challenge. He demanded to know what American intentions were. The President gave him what he had, pleading for rationality.

Markisov scoffed and accused him of attacking one of his submarines.

Yes, the President conceded, reports from the submersible's mother ship *had* indicated a sonar contact with a Russian sub. But, he emphasized over and over, no military action had been taken against it. Explosions of an internal nature had been heard.

Markisov was silent for a long time. Then there was an abrupt disconnect. Further attempts to reestablish the link ran into dead air over Moscow.

As the Qantas airliner, now accompanied by an escort of NF-16B's from the carrier *Enterprise*, neared the outer perimeter of Wake Island's control zone, the President was jolted by a report from Pensacola. All communications with Bonner had been broken. Langenscheidt estimated detonation of the Trident to be four minutes away.

The frantic probes to break through to Markisov continued, bypassing radio links to utilize ground telephone networks out of northern Italy and Poland. Then Pensacola relayed that the Trident had just been defused. Four minutes later, a telephone line through East Germany broke through to Markisov.

The President, beads of sweat rolling down his face,

informed the Secretary that the Trident had gone inert.
Markisov was silent. Then he said simply, "We will wait."

Napah drew her gaze from the excursion boat and
looked at Bonner's profile. "I got a call from Sutter Oil
this morning. They've assigned me to an oil probe in the
Aleutians."

"Oh?"

"I'm supposed to report in San Francisco tomorrow
night." She propped herself onto an elbow. "But you
know what? I think I'm in love with you. God, can you
believe that?"

"Incredible."

Ever since being released from the security quarantine,
she and Bonner had roamed the island of Oahu. He
showed her his island, the places the tourists never saw.
They went tandem hang-gliding off the bluffs above the
Makapuu lighthouse, Napah's joyous squeals bouncing
off the cliffs of Rabbit Island. They hunted mountain
apples in the misty valleys of the Koolaus and went
skinny-dipping in the frigid, milk-chocolate waters of Hanai
Falls with Bonner's cast wrapped in plastic. One afternoon they got deliciously fried on pineapple *swipe* in a
dive in Waipahu, and spent the rest of the night drunkenly repairing Cas's boat. For two days they ran the blue
marlin off Kahuku Point. But mostly they soaked in the
sun, as if their bodies could never get enough of its
warmth. And they made long, languorous love.

"What do you think about that?" Napah asked.

"What do *you* think about that?"

"We're good together."

"Agreed."

"So?"

"So what?"

"What the hell kind of answer is that?"

He laughed and ran his fingers through her hair.
"Honey, if you don't know how I feel about you by now,
my saying it won't make any difference."

"Oh, God, you're a hopeless romantic, aren't you?"
She flopped onto her back. "Well, what do I do now?"

"Go play with the icebergs."

"Just like that?"

"Just like that." From the pavilion "Sweet Mapuana" fused delicately into "Maui Girl." "I've got a little news myself."

"What?"

"You remember Frank Merak at Scripps?"

"Vaguely."

"He's a good old boy who just got promoted to director of their biological-research department. Apparently he's been trying to get hold of me for weeks." He flashed a grin at her. "Wants me to head a team doing deep studies off the French Frigate Shoals."

She sprang up. "Oh, Cas, that's wonderful. You'll be back in research again."

"Yeah, surprised the hell out of me."

Her eyes narrowed. "How come you didn't tell me sooner?"

"I figured it could wait."

"You're going, right?"

"Yes. You?"

She nodded. "I really want to go on this Aleutians thing. We'll be using the new ZAK laser gear."

"All right."

She gently moved his cast and stretched out on top of him. "But you get one thing straight, pal. I'm coming back. I'll always come back."

"Oh? Maybe you've forgotten what you called me once. Strictly a beer-and-pizza man."

"Funny thing," she said, her voice throaty, sensuous. "I've developed a hellish taste for beer and pizza."

Gently Cas put out his cigarette and enfolded her in his arms.

ABOUT THE AUTHOR

Charles Ryan lives in northern California. *The Panjang Incident* is his first novel.